**Also available from Tricia Lynne
and Carina Press**

The Unlovabulls Series

Protective Instinct

Also available from Tricia Lynne

Moonlight & Whiskey

Dear Reader, please be aware this book depicts mild recollections of emotional abuse and portrays a character coping with the aftermath of driving while intoxicated. I've done my best to keep those issues off-page and as non-triggering as possible.

MODEL BEHAVIOR

TRICIA LYNNE

carina
press

carina
press®

Recycling programs
for this product may
not exist in your area.

ISBN-13: 978-1-335-00539-7

Model Behavior

First published in 2022. This edition published in 2023.

For questions and comments about the quality of this book, please contact us at CustomerService@Harlequin.com.

Carina Press
22 Adelaide St. West, 41st Floor
Toronto, Ontario M5H 4E3, Canada
www.CarinaPress.com

Printed in U.S.A.

For Mike,
Thank you for being the order to my chaos.

I love you.

Chapter One

What the hell just bit me in the ass?
Oh, it's my past.

Olive

Ohmygod, your parents should have used a prophy-lactic, you know-it-all, Instagram-famous Kardashian wannabe.

I had visions of all the things I'd rather do than be dressed down by this harpy of a client rolling around in my brain. Like beat my head on my desk. Maybe get a root canal, sans anesthesia, or have a murder hornet sting me in the boob.

Any of those would be a better option. "Are you even listening, Olive? I'm paying your firm to up my PR profile! I want to know why I didn't make it into this month's issue of *Dallas Life & Style*! It's your job! Do your job!"

Jesus Christ, her voice was so high. Could dogs even hear her? I literally had to pull the phone away from my ear. This girl made me want to yank my hair out, but I wouldn't dare risk my perfectly coiffed, tightly slicked-back bun. I settled for tapping my short manicured nails against my desk blotter as I stared at the glass clock on my desk and realized I was precisely four minutes late leaving Russo Image Consulting—the company *I* built from the ground up.

Yet there I was, fuming while being castigated by a flake of a client I wanted to tell to take a flying fuck. But I didn't do that—it was my job to stay in control when everyone else lost their shit. Bad things happened when I didn't. "Crystal, we talked about this. The Spotted column doesn't run pictures of…" *A sloppy-drunk social climber's nip-slip unless you're already a damn celebrity.* "Wardrobe malfunctions aren't going to get you the recognition you want in this city. Philanthropy is a much better option. Perhaps if you volunteered for one of the charities on the list that I gave you. I have several contacts at the Botanical Gardens or the—"

"Oh, no you di'int just suggest I give away my daddy's hard-earned money because you can't do your job."

Pfft. Her daddy was a heavy metal hair band bassist who was a one-hit wonder in the '80s, then sold the rights to his hit to a Fortune 500. Rumor had it, he sat around most days either snorting his money or using it to turn his daughter into an entitled little shit.

Crystal was a piece of work. She was a recent transplant from Vegas with a mid-level social media following. Half of them consisted of her father's fan base, and the other half followed because of her penchant for posting pictures of herself sucking on suggestive foods while angling the camera to look down her blouse, or up her skirt.

It was time this girl had a reality check. "Darling, there are two ways into Dallas society. You're born to it, or you work hard for it. You weren't born to it. If I may be candid, you are a relative nobody in a town where social media influencers are a dime a dozen. You are going to have to put in the legwork we talked about." *Plus, they're worthy causes you could be supporting, you little—* "Unfortunately, I can't do my job if you don't follow through with your marketing plan."

I heard an elegant male snort from just outside my office. That would be Johnathan. Knocking on my desk to get him to look at me, I waved him in. Tall and lean with grape-colored hair and the pants to match, Johnathan strolled in with a wicked grin and sat in one of the modern white leather chairs across from my desk.

Crystal's voice came out nasally and even whinier than usual. "But can't I just not and say I did, or make a big donation or something?"

"No, you can't. Do what we talked about. Clean up your social media presence—get invested in the community and its people. This city is full of old money families, darling. Prove to them that you're both benevolent and elegant enough to belong in their social circles."

I'd let Johnathan, my executive assistant and apprentice, take Crystal on as a favor because they'd attended high school together. When she'd proved to be too much for him to handle, I had to step in. But I was done with her bullshit. You didn't get to be the top PR firm in Dallas without checking out-of-line clients. After all, my name was on the letterhead, and I had a standard to uphold. A hard edge crept into my tone. "Crystal, perhaps Russo Image Consulting isn't a good fit with your brand. There are two other PR firms in Dallas that I'm happy to recommend."

"No! No, I don't want to go somewhere else. You're supposed to be the best, Olive. I want to stay with Russo."

I drew in a cleansing breath. I really wished she

wouldn't. "Then you're going to do what Johnathan set forth in your marketing plan. Separate yourself from the pack. Spend time volunteering and get to know the right people. Put in the elbow grease when necessary. Socialites may party and get photographed a lot, but in Dallas, most also use their influence for the greater good, or to effect change in the Metroplex. You can't buy those sorts of connections, darling. You'll need to set yourself apart from the two hundred other Instagram models at Lizard Lounge on Saturday night. Get your hands dirty, Crystal. That's the photo opportunity *DL&S* is looking for. Get *those* photos, and their Spotted column will follow. Now, I'm going to brief Johnathan and you're going to call Shari, who's on the committee for the Arts District outdoor concert series to benefit breast cancer research. Like. We'd. Planned. He'll follow up with you this afternoon."

I heard the heavy exhale, and the girl seemed appropriately resigned.

Johnathan had specifically picked this cause because Crystal had a music connection and had lost her grandmother to breast cancer.

"Remember, dear, setting yourself apart in Dallas doesn't mean getting photographed…" *Blowing a bouncer in the bathroom at Gilly's.* "…partying all hours of the night. It's about what you do during the day, too."

Johnathan grinned ear-to-ear as I ended the call with the client from hell. "Thank you," he said. "I was in over my head with her. I never should have taken on an old friend as a client. I had no idea what a brat she'd turned into."

Lesson learned, then. Johnathan had a good head for PR, but a problem saying no to people who hit him up for favors. Putting up boundaries was a subject I might have to broach before I could consider promoting him. Standing to my full and generous height, I smoothed my bright white tailored pantsuit. After shutting my laptop's cover, I added it to my briefcase as well as the client-specific binder for my next meeting. "Don't thank me yet. If she doesn't follow through, we'll be cutting her loose."

Johnathan nodded his agreement at the same time his stomach grumbled.

"Dude. Go eat lunch. Where y'all going today?"

"Savor."

"Mmm. I wish I could go with you, but I'm already late for this appointment. Don't forget to put it on the company card." The Friday tradition of taking my staff out to lunch stood, even when I couldn't go.

A few minutes later, I slid into my SUV as the mid-September sun blazed down on downtown Dallas. Luckily, it was early enough that the Dallas North Tollway wasn't backed up. I relished the quiet inside my Audi Q8—which was safety-awarded best in its class—as I signaled and switched lanes to make the exit for the Unlovabulls Canine Rescue Center. For the first time in a long time, I wasn't technically working this afternoon, and my meeting wasn't with a company client.

My friend Lily was a sought-after dog trainer in DFW. She also ran a dog rescue in rural Collin County for dogs with behavior problems that were too much for other rescues and shelters to handle. They'd opened the doors to an amazing facility in March, but in order to maintain it, they needed money.

That's where I came in. I had volunteered my time to plan and head up several fundraising efforts to make sure the rescue kept its doors open and continued to serve dogs in need. I'd come up with a series of high-dollar fundraisers that would do just that, and today's meeting with Lily was to share them, get her take, and lay the groundwork for the events moving forward.

Because my career was so demanding, I hadn't been able to help much while she was getting the Unlovabulls off the ground, something that I felt horrible about, but then I'd also been mourning. Last December—not long after they started renovating the building to house thirty-five-plus dogs—I'd lost my beloved fourteen-year-old rescued Dachshund. When Cassie died, I was heartbroken. Outside of work, she, and the dog sports we'd done together—agility and Barnhunt, rally and Earthdog—had been my whole world. I'd even taken her to the office with me regularly. I knew deep down I was still reeling from the loss, but I had to do something to move on. I wasn't ready for another dog yet, but helping Lily and dogs who were in need, like Cassie once had been? Yeah, that would be good for my heart.

Hands on the wheel at ten and two, I pulled into a spot in the small lot outside the rescue and grabbed my work bag from the back seat. A cool gust of air-conditioning and the scent of antibacterial cleaner wafted over me as I pulled the door open. Just inside the reception area, pictures covered a blue-gray wall—the original Unlovabulls, breeding dogs that had been rescued from a deplorable puppy mill during a raid that Lily and her fiancé, Brody, worked hard to make happen. Because the shelter specialized in aggressive dogs, other shelters would call them when they had a dog they couldn't adopt out who might otherwise be put down.

Turning down the hall, I passed the staff offices when

a cap of wild brown curls captured in a loose bun caught my eye.

"Hey, girl! Working hard?" Dr. Regina Avalos, DVM—or Gina, as most of us knew her—was tapping on a tablet while making notes on the laptop next to it. She glanced up and yawned. "I'll take that as a yes."

"Yeah, burning the candle at both ends lately." I could tell. She had dark circles under her eyes. She'd been avoiding dealing with her divorce by working too much.

Hell, who was I to judge? I was the queen of throwing myself into my job so I could ignore messy emotional stuff. "I thought about driving over to the UKC agility trial this weekend in Fort Worth to root for the home team. If you need a day off, you're welcome to tag along."

Gina rubbed a makeup-less eye. "Mmm. I might do that if I can squeeze in this surgery between now and then. A Neapolitan Mastiff that came in a couple days ago with a torn ACL and a broken canine that's making him meaner than hell. Plus, we've got a Chocolate Lab getting ready to whelp." The lines on her face softened. "But you know Lily and the mama dogs. I'll be surprised if she needs me for that at all. She'll probably camp out in the lobby again." That was our Lily. "Give me a call tonight, okay?"

Sending her a thumbs-up, I continued to Lily's office, where the door stood open. It always did. Lily Costello looked up from her desk, her short black waves brushing her shoulders, the light glinting in her violet eyes. The Unlovabulls Rescue was Lily's baby. Like all babies, it robbed its mama of sleep many a night. She not only loved and fussed over every dog in her charge, but she knew it would take money she currently didn't have to maintain the rescue in the coming years.

I could alleviate that. "Hey, you. No Brody today?"

Her face took on a wistful quality that I loved her for, but it also made me want to gag a little. "He's running a football camp for inner-city high school teams today and tomorrow, working with defensive players on proper techniques to minimize the risk of concussions."

I wasn't surprised. Football player health was something Brody took seriously, and why, Lily said, he'd chosen to retire relatively young. He wanted to get out while he still had full use of both his body and his brain.

Brody Shaw was the former Pro Bowl middle linebacker and hometown golden boy of the Dallas Bulldogs football team. "Everything looking okay as far as his MRIs and such?"

"Yeah, they're keeping a close eye on him because, really, what pro football player hasn't had multiple concussions? But so far so good." She grinned. "He's one of the lucky ones."

I knew what that meant to Lily. Her biological father— also a Pro Bowl middle linebacker—hadn't been one of the lucky ones, and had gone to an early grave.

I had my own connection to football, but I'd avoided discussing it with...well, everyone. I'd never told a soul—especially not Lily—but my college boyfriend had played for the Bulldogs. Drafted by Minnesota out of college, he'd hopped around to a couple teams before landing as a starting tight end with the Dallas Bulldogs a few years back. Which was why I didn't take on football clients. Hayes Walker was... Well, it wasn't a time in my life I liked to think about. Still, on occasion, I wondered about the abuse his body and brain had taken over the years, and if it had anything to do with his decision to retire after last season.

But Hayes's body had stopped being my concern the night he dumped me right before the draft.

Prick.

I still hoped number 89 was taking care of himself. And I still focused on him too much when I watched Dallas play—a little something I'd never admit out loud.

Luckily, Lily snapped me out of my musings. "Hey, do you want to come with me to check on the pregnant mama before we get started on the fundraising stuff?"

I blew out a breath, though I hadn't meant to. My eyes began to water.

"Shit. Olive, it's okay if you're not ready. I've been there. It's ridiculously hard losing a dog. Especially a heart dog. All dogs are special, but on occasion there's one that's just…extra. Joker was extra. He holds a special place in my heart. Casshole was extra, too."

A laugh burst through my lips as I dabbed at the tears threatening my makeup. "That she was. Girlfriend was waaaay extra. I know she wasn't the perfect dog—it's why I gave her that nickname—and she lived a good long life, but still… Even though I knew it was coming, that I could only make her comfortable for so long, it was still raw. Like knowing she had developed liver cancer, that she had six months to a year left with me… it still didn't soften the blow."

Short little Lily put her arms around me and hugged. "Why don't you stay here. I'll run back and check on mama. It won't take but a minute and then we can get to work."

I pushed out a cleansing breath. "No. No, I'll come

with. I need to do this. I'm going to the trial to cheer y'all on this weekend, too."

After a last squeeze, Lily led me through the hall into the sparse reception area and through a set of doors labeled Maternity Rooms. Someone had painted a stork on the windows clasping a yellow blanket in its beak with a puppy peeking over the edge. That hadn't been there the last time I was here.

We came to a stop at a door with a half window. A sign hanging on the glass read Quiet Please. I put a hand on Lily's arm, whispered, "I'm sorry. I should have been here more. I should have helped more with… everything."

Her eyes softened. "Oh, honey. I understand why you weren't. Grieving a dog is hard. They're these perfect little creatures who give unconditional love and don't have an inherently bad bone in their body. They're so pure and bright. I grieve every single dog we lose here. Every. One. I carry them with me every day, and I can't tell you how many nights Brody has had to comfort me through my tears." She grabbed my hand and squeezed. "You're here now, and it's to do the biggest job we're facing. Keeping this place open for years to come."

I nodded, grinned as I squeezed back. I was lucky to have a friend like Lily through all this. She hadn't always been so open and forthcoming with me—neither of us were the type to let folks in willy-nilly—but since she'd made the effort with me, I was trying to with her as well.

When I heard shuffling in the room, I looked down to see a Chocolate Lab pacing and panting, her belly round and swollen, her nipples filled with milk and swaying to and fro. Poor girl was obviously uncomfortable. "Just in the beginning?"

She exhaled. "Yeah, and it's her first litter. It's going to be a long night."

I couldn't help the small grin. Gina was right.

Finally, the Lab settled down on a Kelly green blanket inside the whelping box.

"She's comfortable for now. Let's leave her be. But I need to run into the kennel area to grab some stuff for later. You can wait in my office if you want."

"I can come."

She looked me up and down. "Honey, the white pantsuit and four-inch Mary Jane heels are gorgeous—and thank you for the shoes, because it's not like you don't already tower over me—but you're not exactly dressed for dogs."

Yeah, to say I was on the tallish side was putting it mildly. With heels on, I was over six feet. "I came straight from work." I smoothed my suit. "Besides, if anybody can keep this clean in a kennel, it's me."

"Mkay, Mrs. Never a Hair Out of Place. Let's go."

Pushing open the double doors behind the reception area labeled Staff Only, we were met with the smell of bleach and the sound of barking. Lily ran a tight ship; something I appreciated about her.

One of the volunteer trainers was on his way back in from the training yard with an English Mastiff that decided to shake his head and let fly with a shower of slobber I quickly, and just barely, sidestepped.

Lily chuckled. "Told ya."

I huffed. "Did you see those moves? Not a speck on me."

Each trainer worked with assigned dogs several times a week on any issues they had that could affect their adoption prospects. Some took a week or two to get up to speed, others took months, but Lily and her staff didn't give up. If they couldn't "rehabilitate" a dog, then they found it suitable environments, owners, and living arrangements to channel their issues. She also had volunteers who came in to exercise the dogs—once it was safe for them—give them affection if the dog would allow it, and plenty of mental stimulation so they didn't deteriorate.

Two rows of six by eleven painted cinder block kennels with solid doors lined each sidewall. Dogs milled about in their kennels and made good use of the attached and shaded outdoor runs. The indoor runs were well-equipped and comfortable, and the solid walls and doors tamped down most of the noise. Not just for the sake of the staff, but for the dogs, too. Not all dogs responded well to noise. Lily walked past the bank of cabinets with medical supplies, exam tables, six intensive care kennels, and four computer stations for staff to chart.

Against the back wall, the left led to the surgical wing and the quarantine suites. But Lily kept going to the door on the right. "Lil, I thought you needed supplies." I stopped to point at the stocked cabinets.

"Mmm, Gina and her techs get pissy when you pull from their stuff. I'm going to raid the storage cabinets."

Following her through the door on the right, I eyed the pristine stainless-steel bathing stations and their supplies. A groomer I recognized from the agility circuit waved a quick hello before he picked up the massive paw of a very thin American Pit Bull Terrier and continued to clip the dog's overgrown nails.

Lil whipped open a cabinet against one of the adjacent walls and reached for a stack of black towels. "Oh,

I should grab a clean blanket for the whelping box while I'm back here, too." When she opened a door between two of the wash stations, I heard a soft whine followed by a man murmuring.

I whispered, "When did you put kennels back here?"

Lily kept her voice low. "When we didn't have room anywhere else and had three dogs that needed us. A rescue brought us three that were aggressive, kept outside all their lives and not socialized, but we were full up, so we put temporary kennels in. Then, the shelter that sent them to us went bankrupt and we needed something more permanent, so we did a quick remodel off the supply room. I like to use it for older dogs, or dogs that don't do well with the noise of the main room. There's only one dog back here right now, and I've been working with her. She's spending more and more time in the main area, and I've been exposing her to new noises and situations. Still, she doesn't like pups or overly excitable dogs."

"Did you find homes for the others two?"

She nodded. "This girl has just needed a little more time."

"So, she's back here by herself?"

Lil chuckled. "Never for long. She has one of our volunteers wrapped around her little nub tail. But Gina thinks she's eight or nine years old, maybe. She's responded well to training, but…"

"People want young dogs." I pitched my voice low to match Lily's.

She nodded, leaned against the other side of the door frame. "She gets plenty of one-on-one time, but she's going to need a home that not only wants an older, large dog, but that's quiet. No young kids or loud teens, no rambunctious dogs. I'm being extremely picky about who I let adopt her, but we also just got word that a private rescue in Arlington is closing its doors soon. I agreed to take on six of their dogs that will be adoption ready when they get here."

I could see the worry on her face. It wasn't easy keeping a shelter this size funded.

"Lil, don't worry. I got you on this. I'm not going to let this place close."

Her grin wasn't quite believable, but it grew as that deep male voice crooned to the dog again. Brody must have finished up his camp early and snuck in.

Sidling up to the other side of the door frame, I cocked my head to listen to one of the toughest dudes to ever play linebacker murmur "good girl" and "sweetheart" and "baby cakes."

Lily smiled, bit down on her bottom lip to keep from giggling. "That's one of the reasons I'm being so picky," she said in a whisper.

I leaned over. "Who'd have thought your man was such a softy."

She leaned over, whispered. "Oh, Brody is definitely a softy, but that's not him."

That's when the guy stood, and something about those shoulders and the sandy blond hair struck me as familiar.

When he finally turned, my world tilted on its axis and time ground to a halt between the space of each heartbeat.

Chapter Two

How to Be a Fucking Professional
by Olive Russo

Olive

Hayes Walker's electric blue eyes hit me right in the gut. I was fairly certain the way our chins hit our chests in complete unison would have been comical if I could have seen it from Lily's viewpoint, because I'm sure it took a good twenty minutes before I could actually draw in a breath.

That's when his scratchy bass broke over me and while my nips may have pearled, for a split-second a whiff of anxiety tickled my brain stem. "Olive?"

Then, my boss bitch got control of the situation. "Hayes?"

"Oh my God, sweetheart! I was just thinking about you." His stride ate up what little distance was between us, and before I knew it, I was wrapped in his arms. Warm and huge and gentle. Just the way I remembered. That scent of sandalwood and grass I'd thought about too often in the last decade enveloped me. But it had an undertone to it, something earthy and...well that was being generous. Honestly, it smelled like poo. We *were* in a dog rescue—maybe one of the dogs needed their kennel cleaned—but it was that smell of dog shit that snapped me back into myself. Thank God.

Not before I thought I heard him sniff my hair, though.

No, no, no. This was all wrong. Hayes was not a good guy. Hayes Walker was the bag of dicks that dumped me the night before the NFL draft. By text. From halfway across the country. And the fucker didn't even give me a reason. Hayes was the reason for my spiral all those years ago. Hayes was the reason for *my* twenty-year-old broken heart, and the altogether broken girl I'd become.

You're not her anymore, Olive. You're a badass and you will handle this like the fucking pro you are.

Gently, I let my arms fall to my sides, but it took Hayes a heartbeat to get the hint. Instead of letting go completely, he held on to my upper arms.

"How are you, Ollie? The years have been good to you." His smile was genuine, wide, with that telltale sparkle in his electric blue eyes that had seeped into my dreams more than a few times over the last decade. The years might have been kind to me, but they'd been even better to him. The man was sex and sin blanketed in a translucent sheen of my memories knotted up with current reality.

The tanned face and the lines around his eyes. The tattoos covering his strong arms and the column of his neck. The blond beard that was neatly trimmed and shaped to a point just past his chin. He hadn't had *that* ten years ago. Or the haircut—shaved down to a fuzz on the sides but the top was maybe four inches long and combed back from his face with some kind of product.

But I knew the jaw underneath the beard was strong and square and complemented those sinful lips and high cheekbones. Even the crooked line of his nose was perfection—a hint of the imperfect in the otherwise flawless. Everything about this man had called to me when I was a college girl before he'd had the ink and the fine lines. He'd been the jock, me the good girl, but nobody was able to coax out my wild side like Hayes Walker had. Now I was even less wild, and he was obviously more so, and my traitorous body responded. Breathing? Shallow. Nipples? Painful points. Skin? Goosies. Panties? Damp. As fuck.

"I'm good, thanks for asking. Doing really well, though I never expected to run into you at my friend's dog rescue."

He shrugged in that nonchalant, I'm-cooler-than-hell way he had that I would never be able to duplicate in a million years. "I don't know if you follow football, but Lily's fiancé was my teammate for a few years."

Oh, I knew. I'd just never told anyone I'd known Hayes once upon a time. Including Lily and Brody. Because I'd never pictured this moment happening.

Denial ain't just a river in Egypt, girl.

Ugh. Hayes volunteering at a dog rescue didn't seem like the kind of altruistic thing the completely self-absorbed jack wad of a tight end I once knew would do either.

"Well," Lily cut in, refocusing our attention. Her eyes had gone wide with delight. "This is awesome that you two already know each other!" She shot me a look that said as soon as we were alone, I better 'fess up. "With Hayes as your liaison to the Dallas Bulldogs players, and your co-chair for the fundraisers, it should make all the planning for the events easy-peasy." Lily nudged me with her shoulder as a Cheshire grin worked its way across Hayes's face.

...wait, what?

Shit, shit, shit.

No, this couldn't be happening. I had this weird kind of panic climbing my spine at the thought of getting stuck doing anything with Hayes Walker. Lily was supposed to be doing the planning with me. Not my ex. *Seriously?* I started ticking off all the reasons I couldn't work with Hayes.

1. He dumped me.

2. My broken heart spiral led to two compound fractures, four surgeries, and a criminal record. I'd had to take a hiatus from college, for fuck's sake.

3. This panicky thing in my chest was something I was neither familiar with nor cared for. It made me feel out of control.

4. Hayes Walker was the kryptonite to my control freak.

He had a knack for getting me to let my hair down and do things that were very un-Olive-like. Skydiving and having sex under the stars. Riding the mechanical bull at Cowboys OKC, and two-stepping until two a.m. the night before a final. Flashing my boobs to several members of Oklahoma University's incoming freshman class...who had their parents in tow.

Ollie had thrown away all the to-do lists and parental expectations. Then she'd gone cow-tipping and rode a horse bareback. Got her boots dirty before she slid into her bae's lap while he drove in order to ride him, too. Most of it was harmless, and Ollie was always fun...lots of fun.

Until she wasn't anymore.

Olive didn't do any of that. She was all about lists, planning, spreadsheets, orienting to a goal and seeing it come to fruition. Attention to detail and sticking to a schedule. I needed those things. Olive was a perfectionist who needed control at all times in order to handle whatever her clients might throw at her any given day. Not only was I damn good at maintaining that control, I'd made my PR firm the best in DFW because of it.

Hayes Walker was the fucking king of the unpredictable and I was drawn to him like a bee to pollen.

Which was exactly why I couldn't work with him— never again would I let myself be as out-of-control as I was when he broke my heart.

With quick steps and the click of my heels, I hooked my arm through Lily's and whispered, "Hey, there's… I can't… Hayes…this is…" Unable to articulate why I couldn't work with Hayes, I twisted all casual-like to look behind us at the man in question. He was eyeing me with a crooked grin that could've melted the panties right off my ass.

"You're gonna give me the full tea. After the meeting," Lily whispered in return.

The meeting. That's right. The reason I was here in the first place. To discuss with Lily how we were going to keep the doors open on this amazing dog rescue for the next few years. You know, for rescue dogs. Dogs without homes. Like Cassie. And Brody's dog, CC. Lily's dogs, Mack and Laila. And all the dogs we'd passed as we walked to the back room to get towels. For the Chocolate Lab in labor with her first litter. All the dogs in the pictures that lined the wall of successful adoptions and the ones on Lily's office plaque that

didn't make it after the raid that broke the back of a no-
torious puppy mill. The dogs that Gina busted her ass
for—outside of her own office house—to give them the
best chance at survival. The trainers that volunteered
their time to work with the dogs. The two groomers
who took time from their schedules, the vet techs, the
specialists Lily had on speed dial. Even her students—
Lily's very own dog training students, some of whom
were my friends—volunteered cleaning kennels and
scooping poop. Spending time with dogs and washing
laundry. There were paid personnel here, but not many,
and those who did get paid did it for significantly less
money than they could get elsewhere. They did it because they loved the dogs and believed in the Unlovabulls Rescue.

Apparently, Hayes did, too.

Yet I was over here coughing up one excuse after
another for why I couldn't work with my ex to raise
money for this rescue so many people believed in, including me.

I was fairly sure either Megan Thee Stallion, or Be-
yoncé, or both were about to walk through the door and
make me hand over my Bad Bitch Card.

*Reasons to Help the Rescue
and Get Over My Damn Self.*
1. *The dogs.*
2. *More dogs.*
3. *My friends needed me.*
4. *Did I mention helping homeless dogs???*

Yeah. No-brainer. Dogs win. I had to do this. For
the dogs and the people who were essentially my only

friends. I could work with Hayes. I was a motherfucking professional and that was exactly how we'd behave. Like goddamned adults.

As I moved to the chair closest to the window, Lily opened the soda fridge behind her desk and pulled out two Shiners and a Coke Zero. "Hayes, leave the door open, would you? So I can listen for Iris."

"Yeah, sure." He slid into the seat next to me and Lily handed him one of the beers before passing me the Coke. She knew I didn't drink—not even a little—when I'd have to get behind the wheel, though I'd never told her why.

"So, how are we going to keep the shelter open, Olive?" *Shhht*, went the top on her longneck.

Clearing my throat, I swallowed deep and reached into the bag I'd left in her office earlier to retrieve my notebook. I could feel Hayes's eyes on me and cleared my throat. "I think it would be best for us to break up the fundraising into several events. All except one shouldn't require a large investment of capital for the shelter. But they could yield nice returns. Two or three smaller events will help create buzz, leading up to our pièce de résistance in February. It will require some output of cash, but I think with mine and Brody's connections, we can minimize expenses."

Lily nodded. "I expected as much. Bringing Hayes in will help with that, too, since he has a straight line to the players who want to volunteer."

"And their pockets," Hayes added.

I glanced at him, then back to Lily. "I thought he… you retired."

The I'm-up-to-no-good twinkle he always had slipped from his eyes as he sat his bottle on the edge of Lily's desk. "Yeah… I was kind of forced into that. The Dallas Bulldogs Football Organization offered me a job as an assistant coach this season instead of a ros-ter spot."

Oh, man. Poor Hayes.

Poor Hayes? He. Dumped. You. By. Text.

Still, football was life to him. At least that's how it had been. It was his oxygen. Given the way his smile faded, and how he studied the edge of Lily's desk while flexing his jaw, I'd guess he wasn't doing so well with the change. "Why, what happened?"

"Eh, it's a long story."

Lily cut in, refusing to let Hayes shrug it off. "My stepdad lived up to his name, yet again. He couldn't take a parting shot at Brody, so he chose the next-best target."

Lily's stepdad, Dick Head (yes, that's his actual name. Well, truthfully, it's Richard, but anybody who's ever met the man would call him Dick straight to his face), was the general manager of the Dallas Bulldogs. "When Brody and I were working to find the puppy mill his dog escaped from, and we started seeing each other on the DL, my stepdad found out. Dick tried to use the relationship—along with Brody's shoulder injury—to trade him to another team. That's when Brody started digging into his medical records with the team," Lily offered.

"Right." I nodded. "But what does that have to do with Hayes?"

"When Brody found out my stepdad and the team doctor—aka, my douche of an ex-fiancé—were work-ing together to gaslight players about the extent of their injuries to benefit the team, he didn't get any blowback because he'd already decided to retire.

"But as the players' union rep, Hayes wasn't so lucky. When Brody brought the issue to the commissioner, Hayes got the players' union to open an investigation into Dick and Trey's collusion, and subsequent results on player health."

"Yeah, but Trey lost his license over that, right? He can't practice medicine anymore. And Dick got a pretty hefty penalty." I glanced from Lily to Hayes. "How does that affect you?"

He shrugged a solid shoulder. "The team had to pay a 500K fine and Dick Head got suspended without pay for eight games. He was pissed and wanted to take it out on somebody. Not just because of the fine—the league will watch him like a hawk for years to come. He couldn't take it out on Brody because Brody retired."

Ahh. "But you didn't."

"I didn't."

"My stepdad made sure the team forced Hayes into retirement 'because of his age,'" Lily added.

Hayes's eyes met mine. "They couldn't fire me outright. That would look like retaliation, so they offered me a job as a tight end coach and gave my roster spot to someone younger. They didn't think I'd take the job. But I did." His gorgeous blues fell to some invisible lint on his jeans.

"Hayes, I'm so sorry. I know what football means to you." I sought his eyes, but he turned away and gave me the famous Walker shrug. There was something, though—a sadness? Not something I'd seen often in the younger version of Hayes. There had only been brief flashes of something similar. He wasn't taking this nearly as well as he pretended.

"Tell us what you have in mind for these fundraisers and how I can help?" he diverted.

Right. Blinking away the empathy I had for a man who really had no right to it, I settled into a role I was more familiar with. Boss. "Here's what I think we should consider." I cracked open my folder.

Chapter Three

Hey, women have to do it, too...

Hayes

"I see a few major fundraising opportunities over the next few months capped off with one hell of a gala. The gala will take the longest to plan. Since you gave me carte blanche as far as planning these things, I've already started laying some of the groundwork." Olive faced Lily, studiously ignoring me.

I didn't care, I was mesmerized.

Her voice was deeper than I remembered. It used to be smooth like butter, but now it had a touch of gravel and a rounder tone. Of course, we'd both been kids. She'd been going into her sophomore year when I graduated and headed into the draft. We'd both had a hell of a lot of maturing to do back then. She'd definitely done that, and damn, could a guy get an icepack for the blue balls he was gonna have after this? Because Ollie had fucking flourished.

She'd always been tall—volleyball had been her thing—at nearly six feet with gentle curves and strength underneath. Because I was six foot five, two hundred and forty back then (now I was bigger), I'd always appreciated that about her.

I'd never felt like I was going to crush her. Small girls, especially short girls, had a way of making me feel big and clumsy, like I might accidentally hurt them or something. That was never Olive. Physically, she'd been strong enough that if she shoved me, I felt it. If she locked her legs around my waist and squeezed, I was her bitch until she decided to let me go. I'd added an extra fifteen pounds of muscle since college, but I'd guess Olive was every bit as strong as she was then. Though, now, she was softer, curvier, plus-sized even.

It fucking suited her.

"This is off-the-cuff, but since we'll have the Bulldogs players to work with, I think we should start with a paid photo opportunity at the Texas State Fair. We could include some of the dogs that are ready for that environment. Give an agility demonstration, make it about how taking care of your dog can be fun for the whole family. Maybe even get some of the football players to give it a try with some of the rescue dogs. I know a photographer who will donate her time, and I can get some media outlets to cover it. We can announce our other fundraisers and the gala. Lil, do you think we can get a few of the rescues up to speed on basic agility before then?" Olive asked.

Lily took a swig from her bottle. "Not the dogs here now. They need to focus on becoming good pets first, but I can talk to some folks that have adopted our dogs. I've got a couple of students that have adopted mill dogs from the initial rescue, but there are other logistics to think about that…"

When Lily's sentence dropped off, I could tell she was trying not to piss on Olive's parade.

Olive could, too. Her face softened as her demeanor changed from the ass-kicker who gets shit done to the friend who was a volunteer. "Say it, darlin'. It's why we're here—so you can tell me if any of the ideas I've got chugging along in my brain aren't going to work."

"It's just the fair isn't that far off, Olive. It would be a quick turnaround to get set up for agility, and I don't think I could pull together what we'd need." I could see the worry settle into Lily's face. "We'd have to rent the agility equipment, since I don't have a full setup and the Unruly Dog would need theirs for weekend classes. I don't think I'll be able to find it this late with all the trials planned in October. Even if I could find equipment, I would insist on it being indoors because of the heat; that means special flooring that's safe for the dogs."

"I see what you mean. This close to the fair it will be hard to get any indoor space with enough room for both football players to do a signing *and* an agility course. Hmm." Olive chewed her bottom lip as she nodded. "Let me think about this for a bit. I might have another idea." She gave Lily a small grin to reassure her.

Man, she was pretty. Her angular jaw gave way to rounded cheeks that made her hazel eyes dance. Long neck and wide, strong shoulders that framed generous breasts. They'd always been on the larger side, but not like they were now. The cami-thingy she had on did nothing to hide them either, not that she was trying to. She looked stylish as hell—the bright white of her jacket cut a snug profile around her waist before ending just above the widest point of her rounded hips. Luminous skin highlighted by touches of a peach flush that crawled down her neck and chest.

Adjusting in her seat for the third time, she finally peeked over at me before refocusing on Lily.

She must have felt me watching her, because yeah, I was in awe. She was fucking beautiful, and the idea that my eyes on her was making her a little fidgety had me cracking a small grin.

"Hayes!"

"Huh?" I whipped my head around at the sound of Lily's voice just in time to see her straighten out her smirk.

"Which weekend will work best for the guys on the team?"

"Isn't the fair in October?" I popped my phone out of my pocket, swiping open my calendar.

Olive turned to me just as a whiff of fart assailed my nose. Well, maybe that's why she'd been fidgety. Trying to resemble some semblance of a gentleman, I acted as if I hadn't noticed a thing.

"The fair always opens the last week of September." Ollie's cute button nose twitched ever so slightly as she eyed me with suspicion. "It goes through the third weekend of October."

Hmm. Maybe it was Lily. "The third weekend in October is our bye week. If you can aim for that closing weekend, we should be good."

"Perfect!" Her eyes lit from within. "Closing weekend is super-busy, historically. I'll call my contact on the board and get them to slot us. If I tell him I'm bringing Dallas Bulldogs players with me, he'll make room for us. Hayes, I'll need a list of players that can commit in the next couple of weeks."

I nodded. "I'll talk to the guys."

Lily beamed. "What's in store for the other fund-raisers?"

"You know how the Frisco Sidewinders do a Dog Day? I think we could pull together a celebrity baseball game." The Sidewinders were the Rangers' farm team.

Lily bit the inside of her lip. "It's a good idea, but baseball is a summer sport. That would have to wait until at least spring at Sidewinders' Ballpark since it's outdoors, don't you think?"

I hummed as I thought. "Maybe, maybe not. Pitchers and catchers for minor league report in February, I think, and regular season starts in March or April? It might be chilly outside, but it could still work."

Ollie shifted to look at me and the smell hit my nose again. Lord, maybe we needed a ten-minute break.

"What about the new park in Arlington?" she asked.

"Lone Star Field where the Rangers play?" Whistling through my teeth, I looked up to see Lily shaking her head.

"We can't possibly swing that, moneywise. There will be a shit ton of costs associated with Lone Star. I highly doubt the Rangers would donate all the overhead to open the stadium. The Frisco stadium is a lot smaller."

It's exactly what I'd been thinking.

"What's the baseball saying?" Olive arched a sculpted brow. "Swing for the fences? Let me work my magic and see what I can find out. If neither of those plays out, I know we can arrange a celebrity basketball game at Frisco Athletic Center where the Legends play and the Stars practice. The hockey team owes me a huge favor."

Lily's eyes lit up. "Really? Can you introduce me to Tyler Seguin?"

"Right? I wish." Olive stuck a hand up and Lily high-fived her across the desk. "Sadly, I can't. I bet Brody can, though."

"I already asked. He refused."

"Pfft. Whatever," I added in a soft voice, at which point both women turned to look at me and burst out laughing.

"Let me work my magic before we make any decisions on baseball versus basketball versus something else altogether. That one will require some brainstorming and we have a little time to play with those. That brings me to the gala."

Lily chuckled. "What? No half-naked dudes with puppies calendar? I'd offer up Brody and Hayes."

Ollie tapped her nose. "It's a thought. If we can make a viral thing like the Australian firefighters? That could bring in some capital. Let me research it."

"Heeeeyyy…" I did my best to look offended.

Olive snorted. "Oh, please. The Hayes Walker I knew would drop trou and jiggle his junk on a dare for a six-pack of Shiner. Don't try to get all delicate on me now." With a knowing grin, she shot me a little side-eye, and I saw shades of the girl I'd been in love with. It was a familiar gesture. The kind of thing two old friends shared as an inside joke. And as quick as she picked up the playful look, she dropped it again, seeming to remember far more than the night I'd taken that bet.

Across the desk, Lily's mouth fell open as her eyebrows shot into her hairline. "Umm, exactly how well do—"

"So, the gala." Olive cut her off. "We're going big.

Seated dinner. Silent auction. Gambling for charity. Date auction. Dancing after the festivities until the wee hours of the morning with Jimmy Choos stranded under the nearest table. The whole nine. It will be an event people clamor to get into. Or at least pay out the nose to attend. February is our best bet. It doesn't give us much time to pull it together, but it's the perfect flip side to the Cattle Baron's Ball in October. Society will be ready to get out of the winter blues and into their finery to spend some money."

Lily looked horrified. "How are we supposed to pay for that? You know I prefer every cent in the coffers go to the dogs."

When Olive shifted forward to meet Lily's eyes, eau de poot hit my nose again, and I saw the dog shit I'd apparently, inadvertently, smeared on Olive's pristine white suit jacket when I'd slung a bag of dog poop over her shoulder as I hugged her.

Oh, Jesus fuck, you see the only woman you've ever loved after ten or so years and what do you do? You smear dog shit on her. Way to go, Walker. Way to fucking go.

I had to tell her, right? I mean, of course I had to tell her. I think. Here I was, eyeing her for releasing the Kraken, and she's giving me stink eye that said *Of course you fucking sharted in Lily's office, you Neanderthal.* "Umm, Olive?"

"Lil, I need you to trust me on this. I know you're worried about the money and the logistics of all these events, but you're going to have to let go a little and trust me to make things happen. That's why I'm here. To put in the work so you don't have to worry about a damn thing. This gala will take some capital, but not as much as you think. I've been handing out markers in this city for a long time, darling. It's time to call them in."

I couldn't tell if she ignored me on purpose or didn't hear me.

"Olive, you've got—"

Lily's nose twitched. "I can't let you do that, Olive."

"Yes, you can. I can't think of a better reason. This community, these rescue dogs, the work you're doing here? To know that I'm helping that work carry on in the future? Well, let's just say I'm doing it for completely selfish reasons."

"Ollie, sweetheart, you have dog—"

She shot an annoyed look at me as she wrinkled her nose and caught sight of the trail of brown over the back of her shoulder.

Lily took that moment to call me out. "Hayes, did you drop Sadie's poop bag in my trash can?"

Olive's jaw went slack for the briefest moment before she fixed her face. "No, but he did sling it over my shoulder with a handful of dirty paper towels, and I have dog shit on my jacket, don't I?"

I couldn't help the cringe. My eyes squeezed tightly shut as I tugged at my beard. I'd washed my hands while Lily and Olive gathered the rest of the supplies for Iris. Slowly, I cracked open an eye. "Christ, I'm sorry. I hope I didn't ruin the jacket. I was so shocked when I saw you that I didn't even think about the poop. I'll pay to have it cleaned. Or replace it, or whatever. Sadie's poo wasn't solid, so it was a mess to clean up."

Shooting off the chair, she unbuttoned the jacket before pulling it from her shoulders and spinning it around to examine the stain.

I was so damn embarrassed, and I didn't get embarrassed. I'd just been sitting here mentally accusing her of floating air-biscuits, and I'd rubbed dog shit on her. I'd done a lot of dumb stuff in my life, but I'd never rubbed shit on an ex-girlfriend before.

The *Ex-Girlfriend, dipshit. The one that got away.*

She slanted a look at Lily, who was trying her damnedest not to laugh. Olive flipped the jacket inside out and folded it up before she grinned. "Let's just be grateful you didn't grab my ass, too."

Lily busted out laughing as I dropped my beet-red face into my palms. When I finally chanced a look, she was leaning on the edge of the desk looking sexy as hell with her strong bare shoulders and her lip rolled between her teeth on a stifled laugh. When she caught my eye, she sent me a wink that didn't do a damn thing to lessen my embarrassment, or how much I wanted her.

Thank Christ, she'd always had a good sense of humor.

Chapter Four

Love and Chaos Theory

Hayes

Ollie wadded up the poop-smeared jacket before throwing it in the hall trash can as Lily and I walked behind her to the parking lot. Her hair was longer than it used to be, all sleek and golden brown, perfectly coiffed into a low ponytail with a center part. Not a single fly away. It used to be a little wild. In college, it had a natural wave that always looked sexy as hell after a round of mattress Olympics.

She must use one of those flat iron things now. Not that the ponytail wasn't tripping my trigger. I could picture it wrapped around my fist as I gave it a gentle tug and she whispered *harder, baby* over her shoulder with those big brown fuck-me eyes. Jesus, I was giving myself wood. Looking at the two of us, you'd think I was the one that liked it hard in the sack, but more often than not, it was Olive who liked it a little rough. I tended toward the soft and slow, eye-gazing, emotional-connection-type sex. I was all about the romance. With her, anyway. I'd savored her body. Every touch, every kiss, as I drew out her desperate little moans and pleas until her eyes rolled back in her head and her limbs shook. I'd worshipped Olive. Like the queen she was. Is.

Not that I wasn't game for a good, hard fuck, too. Hell, the first time she bit me, it shocked me. I wondered if she still liked to bite. It wasn't hard enough to break the skin, just enough to leave a shallow bruise. She'd take the crown of my shoulder, the meat of my inner thigh, the skin stretched over my ribs, and bite down with enough pressure to make me hiss, leaving an imprint behind. Fuck if it didn't turn me on watching her full lips spread over her teeth before she sank them into my skin.

Forgetting where I was, I reached down and adjusted my jeans so my zipper wasn't pressing into my cock.

Lily slugged me in the shoulder, reminding me I wasn't in a locker room or on a football field. It wasn't acceptable to adjust my junk while staring at her friend's back. That had always been a bit of a problem for me with Lil—remembering she wasn't one of the guys.

"Oops. Sorry," I whispered.

That had always been me and Olive, though—the odd couple. I was the rough around the edges bad influence straight out of the Oklahoma trailer park. While she was the elegant, buttoned-up overachiever with perfectionist tendencies and exacting parents. I'd blow off class and drive three hours for a theater showing of *Rocky Horror.* She made to-do and goals lists every morning that she had completely checked off every night.

Until we got into bed, that is. But after a while, the wild child I only saw in the sack started to come out and play in other ways, too. I'd rubbed off on her.

If only she'd rubbed off on me a little more then. I wouldn't be between a rock and hard place now.

Before dashing off to get something from her car, Lily gave me a hug and a quick slap on the ass.

"Olive! Wait up!" I yelled. Her shoulders tensed before she ever turned around. "We should exchange info, don't you think? Maybe we can grab a bite and talk through some of this stuff? I've never been on this side of it before, but I'll help any way I can. I actually know a guy over at Lone Star Field. I could call him if you think it would help. I'd like to get caught up on the gala stuff, too."

Nodding, she slipped a hand into her designer work bag and fished out a business card. "If you email me, I'll get you caught up on the planning and we can divide up the things that need to be done. Right now, I need to focus on the State Fair since it's not far off. I have a contact on the board of directors who owes me a favor." I didn't miss the way she was looking over my shoulder instead of meeting my eyes. Or the way she shifted her weight from one foot to the other.

Taking the card, I brushed my fingers over hers and didn't let go. A flush crawled up her neck as her chocolatey eyes widened, the gold flecks catching the sunlight. Goose bumps chased over her shoulders—even though it was mid-September and still hot in Texas—and I could see her heartbeat at the base of her throat.

I still tripped her triggers, too. The flirty grin that quirked my lips was a reaction I couldn't control. "How've you been, Ollie? I mean, you look amazing, and you're obviously doing well for yourself, but I'd love to catch up, talk about old times. What we've been doing the last decade? Why we haven't crossed paths again before now."

She rocked the heel of her shoe back before tapping the toe on the concrete. "I'm swamped at work. Email is best. We can Zoom, but don't have time for much else."

Ahh, she was holding a grudge. Yeah, I'd been a prick. I'd dumped her the night before the draft. In truly immature fashion, I'd told her it would be best if I didn't have any attachments as a pro because I'd be traveling a lot and it would be easier on both of us. That I needed to have my options open.

Fuck, I'd been such a dickhead.

Truth was, I'd loved her back then. When I'd looked at her, I'd seen my future. But as my mother so kindly reminded me, I was my father's son, and he was an absentee, cheating bastard. I couldn't hurt Olive that way. I'd broken it off, regretting it every day since. But here she was. In the flesh. The yang to my yin.

The only girl I'd ever fallen for wrapped up in the amazing, sexy woman before me.

Reluctantly, I let my fingers slip from hers and accepted the card. "Next time, then. I'll email you and we'll get me up to speed."

Nodding, she ran her tongue first over her top lip and then the bottom before a breath escaped from between them.

"It's good to see you, Olive. I've missed you over the years. I'm glad they've been kind to you, sweetheart. I'm not sure if I should hug you or shake your hand so I'll let you tell me."

I could see the debate going on in her head. "You've already rubbed shit on me, Walker, so it might as well be a hug." In the end, I think it was her sheer stubbornness that forced her to walk into my arms. But, God, did it feel good. Right. Natural. Just as it always had. I closed my hands around her back, her warm breath playing over the spot on my neck that had always been hers alone.

She pulled back too quickly for my liking, got in her car, and hands at ten and two, she reversed out of her spot.

I tapped my thumb against the card. It was elegant, modern, sleek—just like her. Olive Russo. Live, and in person instead of in one of my better dreams. The fact that she was still holding a grudge told me more than she could.

Truth. Losing my position on the Bulldogs roster had done a number on me. I knew I was too old to be playing, but football was all I knew. With the exception of taking care of my sister and mother, it was all I'd cared about for the last decade. The only thing I was good at, and Lily's stepdad had taken it away from me.

I still got out of bed in the morning. I still watched my diet and ran with Brody. I still did conditioning and worked hard to stay fit in the hopes another team would need a tight end and come calling. Spending time with Sadie a few times a week had been my only haven because we were kindred spirits. I knew what it was like to be unwanted. We were both too old and had too many issues other people didn't want to deal with.

Everyone wanted the puppies, the younger dogs. The ones that had worked through all of their issues, but Sadie and me... Well, we didn't fall into that group.

Despite my turn in thoughts, I cracked a smile and slid the card into my back pocket as I walked to my Harley.

I had another reason to get out of bed now.

Besides training, and helping at the shelter, the one that got away was in my life again, even if it was only for a little while, and I wasn't going to screw it up.

Olive

The lights on the tollway were just coming on as I drove home, the sky turning dusky orange and soft blue with dark gray clouds off to the west. I was supposed to have drinks with a client after I finished with Lily, but I canceled. Seeing Hayes had left me out of sorts. It was the last thing I'd expected. The shock to my system made me feel like chilled glass in a four-hundred-degree oven—cracked all over and hoping I could hold it together until the heat was off.

I hated that feeling.

Dealing with a client's chaos was one thing. It was my job to make order of the chaos they created, and I fucking excelled. But when the monkeys were in *my* zoo... That was a whole different thing.

Hayes Walker was a special brand of chaos. He was that one monkey. You know the one—that little bastard who was always the ringleader and sucked you into his shenanigans. When I finally got past my shock of seeing him, I felt frozen with indecision—which was another no-no for me. How did one react to such an encounter? Should I lose my shit and go full shrew on him, complete with red-faced screaming? I hadn't heard from him after the night he dumped me—he deserved my wrath. Or should I skip the screaming and opt to rub all my naughty bits against all his naughty bits? The man was yummy from head to toe. Neither was an appropriate response, for fuck's sake.

Hayes... Jesus.

It wasn't like I hadn't seen him on TV over the years. I didn't follow his career or anything, but I lived in a city that revolved around oil and football. Yeah, I caught a game now and then since he'd been traded from Carolina to Dallas. So sue me. He hadn't had as many tattoos back in college, and the hair—OMG, what was that haircut even called? That long on top thing that looked like he put pomade in it to sweep it back off his face. It was goddamned sexy. Made me want to give it a good hard tug while his face was between my thighs. And the beard. Honestly, beards were not my thing. Nothing against Jason Momoa, some guys can pull off the whole scraggly beard thing, but on most, it just looked like something from an episode of *Duck Dynasty*. Give me a clean, sharp jaw any day.

Of course, I knew Hayes had a jaw that could cut glass under his face fur, but his beard wasn't scroungy-looking either. It was frigging curated. Every bit as well-groomed as the hair on his head, the golden-blond length grew a little past his chin where he'd shaped it into a soft point he liked to stroke when was thinking. It smelled good, too. Woodsy; and soft against my cheek. I wondered what it would feel like to run my fingers through it, or feel it tickle the skin of my back as he kissed his way down my spine. Did he have a little comb for it, and beard oil or whatever? I bet he did. He'd keep it right next to the pomade. Was he all neat and tidy downstairs, too?

When I stepped out of my car in my garage, I winced as a familiar ache resonated through my lower leg. A thunderstorm was moving into the area and the rod I had in my shin was my very own weather predictor.

That instantly chilled my musings on manscaping. After slipping my heels off, I dropped my Whataburger bag on the marble counter and pulled an ice pack out of the freezer.

After I shucked my suit for yoga pants and an Unruly Dog Training Center T-shirt, I pulled out my ponytail. Damn, I'd gotten it too tight today. It gave me a bit of a tension headache. Sliding up on a bar stool, I propped my left leg on the one next to me and wrapped the ice pack around my shin, securing it with the attached Velcro straps.

I knew my accident wasn't Hayes's fault. I didn't hate him for it or blame him. In truth, the boy I'd known was kind and generous. Thoughtful, even. Right up until the night he'd dumped me by text like a selfish fucking asshole. Still, all I blamed him for was the broken heart and the bad taste in my mouth.

The accident was mine and mine alone. I was the one who refused to give the keys to my friends outside a dive bar; I was the one who chose to drive drunk after going on the Broken Heart Bender.

I didn't remember a lot of the crash details or feel much pain at the time. I had alcohol and shock to thank for that. But I did remember the sound of the impact. A huge, metallically leaden, whooshing *THUNK*. I'd decided to take a country road because I knew I'd had too much to drink. Except the road got all twisty and winding, and my brain was all fuzzy. I didn't see the curve coming and definitely didn't expect the headlights right around the corner. I was in the wrong lane on a two-lane road and couldn't react fast enough from the curve. The other car swerved, ended up in the ditch. I overcorrected and my car launched off the raised road into the trees. I remembered the green rushing toward me, but I didn't remember the impact, and I don't know how long I was knocked out for.

When I came to, my windshield was broken, my airbag deployed, and both my legs were stuck under the collapsed steering column.

After the firefighters cut me out, I got a glimpse of the bones coming through the skin, and had promptly thrown up.

I bit into my burger, wishing my house wasn't so… still. Sterile. No clicking of doggie nails on the hardwood, no whimpers of *feed me, Mama*, or *play with my toy*. No familiar, strong arms to welcome me home and comfort me when the tears slipped down my cheeks because everywhere I looked, I saw Cassie. She'd been my little piece of the unpredictable in my intricately planned days. I missed her so much—her little yips and warm snout as she burrowed under the covers clear down to my feet.

I hadn't realized quite how alone I was until this moment. Until I saw Hayes today and was enveloped in familiar arms.

There'd been other men in my life, sure, but only one I'd loved. One I thought I'd spend my life with and compared all others to, albeit unfairly. And he'd broken my heart, without warning, because he was a self-centered son of a bitch that "wanted to keep his options open." Which, of course, was code for *fuck a shit ton of women because I'm about to be a pro football player*.

The man actually wondered how we'd never run into each other in all these years? Because that's how I'd orchestrated it. I'd passed on some big-name clients over the years to stay away from football. I'd been carefully avoiding Hayes Walker over the last decade and change. As I glanced around my pristine, well-ordered home, I realized he'd reminded me of something, or really someone.

He reminded me that the wild child inside me wasn't dead, just sleeping. Deep down, for sure, but still there, sawing logs. The one I thought I'd buried for good back in the woods off FM 455.

He reminded me that I missed the chaos.

Chapter Five

It's never "just a dog"

Olive

With a yawn, and my second cup of coffee in my travel mug, I pulled into Gina's driveway and shot her a text.

Olive: I'm here.

Gina: Be right out. Can I bring Boops?

Boops was an awesome dog.

Olive: Of course! Are you going to run?

The back door of my SUV opened before I got the reply, and Boops stuck his head in, putting his paws on the door frame so Gina could lift his butt the rest of the way. "No, not going to run, just watch, but at least he'll be worn out when we get back." She grunted as she lifted the Boopster into the cargo area I had partitioned off with a dog gate. Cassie still had a bed back there, so he'd be comfortable enough.

Boops was a Bassador Retriever. With the body and long ears of a Basset Hound, and the head, coat, and tail of a Black Lab, the dog was beyond adorable. He was a funny little dude who liked to play fetch and chase birds as much as he liked to snooze in the sun and track rabbits. Boops was titled in agility, tracking, and scent work, to boot. Gina had found Boops and his brother Buster tied to the door of her practice one morning, no explanation.

The trial we were going to in Fort Worth was a fund-raiser for canine cancer research, and always fun. There were pros—international competitors and national team members alike—but there were also first-timers just learning the ropes and giving some money to a good cause.

It gave me an idea. I picked my phone up and thumbed up my to-do list in my Unlovabulls folder. Made a note as Gina slid into my passenger seat.

Call Texas Weekly *on NBC 5 about airing a spot on the Unlovabulls—an agility exhibition with a couple Bulldogs players and their own dogs against agility dogs from the rescue with their handlers.*

Hmm. That wasn't a half-bad idea. We could promote the Dallas Bulldogs' appearance at the fair, announce the gala, and show viewers that rescued bullies can be excellent pets. If we could use the Unruly Dog to film, they'd get a little promo out of it as well.

Monday—Call Diane Higgins at NBC 5 and Lauren at the Unruly Dog about using the space.

Boops whined and brought my head up. "We're going, buddy." Yawning again, I pulled out of Gina's drive and followed my nav's directions toward Cowtown.

"Late night?"

I nodded. I didn't really like to talk while I drove—I didn't take calls either—but when I had a guest in the car, I didn't have much choice. "I spent time doing research for the rescue fundraisers. I've got a lot of footwork to do and not a lot of time."

I couldn't see Gina's grin so much as I could feel it. "Are you sure it wasn't a certain football player? Thanks to Brody, we get a *lot* of those around the rescue, and let me tell you, those fellas are more than a little distracting."

I cut a glance at her. "What do you know?"

"Not much, but after I finished the Neo's ACL repair, I spent some time with Lily in Iris's whelping room."

"Everything go okay there?"

"Yeah, the Neo is on crate rest for eight weeks so that the TPLO has time to heal, but he should be okay. A little arthritis maybe. Hopefully I won't need to take the plate out." She had a sigh in her voice that told me she was tired, too.

"What about Iris?"

"Nine puppies. Zero complications. Looks like Iris might like the bully boys, too. The pups are definitely mixed with some kind of bully breed, but it's way too early to tell. Give it a few weeks and I'll be able to pick out what they're mixed with." Gina had a talent for looking at mixed breed dogs and being able to tell most of the breeds that were in the gene pool. "But you didn't answer my question about what kept you up. Elaborate, please."

I shrugged. "Lily told you I know Hayes."

She nodded. "Yes, that you and Hayes seem to know each other well. Or you did at one time. Girl, blonds are not usually my thing, but that man…" She fanned herself. "He's got a Jax Teller thing going and he's built like a Percheron draft horse—big and strong, and still elegant."

I didn't even try to stop the laugh that burst through my lips. "Truth."

"He makes me think of the kind of sex that's border-line illegal in some counties."

That was also truth, but I didn't tell her how apt her description was. Instead, I let a fondly held memory play across my face. He had this thing he liked to do with his finger—

"Umm, spill," Gina demanded. "Right this minute. What were you thinking about?"

I huffed out a breath and grinned.

"So that's how it is." She waved me away. "At least tell me how you know him."

"Hayes and I were a thing in college. We went to Oklahoma University together. You're right about the Jax Teller thing. Back then, though, he was a little more clean-cut. More…boyish." He'd also been my Achilles' heel, but I left that part out. "We broke up right before he was drafted. It was probably for the best. I was only a junior and he would have been a rookie in the NFL traveling all the time." Of course, that's not how I felt back then. Or even how I felt today, for that matter.

"Ahh, two different paths, huh? Well, with my divorce final, I'm ready to get back on the horse, if you know what I mean." Gina's bronze face lit up with delight as she made a giddy-up gesture. I couldn't help the laugh. Not many people got to see this side of the good doctor—her divorce had been long and painful.

"You're ready to start looking for the next Mr. Avalos already?" I slanted her a quick glance.

"What? Hell, no. I'm never getting married again. That boy..." She made a pffft sound. "Because he was definitely a *boy*—whose mama spoiled him rotten, I might add, so he assumed I'd do the same. I wasn't his damn mama. No, I'm just looking to have some fun. Sample the wares. But I'm sticking with actual men this time—a lot less complicated if you ask me. Get in, get off, get out, goodbye. What about you and Hayes? Going to give that another shot?"

"God, no!" *Oophf, methinks thou doth protest too much.* "I just mean that ship has sailed. We're planning the fundraisers together is all." It was time for a subject change. "Did Iris do okay with the puppies? She took to mothering okay?"

Gina sent me a knowing look, but let it slide. "She did beautifully. Started cleaning and feeding them right away. She'd nose them every few minutes to make sure everyone was still there. She was amazing."

That made my heart go all soft around the edges, which must have shown on my face. "Are you ready for another dog, Olive? Cassie's been gone for a while now, and Iris will need a home, plus I know nine puppies that will be looking for forever homes in the next eight to ten weeks."

I shook my head. "Rescues never have problems placing pups. I'm not ready yet. Cassie was such a huge part of my life. Without her, I wouldn't know any of you. I'll admit that I hate coming home to an empty house, but I still see her there, you know? I'm hoping that being around the rescue and the training center more often will help me move past it."

"Mmm. This is why I always have two dogs. It's easier when you lose one because you have the other."

"How has Boops handled losing Buster since the divorce?"

At the sound of his name, Boops let out a hound dog bay that rattled the windows.

"Ahh, I love that sound," Gina said, fondly. "He misses his brother. He wanders the house looking for him and he's started pottying in the house and tearing stuff up. I'm going to have to get another dog since the Basset in him won't do well as an only dog. Not that I'm ready. I miss Buster as much as he does. I love those dogs so much I had a two-year custody battle over them, for Christ's sake. What I wouldn't give to still have them both."

"Divorces, man. They're hell on the kids."

Gina chuckled without humor. "You know, Hayes spends a lot of time at the rescue. He's there at least three times a week cleaning kennels, giving baths, washing laundry. He loves that old Boxer with her white face. I don't know why he doesn't adopt her."

"Hah." Whoops, I hadn't meant to blurt that out.

Gina shot me a side-eye.

"From what I know of Hayes, it might be best. He can be wonderfully considerate, but also impulsive and not always reliable. He never thinks much about how his actions affect others."

She turned her head to look at me. "You're speaking from experience?"

I nodded, and Gina shook her head in disgust. "What the hell is wrong with men?"

"I don't even know."

When we walked into Will Rogers Arena, the smell of air-conditioning and dirt permeated my nose. It was a great place for an agility trial because it was generally used for cattle and stock shows. The dirt was easy on the dogs' joints, and they kept it cold as hell in here. Though it had always been a little hard for Cassie, given her nose and prey drive. She'd had a mind of her own, and when she'd thought better of it, she'd much rather chase rats than run obstacle courses.

Lily wasn't planning on running her dogs today, so I was surprised to see her warming up with her Australian Shepherd, Jet, outside the first ring while another group ran in a second ring.

"Hey, Boops! How are ya, buddy?" Brody's smooth-as-silk bass turned both mine and Gina's heads, and Boops let out his hound dog *Ahhhrrooooo!* as Brody bent to pet him. "Wasn't expecting to see him today. You running, Gina?"

She shook her head. "Just watching today."

With a last pat for Boops, Brody stood, nudged my shoulder.

"I didn't think Lily was running today either." I nodded in the direction of his fiancée.

"She couldn't resist. Came to watch me and CC and got sucked into a demonstration during the break in Ring One. She's gonna run Mack, too. You know, show her students what an open-level dog looks like when competing."

Gina stuck her arm up and waved at someone in the distance. "I see Kate and Carrie with Jasmine and Sasha. Boops and I are going to wish them luck before their run."

Brody barely waited until she was out of earshot to grill me. "So, you and Hayes..." Lily told Brody. I should have told her to keep it to herself.

"There is no me and Hayes, big guy."

"Oklahoma University, huh? You guys were a thing?"

He was fishing. I hadn't told Lily how I knew Hayes, just that I did. Gina was the only one that knew we'd been a couple. Once. "It was a long time ago."

"Yeah, that's what Hayes said. He has a different inflection in his voice, and what looks like hope in his eyes." Brody crossed his arms over his expansive chest, leaned in. "He's not been doing so great since he lost his spot on the team, Olive. He'd never admit it, but he's not been in a good headspace. You know, I've known him for a few years now, and he doesn't talk about women with the kind of reverence he did when he told me about you. There was a light in his eyes I haven't seen in the last few months. I know Hayes does occasional one-nighters, but he never brought those women up or bragged about them like some of the other guys. When he talks about you, though, it's different. He's a regular Chatty Cathy. Said you two were joined at the hip at one time, and then he went on about how great you are. How smart and strong and beautiful." Brody sent me a pointed look.

I quirked an eyebrow. "Should he get a medal for that?"

He shook his head. "Not saying that. He didn't tell me about the breakup, and I'm not asking, but Walker has always had a lightness to him that's been missing since he got cut from the team. The only other time I see it is when he spends time with Sadie at the rescue."

Eyeing him, I made sure he heard my next words clearly. "Brody, I am planning fundraisers with Hayes because I'm the best at my job and I believe in the res-cue. No less and no more. There is a lot more history behind mine and Hayes's breakup than you, or even he, knows. I appreciate that you care for your friend, but whatever he thinks, or that you're trying to deduce, might be between Hayes and me—whatever stroll down memory lane he's hoping for—it's not going to happen. If I were you, I'd discourage him from those thoughts every chance you get."

Brody snorted, wrapped one of those big arms around my shoulders. "Never say never, Ollie. Look at me and Lil."

I wanted to tell him to take a flying fuck but looking into warm brown eyes as they danced with mischief, and at his kind smile, I couldn't be mad. "You're lucky you're cute, Shaw."

"Lily tells me that all the time. Hey, I've got a favor to ask. Lil wanted me to talk her students through her demos, but CC and I won't be able to carry out our pre-game rituals if I do. If I introduce you to them, can you walk them through it?"

Football players and their superstitions. "Sure, lead the way."

Chapter Six

The Long Shot

Hayes

Glorious. It was the only word I could use to describe watching Olive explain the agility classification system to the group of Lily's students. She had on Kelly green and black yoga pants that stopped just below the knees, and a matching green jacket that had the Unruly Dog Training Center's logo on the back. Her warm brown mane was pulled up into a high ponytail, and her makeup-less face made her look younger. When I noticed the dark smudges under her eyes, I wondered if she'd lost as much sleep because of me as I had with her in my thoughts. Huh. Wishful thinking. I wasn't stupid—it was a steep hill to climb if I wanted back on Olive Russo's good side. You know the cliché "you don't know what you got till it's gone"?

Yeah, that.

"They're going to do a Gambler's course. Then Lily's going to run her open-level dog, Mack, for you to see where you would start out."

Olive's sultry voice poured down my spine and set

my dick to stirring in my jeans. *Down, big fella.* But trying to will it away was having zero effect.

"See the ribbon on the ground? The handlers can't cross those lines to get their dogs to take the obstacles behind it. Each dog and handler team will get points for every obstacle they take, but some are worth more than others. Then the dog must take a set sequence of obstacles from behind the ribbon where the handler can't go. They can take the first part of the course in any order, but handlers have to strategize to get the most points. Since Jet is a MACH dog, Lily has more obstacles behind the ribbon than most would."

"What's a MACH dog?" I asked, watching her for a reaction. She didn't so much as flinch, but some of the smile fell from her face as those big dark eyes met mine. Seemed Olive had regained her famous Russo composure after she'd left yesterday. I'd never seen her so thrown off before, but that air of complete competence she'd always had was back in place.

"Masters Agility Champion. It's the highest title a dog can attain in agility."

"So, it's like baseball. Single A, double A, triple A, major league."

"Yes, but agility is Novice, Open, Excellent, and Masters. The AKC has a Premier class, too. It's open to all levels but the courses are difficult even for highly experienced dogs," she said to the group in general. "USDAA, the sanctioning body for today's match, doesn't have a Premier class."

As Olive turned back to the ring, Lily took a lead out on her dog while Jet vibrated with energy. "Jet, break!" When Lil gave the magic word, the dog was off and running, dirt flying into the air behind her. They took tunnels and the A-frame, the dog walk and jumps as Lily's students oohed and ahhed at Jet's speed and skill, and the handler/dog teamwork. But what was really impressive was when they came to the obstacles behind the ribbon pinned to the ground. Lily stopped with her toes an inch off the line while Jet kept going into the special section. Lil began calling out commands to the Aussie as she moved back and forth the length of the ribbon without ever crossing it. "Teeter, Jet. Weave. Go, go, go, go, go," Lil encouraged before pointing to a jump sequence and tunnel, yelling out which way she wanted the dog to turn, and yes, Jet knew her right from left.

When they finished, and Jet ran through the laser timer on the last jump, Lil called her. The dog jumped into her arms with a look that said, *I'm a total badass and I know it.*

It was something to see, but what was even more interesting was watching Ollie out of the corner of my eye. The woman was beyond competitive. Always had been, and there was both a fondness and longing in her eyes, but also a hint of sorrow.

"Hey, Olive?" Out of breath, Lil placed Jet back on the ground.

"Yeah?"

"I tweaked my ankle. Do you think you could take Mack on a standard run for me? I promised I'd show my students what agility looks like for their dogs, and that not even the coach's dogs are perfect."

A sweet smile slipped over Olive's face. "Absolutely."

"Awesome, I'll pull up the ribbon." Lil met my eyes. "Hayes, can you put Jet in her kennel and grab Mack?"

I took the Australian Shepherd with me to where I'd seen CC kenneled earlier and swapped Jet for Mack.

Mack was my bud. The Staffordshire Terrier was aptly named—he was built like a Mack Truck. Short legs, blue-gray coat with that bully-style head. Scars all along his thick body thanks to the puppy mill he escaped from. But he was the sweetest little dude, and so damn goofy you couldn't help but love him. Half the class grinned at his rolling gait and lolling tongue as I handed his leash to Olive. Mack looked like the kind of dog you wouldn't want to get cornered by, but truth was he was a total marshmallow.

Sitting him down between her feet behind the first jump, Olive pulled his collar and lead off, pitching them to me while Lily talked to her class. "Mack is an open-level dog, just barely... I still don't know how we ever moved up from Novice. Blind luck, maybe?" The group chuckled. "Your doggos would start in Novice as well. Mack doesn't have a lead out like Jet does. If Olive doesn't stay with him, he'll take off and make up his own course. He likes to do that, but with standard runs, you have to take the obstacles in order."

It hadn't escaped me that several people had gathered in the bleachers near the course, and it was quieter than it had been when Lily ran. Everyone was watching Olive.

I felt Brody walk up beside me. His voice was low and a little out of breath. CC sat quietly at his feet, her watchful Cane Corso eyes missing nothing. "Olive's agility dog passed away a year ago. She hasn't gotten another dog, yet. It really tore her up. Most of these people running today knew her and Cassie."

Nodding, I watched as Olive leaned down and whispered something into Mack's ear before she took off running on her long, strong legs. Mack followed, taking the first jump, and the clock started its count while Lily narrated for her students. Mack was not Jet, but he was having a blast as Olive ran him to a tunnel and yelled, "Tunnel, Mack. Go!" The first tunnel he made perfectly, then cut back into a second tunnel according to Olive's hand signal. But when the Staffy turned and popped back out of the same end with that big bully grin, everyone laughed. It was precisely why Lily wanted her students to see Mack run. To show them agility could be fun for dogs and handlers at any level. "Go, go, go!" Olive shooed him into the tunnel and goosed his butt.

As he emerged from the tunnel at the correct end, she made for the next obstacle. "Mack, jump!" But the dog simply stood there directly in front of the bar. Olive stopped. "C'mon, buddy. Let's go!" Her face was beyond animated.

Brody leaned in. "Eh, he's not gonna take the jump unless she makes kissy noises."

As if he'd spoken directly to her, Olive made loud kissy noises and Mack jumped over the bar, catching it with his back foot and knocking it down. When they got to the teeter-totter, the little fireplug did something astonishing. He went up the side of the plank that was on the floor but slowed to a stop right at the teeter's fulcrum. Then he just…balanced there, both ends in the air as he rocked on the fulcrum only slightly while he stared at Olive with his doggie grin. Lily's students scrambled to get pictures. "Mack, touch!" Ollie pointed to the end of the board, but he didn't budge. "Mack Truck! Let's go! Touch, buddy." It took a little more coaxing and a lot of laughter on Olive's part to finally get the dog to descend. When they got to the A-frame, he did it all over again, scrambling up to the top with his short little legs, only to stand there like he was king of the hill. Long after the timer buzzer went off, Olive and Mack crossed the last jump. Olive heaped attention and scratches on him just as Lily had with Jet.

Clapping started, more people than just Lily's students, but from all around the ring. Olive looked around.

"The clapping isn't for Mack." Brody joined in, letting out an earsplitting whistle. When I glanced at Lily, her eyes were watery. "Everyone here knows how hard it is to lose a dog, and this... It's the beginning of the healing. You should know she's not seeing anybody, Hayes. I don't know the full story, and after talking to her today, I don't think you do either. The universe is trying to tell you two something here." Slanting a peek at Brody, I noticed his eyes were a little wet as well. "Don't ignore that, my man."

He'd always been a bit of a crier.

But it was Olive's face that held me captivated. Mack danced around her feet as tears fell down her sweet round cheeks and she cupped her hands over her mouth in awe.

"There's plenty *she* doesn't know about the breakup either, but I do still care about her." I knew it the moment I saw her again. The weight on my shoulders lifted, if only briefly. As much as I wanted to give it another shot with Olive, was that even fair to her? I hoped to get contracted with another team. I'd have to move if that happened. Still, I couldn't get my heart to cooperate with my head on the matter.

Brody clapped me on the shoulder, and I let out an earsplitting whistle of my own.

Once people started going about their business again, I made my way over to Olive and Lily just as their hug broke apart and Lily walked away. "Hey," I said, hesitantly.

"Hey." Her voice was a little rougher than normal.

"I don't know much about agility, but I'm fairly sure that run isn't going to win any titles." I let a grin slide over my face.

As beautiful as I'd ever seen her, with red, puffy eyes, Olive let a laugh burst from her lips. "No, definitely not, but Mack is so much fun."

"Brody told me about your dog, Cassie. I'm sorry you lost her. We always had strays around my house." I shifted my weight from one foot to the other. "My mom would get pissed when I'd take them leftovers or whatever and she'd never let me have one of my own. But seeing Brody with CC, I can't imagine how hard it would be on him to lose her."

Nodding, she didn't meet my eyes, choosing to stare at the dirt floor instead. "Thank you. Cassie was the little bit of chaos in my otherwise well-ordered life. Kind of like you were years ago."

As the next round of handlers began walking the course to plan their runs, Olive settled in with her weight on one hip to watch. I could see her formulating her own run in her head. I noticed several people in the ring with arms out, practicing their cues. "Why are so many of them spinning in a circle there?" I nodded at them.

"Huh?" She looked up. "Oh. After the set of jumps, they'll want to pick up the dog on the outside for the next set of tunnels."

"Why not just cross paths with the dog?"

"That works if you're faster than your dog and you can stay ahead of them, or if you have the ability to send your dog to the tunnel sequence without going with them, but if you don't have a send or can't stay ahead of the dog, you run the risk of the two of you running into each other. That's dangerous for both handler and dog. The dog's safety always comes first. They can accomplish the same goal with a quick one-eighty on their feet at the edge of the jump."

"There's a lot more that goes into this than I realized. It's not just teaching your dog to take obstacles, is it?"

She grinned as she continued to watch the handler's walkthrough. "No, it's a little more complex than that. Dogs read body language. There's a lot of subtlety in running an agility course that laypeople don't notice. For instance, see what she's doing there?" Olive pointed to an older lady turning a one-eighty at the edge of a jump. "That's called a post turn. Because the dog has to double back at that jump going in the opposite direction for the A-frame, the dog will read the handler's motion, which way her shoulders are going, and follow her handler's lead. See how she's using her palm with a push motion toward the A-frame? It's called a push. She's using the motion to signal to her dog to push out to the obstacle without having to go with the animal. Instead, she can move to the next obstacle and let the dog take the A-frame on its own. Shoulder placement, hand signals, voice commands, where your feet are pointed, staying in motion without signaling the wrong thing to your dog. It can get quite complicated. Often, when a dog misses an obstacle or gets off course, it's the handler at fault."

I watched her face glow as she explained what I'm sure were fairly rudimentary agility commands. "I can tell you really love this, Olive. Why not get another dog?"

She crossed her arms, eyes searching for some unseen point on the ground. "I'm not ready. Cassie was a heart dog. Do you know that term?" The change in her demeanor, the cast-down gaze as the smile slipped from her face. She was hurting.

"I get the gist. Hey." I paused, waited for her to lift her chin until her eyes met mine. "I'd like to hear more about Cassie. Learn more about agility and about you, how you've been these past years, and how you built your business. All that. Has there been anyone special for you, Ollie? I just want to get to know you again." Reaching over, I grazed her hand with my fingertips, but she wasn't having it.

She shook her head. "Hayes, I'm sure you're a different person now than you were back then. But I am, too. As much as I'm tempted, your brand of chaos is too much. It was a decade ago, and it is now. The only difference is I was blind to it before. I can't get personal with you. We can work together for sake of the fundraisers, but that's where I draw the line." She met my eyes with resolve in the set of her shoulders.

"Can't? Or won't?" I tilted my head.

"Does it really matter?"

"Yeah, it matters. I know I hurt you, but I'd like you to let me show you who I am now. To be your friend, Olive." When she put a hand on my chest, I felt the current run through my body. That magnetic attraction that dogged us years before. It was just as powerful now.

We were polar opposites—being too close to each other would only end with us coming together. Maybe she was right; maybe we couldn't reconnect, but I'd be damned if I could stop myself from wanting to be near her. Wanting to know her. I'd take whatever crumbs she'd throw my way. When her eyes flared at the small touch, I knew she felt it, too—that pull. That attraction, like positive and negative charges.

I'd cut Olive deep. Deeper than I ever knew.

Instead of responding to my statement, she patted my chest twice and stepped around me. "I'll send you the email with the details on the gala tonight."

Winning even this woman's friendship would be a challenge, but I was up to the task. Friends. Just Friends. I didn't want to hurt her again.

Yet, deep down in some part of my soul that came online when she was near me—a part of me I'd thought long dead—I already knew that was most likely a long shot.

Chapter Seven

Throwing down the gauntlet

Hayes

My feet pounded the crushed gravel, my arms pumping as Brody and I hit our stride. "She's closed off. I know I was a dick and I hurt her but come on. There's got to be more to it than what she's said. It was ten fucking years ago. I'm not that kid anymore."

Brody sent me a little side-eye. "And you're sure there's something there?"

I thought about it. Nodded. "Without a doubt, and I know she feels it. Thing is, I'd take about anything at this point. Even if we're only friends. I want to know her again. To spend time with her. I mean, I guess I didn't realize it until I saw her again, but… Things that were out of whack clicked into alignment." *And I'm drowning over here, but she makes me want to kick for the surface again.*

"Jesus." Brody chuckled. "When did we both hand in our man cards? Look, I'd like nothing more than to see you and Olive rekindle a friendship, relationship, whatever. I do see a difference in you when you're around her. You're excited about life or some shit. But I don't know the history between you, and there's a very real chance she may never forgive you for whatever you did."

"I dumped her," I cut in.

"Aww, shit."

Indeed. "We were serious, but she was a couple of years behind me in college. I knew what life on the road would be like the first couple of years."

"You mean the girls." That was Brody for you, blunt as always.

I nodded. "I didn't want her dropping out of school to come with me and I knew the temptation I'd be dealing with. I was stupid, didn't trust myself to be faithful, so I dumped her the night before the draft. In true slimeball fashion, I told her I wanted to keep my options open."

Brody's face scrunched up as he hissed between his teeth. "Ouch. Yeah, that was a dick move."

"What can I say, I was impressionable back then. I should have listened to the voice in my head instead of the one in my ear." I'd never told Brody about my mom, the weight I carried for my family, or that I was counting on another contract to dig me out of the hole I was in. It was nobody's business but mine.

"She loved you?"

I nodded.

"Damn, Walker. I can see why she's not keen on the idea of even a friendship with you."

The way I'd broken up with her… I hated myself for that. I'd loved her back then, thought we'd be together through thick and thin. Me bringing out her wild side while she calmed me the fuck down. Letting my mom get in my head was one of the worst things I'd ever done. Plus, the way I'd played it…yeah, I was a great big bag of dicks. I hadn't really known what to tell her at the time because I didn't want to split up with her, but I'd felt like I didn't have a choice either. Not if I didn't want to hurt her even worse. Sharlene Walker was a force to be reckoned with and the woman had always been aces at twisting me up, even now.

"I don't trust her, Hayes. She's lookin' to ride your coattails and secure her own future."

Oh, like you're not? I'd thought it but didn't have the balls to say it. From the minute my high school coach wrote me the recommendation for Oklahoma University and told Sharlene I had NFL potential, Mama was laser-locked on keeping my eyes on the prize. I was her ticket out of the trailer park and into the penthouse.

"Family comes first, son—me, your little sister and her education." My sister, Jessica, had always been my biggest weak spot.

"Besides, if you're anything like your cheating daddy, you'd be doing her a favor."

Brody tapped me, pulling me from the memory. Stopping, he kicked up his foot to stretch his quad while I dropped down on my haunches to stretch out my hamstring.

"The thing is, Shaw... I loved her, too. Back then."

Squinting one eye shut, he looked at me. "Back then, huh?" A small grin tipped his lips as he let go of his ankle. "Hayes, my man." Brody smacked me on the shoulder. "You are so fucked."

Hell, yeah, I was. Pushing his hand off, I took off down on the trail followed by Brody's heavy breathing. Spinning around, I jogged backward, grinning at him. "What's the matter, bro? A little winded, are we?

Gonna settle into that whole dad-bod thing as soon as the wedding's over?"

"Eat me, Walker." He shot me the bird as I flipped around to watch where I was going.

"You know what you need?" Brody said as he pulled even with me. "Well, you need to apologize to Olive, but if you want to unburn that bridge, you need to make a grand gesture."

"The fuck is that?"

"It's what I did when I begged everyone for money so Lily could open the shelter and quit working for her stepdad."

"Dude, nobody is ever going to top that. The rest of us are screwed."

Brody's smile was huge. "Ha. I know. You don't need to top it, though. You need your own thing to tell her how sorry you are about the way you left things."

Hmm, it wasn't a bad idea. Not just telling Olive I was sorry but going out of my way to do it. "Yeah, but what would I do?"

"You have to figure that out, my man. But you wanna wipe the slate clean? That's how you do it. Show her you're sorry. You need anything to pull it off, I'm happy to help. Just ask me."

"Grand gesture. That's not bad, Shaw. Not bad at all."

"Down. Set. Hut!" Dropping back, I loaded up the ball for rookie tight end Daniel McManus. He had quick, sure feet and was a hell of a blocker, but he liked to get sloppy with the fundamentals. Ten yards. Fifteen. McManus ran the post, cutting inside. As soon as the safeties split, I rifled the ball into his number. He caught it, turned up field and started running, but never ripped the ball in. Coming fast on his right, a kid from the practice squad got a hand on it, nearly knocking it loose.

"Goddamn it. You're killing me, Smalls," I spat the line from *The Sandlot* under my breath. If this had been a real game instead of practice, he would have turned the ball over.

Unfortunately, McManus wasn't my only source of frustration lately. It had been a shit week. Daniel was a general pain in my ass, I still hadn't heard from my agent, my mother had called asking for money, and Ollie was ducking me, purposely cutting me out of any planning.

It had been a few days since the agility trial, and I'd hoped to pin her down to talk through the plans for the gala, and the possibility of a baseball game. The only response I'd gotten was a list of possible vendors and venues along with dates she thought would work for the players and what she'd like me to pull together from the team perspective. She'd relegated me to the bench without seeing the skills I brought to the field, and yeah, my panties were in a wad about it.

Brody's idea of a gesture had merit, but I had to get the woman face-to-face in order to apologize, and she had an excuse to avoid me at every turn. Client meetings, lunch plans, going to the gym, had to take her car in, hair appointment, had a party to attend, yada, yada. I'd even called her office a few times in hopes of pinning her down that way, but she wasn't taking those calls either.

I whistled the play dead. "Tight ends, gather round!" I yelled as calmly as I could manage.

On the upside, I'd gotten to know Olive's assistant, Johnathan, a bit while she'd been avoiding me. The guy was a fount of information that I'm quite sure she wouldn't want him sharing with me. I knew Olive rarely took a lunch break, and expected a lot out of her employees, but in return, she treated them like rock stars. The firm had a couple of problem clients, one of whom Olive had taken on only as a favor to Johnathan. Johnnie also said that Olive dated, but never got serious. Oh, and she still had the dog bed in her office from when Cassie came to work with her—which had been nearly every day.

As frustrated as I was, I couldn't stop myself from thinking about her. Even the lifting and running, the team practices—they didn't help me get my mind off Olive. Spending time with Sadie was the only respite I got, and even that didn't distract me completely. I treasured my time with my sweet old girl. When we played fetch, her wiggly little nub made her whole ass end wag. The way she'd nuzzle into my chest when I dropped down on my haunches. Truth was, Sadie Mae was as close as I'd come to falling for a girl since Olive. I knew the black Boxer was a little long in the tooth, but I still couldn't figure out why nobody had inquired about her. She was an amazing dog. Smart, still playful, pretty, and sweet as pie. I would have adopted her myself if it weren't for football. Probably not the best environment for a rescue dog.

As McManus sauntered up, I slapped his lid with my palm. "Dammit, we talked about this." The rookie who bumped me off the roster still had a lot to learn. He had a huge potential but wasn't good at taking direction. "Catch. Rip. Tuck. Drop-step. These are basics, rook." When I caught him glancing at the sideline, I grabbed his face mask and hauled his head around, forcing him to meet my eyes. "I'm sorry I'm fucking with your so-cial time but you're getting paid to play. The fuck. Pay attention. Jesus, I don't know how you got away with that shit before, but you ain't in college anymore." I knew exactly how. He was a franchise player in the making, but if he didn't get that ego in check, he was going to piss it all away because he was uncoachable. Also, I'd rather light my taint on fire than actually *tell* him that and make the matter worse. "Listen up. If you carry that ball like a loaf of bread at the grocery store, you're going to lose it every time, and as a result, your roster spot. You got me? Because I won't hesitate to make sure you don't see any minutes this season." His eyes widened at that, and I let go of his face mask. "You know damn well you don't haul it in with one arm. That defenseman is going to knock it free every time. Use two hands to catch the ball, dammit. And rip it in with both!"

The overconfident tight end popped up his helmet, sweat shining on his face. The guys weren't in pads today, just running drills at the indoor practice field.

"Coach, ain't nobody here taking this ball from me. I know what I'm doing."

Oh, like hell he did. Arrogant little prick.

It was time to teach him a lesson.

"Tell you what, I'm going to line up across from you. If I fail to get that ball away from you, you can fuck off for the day while the rest of the team practices. But I knock it loose, and you're going to run your ass off until the last player leaves the field. Then you're going to start doing it my way. Got me?"

He pulled his helmet back on. "Come at me, old man."

I rolled my eyes. "Somebody give me a lid." Within seconds, I had a helmet in my hand and noticed players and coaches laying bets on the sideline. Even the team's head coach laid twenty on me.

Daniel got into his three-point stance and I lined up across from him, already seeing his first mistake. His feet were too close together. If I hit him straightaway, I could shift him off balance—he'd never even get a hand on the ball. But that was a lesson for another day.

"Set. Hut," the stand-in QB called. McManus ran his short route as I played him tight. When he turned to make the one-handed catch, I zeroed in on the ball. As he started to rip it down into the tuck, I wrapped him around the waist and put my helmet on the ball.

Forty-five minutes later, I whistled for my tight ends to call it a day while the cocky little shit was halfway through his last lap.

He jogged my way, breath coming heavily.

"How many laps was it?" I said, running a palm over my beard.

"Twelve."

I slapped him on the shoulder. "Tomorrow, you do it my way. Then we're going to work on those feet you had too close together. I catch you doin' that sloppy shit in a game? I will yank you faster than you can say *what the fuck*. And no, I don't care how much the team will be paying you to ride the bench. Got me?"

"Yes, coach."

"Hit the showers." Truthfully, I kind of liked coaching, passing on the things that I'd learned over my career, but I'd barely been able to pay the bills with my player's salary. A coach's salary didn't even come close. I needed to get back in pads and cleats.

Pointing my F-150 in the direction of my apartment, I punched a button on the steering wheel and read the cell number off Olive's business card aloud. Voicemail. Again.

What a surprise. I knew the woman was a badass with a business to run, but she was most certainly avoiding me.

"Hey, Olive. It's Hayes. I made some calls about the ballpark. You know, this would be much easier, and *quicker*, if we could do it face-to-face." Then, I pulled out the big gun. "I get it. You're afraid to meet with me because you're still attracted to me after all these years and you don't think you can keep your hands off me. I know, I know—I've only gotten better with age, and I don't just mean better looking, if you get me. But can't we be adults about this and get some shit done? Assuming you can control yourself, that is."

I'd just thrown down a challenge. If Olive was ever going to respond with anything other than a clipped, toneless email, this would do it. If any semblance of the woman I knew was in that buttoned-up shell, she wouldn't be able to back down from me calling her a big chicken.

When my phone rang almost immediately after I hung up, I gave myself a mental chuck on the shoulder. "Hello?"

"My car is making noise again," came the scratchy, cigarette-soaked tone of my mother. She'd quit smoking thanks to the hypnotherapy I'd paid six large for, but the damage was already done. Though, with the veneers I'd also paid for, you'd never know she'd been a smoker for twenty-five years.

Shit. "Hey, Mom. What's wrong with it this time?" The 7 Series BMW I'd bought her wasn't even a year old.

"It makes a clicking sound when I shut it off. It scares me. I always think it's going to explode or somethin'."

I tried not to sigh too loud as I pulled into my space in my apartment's garage. "Why don't you call and make an appointment to take it in? That's why we got the extra warranty coverage, remember?" In truth, I'd gotten the extra coverage so they'd have to deal with her at the dealership for even a windshield washer fluid top off…and I wouldn't.

But I already knew what was coming.

"I don't want it fixed. It scares me. What if it starts again and then blows up at an intersection, killin' your mama, and you have to scrape my brains off the side-walk? No, I want a new one. A Mercedes. I don't trust these BMWs."

And there it was. "Mom, there is nothing wrong with BMW, or fixing the car you're driving. It's barely a year old."

"Is that what you want? For me to get stuck on the road somewhere when this thing finally dies, where I could get flattened by a semi… Or worse?"

I not-so-lightly tapped my forehead against the steering wheel. "You're being overly dramatic. Take the car in and let the mechanics look at it. I'm not buying you a new car."

There was a pause, and I knew she was fuming, but I wasn't a football player at the moment. And I sure as hell didn't make football player money. Now I was making a tenth of what I had the previous season. It was one of the reasons the team had ousted me. So they could free up my salary. They'd moved me from starter to backup when I tore my hamstring. Add that to the whole thing about player health, and the Dallas Bulldogs sure as shit weren't going to pay me seven figures to ride the bench another season.

"Fine. When it blows up with me in it on the way to the dealership, it's on you." *Click.*

Nothing pleased that woman, and no matter how many times I told her she needed to cut back spending, she ignored me. It was on me. When she came running to me for money, I paid her off, so I didn't have to deal with her bullshit.

I'd adjusted my lifestyle since losing my job, though. When the team cut me, I'd had to do some scrambling to save a bit of a nest egg. The first thing to go was the five-thousand-square-foot house I didn't fucking need. Unlocking the door to my apartment, I shook my head. The house had been Sharlene's idea.

"You're a professional football player! I will not let you buy some dinky little house. What would people think? What would the other players say?"

Umm, I don't care? That should have been my response, but most of the time it was easier to give in to get her off my back.

Luckily, Brody's sublet tenant was at the end of her contract. With four dogs, the apartment wasn't a good fit for him and Lily. Even Lily's cute little house wasn't big enough. She'd put her place on the market and they'd bought a piece of property close to the rescue. As far as I knew, her house hadn't sold. Shame. It was a nifty little place decked out all retro-like with a good-sized yard.

If it weren't for football, I might have considered buying it from her and giving Sadie a home. Dropping my bag on the table inside the door, I grabbed a glass of tea from the fridge and flopped on Brody's big comfy couch with the clicker in my hand. It was quiet, so quiet, though at least the space was cozy compared to my old house. A lot of the time I'd just wander around in the big place wondering how I could feel so...alone. I felt it here, too, but at least the apartment was less cavernous.

Stopping on *Sportsworld*, I watched the injury report with half an eye. Brody had done things right. He took care of his money, rented this place instead of some penthouse, and didn't blow cash on cars and stuff. As much as I was trying to pay attention to the TV, all I saw was Olive in Lily's little kitchen. Only it wasn't Lily's. It was ours. Me cooking pasta as she slid a hand around my middle. *"Did you use the fresh tomatoes or canned?" Olive would say.*

"Canned. How was your day?"

She'd blow out a huff. "Long. I wish you'd use the fresh. Or at least let me make the gravy."

"There's nothing wrong with the way I make sauce." I'd grin over my shoulder.

"Huh. I love you, baby, but your people are not from the boot. You're not paesano—and your gravy sucks."

I'd chuckle, and she'd give me a little butt smack before she moved to the window to watch Sadie lazing in the shade of the red oak.

It was always Olive. In every scenario of happily ever after I'd run through my head, Ollie was the star. Why hadn't I realized that before? Or maybe I had, but I'd chosen to block it out. Tossing the clicker on the table, I took my tea to the kitchen to replace it with something stronger. As I leaned on the balcony's railing and stared into my bourbon, I knew happily ever after with Olive was a pipe dream. Football was my life. It was the only thing I was good at. Who would I be if I wasn't a football player?

Nobody. The thought came swiftly and left a bad taste on my tongue.

Wandering back inside, I set the untouched bourbon down on the table next to the remote and laced up my running shoes.

Sometime later, as the hot sun set on a long Texas day, I walked into the empty apartment again, hoping I'd exhausted myself to the point of sleep. Seemed all I did was toss and turn night after night, only to struggle with getting out of bed the following morning.

I was stepping out of the shower when my phone pinged with a text. After toweling off, I flopped on the bed to check it, and let the smile crawl across my face.

Chapter Eight

Jell-O on a Slip 'n' Slide

Olive

That arrogant sonofabitch!

Though, if I was being honest, that confidence was part of what attracted me to him. The way he seemed so sure of himself, so sure things would sort themselves out on their own. I'd always wished I had that in me. But no. I needed to be in control of the outcomes, not leave them to the powers that be. And when I wasn't in control? That's when the cracks showed.

Picking up my phone, I typed out a text. Because let's face it. I wasn't calling him back and risking him pulling me over to the dark side.

Olive: Don't flatter yourself, Walker! You weren't a good lay in college, the only way for you to go was up. I'm guessing you peaked at average.

Oh, sure, it was a boldfaced lie. Hayes had been a great lay. If he'd gotten better? Oophf, the thought made me rub my thighs together. I wasn't stupid, I knew he'd used the voicemail to bait me into exactly this situation. But what really irked me was that he knew I was making excuses to avoid seeing him, and he was busting my balls about it. I couldn't keep being a coward.

I didn't dodge the hard stuff. Hard stuff was my bread and butter. Yet that was exactly what I'd been doing. After seeing him at the agility trial—and being way too comfortable with his touch—I'd decided distance was my best course. If he left me a voicemail, I emailed him back. Even just his voice on the messages had been enough to make my nipples pearl. Yes, Hayes did things to my body. He always had. I was sure if I could control the environment by keeping things impersonal, then I could control the outcome and maintain a professional relationship.

Truthfully, deep down I knew spending any time at all with Hayes could be a slippery slope to becoming the person I promised myself I'd never be again. There would be no *get him out of your system* bangs, or quickies for old times' sake. Hayes and I didn't work like that.

That's how it would start. Innocent enough. But I'd been down that road before. It wasn't paved with good intentions like folks said—it was paved with compound fractures and class A misdemeanors.

Hayes Walker had an inexplicable pull on me. Being in his orbit was all-consuming. Not because I disappeared or he absorbed me, but because he challenged me to do, be, try, live, in a manner that I'd never entertained pre-Hayes. If I told him I'd like to live in Bali someday, he'd tell me to make it happen. If I said I couldn't possibly, he'd simply ask me why not.

Hayes focused on what was right in front of him. His present was all that existed. There were no regrets from the past or a future to worry about. There had been something I'd only seen a couple of times—a shadow that hung over him—but it was there and gone so quickly I was sure I'd imagined it. Nothing dimmed his light.

That carefree attitude that had drawn me to him. When I got too mired in my life plan, he'd stop me and say, *"You're missing it, Ollie. You're missing the good stuff."* It was a completely foreign concept to me, but the boy he'd been made me see…well, possibility.

It was what I loved most about Hayes when we were together. It could also make him impulsive. Reckless at times. Often, without much thought for how his actions affected others. That shadow, though…the one I'd only thought I'd seen before. It was heavier now. His light was dimmed. Of course, losing your identity could do that to a person, I knew. For Hayes, football wasn't only what he did, it was who he was.

Hayes: Uhh, you wound me! Especially considering the night when the guy in the next apartment called the cops on us because of how loud you came.

I couldn't help the laugh that burst from my lips.

Olive: ME! THAT WAS YOU! YOU WERE ALWAYS THE SCREAMER!

Hayes: Mmm, says the woman texting me in shouty capitals.

True story. My neighbor had told the cops he thought my cat got stuck under the bed again, given the yowls and grunts and hisses he heard coming from the apartment. And that was just Hayes.

Hayes: Remember when I'd do the finger thing that made you sound like a squeaky toy? Always made me feel all caveman and shit.

Hell yes, I did. And it had starred in many a late-night fapping session. I beat the back of my head against the kitchen wall trying to knock the thought loose.
It didn't work.

Olive: I am NOT talking about that with you. I texted to tell you I am looking at scheduling meetings with different venues for the gala in the next few weeks. If you can give me a few days to choose from, I'll try to work it so you can attend.

Hayes: Hang on a sec. Let me run and get my glasses.

Oh, my damn. When had he gotten glasses?
In for the night, I grabbed my wineglass off the island and chugged the rest. "How is he even for real?"

Hayes: Okay, I've got my calendar pulled up.

Olive: Hayes, when did you start wearing glasses?

I knew I shouldn't torture myself. Sadly, that ship had sailed.

Hayes: idk, 3 years ago, maybe? Why?

Sliding up onto one of the bar stools, I took the first step down that slippery slope.

Olive: What kind of glasses?

Hayes: They're just for reading.

Olive: No, I mean what do they look like? I needed a quick save. I'm just trying to picture you in glasses.

Hayes: Oh, well then...

The dots popped up and I knew what was coming next. I'd practically asked for it, but I sure as hell wasn't going to tell him to stop. When the picture came through, my chin connected with my chest. "Holy... Unnphf."

Black Wayfarers with clear reading lenses framed his deep-set electric blue eyes. His hair wasn't styled but combed back away from his face, with a piece slipping down next to the frames. A freshly trimmed beard that looked soft outlined his pink lips.

His chest was bare, the blond hair—a shade darker than what was on his head—had been neatly trimmed. A mound of muscled shoulder bunched thanks to the hand casually behind his head while the other palm held the phone aloft. And those pecs... Jesus. Solid and defined with little pink nipples. The lats with soft delineations between each rib. The triceps. The first row of a six-pack.

And that damn crooked, shit-eating grin that said he knew exactly what he was doing to me.

I slapped my forehead down on the back of the hand

I'd rested on the island countertop. "Christ, why did I do that? That was stupid." Hayes Walker was my very own wet dream come to life.

This had to stop. Now. I wiped the slobber from my chin.

Olive: Hmphf. They make you look like an old man.

Hayes: Uh, huh. Sure, they do.

Olive: I'll email the dates.

Hayes: Wait, aren't you supposed to send me a picture now? Isn't that what the kids do these days?

I quick-snapped a photo of my middle finger flipping the bird and hit send.

Hayes: Ooh baby, you know exactly where I like the finger, don't you, naughty girl? :P

Olive: Goodnight, Hayes.

Hayes: Sweet dreams, Ollie. *wink wink*

Like I said, slippery slope.
Slipperier than my panties and that was saying something.

Chapter Nine

Just a little ambush

Hayes

With a plain black ball cap on my head, I took the glass elevator up to the thirty-eighth floor of a stylish downtown high-rise, a heavy paper bag in each hand. It had taken some finagling to pin her down, but Olive couldn't escape this time. Not only did I need to make things right between us, as the State Fair appearance thing was only five weeks off—if she'd managed to secure space, that is. I'd need time to arrange things on the football players' end, but Olive had done a stellar job of boxing me out of…well, pretty much everything since the meeting at the rescue.

After bribing Johnnie with game tickets for him and his husband, I knew I had exactly one shot this week to catch her face-to-face and make my apology. She'd gotten back from a client meeting about ten minutes ago and had ordered in food, planning to work through the lunch hour.

Something I knew about thanks to my new friend, who giggled every time I called him Johnnie.

The elevator dinged and I walked the short corridor to the frosted-glass doors of Russo Image Consulting. The entry was classy, sleek, and no-nonsense, just like Olive. The receptionist's eyes flared when she recognized me, her gaze raking over me in a not-so-subtle way. I'd dressed in well-worn jeans, a black V-neck T-shirt, and the hat. I wasn't even trying to be modest. I looked good. Olive was still attracted to me, that much I knew, and I'd use every weapon in my arsenal to get her to listen to my apology.

Because, frankly, even though we didn't have a snowball's chance in hell at being together again, I still wanted to know her. To be her friend and learn if the years had been kind. I wanted to know about her relationships, her dog, agility, her business, anything... so long as I could be near her. Was I torturing myself? Yep. Especially given that I hoped to get picked up by another team, but I couldn't control it. Olive grounded me. She always had. Since she'd came back into my life, she was the first thing I thought about in the morning, and the last thing I thought about at night. I wasn't going to let go of that if I didn't have to.

The receptionist showed me back to Johnathan's desk. He smiled instantly, gave me a conspiratorial wink. "She told me to order about fifteen minutes ago. I suggested Pecan Lodge and DoorDash so I could run out to do some errands."

Setting the bags down, I pulled the fifty-yard-line seats out my back pocket. "I can't thank you enough, my man. I hope you and your husband enjoy these." Clapping him on the shoulder, I handed him the tickets.

"Honestly, Hayes, you didn't have to give me these. I would have done it anyway, for Olive's sake. She's a one-of-a-kind boss. I just want to see her happy." A soft smirk covered his face. "With that in mind, you should know my husband is a bodybuilder. If at any point you disappoint that amazing woman, I will have Sven kick your rather tight ass."

With a mental picture of Sven that made me chuckle under my breath, I met Johnathan's eyes. "I promise to do my best not to disappoint her."

With that he punched a button on the phone on his desk. "Olive?"

"Yes?" came her voice through the speaker.

"I'm leaving to run errands, but lunch is here, and it looks…amazing." He sent me a thumbs-up.

"Send the delivery person back and you can take off."

"Will do." Turning to me, he pointed to a set of frosted-glass doors. "That's your cue, buddy. The place is mostly empty except for Jennifer up front. Good luck." He slipped on his blazer and left.

The whole place was quiet. I wondered if it was part of Johnathan's design.

With a fortifying breath, I pecked on the office door.

"Come in." My heart raced at her sultry tone. *Shit, I hope this works.*

She had her back to the entry and a cell phone—on speaker—held lazily near her mouth as she stood gazing out of the floor-to-ceiling windows of her corner office. The desk was glass and chrome, and neat as a pin, without a smudge. Two white leather club chairs sat across from it with a matching couch against one wall, and a fluffy rug with abstract swirls of gray covered the floor under the desk.

I couldn't go any further inside. She simply took my breath away. Her hair was in a bun on her head that looked hastily pulled up instead of well-groomed, and the late September sun warmed her profile against a backdrop of the Dallas skyline. The business-suit-style dress was half black, half white and split directly down the middle with a large cutout over her chest that highlighted her generous curves.

Then there were the shoes. Kicked off under her desk, the red peep-toes had matching soles and heels like toothpicks. A perfect pairing with her lipstick, the only nod to the wild girl I knew long ago. But I didn't want to know *this* Olive any less. Only more.

I cleared my throat.

"Thank you, can you put them on the table in front of the sof—" When she finally glanced up, her eyes widened to cartoon proportions.

"Ma'am, did you say the table by the sofa?"

"What are you doing here?"

Setting the bags down on the aforementioned table, I grinned. "You wouldn't come break bread with me, so I brought lunch to you."

I saw the purse of her lips, however slight and fleeting.

"Okay, I'm back," said the voice on the other end of the call. "I checked with staff, and I think the week of October 3 should work. We'll have to do it in the afternoon and evening. What else will you need from me to get it set?"

"A full open-level course with a beginner's course worked into it. You know, no teeter, no weaves. We'll teach them the A-frame and dog walk, but no tire. We could use a few staff to make sure things run smoothly, but only if they want to volunteer. Of course, you'll need to be there for filming. I'll need to bring the show's producer in to plan their setup. Her name is Margo, and she may be calling you in the next few days to discuss basic logistics. Lighting, power sources, rigging she might need, et cetera. In the meantime, I'll pin down our players. Of course, Lily and Brody will partici- pate. Lily has a couple of the former rescues from the Unlovabulls who've turned into agility dogs in mind. I'll need to talk to my liaison at the Bulldogs to see who might be available and willing to make an ass out of themselves for the cause." Olive cut a quick glance at me, and I couldn't help being in awe of the woman doing her thing. Even if she seemed a bit ruffled by my appearance.

"And you're sure the producer is okay with adver- tising the training center as well?" the woman on the other end asked.

"Yes. You'll have your own interview window to talk about the Unruly Dog and what you offer as far as training and facility. Lily will also get a one-on-one about the Unlovabulls, and I'll be discussing the State Fair appearance and announcing the Gala. After we meet with the producer to work out the logistics, we should be good to go."

"Olive, you're the best. Thank you for thinking of the Unruly Dog for this. I can't possibly repay you for the free PR."

Her face softened. "Please, girl." She waved the gratitude away. "This producer still owed me a favor from a Mark Cuban interview and tour of the Ameri- can Airlines Center I got for her. I'm just glad I can do things for the people and places that matter to me now and then, too. There aren't many training facilities as amazing as yours in the area. I can't wait to show you off to DFW."

As she said goodbye to who I assumed was the owner of the Unruly Dog, her eyes locked on me. There was annoyance on the surface, but banked heat in the depths. She looked me up and down in a way that suggested her body was warring with her brain. "Hayes, you should have called. I'm busy this afternoon."

Her brain won out. "Yeah, I did call. Several times. But after the night you texted me, you pretty much ceased all communications. I have updates to give you and you're leaving me out of the loop."

Her swift glance away told me all I needed. She wasn't proud of herself for it, but she had done it on purpose. "Look." I pulled my hat off, smoothed my hair back before replacing it on my head. "I understand why you're avoiding me, Olive, but you haven't given me the time or space to make it right. I hurt you in a way you obviously never forgot, but I can't apologize if you won't give me the time of day. So, I decided a small ambush was the only shot I had."

"Small ambush," she said with a twitch of her lips. Placing her palm on a bright white leather chair, she slipped into heels that made her nearly as tall as me.

"Tiny, really. Miniscule, even."

The shadowed beginning of a real smile was quickly replaced with one that was reserved for clients and cameras. "It's really not necessary, Walker. It was a long time ago. We were both kids. Kids do stupid stuff. I'd hope we've grown up since then."

There it was. My opening. "Yes, exactly! We're adults now. Grown-ups fully capable of having lunch with an old friend while we talk about fundraiser details. Especially since I made the whole spread myself." Clapping my hands together, I went to the bags and began pulling out food. "Let's see, we've got slow-cooked brisket…" Slanting a peek her way, I watched her mouth fall open. "Might as well kick those murder sticks you call shoes back off and get comfy. I plan on putting you in a food coma, my friend. Got any sweats handy?"

If food was its own language in the South, then brisket was the very essence of Texas twang, and Olive was a Texas girl, tried and true. When we were in college, she and I had driven three hours down to Dallas for good barbecue on several occasions. She's the reason I loved barbecue, and she would know exactly how much effort I put in to making it.

"I… Lily said you were renting Brody's apartment. How could you make that yourself?" She gestured to the foil-wrapped beef in my hand.

"Not gonna lie. Brody and I hauled my smoker out of storage and tried to put it on the apartment's balcony. Once we got it up there, we realized it was probably a fire hazard and my place was upwind. I'd flood the whole building with barbecue smoke. So, we drove the smoker up to his place."

I started setting out the containers of sides. The ranch beans with bacon and jalapeños in them just like she liked. The potato salad I'd made from scratch from my grandma's recipe. Even the pecan pie I knew would make her mouth water.

Olive scrunched her brows, revealing the cutest little worry line. "You would've had to stay overnight at their place to tend it."

"Yep. I did." I'd gotten up every two hours all night

long to check on the meat. Make sure it was staying juicy and tender, putting more wood in the smoker, checking the bark to be sure it was turning good and dark. "Everything is from scratch. Hell, even the sauce is homemade. Sweet with a bite of heat, just like you like. Besides, since Brody and Lily live so close to the rescue, I got to spend some extra time with Sadie." With a shrug, I pulled plates and utensils out of the second bag, along with corn on the cob, a loaf of Texas white bread and a container of barbecue sauce. I'd even thought to bring a lunch-sized cooler with four Shiners.

I could see her wheels spinning. "Hayes, this is—"

"Come sit down and eat with me, Ollie." After moving around the table, I patted the sofa next to me.

Her lips quirked up in a *there's really no way out of this* look.

An answering grin covered my own face. *Nope, there's really not.*

With a heavy breath and a hint of amusement, Olive kicked her murder shoes back off and slid around the end of the couch while I unfolded bibs for us both.

"I am not wearing that, Hayes."

"How much did that dress cost?"

"Yeaaahhh." She bit her lip. "Okay, give it to me."

Instead, I slipped it over her head and leaned back to tie it. When my finger brushed her nape, I saw the little shiver work over her shoulders. I wanted to do it again, to watch her tremble with my touch. But that wasn't what this lunch was about.

"Put mine on?"

"Take your hat off."

I did, smoothing my hair back as it tried to fall in

my face. Her short nails whispered over the base of my scalp a little too slowly. *Payback.*

"I can't believe you made all this. It looks delicious."

"It is. Let's dig in."

"Cocky as ever, I see. I'll be the judge." She began filling her plate as she talked. "About the fair—"

"Yeah, that's creeping up pretty fast. Did you get the space?"

She nodded. "Everything is pretty much set except for your part. I'll need a list of Bulldogs players who are willing to donate their time for this. We only have the space for one day. It's a special *Meet the Bulldogs and Support the Rescue* thing. The Fair Board has agreed to run a few TV spots on their dime because the signing alone will bring people through the gates. Those start next week."

"Wait. My part? You know I can do more than just be your Bulldogs hookup, yeah? I want to do more, Olive. Let me be involved. Make me your fundraiser bitch or whatever. I can do whatever you need me to."

When I turned to look at her, she was staring at her plate, but didn't respond.

"I've got a list of players in my office at work. I'll email it to you tomorrow. We're up to nineteen, I think? A hefty chunk of them are starters. Names everybody knows and wants to meet."

"Um, wow! I hadn't expected so many would want to help."

"Yeah, now that I know things are a go, I'll be able to pin down a few more. Logistics for that many players will take planning. I'll also need to work with some of the Bulldogs staff to handle players' needs that day. Will you all bring any dogs?"

She nodded with a sheepish look on her face. "Yes, Lily is pulling together some of the rescue's former pups with a select few she thinks are ready for adoption. Did you call your contact at Lone Star Field?"

I nodded. "I think it's going to be out of our price range given the budget you emailed me and what's allocated for the Gala. Celebrity games just don't pull in enough people to fill a stadium that size. We'd get a decent-sized crowd, but ticket sales would barely cover the overhead. They'd be willing to kick in a little, but they can't donate all the manpower and overhead for a nonprofit this size."

"Hmm, did they give you a breakdown of the numbers?" She added a dollop of potato salad to her plate.

I nodded, pulled the Shiners out of the lunch cooler. "A rough estimate. I can email it to you when I send over the players' names, but I think you'll agree it's a dead end. We might be able to pull something together at Dr. Pepper Ballpark. Smaller, lower overhead."

"Send me the estimate for Lone Star for future reference, but if you say it's a nonstarter, I'm good with that. Besides, I've got something else in the works that's not a fundraiser itself but will bring in a crowd for the fair."

After twisting the top off, I offered her the beer.

She shook her head. "No thanks. I'll have to drive home in a couple of hours." Sliding off the couch with complete grace, she grabbed a reusable bottle from her desk and tipped it to her lips.

I did the same just to keep from staring.

After returning her plate to her lap, she pulled her feet up on the sofa and slid back. "Do you know anyone at Dr. Pepper Ballpark?"

I nodded, swallowed. "I can give the team manager a call. He's a Bulldogs fan."

She forked up a couple of pieces of brisket and ladled sauce over them. "Who do you know on the team that could lend me an afternoon or evening and would be willing to make an ass out of themselves for a good cause?"

"Hmm." I heaped potato salad on my plate. "Ahh, Jackson. Shane Jackson. What for?"

Olive placed a napkin over her lap. "That other thing I'm pulling together."

"Okay." I gave her an expectant look. "Wanna tell me?"

"Do you ever watch channel five news at eleven a.m.? The show that's on the second half of the hour. *Texas Weekly*?"

"They're the ones that do the things going on around Dallas shows and focus on locally owned businesses and happenings? I've seen it once or twice."

A sly smile worked over her lips. "I've been working with their producer to quickly pull together an episode on the Unlovabulls." She leaned forward, sipped from her bottle. "Well, actually it would be a combination piece featuring the Unlovabulls Rescue at the Unruly Dog's training center. We'll have an agility demonstration with dogs from the rescue, as well as a couple of pros like Jet running the course, and a few celebrities who don't mind making a fool out of themselves. It will be an introduction to agility piece that features the rescue as a nonprofit along with the stellar local dog training facility. Then to wrap it up, we'll announce the gala happening in February along with launching its website, and hype the State Fair appearance. But we'll need to film in the next couple of weeks to get it to air at least two weeks before the fair. It's been cutting it close trying to make sure all the cogs line up just so."

"That's actually kind of brilliant. Pimp the rescue, the appearance at the fair, and the gala on a local TV show? Fricking ingenious. I'll ask Shane, but I know he's in if he can run with his own dog. And you can use me, too, if you want. Since I'm not playing, you might want someone who's still on the field. Maybe one more celebrity. What about Isaiah Bolton from the basketball team? I can give him a call. Or maybe an actor or something. Seriously, you don't need my opinion. You're the pro here." I turned back to my brisket.

"Don't sell yourself short, Hayes." I could hear the bit of concern in her voice. "I do need your opinion and input. You're smart, you've had good ideas, and you followed through with the work. I realize I've kept you sidelined so far… I'm sorry for that. It wasn't very professional of me, and I should have looped you in on this as soon as I had the idea. I'd love to have you be one of the celebrities. I can tell you're dedicated to helping the rescue, and I promise to stop being so short with you. We are equals in this and I haven't been treating you like my equal. I have been cutting you out. I promise that stops now."

She said it like she thought I needed to hear those things, and it was making me uncomfortable as fuck. I nodded, waved her off. "So that gives us *Texas Weekly*, the Texas State Fair, and the gala."

"Yeah." She sighed. "I wish we had one more, but we can work with these and still generate enough capital for the shelter to operate for the next year at least."

That gave me an idea, but I'd need to make some

calls before I brought it up to Olive. "Sounds good to me, now eat the rest of that 'cue before it gets cold."

With a tiny smirk, she stuck her fork into the meat she'd drizzled with sauce, and it fell apart on her plate as I tucked into my own.

"Mmmmmm, my God. Hayes, Jesus, that's good."

Holy. Shit. I squeezed my eyes shut. The sounds she made were passion and pleasure and sin, and my cock went hard enough to slice through steel. When I pried my lids open and turned to look at her, I really wished I hadn't. Her eyes were closed, her lashes fluttering as she licked her lips. *Are you trying to make me come in my pants, woman?*

Olive was my own personal thirst trap. I had a near perfect memory of what she'd looked like years earlier as she came apart with me inside her, and the look she had now was damn close. I shifted, slid back against the sofa, trying to give my strangled dick more room.

"Good?" I asked, voice coming out too low and too rough.

Her eyes snapped open at my tone, darting first to me and then to her plate. "It's amazing, thank you for making all this. And all the trouble you went to."

"Olive, look at me." I turned toward her, pulling a knee up on the couch, my plate balanced on the other. When her rich brown eyes met mine, I blew out a breath. "I'm the one who owes you an apology. I want you to stop avoiding me. Which is one reason I ambushed you. But I *needed* to tell you how sorry I am. The way I treated you…" Goddamn, I was tripping over the words. "I was young, and stupid, and it was selfish… I'm so very sorry for the way I left things between us."

She set the plate side, a line forming between her eyes. "Hayes, we really don't need to—"

"We do." I reached for her arm, but she moved to stand and look out the window. "The things I told you, the way I did it. I was an atrocious fuck stick. I'm ashamed of myself for how that went down. I could make excuses, but really, it's all on me. I've made tons of bad decisions in my life." *You have no idea.* "Done some really stupid things. But breaking up with you the night before I was drafted takes the cake. By far."

Chapter Ten

Reality check: Table four

Hayes

Standing, I moved behind her to lean my butt on the edge of her desk as Olive pinched the bridge of her nose. "Dammit, Walker. Why can't you just let it go?"

"Because I can tell it bothers you. And it bothers me, too." She jumped a little at my voice, as if she didn't hear me move across the room. "It's weighed on me. For years, Ollie. We were so good together. So…right." I had a hunch we still would be, and I wanted that so bad. To be with Olive again. But I knew that wouldn't be fair to her. "Sweetheart, I'm not blind. I know the chemistry is there between us now, and I know you can feel it, too. For fuck's sake, I wish I didn't feel it. But if we stand any chance of moving past this, even just as friends, which is all I'm asking here, then you needed to hear me say I was sorry as much as I needed to say it. I want that, Olive. To be your friend." My voice came out low, soft. "To not have you so uncomfortable around me that you completely cut me out. I realize I'll never again get to say that you're mine and I'm yours. But let me in a little. We were just as good at being friends as we were being lovers. That's all I'm asking. To get to know my friend again."

When she finally turned to meet my eyes, the glassiness in hers caught the afternoon sun and sent a literal pain through my chest. But she also had pink in her cheeks and barely bottled temper in the clench of her jaw.

"I'm so sorry, Olive. I'm sorry if I hurt you."

Then the lid came off the bottle. "Well, fucking of course you hurt me, Hayes! We weren't just a fling. We'd talked about growing old together, about getting married and having a family. We'd talked about us in terms of lifetimes instead of years. I was completely in love with you, like, soul mates and shit." She threw an arm out, poked a finger at me. "Then you dump me out of the blue like it was no big deal. You have no idea how much that broke me and how long it took me to put myself back together." Throwing her arms up, she turned back to the window.

"I loved you, too. Please don't doubt that. I loved you. Very much." *In fact, I might still.* I shut that thought down as quickly as it popped up.

She huffed, craned her head to meet my eyes. "It sure as hell didn't feel like it that night. What really gets me is the why of it. Why, Hayes?" I could see the pleading in her eyes. "It was just so out of the blue. Yes, you could be impulsive and even a little reckless at times, but I'd never thought of you as selfish before then. You'd always been generous and caring. Your heart was so big, and you just…turned it off and walked away. You stomped all over my heart without a believable goddamned explanation. Were you really that selfish? You wanted to play manwhore for a while? Because I'm not sure I ever bought that excuse."

An angry Olive was a fucking hot Olive, but when she poked me in the chest with her index finger before taking a step away, I resigned myself to accepting the pain because I knew it would be absolutely out of line to try and adjust my junk. Besides, she needed this. She deserved this. To get it all out. To yell at me, and poke me in the chest, and maybe even slap me across the cheek. She deserved her due, and I'd had no idea just how long she'd been holding on to the pain and anger I'd caused her. But I couldn't tell her why.

I watched her in reverence as she tried to reel her temper in. "If that was the case, why did you lead me on for a year and a half? Why make plans with me you had no intention of following through on when you could have slept your way through the entire female student body of OU?"

My voice came out soft. "I had every intention of following through with you, Olive. Every intention of seeing those plans through." I crossed my arms so she couldn't see the tight balls of my fists. I was so frustrated. Disappointed in myself, in my family. "Damn it, Olive, I don't think I ever really moved on from you. We had the best kind of relationship. I just happened to be hot for, and fell in love with, the girl that became my best friend. But there were things… I had obligations, and the last thing I wanted was…"

For my mom to be right, and for me to end up hurting you even worse than I did.

I wanted to tell her more, but I hid that part of me. From everyone. Not that I grew up poor, but how my mom treated me. How I *let* her treat me. Telling me I'd never be good for anything but playing football. That I was a constant reminder of a man I barely remembered who'd cheated on her and walked out. That *I* owed her for *his* sins.

My sister was spared our mother's ire, but she had a different dad. Lisa wasn't the spitting image of the man who'd broken our mother's heart. I'd always done a damn good job of making sure Sharlene Walker aimed her bullshit at me and not Lisa.

At least, until she found out I had potential. After my high school coach told her I had a chance at going pro after college, Sharlene made sure I ate, slept, played, and shit football twenty-four seven. Playing football was all I knew. It was all I had. And it had been taken from me.

Besides, *I* made the decision to break up with Olive, not my mother.

You let her manipulate you into it.

Only, I didn't want Olive to know any of that. I was embarrassed by it. Ashamed of it. That I had little to show for my career in the way of savings and I was pretty much useless if I couldn't play football. Or, that my mother had drilled that into me for so long that I believed it. It made me feel weak, that I'd needed Sharlene's approval and bent over backward to avoid rocking the boat.

Nobody needed to know how weak I was.

"I'm sorry, Olive. So fucking sorry, and I understand if you have no desire to want to know me away from the fundraisers. I'll back off and leave you be, but I've never forgotten you, never stopped thinking about you. You were never just my girlfriend. You were my best friend, and I'd like the chance to get to know you again."

I looked up from my crossed arms, willing her to see my sincerity. "I'll take whatever you're willing to give."

That's when my phone rang. My agent. "Umm, give me a second. I've got to take this."

Nodding, she slipped back onto the couch, extending her legs, and I noticed a grouping of faded but jagged scars on one shin that weren't there years before. "I'll be right back."

I stepped into the hall. "Aaron, hey." As much as I knew I needed this call, I wasn't sure I wanted it.

"Hayes, my man. How've you been? How's the coaching working out?"

"Ehh, not bad. I don't mind coaching. Maybe not at this level." I even kind of enjoyed it on most days, when McManus wasn't an asshole. "But it's not paying the bills, Aaron."

"You're still getting your workouts in? Staying fit?"

"A few days ago, I laid out Daniel McManus while we worked on pass blocking. Does that answer your question?"

He whistled. "Damn. That's a yes."

"I'm lifting, drills, running. I still have access to the Bulldogs training facilities; I just have to do it before everyone gets there or after they leave. Darius, the head trainer, he knows where my head's at and has been working with me after hours."

"Good, good. How's the knee and the hamstring?"

I blew out a long breath. "What do you want me to say? The hamstring is fine. The knee is a football knee, but I'm taking care with it. Doing what I can. Hell, we all play through the pain. You know that. Now, why the fuck are you calling. Tell me something good."

"Direct as always, Hayes." He chuckled. "I got a line on New York."

I nodded even though he couldn't see me. "I saw Butler go down last week." Their starting tight end was out for at least the rest of this season, maybe for good. "But they moved Taylor Jones into his place."

"They did, but that leaves them short, and from what I hear, they want experience in the position. Not another draft pick. They need to be three deep at tight end, and their rookie, Antoine Kahele, he's not ready yet. I'm guessing they want someone for second string and special teams that can help bring Kahele along."

Damn. It wasn't a starting position, but it would bring in a hell of a lot more money than I was making now, and I'd still see a decent amount of field time. It would mean leaving the rescue behind, and Olive. I hated that. I liked Dallas. I had friends I cared about and liked volunteering at the shelter. But if I left, I wouldn't be toting a clipboard and whistle anymore either. I'd be back on the field, doing what I was good at. Playing paid the bills. I just wasn't as excited about the prospect of getting back on the field as I thought I'd be.

I was getting way ahead of myself. I wasn't the only unrestricted tight end in the league. And I was an old man by football standards. Maybe too old.

My phone pinged with a text, and I pulled it away from my head, switching to speaker as I read it.

Sharlene: I checked, and you still haven't transferred my rent money to the leasing company. You need to deal with that, and I need to write a check for your sister's tuition soon.

Son of a bitch. The woman thought I was made of money and what little I'd set aside was going to start dwindling soon.

"Hayes, you there?"

"Yeah, I'm here. I'm definitely interested if you can get me a tryout. When do you think you'll hear from them?"

"It's early yet, and like I said, this is all rumor so far. They could go another way, but I wanted to give you a heads-up, so you keep your ass in shape."

"Will do, boss." I ran a hand over my beard.

After I let Aaron go, I shot my mom a text.

Hayes: I'll take care of it, but I don't make what I used to. You're going to have to cut back on spending.

The response came immediately.

Sharlene: And whose fault is that?

I didn't bother answering. Damn her. If I wasn't careful, I was going to end up a cautionary tale for new football players like Lily's dad had. *Welcome to the NFL, rookie. Don't plan for your future, don't take care of your money and body? You'll end up like Hayes Walker. Old, in a wheelchair, and flat broke.*

If I didn't want to be that guy, I had to start dealing with my mom instead of ignoring the problem. I also had to dig myself out of the financial hole she helped put me in.

I adjusted the bill of my hat, watched Olive finish a piece of pecan pie through an unfrosted section of the glass wall. A year or two playing with New York just might do the trick. Then, maybe, I'd be worthy of the girl in the glass office. Olive didn't need to know about my money woes. Deep down, I knew I should leave her alone and walk away. I didn't deserve her, even as a friend, but Olive Russo was under my skin. I needed to make the most of the time I had with her, because when I left—whether it was as friends or something more—it was going to tear me apart at the seams.

Olive

I watched Hayes pace around while he was on the phone. He was agitated. Worried. At one point something like hope lit in his eyes, only to be quickly doused with a scowl.

The man was an enigma. He was a beast on the football field, so sure of himself and how good he was at his job. Off the field, he'd always been easygoing, quick with a smile, a joke at the ready, and easily brushed off the stuff that didn't matter. Hayes had always been one to get a wild hair up his ass and drop everything else. Maybe that wasn't who he was anymore.

He was carrying something. Hayes had a heaviness that had nothing to do with his size. It made me want to help him, to unburden him. To be his friend. He'd been right when he'd said we were best friends. We'd told each other everything, once upon a time. Or so I'd thought.

He'd said he had obligations that I wouldn't have understood. Noodling on it, I remember seeing those fleeting moments of something darker in Hayes. Something encumbering and burdensome. I'd written it off in college—everybody had bad days—but maybe I'd been too quick to dismiss it, or too eager to glaze over it. The woman I'd become saw something the girl I'd been hadn't been able to see.

One thing I knew, Hayes hadn't told me everything then, and he wasn't telling me now either. A decade ago, I may have had the right to know. Now, not so much. But I couldn't see him so heavy like this and not try to help. Especially if we were going to move forward. As friends.

Yes, I was irked that he still hadn't given me an explanation for dumping me, but it was painfully obvious that whatever his reason, he was sorry.

As he pulled the door to my office open, he stroked that soft-looking beard.

"Everything okay?" I asked, setting my plate aside to work my ankle in circles. The shoes I'd chosen today weren't doing my arthritis any favors. But it was maybe the first time since the accident that the pain didn't make me think of the Broken Hearts and Bad Decisions tour. It felt like a new beginning. Something I hadn't even realized I needed until Hayes made amends. "That call seemed pretty intense."

He fixed on a quick smile that was transparent now that I was seeing him more clearly. "Yeah, just work stuff." Flopping down on the sofa, he stared unseeing his half-eaten plate.

He was holding something back again. I saw it in the set of his shoulders, the lines on his face, the sadness in his eyes.

I had to be smart with how I handled any kind of relationship with Hayes, including a friendship. As much as I wanted to be all in on the idea, something told me to be prepared for the worst with him. From him. I'd do well to control my emotions both for and with this man, or I might get burned again. Soul mates were simply best friends who managed to fall in love. I couldn't let that happen. "How do you like coaching?"

Hayes leaned forward, planting his elbows on his knees. "It has its moments, but at this level, it's a pain in the ass. Too many divas making too much money who bitch about every little thing."

"Hmm, I know something about that, working in my field." Sliding forward, I started to pick up the trash. "Thank you for all this. And for the apology. I didn't realize how much resentment I was still holding on to until today."

He pushed out a humorless laugh. "So you know, I didn't dump you, sweetheart, like you said earlier. We broke up."

"No, no. I'm quite certain you dumped me. Flat on my ass." I chuckled. "I know you may never share with me the why, and that's yours alone, but I needed the apology. You always did know when I needed to talk. Even before I did."

"That's what friends do. But this wasn't selfless, trust me. I needed to say how sorry I was—am—too. It's right there at the top of the stupidest shit I've ever done."

Reaching over, I wiggled my hand under his arm and into his palm, giving it a soft squeeze until our eyes met. A lot went unspoken in that look. It didn't do either of us any good to dwell on what might have been, yet neither one of us moved.

When Hayes leaned back against the sofa, he pulled my hand with him, toying with my short nails. "Has there been anyone else? Not that anyone could follow me, but…" His lips split in a crooked grin.

Extricating my hand from his, I gave him a decent shove in the shoulder. A very hard, strong shoulder. "Cocky asshole."

When the laugh broke free of his throat, I saw the boy I knew in the man he'd become. "Damn, you're strong."

"Still strong enough to kick your ass." I winked.

"I don't doubt it for a second, but you didn't answer the question." He nailed me with those electric blue eyes.

"Eh." I gave a noncommittal shrug.

"I see how ya are. Playing it close to the vest." Turning his attention to the food, he started packing up the leftovers.

"I miss the friendship, too, Hayes. But I needed that closure before I could consider being your friend again."

He paused, looked as if he was mulling something over. "I'd like that. If we could try, at least."

My heart skipped and my breathing kicked up as I eyed my scars—probably a little too obviously—and hesitated. They were a constant reminder of how close I'd come to losing everything and how hard I'd worked to become the woman I was. That's the thing. You never really knew how strong you were until your mettle was tested. I swallowed the nerves. "I don't know what's going on in your life, but I'd like to get to know you again. I'm here if you need an ear, Walker. I won't keep avoiding you."

Something flared in his eyes that was just as quickly gone. Instead of saying whatever was on his mind, he stuffed leftovers back in their bags. "What happened to your legs? The scars?" He nodded at them outstretched on the cushion.

I pulled my legs up, tucking them to the side of my hip, not ready to go there. "A story for another time."

Hayes nodded. "I...things are complicated for me right now. I'm not sure where my own head is at but thank you for offering to listen." Something in his gaze hardened just the slightest. I saw the wall go up between us as he pasted on the smile I'd once found charming, that I was beginning to learn wasn't nearly as easy as it had once seemed.

"Well, the offer stands," I said, patting his knee.

With the food put away, it was time for me to get back to work, as evidenced by the speaker on my landline. "Olive, I'm back. And Trevor Cote is on one. Apparently, there's an issue at the cologne shoot. Something about him taking his shirt off being in the contract."

I couldn't stop the eye roll. "Okay, thank you. Tell him I'll be a minute."

"Ahh, back to the grindstone," Hayes remarked. "I should go so you can get back to kicking ass and taking names."

I nodded. "No rest for the wicked."

"I'll send the email from Lone Star Field over tomorrow. I don't know if I'll have time to visit all the gala venues with you, but I'd like to make a couple, at least."

"How about I pre-screen them, and you and I can go back to the top two or three and make the decision together."

That gave him a genuine smile as he turned to open my office door. "Thank you for that."

"Oh, hey don't forget the food. You didn't even get to have any pie."

When he turned, the look he gave me was tender, affectionate. "I made it for you, sweetheart. It's all yours."

Chapter Eleven

What's a twunt?

Olive

I was enjoying a bath and a glass of wine when my notifications started pinging from the girls' group text.

Lily: Did you have a lunch date today?

Of course, she'd known what Hayes was going to do.

Gina: Ohhh, who?

Oh shit, here we go, I thought.

Olive: Yes. I heard Hayes fed y'all, too.

Lily: OMG, the guys were so cute! Brody and Hayes stumbled around my kitchen mumbling about grand gestures. What the hell was that even about?

Gina: Hayes??? Yeah, Olive. Tell Lily exactly how well you know Hayes...

Shit.

Olive: Hayes and I were a thing in college. It got serious for a while, but it didn't end well.

Gina: Are y'all gonna start bumping uglies again? Is that why he brought you lunch? Did you have yourself a little afternoon delight?

I grinned. The woman seriously needed to get laid.

Olive: No. Besides. I'm fairly sure my vagina has cobwebs. But if y'all are going to continue the inquisition, I have leftover barbecue if you want to come over and get sauced...

Lily: 😊 Girl, I'm out the door.

Gina: Can I bring Boops? I was gone all day. I don't want to leave him alone again.

Olive: Of course! Boops is always welcome here.

I loved that little doofus. It would be good to have the pitter-patter of doggie paws in my house again.

Olive: Lil, your dogs are welcome, too. ♥

Thirty-five minutes later there was a knock on my door. When I pulled it open, Boops, Mack, and Laila—Lily's young Bulldog foundling—crashed in, nearly knocking me on my butt. But it wasn't Lily at the door. It was Brody.

"Surprise," he said. "Don't worry, I'm not staying. She just brought me to do the heavy lifting. Then I'm out so y'all can drink yourself into oblivion." The man was carrying one of those big margarita machines. "Where can I set this?"

"Uhh, I have plenty of wine. She didn't have to bring that."

Brody shrugged. "I do what I'm told."

"Uhh, yes, I did have to bring it! That thing is amazing," Lily said from behind him. "Besides, we're not sucking down all your good wine when tequila is quicker." She held up a bottle of Don Julio in one hand and Tres Agaves Mix in the other. Sliding around her fiancé, Lily pecked his cheek. "Put it on the kitchen island, Shaw."

He did as he was told while Lily wrapped me in a hug, her Cookie Monster pajamas soft against my cheek.

"Incoming!" Gina yelled from behind Brody's big body while the dogs did the zoomies around my living room. "Where can I put this? It's heavy as fuck."

Brody didn't hesitate, he turned and took a box from Gina, carrying it to the island before going back outside.

"I brought snacks *and* wine!" Gina beamed while I took in her state of (un)dress. Pajama pants with reindeer on them even though it was September. Puppy dog slippers and a T-shirt that read I'm only talking to my dog today. Even her hair was pulled into braided pigtails. "Those pajamas, Olive. Love them."

My pink satin pajamas had little brown Dachshunds all over them. "Thanks. Did Brody just leave?"

"Nope, Brody had more to carry in," he said as he came back in with a bag full of food. "I'll be back in the morning to collect these two. Because they'll be hungover, I'm sure."

He walked over and gave his fiancée a kiss. "Love you. Have fun."

"Brody, you can stay and have a drink with us if you want?" I couldn't help it. Southern manners.

"Yeah, Brody." Gina made a thrusting motion with her hips. "I've got a pocketbook full of dollar bills. Wanna be our Magic Mike? I hear it's an XXL."

Ohmygod, she was so crude. It actually reminded me of Hayes, the way Gina had no qualms about letting her hair down. I was no prude—I thought shit like that all the time—but my job demanded I kept it to myself. It was second nature. With these women, I didn't have to do that. I could say what came to mind, wear the sloppy PJs, drink too much tequila inside the safety of my home, eat Cheetos and licorice at the same time, and Gina and Lily would never judge me. Something in me loosened and I pulled my hair out of its ponytail as I cackled at Gina.

When Brody looked at me like I'd lost it, I realized something else. I didn't let myself laugh much—like, throw my head back and really let go. That changed tonight.

Lily cued up her phone. "Siri, play 'Pony' by Ginuwine." The music started and Lily hooted at her fiancé. "C'mon, Shaw. Shake what your mama gave ya."

"Nope, only you get to see my XXL, darlin'. See ya, ladies." He headed toward the door but stopped along the way—first next to his fiancée where he stuck his butt out for her to smack, then again for Gina who laughed as she swatted his ass. Finally, he stopped in front of me, lifting the shirt covering his rump so I

Model Behavior

could take a whack. I met Lil's encouraging eyes as she gave me a subtle nod. So, I smacked the hell out of Brody's butt.

He yipped. "Ohh, that one was good, Olive. It popped just the way I like. I always knew you were a Top. It's the ponytail that gives you away." He winked. "Night, ladies."

The door shut behind him as dogs danced around our feet. "Hi, babies, hi." I bent to pet everyone before I got a dish of water to set on the floor.

Lil picked up where our texting left off as she plugged in the margarita machine and got to work. "I love Hayes, Olive, but if you're pissed at him, girl code demands we must be, too."

"Yasss! I mean, if you hate him, we hate him. End of story," Gina said as she was bent over stuffing wine into my cooler.

I raised an eyebrow. "Isn't that a little immature? Just because I have issues with Hayes doesn't mean y'all have to."

Lil stopped and met my eyes. "Look, I'm still learning to let people in, but I figure you two are as close as I've ever gotten to having a girl squad. So, fuck yes, it's immature, but chicks before dicks. Hoes before bros. Bitches before...well that's not a good one."

"Exactly," Gina put in. "Where do you keep plates and glasses?" I walked over and showed her, then helped her arrange an assortment of snacks on two platters. She'd brought Milano's, Chips Ahoy, and Cheetos and potato chips. Lil had managed to bring meats, cheeses, olives, and strawberries and grapes.

"Are we getting high?" I asked as I watched them

set out the spread. "This looks like the shit I ate in college when I got high."

Lil and Gina looked at me with wide eyes, then Lil blinked like an owl. "Well, I hadn't thought of that. I haven't gotten high since my sophomore year. I wonder if we know anyone who can get edibles?"

"Gurrrl," I said to Lily. "This is Texas. That's still illegal here. I wasn't actually suggesting we get high."

Gina snorted. "I would have never taken either one of you for potheads, but especially you, Olive. Nobody would tell on you, babe. Safe space." She motioned around my kitchen. "But tonight, let's stick to the liquor. There's always next time."

An evil smile spread across my face as I felt the stirrings of the girl I'd once been.

Two margaritas later, the three of us were curled up on my leather sofas, snacking and watching a movie on Netflix that had little plot but for the hot Italian dude and the even hotter sex scenes. Boops had settled down with his mom in the corner of the sofa, and Laila was curled into Lily's outstretched legs on the chaise. Lying half across my lap, half across the couch, belly up, Mack snored like he was trying to suck golf balls through his nostrils—and succeeding—as I stroked his belly. He was an exceptional cuddler—something I missed, terribly. Which was probably why his mama brought him.

A fond look crossed Lily's face. "No matter how bad my day, my mood, an argument with Brody, or how stressed I get at the shelter, that derp always makes me smile."

I met her violet eyes. "I can see why. Casshole wasn't a derp. Ever. She was a perpetually unimpressed old lady. If she could have spoken, she would have yelled, 'Hey, you kids! Get off my lawn!'"

"Cassie was awesome," Gina added. "She was exactly the kind of bitch I aspire to be someday. Speaking of men, what's up with Hayes?"

I huffed out a laugh. "We weren't speaking of men."

"No, but somebody had to bring it up, and I'm feeling pleasantly plied with alcohol and slightly horny from this movie." She crunched a potato chip, and Boops's nose twitched, but he didn't open his eyes.

Lily popped a grape into her mouth. "I can't picture you and Hayes together."

"I know, right? I'm organized to the point of anal, I have my plans and to-do lists, my goals, and I like things done my way."

Lil snorted. "That is sooo not Hayes."

"Which is why it worked. My parents were exacting, meticulous people. My dad is a goddamned federal judge and all that comes with that. He and my mom demanded perfection twenty-four seven. They were all about the overachieving and pushed me to do the same. There was this huge amount of pressure my father put on me to be the judge's model daughter. If he got disappointed in me because I got a B in a class, I would literally go to my room and cry, then get lectured for showing emotion at all. He was so controlling, so concerned with presenting the perfect picture for his own career. A lot of the time, I felt like I was a PR decision so my dad could keep climbing the judicial ladder."

Sad thing is, I wanted to please him, needed that approval from him, but nothing was ever good enough. It was exhausting. "Then, I went away to college and didn't have him…well, judging me. I met Hayes, who was sooo different. He took things as they came, he was spontaneous, and always in the moment. Hayes gave me the chance and space to explore a way of being where I didn't live for my parents' approval."

Gina popped one olive into her mouth and slid a second one under Boops's lip. "How did you meet?"

I chuckled. "Frat party. I didn't go to many parties, but my roommate dragged me out. This dude the size of a small mountain plucked a half-warm beer out of my hand as I was about to sip, because someone had handed it to me. I didn't know any better. It wasn't like my dad let me go to parties. Anyway, the beer splashed all over my white shirt."

"Which, of course, turned see-through," Gina offered.

I nodded. "Hayes gave me his hoodie to cover up with before he proceeded to lecture me about taking drinks from strangers."

"Did you know who he was?" Lil asked.

I shook my head. "No, but I knew he played football—he had on an OU football T-shirt that they didn't sell to students. I told him my roommate had ditched me and I was going to walk back to my dorm because I had an early volleyball practice. He offered me a ride. I was all, 'Look, dude, you may be some hot-shit football player, but I'm not dumb enough to get into a car with a strange guy who's big enough to make *me* feel small.' He suggested I text my roommate that a guy named Hayes Walker was taking me home, then told me to take his picture and send it to her."

Deepening my voice, I pretended to be Hayes. "'Now, if you come up missing, they'll know who took you. I'd have to be pretty stupid to try something, yeah? Besides, riding with me is safer than walking across campus by yourself, sweetheart. I promise I won't try anything… without asking you first.'"

Lily chuckled. "That sounds like Hayes."

"We didn't go back to the dorm but ended up on the South Olva, lying on a blanket in the grass, talking about everything. After that, we were joined at the hip."

"You're all moony over there," Gina added. "What went wrong with you guys?"

I shrugged. "He didn't tell me. Still hasn't, actually. At the time he gave me a reason I didn't believe, but I believed him today when he told me he was sorry. We were together nearly two years. We made plans. He knew he'd go to the NFL, and we'd have to do long distance for a while, but I could do my post-grad wherever he landed." I sniffed, looked down at Mack as I took another swig of margarita.

"Y'all were serious," Lil threw in.

"Yeah. We'd talked marriage. Not right away, but after I'd finished my post-grad, and he was settled with a team. Out of the blue, the night before the draft, he just…dumped me. By text. He said he didn't want to go into his career with attachments. That he needed to keep his 'options' open."

Gina harrumphed. "Translation: 'I want to fuck a supermodel.' And a goddamned text?"

"Un-fucking-believable," Lily added with a shake of her head.

"I was heartbroken. Being with Hayes unleashed this whole other side of me, an Olive who did crazy shit and took chances I never would have taken without him. I went skydiving, for Christ's sake. On a goddamned whim. After the breakup, my grades plummeted. My volleyball coach benched me, and I spiraled."

Out of the corner of my eye, I saw Lily peek at my scars. "I can see why you think he was a douche. If you think he lied to you when he dumped you, aren't you curious why he did it?"

I nodded. "But he had the opportunity to tell me today and didn't. Or maybe 'I wanna fuck a supermodel' was the truth." That excuse might have made things easier—if I'd thought for one second Hayes was that type of guy. But it didn't line up with the person I knew.

"I'm empty." Rearranging Laila, Lily got up to refill her margarita glass. "Anyone else?"

"Yup." Gina stuck hers in the air.

"I could use another, too."

Taking all three glasses, Lil set to work in the kitchen. "So, the barbecue was his version of an apology for being a douche."

Gina popped a Cheeto in her mouth. "What's a word worse than douche? Because what he did to you was way more than douchy."

I shrugged. "Wank stain?"

"Yes! Yes, Hayes was a stain of the wank! Like my ex-husband, Wyatt. Wyatt the Wanker."

In the kitchen, Lily chortled as she filled the last glass. "Twunt. Hayes was a twunt."

Gina hit pause on the remote, rotated on the couch. "What's a twunt?"

Lily walked back into the living room carrying our margs. "You know… Like a cwat, but a twunt."

When it hit me, I cracked up. "Yes, yes. Twunt totally fits."

When Gina figured it out, her whole face lit up. "TWUNT IS MY NEW FAVORITE WORD!"

Lil drank deep, pulled Laila back onto her lap. "The real question is, is there anything left between you?"

I didn't hesitate. "No. Sparks or not, I'm drawing a line. I was in a dark place for a long time after Hayes. I don't blame him for my spiral—that's all on me—but he's a catalyst to chaos. Hayes pushes my buttons like nobody else—he's kryptonite to my self-control—and I'll never let myself get out of control like that again." That was the moment a sleeping Mack slipped off my lap, headfirst, and hit my white shag rug with a thud. I slapped a hand over my mouth, laughing. The dog didn't move—he just kept right on snoring.

Lily waved it off. "Trust me, didn't hurt him none."

"Lily! That's not nice." Setting my drink on the end table, I slid down on the floor with Mack, rubbing his pointy little ears. "Mommy didn't mean it, buddy. You are the goodest good boy. So sweet and kind and the best snuggler."

"Oh, he is all of those things, but Mack is not the brightest crayon in the box."

Picking up his dead-to-the-world doggie head, I put a kiss on his snout. "Ignore her. She didn't mean it. You can come live with Auntie Olive if you want."

"Welp, I'm officially shitfaced," Gina volunteered.

"Ohh, me too!" I put my hand up. "Who wants left-over barbecue from the twunt?" Pushing off the floor, I made for the kitchen.

Chapter Twelve

HBIC

Olive

As I sat at my desk and sipped my protein shake, I was still in a little bit of shock. Not from Hayes, but from Lily's revelation the night before. She and I had woken up at my place—with atrocious hangovers—to Gina whipping up breakfast while she swung her hips to Cardi B and Bad Bunny.

"So, I have a favor to ask," Lil had said as she pushed up on one of my bar stools with her eyes squinted against the light. "Brody and I decided to forego the big fancy wedding. We're gonna do it at the ranch. Barbecue and hoedown-like. Dogs welcome, people tolerated. Straw bales and picnic tables, and a local band, which I'm having a hard time pinning down." She'd hesitated, fidgeted a little. "I was kind of really sort of hoping you two might be my bridesmaids?"

"Ohmygod, yes!" Gina had yelled.

Lily and I had sent her simultaneous death stares.

Lil had turned her eyes on me, looking a bit nervous.

"I'd be honored, my friend. Absolutely honored."

I was following the shake with a sip of water when the intercom on my office phone beeped.

"Yes?"

Johnathan's soothing voice came through the speaker. "I have the manager for Brother's Keeper on line one."

"Put them through. After this, I'm done for the day so I can make it to the Unruly Dog on time."

I stuffed my iPad into my work bag before I picked up the phone. "Tell me something good, Jimmy."

"Yep. We rearranged, gonna be able to do your friend's wedding."

"That's what I wanted to hear! Now, what do you need in the way of a deposit? This is my gift to the bride and groom."

After we discussed money, I moved on to music. Brother's Keeper was a sought-after cover band whose manager would double as a DJ for their set breaks. "I am not kidding, Jimmy. Country, classic rock, top forties, even some newer pop if you have it in your repertoire, but I hear a single note of 'All My Ex's Live in Texas' and I will have you by the short and curlies."

As I slipped into my shoes prepared to beat feet to the Unruly Dog in Frisco, Johnathan whizzed into my office with his laptop, shutting the door behind him. The look on his face said it all.

"What is it?"

He sat the open computer on my desk, browser opened to *The Observer*.

I flopped back in my chair. "Goddamn it. Fucking Crystal."

The call from Shari Jones, the head of committee for the Arts District fundraiser, came while I was still looking at the article. During Saturday's concert, Crys-

tal had been photographed screwing Michael Seaton—
the husband of wealthy socialite from old Dallas money,
Amanda Baker-Seaton—who also happened to sit on
the Arts District's Summer Concert Series Committee
to Benefit Breast Cancer. The event Crystal was supposed to be volunteering for. It was obvious, too. The
married man's ass crack had been blurred out, but Crystal had her skintight dress around her waist while she
bent over a hard-sided box just *barely* backstage. Whoever had taken the picture sure as hell hadn't needed a
telephoto lens or a backstage pass.

"Hi, Shari, yes, I just saw it. I'm so very sorry about
this."

"Olive, I took her on in good faith. Not to have her
screw my friend's husband and break up their marriage." Truthfully, that was neither here nor there. The
man screwed around on his wife all over town and everyone knew it. But now she had evidence, and if the
socialite planned on filing for divorce, I suspected it was
because evidence of cheating and her prenup would get
her out of paying him maintenance. "The fallout from
this will be huge! Plus, the bad publicity this tramp is
bringing to my committee? This could damage my reputation, not to mention Amanda's!"

"Mine, too, Shari. I'm going to cut her loose immediately, and make sure the committee is insulated from
any more fallout. I'm sincerely sorry about this and you
can be sure it won't happen again." This little twunt was
done screwing with my, or anyone else's, reputation. It
was time for her to take her ass back to Daddy. When I
was done, nobody in Dallas would touch Crystal Vincent, even with a hazmat suit and black light.

"Want me to pull the contract?" Johnathan said after Shari finished my ass-chewing.

"Yes, and call Lily at the Unruly Dog to let her know I'm going to be a little late. I'll have to call Anthony at *Dallas Life & Style* tomorrow; we're shooting the *Texas Weekly* show tonight. Oh, get me Crystal's number, too, please."

I couldn't believe how quickly October had snuck up on us and I didn't have time to deal with Crystal's petty shit. The State Fair was in full swing, which meant the countdown was on, and things were starting to gel. Like the TV show. The producer would have to burn the midnight oil to get us to air in only two weeks' time, but it was worth it.

A dog person through and through, Margo had taken a cameraman and gone out to the Unlovabulls Rescue to get footage she could cut in with the training center footage. She'd also asked if she could come do a short follow-up with Lily and Brody during the fair event to run during the news at six and ten. Above and beyond. By the time this thing aired, I'd be the one with a red mark in my ledger.

Johnathan nodded, and hurried after the things I'd asked him for, quickly dropping them at my desk as I formulated my plan for damage control on my notepad. Five minutes later, I had a workable plan for skewing any fallout away from the charity committee. Was I throwing Crystal under the bus? Pfft, she'd walked in front of it and painted a bullseye on her chest. I simply wasn't going to nudge her out of the way.

Tapping the speaker button on my landline, I put in Crystal's number as Johnathan sat in one of my club chairs to listen.

She answered the phone with "Olive, I can explain."

"You can explain being photographed having sex in public with Amanda Seaton's husband at a fundraiser?"

"No, see…he came on to me, Olive. I swear." Oh my God, that voice. It immediately started to give me a headache.

"It doesn't really matter who came on to whom. From the look on your face, I'm going to assume it was consensual, yes?"

"Well, yeah."

I closed my eyes on an extended blink. "Crystal, something like this doesn't just damage your reputation. My reputation is on the line. Shari's is, too. This indiscretion is going to incite a divorce worth millions of dollars, not to mention the bad publicity for both the husband and wife, and the Arts District Charity Committee, as well as the bad word of mouth for me because I couldn't *keep you in line*, so to speak."

"Wait a minute. Your job is to make me look good, no matter what I do. Do your job."

"Oh, no, it's not. Not anymore. I've tried with you, and it is not my job to be your glorified babysitter, and continuously sweep your indiscretions under the rug. Frankly, as I've told you before, you are a relative nobody in this town. My job was to open doors to Dallas society for you, operative word being *was*, which I did to the letter of our contract. I am not under contract to handle crisis management for you and frankly, I only took you on as a favor to Johnathan. It was your job to make the most of the opportunities we provided for you. Instead, you've managed to use them to cause a scandal and become a liability to Russo Image Consulting. Given that we've fulfilled our end of the contract, and you've failed, on multiple occasions, to follow through with your end, I'm severing all ties with you, Ms. Vincent. Effective immediately."

"You can't do that! I'm paying you!"

"Frankly, darling, there isn't enough money in the world. My reputation is the cornerstone of my business, and you've threatened that while possibly damaging a long-term relationship with a valued contact of mine. Because of that, and according to the terms of our contract, I'll be sending you a full refund."

"Fuck you, then! I don't need your shitty-ass PR firm. I'll just go elsewhere."

"Good luck with that."

Crystal huffed. "What, you think you're going to try to blacklist me? ME? Stuck-up bitch."

I chuckled under my breath. "No, Ms. Vincent. I would never burn a client with other firms. You've done that all on your own. There isn't a PR firm worth its salt that's going to touch you after this debacle. Amanda Baker-Seaton is a force to be reckoned with. I'm afraid you picked the wrong woman's husband to screw in public."

The noises that came out of her reminded me of a strangled cat. "Wh... What am I supposed to do now?" I could hear the waver and the oncoming blubbering. Time to wrap this up.

"My advice is to buy a return ticket to Las Vegas."

"My daddy will crush you, you bitch."

That was it. I'd been called bitch one too many times. "Your father should have spent a good deal more time raising his daughter to respect herself, and others, and less time snorting his royalties up his nose. Somehow,

I doubt your daddy will give a good goddamn about any of this."

"My grandfather is—"

"I don't care. We're done here, Ms. Vincent. Good luck to you." With that, I hung up on her.

"And that's how it's done by the master." Johnathan grinned. "She deserved that spanking. She's no longer a client, or a friend, and I'm good with that."

I sent him a wink. "Good to know. Now, get back to work, groupie, and run my office because I'm late for a TV show. Make sure you have accounting send Crystal her refund."

Most clients came to me to improve their image. Perhaps they had PR issues in the past they wanted cleaned up. Or perhaps they'd found themselves embroiled in scandal after scandal. My qualifier was that I didn't turn away from scandal, but my clients must make a concerted effort to follow the plan we laid out for them, which they agreed to up front. I also didn't drop clients for getting themselves into scrapes. It was my job to help them get out of them. However, Crystal was different. I couldn't have clients damaging my relationships with important and influential people in the DFW area. And I sure as hell didn't have to put up with verbal abuse, complete disregard for the public relations plan, and be expected to play nanny to a brat for one quarter my normal contracted rate.

In the history of Russo Consulting, I had only cut one other client loose—a local shock jock who'd beaten his girlfriend so badly he'd put her in the hospital. Letting clients go wasn't something I did willy-nilly. I understood what it felt like to be the one sitting across the desk with the DUI in hand and a lead balloon full of shame in your stomach. Still, I had lines I wouldn't cross. Abusers of any kind, rape, manslaughter, or murder.

It was one thing to take on someone who truly wanted to turn their image around. It was another thing entirely when someone hired me to continuously sweep bad behavior under the rug to my own detriment.

Stuffing my notepad into my bag, I headed for the Unruly Dog. A state-of-the-art center, the staff, trainers, and even the owner, Lauren, volunteered at the rescue regularly. Not only was it a top-notch place that deserved more due, it was the perfect setting to demonstrate what the Unlovabulls rescue dogs could become with a little love and patience.

Grabbing my work bag, and the bag with my change of clothes, I locked up and headed inside. I saw Margo was with Lauren running cables to a power source as one of her camera people put the last touches on a bit of scaffolding set up on the agility ring.

My squad was sitting on the bleachers, drooling every time the cameraman on the scaffolding reached above his head and his abs peeked out.

"Working hard, I see," I said as I sat my bags down on the metal seat.

"Well, yeah. This is thirsty work." Melissa motioned to the poor dude, and all I could do was shake my head and chuckle.

"Hey, Lily was looking for you," Kate added without taking her eyes off the peep show.

"Okay, thanks."

"Olive," Lauren said. "Can we talk in my office?"

Uh-oh. Time to go to work. "Sure, can I put my stuff in there?"

As we walked to her office, I scanned over the room. Things were coming together. Lauren shut the door behind us. "You can put your bags on my desk."

"What's wrong?" I dropped the bags and leaned on the desk.

"One of Margo's camera people wants to take down the Unruly Dog banners in the agility ring because they're not *aesthetically pleasing to the camera*." Her cheeks were pink, her mouth pinched. "They think it looks too much like product placement. Those banners are in there all the time and they're a pain in the ass to get down from the rafters and put back up!"

"Yeah, no. I won't let them do that. Let me have a talk with Margo."

"Good, because they've already brought a ladder in. I let them put holes in a brand-new five-hundred-dollar competition-grade tunnel so they could mount a GoPro inside, for Pete's sake. They showed me what the footage will look like, and it's nifty, so I told them they could, but now they want my banners pulled, too? I'm not sure we can get them down without tearing them up, and cloth banners like that? Those things were nearly three grand apiece!"

Okay, Lauren was losing her shit. "Let's go find Margo before they do any damage."

As we walked back through the bleacher area, I realized I hadn't seen any of the football players. They should have been here by now. One fire at a time.

"Margo, got a minute?"

"What's up?"

"Get your guy down off the ladder. The banners stay put."

She set her shoulders for an argument. "They don't

look good on camera. It's like one giant advertisement
and it's visually overwhelming."

I shook my head. "No. We talked about this. Lauren
is letting us film here for free, they canceled their evening classes for this and are losing money because they
have to refund those clients. Their staff are here purely
as volunteers. This is also one of the premier training
centers in Texas, and the only purpose of your show is
to highlight area businesses like this one. Those banners are a fixture in this ring. They stay."

"I don't think—"

I stopped playing nice. "Mark. Fucking. Cuban.
Margo."

Crossing her arms, she fixed her eyes on the floor.
"Okay. Like we discussed."

"Thank you. I'll want to see the piece before it airs.
And the GoPro stays when you leave."

Her head came up. "What? You're not keeping
my equipment. That's a four-hundred-dollar camera,
Olive!"

"That's a five-hundred-dollar tunnel you put holes
in, Margo."

She grinned. "Always a hard-ass. Okay."

"Just doing my job. Still on for lunch next week?"

"Of course, but you're picking up the bill."

"Now, *that* I will do." When I turned, I saw Lauren
beaming, the rest of my posse with their eyes wide, and
Lily fidgeting over by the bleachers.

After walking over, I lowered my voice. "Okay, Lil.
Lauren's office?" She nodded. "Oh, have any of you
seen the fellas?"

"Brody's on the way," Lily answered. "When I talked

to him at the rescue earlier, he said he was bringing Shane and Jensen with him."

"What about Hayes?" I scanned the area. "Anybody seen him?" I'd emailed him the details. Maybe I should have called him instead. It would be just like Hayes to blow this off because he got a wild hair up his ass to go try roller derby.

"I thought I saw him not too long ago," Kate piped up. With a little smirk, she winked.

"Who told you? Gina?" Who wouldn't be joining us. Wednesdays were the night she kept her practice open late.

"Brody. When I was at the rescue earlier."

Fucking gossip! I knew I'd made a face before Lily even said anything, and that was a no-no. My poker face was an essential part of my job, but I was fixating on a man, not the work.

Kate cringed. "I don't think he knew it was a secret, Olive. Don't be too hard on him."

Lily cracked a grin. The first one I'd seen from her. "He's got it coming. Those guys gossip more than a knitting circle."

Drawing a deep breath through my nose, I reset my face and smiled at my friend. "It's fine. I'll talk to Brody later." It was not fucking fine when my past with Hayes interrupted my composure.

Lily led the way to the office, but I already knew what was coming. She closed us in, and I could see the cracks in her surface. Picking the skin on her thumb, constantly shifting her weight between legs.

A big piece of what I did required me to be observant. I needed to know how my clients would react in certain situations or settings. Unfortunately, Lily hadn't had time for any media training, but I had a plan. "You're nervous about the interview?"

"I mean, yeah. I... Media is not my thing. It's god-damn triggering to have that camera and microphone stuck in my face. It's like being a little girl and watching them hound my dad after a game. Can't you work it into your interview? Or Brody? He's used to that stuff. You know what I'm like when I get nervous; I babble, usually in doggie voices and shit. I'll screw this up, I—"

"Shhh, Lil," I said in a calming voice. "It's okay. I don't want you to be anxious about this. If you don't want to do it, Brody can. The reason I suggested they interview you is because you *are* this rescue. It's your baby from the ground up. You can speak to it, and the dogs, with passion and on a level even Brody can't."

A knock on the door interrupted me. "Olive? Brody's here with the hot guys." It was Kate.

"Okay. What about Hayes?"

"He's not with them."

"Thanks." Goddamn it, had he showed up and left? And why was I letting him get under my skin? *You expect him to flake and you need him not to, because reasons.*

Kicking off my heels, I slid up on the edge of the desk and turned back to Lil. "What if you and Brody do the interview as a team? If it's not working for you, Brody can take the lead, or he can be there to fill in any gaps and just give you support."

She shifted her feet, crossed her arms over her chest. "It's still a lot; what if she tries to ask me about my dad, or Dick Head, or if she brings up the Fantasy Suite stuff, or..."

Reaching behind me, I fished in my work bag until

I found what I was searching for. The previous year, Brody had been embroiled in a scandal when several of his teammates held an orgy in a swanky downtown hotel. One of the women who attended leaked pictures to the press doctored a photo to look like Brody. "The host isn't allowed to ask you about your father's issues, your stepfather, or any personal information about your relationship with Brody beyond what the media already knows. The Fantasy Suite scandal is also off the table. I spoke with Margo, and she understands that the show host has to stick to topics I preapproved: dogs, rescue, agility, training, the appearance at the fair, donations. It's a feel-good piece, Lily. I promise they won't and can't come at you like the reporters used to do to your dad or Brody."

I handed her the notecards in my hand. "Plus, you can practice your responses. Here are the questions I approved, with a couple of suggestions from me for talking points. They may not ask you all of them, they may rephrase them, but you'll be prepared."

"My dad is on here, but only in reference to his legacy in Dallas football." Glancing up at me, she beamed. "This is… Yeah, I can do this so long as I have an idea of what's coming. I'd still like to have Brody there to back me up, though." She shuffled through the cards.

"Absolutely."

She hit me with a pint-sized tackle hug that might have taken out someone Gina's size. As it was, her face was smothered in my boobs.

"It's my job to make you look good, my friend. I'd never hand you over to the wolves."

As soon as Lily left with her cards, I hopped down and started pulling out my clothes. I'd been here ten minutes and already put two fires out. "Damn, I'm good," I whispered as I stripped off my blouse and unbuttoned my pants.

"Hayes, where the hell are you?" I said to myself. "You'd better not flake on me."

"I'm right behind you."

Chapter Thirteen

The fuck just happened here?

Hayes

"Ahh!" The little squeak was so cute. Olive jumped, and I felt bad for a split second. Before I realized her pants were on the way to the floor.

"Jesus." I tried to look away, but if I was honest, it was too late. I'd seen those amazing cheeks and they were tattooed on the inside of my eyelids.

"Holy fuck." She spun to face me, clasping her chest. "Not. Cool. Walker. What the hell are you doing in here? How did you get in?"

I couldn't help the grin. "Don't you want to put some clothes on?"

"Don't *you*?"

Yeah, that was my girl. *Wait, my girl?* "I would have gotten dressed in the bathroom, but I left my bag out here." I nodded to the bag sitting in the corner chair, wiggled my eyebrows. "Didn't realize you'd be getting naked in someone else's office."

"I *thought* I was alone, so I locked the door and

started to change. Does Lauren have a shower in there? I thought it was storage."

"No, darlin'. I washed off in the water fountain, wrapped a towel around my waist, then purposely waited for Lily to leave just so I could flash you my pecs." Tacking on an evil laugh for kicks, I bounced said pecs à la the Rock, and damn near dropped my towel.

"Smart-ass." The throaty chuckle that worked through her lips would have been worth the embarrassment of her seeing my semi. "Careful, there, buddy. You almost dropped that thang."

"Sorry I scared you."

She turned back to her bag and flashed me her ass again. "Christ." I looked at the ceiling. "Olive, you're flashing me your ass."

"Isn't anything you haven't already seen. Why are you in Lauren's shower?"

Shoulder rested on the door frame, I literally had to shake my head to think straight when she bent to pull a pair of khaki shorts up her legs and her panties rode up her cheeks.

Great. Now I had a full fucking hard-on. In a towel not even big enough to tuck in around my waist.

"Umm… Came straight from practice and Lil said I smelled."

"Mmm, I used to love that smell." The words fell out absently as she pulled something else out of her bag.

She was driving me to an early grave. "Are you doing this to me on purpose? I have to say, it's not very friendly."

She threw her head back and laughed. That laugh was life. It was a siren's call, and I was starting to get close to the rocks.

"Nope. I'm just in a hurry. Though, it might be a little fun." With deft fingers, Olive reached back and popped the hooks on her bra.

My palm was rough as I scrubbed it across my face and my hard-on kicked against the terry cloth.

"Don't know if you heard but we're filming a TV show here today. I've got lots to do." She pulled some other kind of bra contraption over her shoulders like a jacket. That's when I saw the side curve of her breast.

I growled. Fucking audibly. And it wasn't friendly. It was predatory. "Olive."

She picked up on the change in my voice, because as soon as the bra was zipped, she spun to look at me. Those dark eyes of hers slithered down my neck, over my pecs, down the abs I worked fucking hard for. Everywhere her gaze touched me, I lit up. The pink in her cheeks spread down her neck, over her chest. She wanted me, too.

Fuck, my cock jerked again, and she tracked the movement, her lips parting a hair's breadth.

"Umm," seemed to be all she could get out.

"My eyes are up here, Ollie," I said with a cocky grin. Quickly, she flipped her gaze up to mine. "At least *I* tried not to look."

"Whoops." She chuckled, leaned her ass against the desk. "Busted."

Leaning over to the chair in the corner, I pulled out my boxer briefs. "Two can play this game, my friend." I turned away from her and dropped the towel. "An ass for an ass."

Her intake of breath made a rumble of laughter escape my chest. "That was nice, what you did for Lily."

When I bent to pull my drawers on, I was careful not to flash her the frank and beans.

"Mmhmm, s'my job."

"I heard what you said. About me flaking?" Reaching down the front of my underwear, I adjusted myself, trying to get my hard-on to cooperate. "Did you really think I'd flake on this?" I turned back to her to read her face.

She shrugged. "It crossed my mind."

"Have I been anything but dependable up to this point, Ollie?"

She let out a derisive snort as she pulled a Kelly green polo shirt over her head. "I... I'm just..."

"Waiting for the other shoe to drop. For me to screw up again so you can tell me 'I told you so.'"

I took the couple steps across the room. I knew I should have given her space, but my brain was offline, and my signals were all mixed up. I needed to be close to her, to feel her skin under my fingertips. To have her know why I was so reckless back then. But I was also a little pissed. She was judging me now for things I'd done then.

Olive put a hand up between us. "Look, it's going to take me a minute. The Hayes I knew would blow off a midterm for a taco truck in Corsicana. I'm trying here, Walker. I'm just having trouble separating past from present with you around. You make it hard for me to compartmentalize."

"Ahh." I took another step forward—one I knew I shouldn't take—and pressed my chest against her upheld palm. "Which box do I belong in, Olive?" That was the thing, though. I deserved her derision and the skepticism. I *had* been that guy in college. I'd had my reasons—it was the first time in my life I had been out of my mother's reach, and I did my damnedest to make the most of it—but Olive didn't know that.

"I'm not sure." She shook her head. "You get my boxes jumbled up. I don't know where you belong."

Leaning forward, I got close. Close enough to feel her warm breath fan against my lips. Only a cool whisper of air separated my mouth from hers. The tension, that anticipation, her elevated breathing, mine too. I would have given anything to touch her and ease the knot under my breastbone. "I belong right here, right now. With you." I knew it hadn't been long, and after what I'd done to her… Yeah, a meal and a conversation weren't going to wipe it all away. Especially when we obviously had more between us than attraction.

So. Much. More.

"Olive." I could see her pulse against her neck and her chest rise and fall. The ache as my stomach clenched, my body begging for more of her touch. To feel her pressed against me. I wanted this woman so bad my hands shook, and my skin felt too sensitive, my muscles too tight. Her palm was a brand over my heart that might as well have said property of Olive Russo.

What's more, the way her pupils dilated, her quick, shallow breaths, the flush on her throat and dampened lips. Everything about her was calling out to me.

But how could I do that? How could I kiss Olive if I couldn't keep her? And I couldn't keep her when I had to take care of a mother and sister who needed me. I couldn't do that to Olive. I *wouldn't* do that to her. To either of us. I knew what kind of pain that would bring. I knew I'd never gotten over Olive—I knew that way down deep in my bones. It wasn't just her heart I'd broken that day. I laid waste to mine, too.

Turning on my heel, I breathed deep to steady myself before I snatched my athletic bag off the chair. Storming back into the bathroom, I slammed the door behind me angry at myself, at what I'd done, at who I was and how I felt.

Because I was falling for Olive and I knew I couldn't have her.

Olive

I couldn't…it was overwhelming. There had been so much familiarity and heat with Hayes, and the look in his eyes… Something broke open in me. Each time I was around him, it opened a little more. Something reckless and passionate and dormant came awake with an aching and hunger. It wasn't a feeling I could prioritize on a list, or sort through the pros and cons of, because it just…was. Hayes muddled up all my compartments. Ex-boyfriend or current friend. Attraction, affection, passion and control, betrayal and love and excruciating pain. Emotions of all sorts got all mixed up around him and I couldn't sort them out.

I suspected that's why I couldn't breathe in the little office. The knot of feelings and memories in my head and heart that I was fighting to untie, but it wouldn't come undone.

Those feelings were unmaking me. My skin felt like the buzzing of bees. My breathing, too shallow. My head fuzzy, and my body uncoordinated.

I need to get out of there, get distance to collect myself into some semblance of the woman I knew. Stable. In control.

After coming out of the office, I slipped through a staff exit that led to a picnic table under a tree. As soon as the early evening air hit my lungs, the tension began to ease. The bees flew away.

What the hell just happened to me?

The door flew open and out walked Gina. "Whatcha doin' hiding out here? With all your stuff. Barefoot. And your zipper is down."

I looked down at the gaping hole in my khakis and snort-laughed. Just like that, the knot eased, as if the problem wasn't the knot, but me pulling at it and only making it tighter. "Ahh, I just needed air. What are you doing here?"

"My last client canceled so I thought I'd come lend a hand. You sure you're okay? You look a little…undone. That's not like you."

Again with the door, and out flew Lily, still looking nervous as hell, with Laila in tow. "Oh, I didn't think anybody would be out here. I… Laila needs to potty. I think."

I patted the bench next to me. "C'mon, we'll have our panic attacks together."

"Umm, wait, what? You?" Lily's eyebrows shot up as she took the seat next to me.

"Yeah. I think that's what happened. I think I've just exceeded my quotient of Hayes for the day."

"Ahhh, now I get it," Gina said, lifting Laila into her lap for smooches. "What happened?"

"Let's just say Hayes and I had a moment."

Gina nuzzled the Bulldog. "We can all tell you two still have the feels. I actually think it's kind of sweet."

"This, from our resident cynic?" Lily sent her a side-eye.

Gina shrugged.

"Why don't you see where it goes?" Lil nudged my shoulder. "What can it hurt?"

Me. It can hurt me. "It's a lot of history. A lot of good times, sure, but a lot of painful memories tangled up in that, too. I don't know if I want to be a part of that again. Hayes was always mercurial. What he wants today will likely be different tomorrow. My life is well-ordered, and Hayes is chaos."

Lily took a long look at me. "That doesn't sound like the man who comes to the shelter four or five times a week to play with the sweet old Boxer *he* named Sadie. Or the guy who showed up on my doorstep because he didn't have a place big enough to make you barbecue. Maybe he's not the same person he was then. People change, Olive. Look at me and Brody." I really thought about Hayes. He had been dependable this time around. Helpful. He'd held up his end, and if something needed done, he did it. He never shied away from the work. Even Hayes said he wasn't the boy he had been. That he had obligations I didn't understand. "Besides, a little chaos sometimes can be a good thing, too. Look at Gina."

"Hey! Okay, yeah, I'm my own brand of chaos. I happen to love that about me."

"I do, too," I said, winking at her.

Was I really considering Lily's suggestion? Not drawing lines and seeing where things went with Hayes? Part of my job about creating second chances for people, but I'd just had a panic attack at the mere possibility of kissing Hayes. All those wires crossed up—past and present—with need and fear all combined with the crunch of metal and excruciating pain.

It was a lot for me, keeping everything in my life just so. My image, my business, my house, my clients, and their bullshit. Shouldn't I have a little chaos in my life? That chaos had once come in the pint-sized package of a Weiner dog. I'd invited that in and fallen in love. She was the one that made me laugh at myself and reminded that you couldn't plan every detail down to the minute. That sometimes you needed to roll with things and enjoy the ride without picking at the knot and making it worse. "I'm not sure what I want. As cliché as it sounds, I need time to think."

Lil nodded along with Gina. "We wouldn't expect any less."

An hour later, we had the football players up to speed with very basic agility and Lily had rocked her interview.

"We're really excited about the appearance at the Texas State Fair on October 19, and I can't tell you how grateful we are to the staff, players, former players, and the coaches of the Dallas Bulldogs who have helped us pull it together. We couldn't have done it without them. I'd like to send a special thank you to my co-chair, Hayes Walker. He's been invaluable."

The *Texas Weekly* show host took a glimpse at her notes. "What's in store for people who'd like to go to the appearance?"

"We'll have twenty-four players participating in a signing in exchange for a minimum donation that goes directly to the Unlovabulls rescue. We'll also have photographs with the players of your choosing. Thanks to Charlie Delaune Photography, and the players who've waived any normal appearance or photo fees, all proceeds will directly benefit the rescue."

"Wow," the host remarked right on cue. "That's really exciting! Bulldogs helping Bulldogs. I love it! But, Olive, I sense you might be excited to tell us something else."

"Absolutely. We're thrilled to announce our inaugural fundraising gala, Love for the Unlovabulls, coming to a venue in downtown Dallas this February, after football season of course. The evening will be loaded with fun and entertainment, including a plated dinner, a silent auction, a date auction with prominent men and women of DFW, and so much more. Long after the plates are empty, the auction items are spoken for, and the Jimmy Choos are left under the table, we'll dance the night away. More information about auction items will be available in the coming months, but I can let it slip that at least two of the lots will be a trip for two to Paris with five-star accommodations, and a brand-new custom-kitted Audi R8 Spyder."

"Oh, my! That's fabulous! Sounds like *the* place to see and be seen next February. Where can interested parties find more information?"

"Our website just launched this week at TheUnlovabullsGala.com. More information will be available in the coming weeks including venue information and price points as well as a way to donate directly. All proceeds will go to funding this amazing shelter and the work they do to help rescue dogs become healthy, well-adjusted, loving pets that people will be proud to call their furbabies."

"Cut," Margo yelled. "Olive, top-notch. Let's reset for the agility. Twenty minutes, people."

I skimmed the room as the worker bees began moving around the agility ring with their camera equipment. When I saw a PA trying to move the A-frame by himself, I went to stop him, but Lily was on it.

"Dude! You can't move that! The course is set just so to be safe for dogs and people!" She rubbed her temples, but Brody was already striding across the room.

"Think he'll get her to keep it together a little longer?" Hayes asked.

"Lily's tougher than she looks." I couldn't bring myself to look at him for fear it would send me into another spiral.

"Oh, I know," he said. "When she was a Bulldogs trainer, she had half the guys on the team scared of her wrath." He nudged me with his shoulder, nodded at the bleachers. "Check it out."

I glanced over only to see Gina flirting with Jensen Bishop. Jensen had replaced Brody on the team. "Am I going to have to have a talk with him?"

"Nah. He's one of the good ones. A little naive, on the shy side, but not a player in the sense you're thinking of. He's got a good head on his shoulders. Much better than I had at that age."

I heard the regret in his voice, and finally turned to look at him. The sexy mouth and square jaw. The blue eyes and blond beard and all that ink. Nope, I didn't panic. I didn't run screaming from the room, or hyperventilate, or feel like my own brain was eating itself.

"Olive, I ah—"

"Hayes Walker, you're running with the Boxer, correct?" a production assistant interrupted.

The annoyance on Hayes's face only lasted a split-second. "Yes."

"We need you to go over things."

Hayes nodded. "Give me a minute. I'll be right there." Turning back to me as the PA disappeared, he lowered his voice. "I'm sorry about earlier in the office, getting in your space like that. We're supposed to be friends, not... I just... I still feel...things, and I'm not sure I can handle being in half-naked proximity to you without wanting...things."

He was flustered. It was adorable. "Hayes, I know what you're trying to say, and thank you."

"Guys," Brody yelled.

Hayes gave Brody a death stare before turning back to me. "I just needed to say that."

"Thank you." I patted his chest. "And for the record, I never should have said that you'd flake. My job is all about creating second chances and what I said totally undermines that. I'm not going to say it will be easy, but I am trying, Hayes. I just need time."

He nodded, almost shyly. I may have actually swooned. On the inside. Definitely not outside.

As soon as we walked up to the group waiting on us, Margo started in. "The concept here is pro athletes versus pro athletes of the four-legged variety. We're going to film each of you doing two runs, and cut the final product to make it look like a competition between the Bulldogs and the rescue dogs. I want to show off what the rescues can become with the proper training and care, and I'm going to do it totally at your expense." The players nodded all around. "Don't underestimate us, Margo," Shane said. "Some of us have pretty quick feet."

Lily, Brody, and I gave each other a knowing look. They had no idea what they were in for.

Hayes lined Sadie up with the first jump, just like Brody taught him. Sadie knew the fundamentals, but she was a true beginner.

"Sadie, jump!" Hayes yelled, and she took the jumps beautifully, trotting from one to another at a leisurely pace. Lily had set the bars low for her aging knees and hips.

When they got to the A-frame, Sadie ran around it instead of up it. "C'mon, girl, up! You have to go up." Hayes turned back to try again.

They both made another run at the obstacle and Sadie ran around and looked at him like, *Around is much easier, idiot.*

Then there was the last tunnel. She went in but didn't come back out. "Saaadiiiie, come on, honey, let's go! Sadie Maaaaeee!"

I looked over at the playback on the GoPro in the tunnel, a little worried that maybe she'd mentally shut down.

"She's fine," Lil said, walking up behind me.

That's when I saw her exaggerated nose and tongue on the TV monitor, sniffing and licking the camera. When I glanced back to the ring, Hayes was literally scratching his head. "Do I go in after her?"

I was about to yell no when Lily yelled, "Yes! You should go in."

What the... But when I glanced at her, she had an evil grin on her face. "It's TV. Hayes should get to make an ass out of himself. Besides, I know Sadie loves tunnels. She plays in the one we have at the rescue. She's a tunnel sucker."

A tunnel sucker was a dog that ran into the mouth

of any tunnel they passed whether they were supposed to or not. My lips quirked to one side. "You are evil."

"Look." She tipped her chin at the ring.

Hayes was on his hands and knees with his ass in the air, his shoulders too wide to go in. I snort-laughed. "Ohmygod, that's priceless."

I wasn't the only one who thought so. Brody and Shane were heckling him.

"He's got a real affinity for that dog, Lil. Why hasn't he adopted her?"

"I know he does. Old dog, past her prime, nobody wants. Old football player, past his prime, nobody wants. Not hard to see the parallel." No, not hard at all. "He does want to adopt her, but traveling half the year? It's hard on the dog unless you have someone you trust to take care of her."

I scoffed. "Surely, you would watch her."

Lil shook her head. "We can't. Sadie doesn't get along with Laila and Mack. They're too much wiggly energy for her to handle. She gets overwhelmed and then aggressive. Maybe if he had someone else to help... He wants Sadie to have a stable home with people she trusts. It's what she deserves. But when she finally gets adopted—and she will—it's gonna break Hayes's heart."

Turning back to the ring, I moved up to the half wall, put my finger and thumb in my mouth, and whistled three short blasts. Sadie popped out of the end of the tunnel opposite Hayes, took the dog walk and three jumps on her own on her way to me. Her little black brindle nub tail wiggled her whole butt when she put her paws on the wall to tell me hello.

"Hey, baby girl. You're such a good girl, you did so

well!" I fished her ball out of my pocket and threw it across the ring smiling as she took off after it. "Walker, you can come out now!"

"Yeah!" Brody yelled. "We can't wait all night for you to pull your head out of your ass!"

"Jesus," Lil whispered, shaking her head. "I hope they can edit Brody out of that."

Jensen went next and didn't fare any better. He ran Mack because he didn't have a dog of his own. When Mack refused to take the jumps, Jensen was just as stubborn about making kissy noises; Jensen started jumping over the bars himself hoping Mack would follow. It was both completely ridiculous and hilarious but would make for great footage. He was doing exactly what we wanted—making an ass out of himself. When Jensen tripped over the corner of a tunnel, landing on his butt, Mack flew over to him and sat on his chest. The big man just lay there, laughing.

"Oh! Jensen, close your—" Lily shouted, but it was too late.

"Gack. This dog just slipped me the tongue."

"That's the only tongue you've pulled this year!" Shane shouted.

"Oh my God," Lily whispered. "They can't air this shit."

Margo stepped in next to her. "Don't worry. I am an editing god."

The whole experiment had become exactly what I'd hoped for—a comedy of errors that was completely endearing for both the dogs and the players. This was going to be perfect.

Shane fared better than Hayes and Jensen. Then again, his Lab mix had picked up on the training quickly. Shane also had an instinct about where to be and when to be there. Wide receiver—go figure. He and his dog had real potential as a team.

Next, the pros were up. On a full course, not the simplified course the players had run. CC took the weave poles like a rocket, rode the teeter-totter to the floor, and flew across the dog walk with her long legs. Corsi were surprisingly agile and fast for big dogs. When she finished her run, Brody pulled a tug toy from his waistband and CC latched on to it. Brody swung her around off her front feet—not easily done with a one-hundred-and-forty-pound dog. No wonder Brody stayed in shape.

Next was Kendra running Ramsey, the Dogo Argentino she'd rescued after he'd graduated from the Unlovabulls. He was every bit as fast as CC and more body aware. So was his owner, who was cleaner with her signals than Brody. Ramsey's stunning white coat, his square head and powerful chest would make for excellent footage.

Finally, it was Lily's turn, but not with Jet. The point was to highlight rescued bully breeds and what they could accomplish with the right training and care. Obviously, the deck was stacked. Lily ran Tucker, an American Staffordshire Terrier with a jet-black coat, a white patch on his chest, and cropped ears and tail. He was one of the dogs that had come from the shelter that closed. Lily took on his training herself, and he was ready for adoption, but large, adult, black bully breeds were the least likely to get adopted out.

Tucker had taken to agility with ease and I had no doubt he could compete at a high level with the right owner. Lily knew it, too. She was keeping him at the rescue until she found a proper agility home for him.

Personally, I thought Tucker might be going home with Lily permanently if he didn't find a home. The Pit Bull did not disappoint, flying over the jumps with grace and speed, sending to the tunnels from several yards away. Over the top of the A-frame with his feet barely touching the wood, and across the dog walk in four or five strides.

Lily and Tucker pulled in a ribbon-worthy time and showstopping performance.

As we wrapped up and cleaned up, everyone exhausted from a long evening, I kept my eye out for Hayes. But he was good to his word. He gave me space, which was exactly what I needed to sort out what happened earlier. In fact, at one point when the cleanup was done, I looked up hoping to catch a glimpse of familiar blond hair only to find out from Gina he'd slipped out, quietly, with Sadie in tow.

I guess I wasn't the only one who needed time and space to think.

Chapter Fourteen

*"Sometimes you need a second chance,
because you weren't quite ready for the first."*
—Unknown

Hayes

In no time the third weekend in October was on us and
so was the Texas State Fair appearance.

By the time I got there at the ass crack of dawn,
Lily was already directing traffic. "Good, Hayes, you're
here. Jensen could use some help with the dog and team
supplies—kennels, water, toys, ex-pens, props, et cetera, and the photographer needs help getting her rig set
up since her assistant didn't show. Either delegate or be
everywhere at once."

Between the *Texas Weekly* show airing and the short
TV spots the fair committee had paid for, the signing
event had turned into a huge thing. The team was getting so much free publicity from the event and its adver-
tising even Dick Head had latched on to the "Bulldogs
helping Bulldogs" thing and decided to send the cheer-
leaders to the signing. Would wonders never cease. He
didn't really have a choice but to go along. We had so

many players coming to help, the fair committee had given us indoor exhibitor space with private parking.

I sipped my gas station coffee. "Tell me where you want *me* to go first, and I'll find guys to do the rest."

Lil paused, caught her breath. "Help the photographer because I know you won't hit on her. Delegate the heavy lifting until that's done. Olive or Brody will call when they get here with the first group of dogs and their handlers. I'm sure they'll need a hand. Carrie and Melissa are bringing another group later in the day so it's easier on the dogs. We're only doing four hours at a time for them and their handlers."

"You got it, boss." I took a step back, cupped my hands over my mouth. "Listen up! For those of you who don't know, Lily Costello is your coach for the day. She has zero problems keeping your asses in line. She says jump, you say how high. And before you think about giving her any lip, I suggest you consider who she whipped into marriage material." A chorus of laughs followed along with someone yelling, "We love you, Lily!"

"I know!" she returned without missing a beat.

After I tapped a few players to help haul shit in, I went to help the photographer get her stuff set up. Apparently, Charlie was short for Charlotte, and the woman was muttering to herself, hurling violent curses at no one in particular. At least I'd make a big target for her.

Olive and I had a plan. We'd worked with the fair committee to schedule volunteering players for two-hour sessions. The fair staff were handing out the schedule at the front gate as well as posting it to the website so visitors would know when the players they wanted to see would be signing. Anywhere from five to seven players at a time would sign autographs, take pictures, and pose with the pups and the people for a healthy donation fee.

My players knew they were supposed to chat the folks up, too. Especially if they paid for photos. We had volunteer Bulldogs staff—including security—handling the players' needs, and Lily had plenty of people to take care of the dogs. The most impressive part? Everybody that was here genuinely wanted to be here to help the rescue. It was a thing of beauty, and all the pieces were falling into place.

Except for one.

I hadn't seen Olive since the *Texas Weekly* taping. We'd both been busy with our respective jobs, but we talked by phone and traded emails about details for the events and going to visit venues for the gala. She'd been true to her word about not cutting me out of the planning.

As I secured the photographer's green screen with zip ties, I got the call from Brody that he and Olive had arrived with the first group of dogs and handlers. Nobody would be allowed to adopt a dog today, but they'd know how to put in an application, and how the adoption process went.

As I walked down the short slope to the parking lot, I nodded to Daniel McManus, who was carrying two large, folded dog kennels in each hand.

Glad to see I won't have a problem with that one today. His tune had changed a bit since our little showdown. Respect was earned on the field, and I guess I'd earned his.

Brody had Mack and CC leashed around his wrist

as he pulled dog stuff from the back of the SUV. "Hey, man. I've got Smalls if you can get Biggie. There's another dog in the side door, too. Plus, Olive's got Dogzilla and Kevin." I pulled Biggie out of his kennel and lifted him down to the ground. Not an easy feat given he was nearly two hundred pounds of English Mastiff. His buddy, Smalls, had the same fawn brindle pattern, the same goofy look on his face, but she was an English Bulldog and weighed in at closer to forty pounds. The two had come into the shelter together, a bonded pair. They were inseparable and that's the only way Lily would adopt them out.

Walking around the side of the SUV, I gave Brody a dirty look. "You gave Olive Dogzilla? What the hell, Shaw? You or I, either one, couldn't control Dogzilla."

Brody cocked his head and tipped his chin, motioning for me to look behind me. I turned, and there was Olive with a perfectly behaved Neapolitan Mastiff on one side and a perfectly behaved Miniature Bull Terrier on the other. Son of a bitch. How did she do that? Dogzilla still gave me nightmares. He'd once launched his head straight into my balls. I'd never been hit in the nuts so hard in my life and Brody had laughed his ass off at me while I'd had to ice my junk.

"We gave him to her because he always behaves for her." Then it happened. Zilla saw me. He started scratching at the pavement, pulling on the leash like a bucking bull thrashing to get out of the chute. His butt started bouncing around with nervous energy, and finally he lunged, yanking his leash out of Olive's hand.

"Oh, shit." I nearly went into a three-point stance trying to figure out the best way to protect my jewels, but at the last minute I chose a half squat, full ball-cup combo and braced for impact as the Miniature Bull Terrier barreled toward me.

Poor guy had been left in a kennel not far off the highway near an unsanctioned weight-pulling event, and. Zilla. Was. Strong. Apparently, just not strong enough for his owner. They hadn't taken care of him either. He'd had muscle tears all over his body and a lot of fear aggression.

Zilla was a good dog now. Still, for whatever reason he got a kick out of loading up that egg-shaped head and clocking me in the seven-ten split. Just me. Only ever me. Because I'd made the mistake of wrestling with him once, and he'd decided I was his favorite toy. Oh, to add insult to injury? He'd jumped around like a doofus hoping to get me to play while I rolled into a fetal ball and tried not to throw up.

"Oh, shit. Oh, shit." I squeezed my eyes shut and dropped Biggie's leash, who was completely nonplussed. But Zilla didn't make it to me. An earsplitting whistle pierced the air. I cracked one eye open, cupping my junk in my hand. Dogzilla had slid to a stop about six feet away and just…sat down.

"Oh, that was hilarious." Olive chortled as she drew closer with the Neapolitan Mastiff named Kevin. Then she bent to pick up the Zilla's leash and kept right on walking.

When I finally turned to Brody, he had a hand on his stomach from laughing so hard. "Ah, Christ. That made my day. Pick up Biggie's leash and don't forget to get Sadie."

I stood fully. "Wait, you brought Sadie? Why would you do that? Won't this place be too much for her? She'll get overwhelmed."

"Okay, mom. Sorry, but the dog trainer, you know, my fiancée, said it would be good for her to spend time with people besides you and her. She thinks Sadie is ready for a new experience. She did great at the TV shoot. She's not going to be in pictures or anything, she's just here to soak in the sights and sounds, and if she doesn't do well, Kate is on standby to take her back to the rescue."

Shaking my head, I pulled open the side door. I understood. I wanted her to find a family. She deserved a forever home and all the love they could give her.

She deserves my home. Not some stranger's.

That thought put me in a mood as I helped finish with setup. What if I could give her a home? I was a damn good coach, and I liked living in Dallas. Did I even want to play football anymore, or did I do it because I had to?

That was simple. If I played again, it would be because I had to, not because I wanted to. It was the motivation behind playing that was complicated.

I knew if I still hoped to get on with a team, Olive was off-limits. I couldn't hurt her again. Hell, I couldn't do it to myself. I'd broken more than one heart that day. But my own feelings and emotions always seemed to get pushed down my priority list.

Olive thought I did the things I did because I was selfish and impulsive. Impulsive, I would cop to, especially in college, but never selfish. I did the things I did then, and now, for my family. I'd always put them before me. Before everything.

Yet, if I stayed in Dallas and set some boundaries with my mom… I could be more than a friend to Olive, if she'd have me—if I could get her to see me as I was

now. The more I thought about it the more the idea felt
right.

Sharlene will torture you with guilt...

Hell, my mother would find a reason to torture me
anyway. Besides, if I didn't have the money to give her
because I wasn't playing, I didn't have a choice and neither did she. I'd have to face her guilt, but she'd have to
face reality. Sharlene resented me half the time anyway,
and that was being generous. I wanted a relationship
with her, but the one we had was all kinds of fucked up.
The sinking feeling I usually got at the thought of her
wrath was replaced by anger. My mother was grown,
capable, and didn't have a job. She drove a 7 Series
BMW and lived in the Arts District while forwarding
me her Neiman's bill every month.

I couldn't afford to do that anymore, had to make
lifestyle changes, but she refused to acknowledge it
had to stop.

That's fucked up, homeboy.

Maybe it was time I started thinking about the future
and what *I* wanted. Even if I got an offer to play again,
it wouldn't last long. A year, maybe two. I couldn't play
forever. Was that worth walking away from my life
in Dallas and the woman I'd fallen for all over again?
Every day it was less likely that the call would come.
The decision to play and leave, or stay and live, was
being made for me. The interesting thing was I wasn't
upset about that. It was a relief.

What does that tell you, Walker?

I had a little money stashed. Not much, but it should
get Jess through the last year of medical school. After
that, she'd start her residency and have a salary of her

own. Maybe I could even put a down payment on a small house with a yard for Sadie.

Was I doing this? Crossing playing football off the option list?

A few hours later, I was sitting on a metal chair with a black brindle Boxer between my legs, back off to the side of the signing as I watched things run smooth as silk. Truthfully, I didn't want to be up where I'd have to sign autographs or field questions about coaching versus playing. About how retirement was treating me and all that bullshit. Not with thoughts and questions whipping through my head like a tornado in a trailer park. All the questions I should have asked myself years ago. Hindsight was a motherfucker.

Sadie had done great today. Lily was right. Maybe I just didn't want to see how well she was doing because then I'd have to face that someone could come along and take her from me. I think she felt my turmoil. The sweet old girl kept nosing at my hand and leaning against the inside of my thigh.

Or maybe we were comforting each other, both of us facing some pretty heavy shit.

"You've been awfully quiet today." Olive sat down in the chair next to me and Sadie stood to tell her hello. "Something on your mind?" She stroked the Boxer's snout.

I'd watched Olive buzz around today with nary a break and I was in awe. She was the hub for all the activity. Every question, every hiccup, Olive was the go-to, even for Lily. Olive never tired, never lost her cool—she simply directed traffic and kept the wheels spinning smoothly.

"Honestly, I'm in awe. What you pulled together

here. All these moving pieces, and watching you work? You're the calm in the storm."

She scanned around at the players signing posters, Kevin the Neo posing with Shane and a family of three for a photo. "What *we* pulled together. We needed each other to do everything on this scale so quickly. There's no way I could have done this without you. No matter how many contacts I've got in my phone, I couldn't have pulled together all the players and staff from the Bulldogs to make this as successful as it is. That was all you, buddy."

"We did do it together, didn't we?" The thought made me grin. "I guess I underestimate myself sometimes. I think I underestimated Sadie, too." I patted her neck.

Olive nudged me with her shoulder. "Why haven't you adopted that dog? I, and everyone else at the rescue, can see she belongs to you. How come you haven't taken her home with you yet? Especially when we both know it's much harder to adopt out a senior dog than a younger one."

I let out a humorless chuckle. "Yeah, I know all too well what it's like getting passed over for the younger Bulldogs that have plenty of play left in their legs. But me traveling and gone half the season? What would I do with her? She doesn't get along with Laila and Mack and I wouldn't feel comfortable boarding."

"What about your mom? Would she take her when you travel?"

"Ha!" I hadn't meant that to come out quite so loud. "My mom isn't a dog person."

Olive turned to face me, her knee brushing up against mine. "Tell you what, Walker. I'm not sure I'm ready to be a full-time dog parent again, but if you decided you wanted to adopt this beautiful little girl, I would be happy to be your backup puppy parent. When you have to travel with the team, she could stay with me. You'd have peace of mind while you're out of town, while I'd get a part-time snuggle puppy. I'd even take her to work with me. She'll be fine there if she can handle it here."

My eyebrows shot into my hairline. That was an idea with more than a few perks. The biggest and best would be making Sadie mine, but it would put me in close proximity to Olive, too, even after the fundraisers were over. It felt like things were falling into place in my life, maybe too easily. Perhaps I should give it a little more thought.

Dude, don't look a gift horse and all that. "You'd do that for me? Are you sure you're ready to have another dog in your life?"

"I think so. I'm not necessarily ready to commit to my own dog, but getting to spend all that time with a sweet girl like this? No-brainer. Besides, you're obviously completely smitten." She stroked Sadie's graying cheek.

Not just with the dog. "Is it that obvious?" I dropped my head forward so she couldn't read my face.

Olive shoved her knee against mine. "Well, I never thought I'd see the day Hayes Walker loved something more than he loved himself."

Deep down, I knew she meant it as a joke, but she wouldn't have said it if she didn't think there were some truth to it, and that cut me. I couldn't get her to believe I wasn't the selfish bastard she thought I was, no matter how much I told her that I'd changed. My whole life had been about being the person my family needed me to be. But she didn't know that, did she?

Maybe it's time to show *her the man you are instead of the one she thinks you are.*

"Ollie, go out with me." It wasn't a question, and it came out of my mouth straight from my heart, not my head.

"Hayes—"

"Olive, we have a problem," Lily interrupted. "Sorry, you guys look like you're into something here, but this can't wait. The power to the camera and green screen went out. We've got people that have already paid standing around waiting for their photo op because nobody can figure out why, and they're getting antsy."

Olive popped out of her seat, already pulling up a number on her phone. "Hi, Mary. It's Olive Russo. I need maintenance over here ASAP."

As she started to move away, I reached for her hand, slipping it in mine. "We're not done, Ollie. We need to talk."

Nodding, she took off, already talking into the phone again. But she looked back and the expression on her face was…not cool, collected Olive. I'd ruffled her smooth-as-glass exterior. Not that I'd meant to.

With my football career almost certainly a thing of the past, it was time to turn the charm on full blast. Plus, I had a killer ace up my sleeve she knew nothing about. Something big. I'd planned on telling her about it when it panned out because I didn't want to get her hopes up in case it didn't. A part of me also wanted to make it happen on my own just to prove to myself I was good for more than football. Popping out my phone, I hit a number in my contacts Olive would faint if she knew I had.

"Hey, Tommy. It's Hayes. Listen, do you still have those tickets you offered me?"

With her tongue lolling slightly, Sadie pawed at my hand. As I patted her chest, I whispered in her ear, "Yes, sweetheart. I know. I love you too, good girl."

It was the first time in a quite a while that I felt like I had a heading.

Sometimes you just had to say fuck it and go after what you wanted in life.

Chapter Fifteen

What's a comeback if not a
cleverly marketed second chance?

Olive

I'd been worried about him all day. Hayes's normally stoic exterior was very obviously shaky. He'd been reserved, brooding even, instead of pasting on the smile I now saw through.

"Ollie, go out with me."

Shit. I hadn't expected that when I sat down next to him to fish out what was bugging him.

"I'm sorry, Mary, what did you say, fifteen minutes?" I was distracted. I needed to pull my shit together. After we hung up, I avoided looking at Hayes, but I could feel his eyes on me as I moved around answering questions here and there, checked on the rescue dogs, made sure Lily was handling things okay.

"We're all set here. Things are back up. It was a breaker in the maintenance room. You have any more issues, you call me directly." The maintenance guy handed me a card.

"Thanks for getting over here so quickly. I'll do that."

"Hey, Olive. We've got a thing." Johnathan's voice pulled me in.

"What's up?"

He leaned in lowering his voice. "Matthew McKinley is here with his son asking to meet the players."

Holy shit! "The movie star?"

Johnathan nodded. "He didn't warn anyone he was coming, and fair security snuck them in. We can't put him in here with the general population or this crowd will go insane, and we can't pull the players off the floor from signing. But he's also offering to make a major donation."

Cha-ching! "This isn't a problem, it's a good thing! Where is he?"

Johnathan led the way through a set of curtains where we had an area for the volunteers and players to take breaks. "He came in through the side door, the one we've been using to take dogs out."

There, on a metal chair, he sat, his son on his knee. "Well, butter my butt and call me a biscuit. Go get Lily and Brody, and tell them to bring Mack. And tell Hayes, and have him pull a couple of his superstars. Have him bring Sadie, too. Oh, and as soon as Charlie gets caught up, have her slip back."

"On it."

The movie star stood up from the couch, settling the toddler on his hip. "You must be the big boss around here. Hi, you can call me Matt. This here is Bodie."

"I'm aware! It's lovely to meet you, Matt and Bodie. So, I hear you wanted to meet some of the players today." I tugged on Bodie's Bulldogs jersey. "Big fans, are you?"

"Indeed. We saw the *Texas Weekly* show last week

and thought we'd come by to see if we could meet some Bulldogs and some real dogs. We've got a soft spot for rescues, and we were hoping you could help." His voice curled higher just a touch when he elongated the middle of the word *hoping* in his Texas twang. Then there was the smile. Those dimples the whole world knew.

"Tell you what. I can make that happen, but we can't pull all our players at once. What I can do is send them in a couple at a time for a few minutes each if you can tell me which ones you'd like to meet."

"That works."

"Would you mind meeting the rescue's founders and taking a few photos with them?"

"Not at all an imposition. I'd like to meet Brody, and Lily's dad, man…that's Dallas football legacy, right there. I'd planned to write you a check today either way, players or no. Got to support a rescue like this. Especially in my hometown." Damn. This day had just gone from great to fantastic. I had no doubt that when we got a look at the figures from today that Lily would be downright shocked. A thought that made me smirk as I introduced Lily, Brody and Mack to the Academy Award–winning actor.

As the day wore down and the sun started to recede into the horizon, we began cleaning up from the long day. Everybody was tired, running on caffeine, and still riding an adrenaline high, including me.

Our movie star was long gone, but had posed for a bunch of pictures with rescue dogs, staff, players and their families, and written me a big fat check before he left. He may have shown up unannounced, but he was beyond gracious.

"I still can't believe a fricking movie star just showed

up and wrote a check." Lily's smile hadn't left her face all day. "I'm so glad you were here. I would have fangirled. Hard."

I chuckled at that. "The good thing is, where there's one star, there's more. And Matt asked me about buying a table for the Gala. Hey, have you seen Hayes?"

I didn't miss the little smile. "He's got Sadie back in the other room playing fetch."

Pulling the curtain to the side, I watched as he fired a tennis ball the length of the room. "I thought you played defense. That looked like a quarterback threw it."

"Huh, *played* being the operative word. And no, that didn't look like a quarterback threw it, but you always were kind."

Sadie dropped the ball at his feet. "Do you miss it?"

He picked it up and threw it again. "Playing? Yes. What playing did to my body? Hell, no."

I watched after Sadie as I stood next to Hayes. "I bet she'd have made a great Frisbee dog, maybe even fly ball, when she was younger."

"They always say shit like that about us has-beens, don't they, girl? Drop it." He scratched her head, and Sadie spit out the ball. "If only we were younger, if only our knees still had all their cartilage. If only time didn't march on and forget about us." He stared at the ball in his hands with a distance in his gaze. Sadie sat patiently, looking up at the man she so obviously loved with soft brown eyes and a face going white with age. These two needed each other.

Gently, I pulled the ball from Hayes's hand and gave Sadie a scratch. Then I launched it across the room. She looked after it but didn't go. "Oh, Hayes. This little girl is sweet on you."

That made the laugh lines appear around his eyes. "Go get it, sweetheart."

Finally, she darted out after it.

"I'm sorry about football. I just want you to know that you are so much more than the game. I've always thought that." Today couldn't have been easy on him, at an event with players who used to be his teammates, but now he coached them.

Hayes nodded. "I mean, yeah. I'm a football player. I'll always be a football player. But it's the way it got taken away from me, and the reason I even played so long in the first place." He shook his head. "I loved playing. I wanted to play solely because I loved it, and I wanted to leave on my terms. That didn't happen. Sometimes I'm a little jealous of Brody for that."

Sadie brought the ball back to me, but I noticed her starting to limp a little on her right hind leg. "All done, sweetheart." Breathing heavy, her black coat shined in the light as she circled and lay down next to Hayes's leg. I studied the man's face. The lines etched into his forehead. The aching set of his jaw. This man was broken, and my heart squeezed for him. Weren't we all a little damaged?

Creating second chances was part of my job, yet I hadn't given Hayes another shot. Not really. I'd kept him at arm's length because I still expected him to be someone else. I had my own sins to atone for, after all, and I understood what it was like to have someone make you pay for them continuously. I didn't want to be like my father—a man who would always hold my mistakes over my head; a man who I'd had to push to the periphery of my life so I could make peace with my sins…

"One date, Olive." He turned his head to me. "Let me show you I'm not who you think I am."

"Oh, I know you've grown up. You've been great with the fundraisers and planning." My gaze shifted to my feet.

"No, on some level, you still believe I'm that guy. I understand why, but we've both had one foot out on this since we came back into each other's lives because we're worried about what *might* happen. I'm putting the other foot in. Now. Let me show you that I was never really that guy."

Hayes was right. We'd both been so worried about what *could* happen that we'd been torturing ourselves with it. Was that any better than what might, or might not, actually happen down the road?

"I have tickets to see one of your favorite bands tomorrow night." His grin was slow, sly.

Everybody knew about the Urban Legend concert tomorrow night. They'd just been an up-and-coming alternative rock band when the two of us were in college, but now they headlined sold-out shows all over the world. I was a huge fan, and he knew it.

I pushed his shoulder. "You didn't…"

"Wanna go see Urban Legend with me tomorrow night?" He winked and I could see the shadow of his dimples under the beard he stroked.

"You're not playing fair, Walker." My mind was already made up. It had been before I went looking for him.

Turning to face me fully, I could see the amusement dance through his eyes. "One night. Let that sleek ponytail down and have some fun with me, Ollie."

I didn't answer. Pretended to think about it, though

I'd already weighed the pros and cons. The con list had won out, but I was going to give this man the benefit of the doubt. Second chances and all that.

He shifted his weight, put a hand on his hip as he cocked his head. "How long are you gonna stand there and pretend to think about this before you say yes?"

"Ugh. You suck."

"Is that a yes?"

For the first time in a long time, I didn't think. I shut my brain off and did what felt right. "You know, I think about us in terms of order and chaos. I always thought of me as the order in the relationship, and you were my chaos. But you know what I'm learning?" As I turned fully to face him, I took a small step forward. There was anticipation and fire and yeah, a little bit of the panic coursing through my veins.

"What's that?" He looked down at me with hooded eyelids.

"That maybe there's nothing wrong with a little chaos. Maybe that's what makes life interesting." I moved a little closer, tipped my chin up.

"Olive…" My name was a whisper on his lips. Lips that were parted, and cheeks that were pink, and a chest that rose and fell a little too quickly.

Like I had a thousand times before so many years ago, I raised up on my toes and brushed his lips with my own. Once, twice. Sweet and soft and painfully slow. Testing the waters with warm, sweet breath and flames igniting in my abdomen.

Hayes's big hands came up to frame my jaw, his thumbs bracketing the edge of my lips. "Can I kiss you?"

I didn't answer. I couldn't. Afraid of what I might

give away in my voice. Instead, I slid my palm over his beard, soft and golden. Tilting my head, I pressed my lips to his fully.

At first it was perfectly sweet and comfortable. Not comfortable boring—comfortable like coming home. The soft moan that worked its way up his throat. Like he'd been waiting for this moment for years. The tickle of his beard against my face, new and not at all unpleasant. When his lips parted, I sank into Hayes. His mouth, his chest, his warmth and orbit. The flawless dance of push and pull, tease and retreat.

I was awash in the sensation. Tonight's second first kiss. The memories of our first kiss so many years ago under the stars. Then our last kiss, the way he brushed his thumb across the corner of my mouth then pressed his lips against mine, and I had no idea it would be the last.

The anxiety started to climb my spine and the bees started to swarm under my skin. My tentative grip on control loosened, as I picked at that knot in my brain. But instead of pulling at it like I had earlier, I ran my fingertips through his beard and let the knot loosen as I placed one more chaste kiss against his parted lips before I stepped back.

His eyes were weighted, his lips pink and wet, his breathing audible as I stepped back and bent down to tell Sadie goodbye with a scratch on the head. When I stood I patted his chest.

I felt the warm fuzzies all over when he hit me with a smile that was a little cocky and a lot *I told you so*. He didn't say anything, and I didn't look back as I walked away. I wanted that image of him with his crooked smile and light in his eyes. With no lines on his forehead and that ever-present weight on his shoulders a little less heavy than before.

I'd felt some anxiety when I kissed Hayes. But it wasn't like it had been back at the training center when warmth and the fond memories were choked out by the recollection of pain. Nope, not even close. In fact, there was something else there, too.

"Was that a yes?" he asked as I pulled the curtain back on the room.

Desire. And not just for Hayes, which, duh. But to live my life instead of watching it go by while I made a to-do list.

"Yes."

Chapter Sixteen

Crimes and Punishments

Olive

When I'd texted Hayes my address, he'd asked me if it was okay to take his Harley, and I vetoed it. Pickup truck it was.

There were butterflies in my stomach. I couldn't remember the last time that had happened before a date. Choosing to wear my hair in a loose braid, I'd also opted for a frayed denim skirt that showed off my legs, a faded black concert T-shirt I'd had in the back of my closet, and my favorite cowboy boots. While I was swiping on my red lipstick, the doorbell rang.

"Okay," I whispered. "You can do this. Just a little bit of chaos."

When I pulled open the door, I remembered why there was no such thing as a little bit of chaos with Hayes Walker. Jesus, the man was hot—worn gray T-shirt that hugged his body. A thin leather jacket that highlighted the V-neck of his shirt and the ink on his neck. A pair of jeans that were old, frayed, and fit him like a fucking glove. And not a single blond hair out of place, the sides of his head freshly trimmed. Plus, those blue eyes and the smirk.

My mouth literally watered, and the bastard absolutely knew how good he looked. He brushed a hand over his beard and looked me up and down. "Fuck. We can skip the concert, and I can come in? I know damn well you wore that skirt to torture me."

Laying on my own smirk, I didn't bother denying it. "No, not again. Last time we were going to see Urban Legend, we never made it out of my apartment because of that damn smirk of yours. I'm not missing them a second time. Frankly, you weren't that good of a lay." After pulling on a jean jacket, I grabbed my little cross body and brushed passed him, letting my breast drag along his chest on purpose.

I tried to bite my bottom lip to keep from smiling, but he caught it anyway. "Liar." He followed me to the curb as I looked back with a chuckle. I was, indeed, a liar, but giving each other a little shit had always been our sweet spot, and it was just so easy to slide back into.

He let out an exhale that made me smirk as he opened the truck's passenger door and offered up a hand to steady me as I climbed in, which I ignored. Once I was in place, he stared after me with a pained look on his face.

"What?" Then I realized why. I'd basically just put my ass in his face in this miniskirt. "Oh."

"Yeah, oh." He blew out a breath, brushed his beard again. "You're not about to make this easy on me, are you?"

I shrugged, but noticed the way he eyed my scars before he shut the door.

We'd barely gotten to the tollway when he asked. "You ready to tell me about those yet?"

I'd expected this would probably come up when I'd decided to wear the skirt. The first tingles of anxiety started to build under my skin, and I gripped the seat with my hand to try and hold it back. I'd associated my accident with Hayes for the last decade. I didn't blame him for it. He wasn't the cause. But there was a correlation I couldn't let go of.

I make bad decisions after the breakup, and this one was the worst of all. It was impossible for me to ignore that parallel.

"Hey." His face softened as he took my hand, brought it to his lips. "I can see it upsets you. If you're not ready, I understand."

Oh, for fuck's sake. If that didn't melt the ice around my heart nothing would. "Car wreck," I blurted without thought or filter.

"A...car wreck? You got hurt in a car accident. How long ago? I wish I'd known. I... It was bad?"

A slightly maniacal laugh bubbled through my lips. "Yes, it was bad. It happened about twelve years ago. And, back then, I wouldn't have thought you'd wanted to know."

"Of course I would, I loved—" Confusion crossed his face. "Wait, twelve years ago?"

"Yes." I watched him closely.

Hayes's confusion morphed into anger. Jaw cracking, he clenched his teeth, his grip on the steering wheel becoming a choke hold. "Tell me what happened."

Dragging in a breath, I straightened my shoulders, fixated on the road, and pushed the tingle of panic down. "After we broke up, I didn't do well. I stopped going to classes and my grades slipped. My volleyball coach benched me. I started going out a lot. Parties, bars, whatever. Anything to run away. There I'd been with my perfectly planned-out life before you came along, but then you showed me I was watching my life go by instead of living it. How wrapped up I'd been in my parents' expectations for me."

I saw him stroking that beard in my periphery.

"I'd been in love with you, and I missed you, and I was heartbroken. But I tried to fill the gap by chasing the feeling I got when I was with you. I did reckless things trying to capture that again, but it wasn't the same. When I realized it was never would be, I started drinking a lot. Hanging out with the party crowd."

I absolutely couldn't watch him. I didn't want to see his disappointment in me, or for him to see my own disappointment in myself. Focus trained on the road, I brushed at a tear sliding down my cheek. "A couple of months after the breakup, I was back home with my folks. The semester was over, and they had been livid with my grades. We got into an argument, and I left the house angry. Met some friends at a shitty little roadhouse out in the country." Heat was burning my cheeks as I slanted my head to take in Hayes from under my lashes.

He picked up my hand again. Kissed the back. "Olive, I'm not going to judge you. Lord knows, I've made more than my share of mistakes, but you don't have to keep going if you're not ready."

I pulled my hand back. "No, I do. I need to tell you this. I have to."

"Okay. Can I hold your hand, though?"

I nodded, slid my fingers between his. "I'd had

way too much to drink that night, pounding shots. My friends told me to slow down, but I didn't. I danced; I took a shot. I kissed some woman's husband right in front of her and took another shot. I was just sloppy, sloppy drunk and they'd asked me to leave. I'd never been tossed out of a bar before, but I didn't go easily. I kicked and screamed the whole way. My friends followed me out and tried to take my keys, but they were way smaller than I was. They would have had to wrestle me down and get the bouncer to sit on me. Given that I'd scratched the shit out of his face, dude was just glad to be rid of me."

I knew my hand was shaking in his palm, but there wasn't anything I could do about it. "I got in my little car deciding to take the back roads home in the dark to avoid the cops. No streetlights, and those back roads get all twisty." Taking a deep breath, I blew it back out, trying to steady myself for the next part. I wasn't sure I'd ever told anybody this in its entirety that hadn't been there for the aftermath. "I was going too fast when a sharp curve came up. I swerved into the oncoming lane as another car came around the turn toward me. I yanked on the wheel and overcorrected. The road was elevated, and I shot off the curve right into a tree. I don't remember much right after that except for the sound the car made on impact—I blacked out. When I woke, I had burns on my face and the taste of powder in my mouth, both from the airbag deployment. The steering column had gotten crushed around my legs and trapped them. When I came to, the fire department was already there. They had to cut me out with one of those big saws as I sat stuck in that car alone." I'd felt so empty.

"The other car had landed in a ditch, but the driver

was by himself, thank God, and only had minor bruises. I could have killed someone, Hayes."

He squeezed my hand. "My God. Olive, I'm so—"

I knew he wanted to talk, but I needed to get through it all at once. "Let me finish. When they finally pulled me out, they'd tried to keep me from seeing my leg, but I got a good look at the bones coming through the skin before they covered it up. The tibia broke through near my knee. The fibula just above my ankle. It took four surgeries to put them back together. I have a rod in my tibia now that will always be there. For months I had an external fixator for the fibula because it broke into several pieces. Do you know what those are?"

Hayes nodded. "Mine were two stainless-steel halos around my leg with forty-four pins that went through my skin to set the bone."

I looked out the window. "I was in that thing for months. The recovery was slow and so damn painful. The whole event was this shameful little secret I carry that's never far out of my mind."

Pulling into a parking place in a VIP lot outside the venue, Hayes put the truck in park. He stared straight out the window, but I could see the anguish. He was going to blame himself. "That must have been terrifying. I'm so very sorry, sweetheart. I was such a little shit head back then. I can't believe all this happened and I was never there for you. Had I known…"

"Hayes, it was not your fault," I said, putting a hand on his big shoulder. "I made these decisions. No one else. But at the TV shoot? When we had that moment in the office, and you slammed the metal door? It's eerily similar, those sounds—a door slamming, and a car hitting a tree. The thick whooshing, the violently metallic *thud*. They only differ in their volume. You slammed the door, and I was in that car again seeing flashes of green whiz by, and hearing the impact while I smelled the copper tang of blood.

"All of it came back. Not just the physical pain, though it was fucking excruciating. The heartbreak, and my behavior after. The hole your absence left in me. All of it. Along with the thought that you bring out a side of me I keep locked down because I'm afraid of what might happen if you break my heart again."

And I missed the girl I'd been with Hayes so much. Not the one who got out of control, but the one who threw the lists away and *lived*. Now, there was always the *but* in the back of my mind. But what will happen if I get out of control—would I be able to rein myself in? If this man broke me again, who would I become?

I wiped at my tears with my free hand. "I missed a full year of school, Hayes. I have a permanent record— a DUI in Texas is a class A misdemeanor. So is reckless endangerment. I nearly did jail time and lost my license for a stretch. My dad had to call in favors to keep everything as quiet as possible."

I felt the shame wash over my face. "My parents never looked at me the same again. I became a complete disappointment in their eyes. My dad, with his reach… it kept me out of jail. But you've met him. He's demanding. Exacting. He expected perfection, and I fell short in his eyes. He never let me forget how close I came to ruining his shot at Federal District Court Judge, that he had to bail me out and bury the whole thing. He didn't do it for me. He did it for him." I shook my head, my eyes blurring up again. "I…I have a relationship with my parents, but it's superficial. Holidays, birthdays. I had to push my dad to the periphery of my life in order to make some kind of peace with what I'd done and try to move on."

Unbuckling his seat belt, Hayes turned to me, brushed the tears from my cheeks. "I can't imagine how traumatic that must have been, and I understand if you don't think you can see me again, sweetheart. But that feeling...feeling like you're living your life? That's completely different than letting yourself get out of control. There's nothing wrong with living a little. It's okay to let your hair down and have fun without letting it go too far. I know you probably don't need me to tell you that, but—"

I felt the ire rise along my spine, my face going from soft and watery to angry in the snap of fingers. No, I didn't need a lecture from the king of impulsive on how to live my life. "You're right, Hayes. I don't need you to tell me shit about how you think I should behave. Maybe I am a control freak, but I'm trying to find some balance, or I never would have kissed you at the rescue. You, however, do the whole *roll with it* thing and never have to think about consequences. Do you even learn from your mistakes? Because you sure as hell don't worry about how your behavior and decisions affect the future." I turned in my seat and let him see all my anger. "Tell me, do you ever think about the consequences of your actions, Walker? Do you ever consider how your behavior affects the people around you? Because the Hayes I knew walked away and never looked back."

His face turned dark, lines forming around his eyes as he ground his jaw together.

I'd done poked the bear, but the bear deserved it.

Chapter Seventeen

Bali is always a good idea

Hayes

That hurt, but I deserved it. I'd never been particularly good at saying the right thing at the right time. I was angry. Not with Olive; with myself for being the sono-fabitch who did this to her. She stared at me waiting for some kind of response, but I didn't know how to respond. I had no idea how badly I'd really hurt her. I'd destroyed the only woman I'd loved because I was reckless and impressionable. Olive was incredibly strong to be able to put herself back together after the accident. My own stupidity had essentially ruined her relationship with her parents. I remembered meeting her dad and thinking, *Jesus, I get it now. Why Olive is so hard on herself.* The man was critical of everything. He held her to impossible standards. I can't imagine the emotional hell he put her through after the accident when she was already nursing a broken heart and a broken leg.

She could tell me this wasn't my fault, but I would always know it was. That I caused the kind of suffering that would always be a part of her.

I'd never forgive myself for that.

I'd let my own knee-jerk reactions own me over the years. My family's interest ruled my choices and I did my best not to think about how those decisions affected anyone else, including me. I'd shoved it all down, each time, the self-loathing, the guilt. What had that got me? Close to going broke. Definitely a little broken. And feeling like a weak-ass motherfucker for not saying no to a long list of demands I should have never had to answer for. Not at ten years old and not at thirty-four.

Olive's questions were legitimate, too. I hadn't thought about the future. Not until the money was nearly gone. I didn't learn from my mistakes back then either. Instead, I ignored them and shoved them down with everything else. But she wouldn't understand the why of any of that.

How could she if you don't give her the whole picture, dumbass?

I steadied my voice. "Yes. I think about the consequences of my actions. It's my priorities that were fucked up then. But I think I had to get to this point before I could see the big picture."

Her face softened. "What are you trying to tell me?"

I let out a humorless chuckle. "I need you to understand where my head was at when I broke up with you."

Her dark eyes melted through my shell.

"I was never that guy who didn't have a care in the world, Olive." I looked out the windshield into the parking lot lights, but all I saw was the boy I'd been once. My mother standing over me constantly browbeating me for anything and everything that was wrong with her life. How good it felt when she found out I had talent, and all of a sudden I was special in her eyes. Football made me worthy of love, and I'd been chasing her approval ever since. Football was the key to my mother's love. God, that was all kinds of fucked up.

"We were poor, and my dad left us, you know that. What you don't know is that my mom was fucking excellent at using that to twist me up. Most of the time, I felt like Sharlene blamed everything wrong with her life on me.

"Until my high school coach told her I had a shot at playing pro. It was like I found the magic words to unlock my mom's love. I was special, worthy...so long as I stayed focused on football and what it could do for my family. But it wasn't her love. When Sharlene looked at me, what she saw was a grouping of dollar signs and a way out of that Oklahoma trailer park. As I got older, went to college, went pro, I knew I was buying either her approval or her absence, whichever would cause me the least amount of strife. Going along was easier than dealing with her guilting me and telling me I was just like my father.

"The night before the draft, I was sitting in a hotel room in Vegas worried what team I was going to go to, and if it would be somewhere near a college where you wanted to go to grad school. I was concerned about how hard my rookie season might be on us with the travel, the long distance, all of it." I shook my head. "I made the mistake of giving it voice and Sharlene took advantage."

A soft palm brushed the back of my hand, and I immediately flipped mine over, running my fingers together with hers. I didn't want to look at her. If I saw the pity that must be there, I didn't think my pride would let me continue. But when I glanced up, it wasn't pity I saw. It was empathy.

"I think she knew if I stayed with you, she wouldn't be able to manipulate me anymore. So, she told me I was being unfair to you. That I'd end up cheating on you because I was my father's son and I'd break your heart even worse. 'Might as well be sooner than later,' she'd said. Looking back, I know she saw you as competition for the money I had the potential to earn."

"Hayes. God. I had no idea. Why didn't you just tell me back then? We could have worked it out together, figured out how to deal with her. Together." Her eyes had gone watery.

"I was a little ashamed, didn't want anybody to know how my mom treated me. Christ, how she still treats me. I mean, fuck. I'm a grown-ass man, and the woman still knows exactly what buttons to push to make me—" *Feel fucking worthless.*

Shrugging, I toyed with Olive's fingers. "Playing football is all I know. I don't really know who I am if I'm not Hayes Walker, football player. I never focused on the future, on retirement or what came after, because that was the day I became worthless."

"Hayes, no, baby. Never."

I put a hand up to stop her. I didn't want my ego stroked at the moment. "I don't blame everything on Sharlene. I let this happen, Olive. I continued to let her play me because it was easier to pay her way or pay her off. If I kept her happy, she left me alone."

"You wanted her approval, like I wanted my dad's. Just for different reasons."

I nodded. It was almost a relief that the money was

gone. If I was broke, my mom couldn't use it to emotionally blackmail me anymore.

Looking up, I gave Olive the half grin I'd perfected
over the years to hide the pain.

"Hayes, you realize what she did was abuse, right?"

Not able to answer, I shrugged it off.

"What about Jess?"

"She treated Jessica the way she treated me once,
when I was in high school. Jess was a kid, and I got in
Sharlene's face, told her I'd leave and take Jess with
me. She didn't do it again after that. I think having a
different dad than I did helped, but also, she knew Jess
was my last straw. That if she focused on me and left
Jessica alone, I'd go along to get along."

I grinned, a real one this time. "You know, Jess is
in medical school now at Columbia. Wants to be an or-
thopedic surgeon."

Olive beamed at me, took my hand between both of
hers. "That's wonderful. I can see you're proud of her."

"I am."

"But what do you wanna be, Hayes? Has anyone ever
bothered to ask you that? Seems like everyone told you
to play football because that's what you were good at,
but is that what you wanted?"

Slipping my hand from hers, I stroked my beard.
"I'm not sure I've ever given it much thought. Football
was there, you know? It was easy and what everyone
else wanted from me. I enjoyed playing, and it gave me
an excuse to not have to think about anything else because it was all laid out for me." But it wasn't all laid out
for me anymore. I didn't have anyone to tell me what
path to take, or give me the answer to my problems.
But if I didn't draw a line with Sharlene my own damn

mother might drive me to financial ruin. Because football didn't really seem like an option anymore.

I needed to start making decisions based on what I wanted and needed, not what kept my mom off my back.

Olive wiped at her cheeks. Seemed to consider her next question carefully. "Do you like coaching? I know you like spending time with the dogs at the rescue, and you've been a quick study as far as fundraising. Have you thought about who you want to be now that your playing days are over?"

Truthfully, I did like coaching. Taking someone and watching them develop their skills because I could share my knowledge? Yeah. "I like teaching the young guys on the team, always did, even when I was playing. And I do like going to the rescue, spending time with Sadie and the others. Besides being with you, it's my favorite place to be."

"It makes you happy."

I bobbed my head. I didn't want to leave what I had found here. The NFL wasn't beating down my door, anyway. If I wanted to make the dream a reality, the boundaries with my mom were essential. I just wasn't sure I was strong enough to deal with my mom and everything she'd throw at me if drew those lines. "Coaching is a hell of a lot easier on my body than playing. I don't know about coaching at this level forever, but maybe college or high school."

Olive's face became a mask of determination. "Hayes Walker, what I'm trying to tell you is that you are more than just a talented football player. So much more than your goddamned mother ever let you believe."

Pushing forward, she settled her palm on my shoulder. "You are kind and generous. Smart and passionate. You have a laugh that makes the world a better place. You can be thoughtful and caring, and you love deeply. You have the biggest goddamned heart of anyone I know. You were dealing with so much more than I ever realized back in school. Someone should have told you all of this long ago, but you can do and be anything you set your mind to. If it's coaching you love, then that's what you should do."

I dropped my head to stare at my lap. She made it sound easy.

"Trust me, Hayes. I know a little something about trying to live up to your parents' expectations. At some point, baby, you gotta let that shit go and get on with your own life." She chewed on the inside of her cheek a moment, seemed to consider something, and nodded as she made up her mind. Ollie leaned across my lap, pushed the button on the driver's-side seat to slide it back while her body covered mine.

I quirked my lips at my lap full of woman. "Olive, what the hell are you doing? Are you about to give me road head or something? Not that I'm complaining."

"Shut up, Walker," she shot back. In a truck too small for two people as tall as us, she managed to shimmy her legs over mine until she'd straddled my lap, my hands landing on her hips as my future stared me in the face.

"I'm going to tell you something. No, first I'm going to remind you of something, then I'm going to tell you something, and I want to look you in the eyes when I say it."

"You have my undivided attention, sweetheart." God, she was everything.

"Good. Do you remember Bali?"

"Huh?"

"The first night we met. That party where you took the beer away from me and wouldn't let me walk home alone."

My lips quirked at one corner. "Yeah. We ended up on the South Oval, lying on a blanket in the grass."

"Mmhmm. You asked me if I could live anywhere before I died, where would it be."

"And you said Bali."

"I said Bali, and you told me I should go. But I told you I couldn't just drop everything to go live halfway around the world." She cocked her head to one side.

"And I asked why not."

"It took me a while to really get what you meant by that, but after the accident, I finally did." She kissed my cheeks, first one then the other.

My grip instinctively tightened on her hips. "I was telling you to live your life for you, not to please someone else. That if you wanted to be driven, then be driven, and if you wanted to get a little wild, then get a little wild."

"I'm so glad you put it that way." Kissing the corners of my mouth, she dragged her palms along my shoulders. "You weren't reckless, Hayes."

"I mean, yeah. Sometimes I was. But it's because it was the only time I felt like I was living for myself. When I was out of my mom's reach. I took full advantage of that, and without you forcing me to study I probably would have lost my scholarship before I graduated."

"Exactly. And now look at us, Walker. Right back where we used to be. Actually, probably worse off than before. For a long time, I thought you were bad for me. That you were my kryptonite and set loose a part of me that would take over and be my downfall. Now I think it was the exact opposite. We were actually good for each other. We tempered the worst of each other while bringing out the best. So, I'm going to toss your question from all those years ago back in your face. Why can't you move to Bali, Hayes? Why are you living your life for someone besides you?"

It was exactly what I was doing, and I hated myself for it. Fuck…this woman had always seen right through me, and nothing had changed. Olive saw me for who I was and who I wanted to be even when I didn't.

I needed to realign my priorities and stop trying to win the approval of a woman who clearly had no love in her heart for me. As for Olive…well, she was straddling my railroad spike of a cock in the front of my pickup truck in a public parking lot. And I was quite sure *that* move was meant to signal that she'd be letting her hair down more often.

Peeling the corner of my jacket away from my throat, she slid her lips up the column of my neck, stopping at my ear. When she skated her hands down my chest and under the hem of my shirt to scrape her nails along my abs, I sucked air between my clenched teeth.

"Jesus. Olive, be sure you want this. Because you and I will never be light and casual. We have two speeds. Stop and Go. I need to know you're willing to give it another go with me, because I can't do this with you then go back to being your friend tomorrow. Be sure, sweetheart."

"Oh, I'm sure, and there's no time like the present."

When she rolled her hips along the length of my hard-on, I hissed. Or was it a grunt? It was one or the other. "Christ, woman."

"My, my, when did you get so religious?" Her voice was husky, heavy as she rocked those rounded hips again, the heat of her obvious even through my jeans.

"Olive—"

"Shut up, baby. Kiss me."

I did not have to be told twice. Sliding my hand into her braid, I gave the hair at her nape a tug and licked a line up her throat until my lips met hers and she gasped into my mouth.

The kiss wasn't easy and sweet. It was hard, hot, and wicked. Our lips met, our tongues twisted and tangled, pushed then retreated. Then pushed again, trying to swallow each other down. She was wet and warm and every fucking thing I'd wanted for over a decade. Everything my life had been missing. Then she bit my lower lip, and a strangled moan rumbled in my chest. I damn near came in my jeans.

I put more pressure on her braid, forced her head back so I could see her face. Olive's eyes were heavy and glowing with gold flecks in the recesses of all that warm brown as she met me head-on. Her chest heaved, a pretty flush crawling along her neck, her pearled nipples scraping over my pecs. Then I smelled her. The arousal of that pretty fucking pussy of hers I wanted to taste. Wrapping her hair around my fist, I ran the fingers of my free hand down her neck, let my thumb linger on the base of her throat before dragging my tips between her breasts over the cotton of her shirt. When I brushed my thumb over one stiff nipple, she let out a sound that was pure seduction, her hips jerking forward without thought as I lifted my ass to push against her.

The skirt was short to begin with, but with her across my lap, I'm sure her ass cheeks would be sitting on my knees and fuck, I wished I could feel them against my skin. But I could only do so much at once, and I knew my girl. If I let go of her hair, the control would shift, and she'd take advantage. Instead of grabbing onto Olive's ass, I trailed my fingers over her stomach, teasing and testing, watching her body shift and coil. Goose bumps broke out on her arms as the scent of her intensified the closer I got to the apex of her thighs.

"Where do you want my fingers, sweetheart? Tell me."

"Hayes…" The look she sent me was *don't play stupid, buddy.*

"Have you gotten so shy over the years? Are we going to have start from the beginning?"

"Look, Walker, just because you were my first, does NOT mean you were the best." She quirked her lips to one side, smugness written on her face.

"Is that so?" I pushed my hand under her skirt and gave her clit a tap through the damp fabric of her panties.

Moaning, she jerked up and back, setting the truck's horn to blasting.

Olive lurched forward against my chest. "Oh shit!"

"Um, Olive?" I wiggled my fingers, which were trapped against her core, causing her to both gasp and laugh.

"Do that again," she said, breathless.

I did, but I also couldn't ignore that people were beginning to stare at my truck as they made their way into the concert. "Olive, as much as it pains me to say this, we're going to miss the concert if we don't stop."

"Damn it." She scanned the parking lot, noticed the people staring. "I guess as a PR manager, it would probably be bad for me to be seen riding someone in the parking lot outside a rock concert." The face she made was annoyed as hell. I tapped my lips against her nose. Damn, she was cute.

As I helped her move off my lap back to the passenger seat, I winced at how fucking painful my cock was. With a quick flick of the visor, Olive set to repairing her makeup. "Shit. My hair's a mess."

"Take it down." I almost didn't recognize my own voice.

She grinned. "Yes, I think I will."

Chapter Eighteen

SAY WHAT, NOW?

Olive

After Hayes opened my door, he took my hand and didn't let me go for the rest of the night as if he was afraid I'd disappear. I understood how he felt. I was half-afraid I'd wake up from this dream and he'd vanish, too.

The outdoor venue was gorgeous and well-appointed. It was probably a little too chilly for the skirt I was wearing, but, legs. If you got 'em, flaunt 'em. Especially if they drive your date crazy. Soft lights sparkled as we passed catering tents on our way to the VIP lounge near backstage. It didn't escape me that we were drawing some attention—Hayes was Hayes, and he was still revered in this city; I was six feet tall, and my body was not the kind anyone would ever call slight—but the eyes on us didn't stop Hayes from bringing my hand to his lips, or the way he barely took his gaze off me.

So much made sense now about our breakup. In college, I'd thought Hayes was impulsive, thoughtless, careless with my feelings, while he believed he was protecting me from the man he would become. Had he taken my choice away? Absolutely. But he'd done it because he thought he wasn't a good man and was saving me from even more heartache down the line.

"Drink?" he asked, leading me to an empty spot on an outdoor chaise. "Whiskey sour, right?"

"No. I don't drink unless I'm in for the night."

Bending to my ear, his warm breath sent shivers down my spine. "Oh, I fully intend to be your designated driver, sweetheart. I'll be sticking to soda all night. But if you'd rather have a Dr. Pepper, it'll make my cock that much harder later when you start swinging your hips to the music and rubbing your ass against me. Because I'll know you're completely sober." He stood up, hitting me with the Hayes Walker shrug and a dirty as hell grin.

Heat crawled over my cheeks and licked down into my lower belly. "Dr.—Dr. Pepper would be good."

As I watched him walk to the bar, my thoughts drifted back to what he'd told me in the truck. It made me both sad for him and angry on his behalf, but I knew Hayes well enough to know he didn't do pity. It's likely why he'd never told me how his mother treated him before tonight or why he hadn't shared his reasons for breaking up with me. That, and probably embarrassment. Lord knew, I knew something about burying the secrets you were ashamed of. But Hayes blamed himself for the way his mother treated him, and that was all kinds of heartbreaking. He thought he'd let it happen, that he was as worthless as his mother told him he was if he couldn't play football. Which couldn't be further from the truth, but I could see how losing his position on the team would exacerbate those feelings and thoughts. I'd guess it was also why he connected so deeply with Sadie.

And his own goddamned mother had sown the seeds of his self-doubt. That made me fucking livid.

Studying Hayes's broad back and heavy shoulders as he stood at the bar, I watched him talk with complete strangers as if it were the most natural thing in the world. The minutes added up while he spoke with a teenage boy and his father, eyes never straying as the young man gestured in a way that surely meant they were discussing football. Hayes set our sodas on the bar and planted his feet, showed the boy where to grab a defender to pull them forward and throw them off balance. His face was animated, a light in his eyes that I'd seen when he was with Sadie.

Yet his mother had the nerve to make him believe that he was less than. Not good enough. Not worthy of her love and affection unless he could play football and take care of her. A grown-ass able-bodied woman living off her son's talent! Did the heifer even have a job? Did she pay for anything, or did she guilt her big-hearted son into it?

I wanted to strangle that shrew.

"Hey, everything okay? You look like you could do murder right now. Did someone hit on you? Whose ass do I need to kick?" Lips tightening, he scanned the area.

What's more, Hayes was embarrassed by how his mother treated him. I could see it in the way his shoulders curled when he told me. He knew she manipulated him and hated himself for it because he thought he *let* it happen. *That narcissistic bitch!* Whether Hayes knew it or not, he was a victim, though I knew him well enough to know that was better left unsaid.

I may have needed a little chaos in my life, but Hayes needed a plan for his future, and that was my wheelhouse. If he wanted it, I'd help him develop it, and be there to cheer him on as he went. I'd be the best fucking cheerleader he'd ever had.

That thought alone made my face soften, and the smile return. Taking my cup, I set it on the table next to the chaise, and marveled at how the lights in the outdoor space reflected in Hayes's blue eyes like lightning in a bottle. "No. No murder at the moment. You're awfully patient with your fans."

Sliding down next to me, he put a hand on my knee. "That kid is a junior in high school. He said during his tryouts, the guy lined up across from him was just too big, too strong for him to hold the line, and he didn't make first-string. So, I showed him how to use a bigger player's body weight against them. It's not always the strongest player that's the best, but the player who can call on finesse when strength won't work."

"That boy thinks you're a god now." I nudged him with my shoulder. "His dad does, too."

His eyes skimmed the crowd in an attempt to avoid mine. "Ehh. I just know a few tricks."

Sliding my hand into his, I leaned my forehead on his shoulder. "You are an incredibly kind man, Mr. Walker." If I had to tell him that every day until he believed it, I would.

I'd meant what I said earlier—it took me a long time to come to the realization, but Hayes wasn't bad for me. He wasn't the selfish jerk I'd built him into in my mind over the last decade. In truth, he was selfless. Impulsive, yes. Did he always think things through? No. But he constantly put his own needs behind his family's needs, even behind my needs, as misguided as it had been at the time. This man… Once upon a time, he'd brought out the best in me by helping me find balance in my life. It was my turn to help him.

He didn't speak, simply toyed with one of my rings, running it around in circles. But I wasn't letting him off that easy. Leaving our palms pressed together, I slid my free hand along his beard, turning his face to mine. When our gazes met, that amazing blue took my breath away.

Leaving my hand where it was, I stroked the corner of his mouth with my thumb. "Incredibly. Kind." With that, I leaned in and brushed my lips against his. Once. Twice. Until our mouths came together like they'd never been apart. Warm and soft. Heartbreakingly gentle. It wasn't meant to ignite passion, but to share with him that truth.

Gina wasn't wrong. My life needed a good helping of chaos, and I was ready to let it in…or out, as it were. Not only was I quite certain I'd never gotten over Hayes, but I was also starting to realize that a good part of my anxiety didn't come from the accident, or even me allowing myself to get out of control. It stemmed from some place deeper and much more profound. Love.

A love I'd never really let go of. Maybe it had gone dormant for a while, but it wasn't sleeping anymore.

As Hayes slid his rough palm over my cheek, into my hair, changing the angle of our kiss. I'd never had the pleasure of meeting Sharlene Walker, and God help her if I did. The woman had better pray that never happened, because she was gonna have a come-to-Jesus with my size-nine-and-a-half boots so far up her ass she tasted leather.

Nobody hurt the man I loved. Not even his mother.

The urge was there to go deeper, open our mouths and let our tongues play together like randy teenagers at a make-out party. Instead, I nipped his lip to elicit a grin, then leaned my forehead against his.

"I wasn't sure I'd ever have another kiss like that in my life." My voice was husky to my own ears.

"You're the only one I've ever wanted to share that kind of kiss with." His voice was a deep rumble that reignited the ache in my core.

Sliding my hand against his sternum, I let him see my heat. "Hayes, let's skip the concert."

He smirked. "Wait, why would you want to do that? I'm not even that good in bed, remember? What was it you said?" He squinted, pretended to think about it. "Average. I believe that was the word."

"I'm fairly sure it was something like the only place for you to go was up."

"Oh, sweetheart. I'm definitely going up, but I will not be blamed for you missing this band again. Even though, if I remember correctly, you were the reason we missed the last concert. Not me."

He wasn't wrong. I let my hand drift down his stomach and let my intention play out on my face. Most of the crowd had made its way to the stage. The way we were turned into each other, our foreheads almost touching, his jacket unzipped, my hand was hidden from sight.

"You're up, huh? Let's see, shall we?" Moving my hand further down, I drifted my fingers over the front of his jeans. He was definitely up.

Hayes let out a small groan as I ran my palm along his zipper. "Shit, Olive." The hand he had at the small of my back shot between us and covered my own. First, he increased the pressure I was putting on his bulge, then he slid my palm to his thigh.

"I think you're right, Walker. I should definitely see this concert." Quickly, I stood.

Hayes chuckled, taking a peek around before rearranging his junk. Standing, he took my hand. "Shall we?"

We weren't crammed against the stage like most of the fans. There was a small VIP section down front to one side with maybe fifty people milling about. It had a dozen high-tops, several comfortable chairs right near the stage, and a bar of its own. Many of the people milling about were folks I knew or recognized. Others Hayes seemed to throw a nod to in greeting, but mostly people left each other alone.

When the band finally came out and opened with their first big hit, I found myself leaning against a metal barrier, singing along, and shaking my butt with Hayes's ever-steady presence behind me.

His hand was always on my belly, my hip, my back or arm, his warmth a blanket from the worst of the chill. Occasionally, he'd brush my long hair back and place a kiss on my neck or ear that drove me goddamned insane. I pushed my ass against his front to drive him equally batshit, or lean into his strong chest pushing my hands under his jacket and around his waist to snuggle into the crook of his arm.

I was having an amazing time, and from the look on Hayes's face, he was equally sexually frustrated as I was, but also having fun torturing us both.

"I'm ready to go whenever you are," I said close to his ear.

"Don't you want to go back to meet the band? I have backstage passes."

"I don't need to meet them. What if they're assholes in real life? I don't want them to ruin the illusion. Besides, I'm cold and I know how I'd like to warm up."

"You do, huh?" Hayes placed a kiss on my cheek as he moved a hand down to cup my ass. "That what you had in mind?"

"Baby, what I have in mind involves a lot less fabric and a lot more skin."

Hayes looked over my head, glancing around before he tucked me closer and slid his hand from my ass down to my naked hamstring, then back up under my skirt to tease the edge of my panties. "Better?" he asked, all deep and growly.

Goosies raced down my legs that had nothing to do with the cold. My body arched back of its own accord, seeking more of that skin-on-skin. Then he did a thing with his finger. Slipping it from the seam of my ass forward to the damp gusset of my underwear, along my sensitive lips.

I arched to make it easier, practically purred as my mouth parted. If I'd gone commando, he'd be teasing my entrance… "Hayes."

"Fuck, Olive, you're so wet, sweetheart," he whispered as he kissed my hair. His sweet breath fanned over my cheek. But instead of capitulating to my demand, he moved his hand away and smoothed down the back of my skirt. "One more song. There's something I want you to see, then we'll go backstage for a bit and maybe find a dark spot."

My only answer was a frustrated noise.

When the band had finished their song, front man

Tommy Jane took a moment to speak directly to the crowd. "Thanks for coming out tonight, DFW! There really is no place like home. Which makes this announcement even more satisfying. The guys and me… Well, we're huge Dallas Bulldogs fans." The singer's eyes flicked in our direction.

"What's going on?"

Hayes shushed me. "Listen, you'll see."

"So, when my friend, and legendary Bulldogs tight end, Hayes Walker, gave me a call to ask about us about playing a benefit concert, of course we were all in."

My mouth fell open and I turned to look at the former tight end in question. "Wait, what? What did—"

The man with the microphone cut through. "Y'all are the first to hear it. We're going to be back this way next summer at an undisclosed location for a very intimate unplugged concert to benefit the Unlovabulls Canine Rescue Center. Wanna know when and where?" The crowd roared and I turned around to look at Hayes, my eyes huge with shock and beginning to feel watery. "Ohmygod, Walker!"

His grin was gentle, remarkable as he turned me back to the stage.

"Well, I'm not telling." Tommy chuckled into the microphone. "But they do great work over there at the Unlovabulls making sure abused and neglected dogs get the skills and socialization they need to become great family pets. I've got a rescue dog myself…my boy, Meatball, is a bulldog mix, and I can't imagine life without him. Listen up. If you want tickets to this benefit show, you're going to have to watch our website for more details. Because these tickets are being sold by auction and it's going to sell out. Fast. One night, intimate setting, and good music for a great cause. What do ya say, who's gonna bid on those tickets?"

The crowd went crazy as Tommy tipped his head to Hayes, who returned a little wave.

"That ought to bring in quite a bit of operating capital for the rescue, don't you think?" There was pride in the look on his face.

My heart soared. Our third fundraiser, and it was brilliant. It would be a huge draw. I was ecstatic. "This is amazing! It will be after the gala for sure. How many tickets are they going to auction? How did you pull this off? Are you sure they have a venue? There's so much that needs to be done."

"Shh, Ollie." Hayes rubbed my arms. "Just soak it in. Enjoy it. I've got this all taken care of. The band has the venue covered, all you have to do is go to the concert with me and collect the check for Lily."

"But...how? I mean, I'm sure these guys get asked to do stuff like that all the time."

His lips lifted at one corner. "Well, it's not totally free. I know Tommy, he's a big football fan. He and I agreed to a swap. They were already heading back this way for a concert, so everything was in place. It was meant to be a test show for some material from their new album, but the band agreed to make it a full show and donate all the proceeds to the rescue. They're even going to cover the costs of the venue."

"How did you get them to commit to all this?"

Hayes gave me that famous shrug. "Urban Legend does a lot of work with local substance abuse counseling programs. Next year, they're holding a weeklong camp for kids affected by parental substance abuse. I pulled some Bulldogs players together and we're going to spend a day hosting a football clinic during the camp."

"Hayes...this is..." Great. I was going to cry again, a lump in my throat choking my words.

He brushed a thumb over my cheek. "Yeah. I know." He didn't say it to be smug, but as if he were pleased he'd accomplished it on his own.

How this man could ever believe he was worthless unless he played football was totally beyond me. "So. Incredibly. Kind."

Once the set was over, we headed backstage, and I got to meet my favorite band to thank them for playing a concert for our shelter. And gawk at my teen crush, Tommy Jane.

"We're happy to return the favor Hayes is doing for us. The Bulldogs guys will be a huge hit with the kids this spring. He told me you're having a silent auction during the Gala. I'd be happy to give you some things from the band, too."

That gave me an idea. "Yes, I'd love that! We're also having a date auction. Will you be in town the second week of February? Because I'd love to have you and the rest of the band take part in it."

Tommy grinned. "Depends. Will you also be up for auction? Because I could be swayed if I might win a date with you, Ms. Russo."

I felt my cheeks heat. *Oh my fucking God! My teen-age crush is hitting on me!* I think I actually giggled like a schoolgirl, but before I could answer, Hayes was all over it.

"Hey, man. I like you and all, but I'm standing right here."

Tommy gave me a quick wink, then met Hayes's less-than-friendly stare. "I know. You're big. Kinda hard to miss, my man. I've got to make the rounds, but Hayes has my number, Olive. Give me a call and we'll see what we can work out."

With a quick salute, Tommy was off to his throngs of admirers, and I couldn't stop beaming from the encounter.

"Little fucker. He's lucky I like him. Most of the time. And that he said yes to the concert. I should smack him around for that."

I turned, bracketed Hayes's jaw with my palms giving him my cheekiest smile.

With a chuckle, he tipped his head to the side. "You're enjoying this."

"Yes, yes, I am." Gliding my hands around the back of his neck, I leaned my torso against his. "But I'm going home with you."

"It's time to find that dark corner." Pulling my arms from his neck, Hayes took my hand. Toward the opposite end of the stage, he found what he was looking for—a spot away from the lights behind a stack of equipment cases.

Backing me up to one of them, the man propped one hand on a case and moved the other around my waist underneath my jacket. I watched as his heart beat in a steady rhythm against the base of his throat.

I ran my fingers through his short beard, rubbing the hair between my fingers. "Your face fuzz is softer than I thought it would be. And it smells nice."

"Mmm. Glad you approve." Dipping his head, he dragged his nose up the side of my neck, making me shiver. When he placed his open mouth against the exposed part of my collarbone, my channel tightened around the emptiness. "You still taste the same. Smell the same. Like vanilla with a hint of something spicy. I can't tell you how many times I've thought about tasting your skin over the years. How many times I've jerked off just remembering how you smell." Slipping his hand from my waist to my ass, he palmed my cheek through the denim.

Dear God. If I hadn't already been wet... "I've thought about you, too, baby." Tickling my nails down the side of his neck and over his chest, I ran my thumb over the flat disc of his nipple while sliding my other hand underneath his shirt to brush his abs. He hissed at the temperature of my fingers. But, Jesus, the man had a set of abs. With those muscles at his hips, and his shallow belly button, the sexy dip at the base of his spine just above the incredible globes of his ass.

"Did you get yourself off thinking about me, Ollie? Did you make yourself come while you thought about me between your thighs?"

"Hayes, Jesus."

"I didn't just get off to your scent and the taste of your skin, sweetheart. It was the feel of your mouth on my skin, the way your legs hooked behind my back with ease. Your pulse jumping under my palm as you got close. How you taste..." Notching his knee between my legs, his eyes were intense as my mouth fell open on a breathy moan. "...right here."

"Mmm, that feels good."

"Not as good as me sinking into that hot pussy of yours while you squeezed me tight. The way you'd rock your hips when you straddled me."

"Yes. So often, baby. I'd think about how well you fit me. Fill me. Your mouth on my body and my mouth around your cock." At some point I started to rock my hips against his thigh and the friction of denim against wet cotton was just enough that I was starting to climb.

With a quick twist of my wrist, I had my hand over the bulge in his pants.

"Shit. Olive." He pulsed against my palm, his body jerking when I stroked him through the denim. "I remember everything. Every detail. How your face looks when you come, how your body shakes. The way you start to pop your hips when you get close." Hayes ran the tip of his tongue over the shell of my ear. "Because every time I came. Whether it was alone, or not. There was only one face I saw. Yours."

Pushing his knee harder against the juncture of my thighs, Hayes found my nipple under the fabric of my shirt and circled it.

"Ahh, just like that."

"Are you gonna come for me? Am I going to have to cover your mouth with mine so nobody can hear your moans?"

"Yes."

That's when I felt something catch against his fly inside his jeans, and he growled "Jesus, fuck," against my throat.

It was that growly sound that did it. "Hayes, it's… Ohh," I whispered.

His mouth met mine precisely as he plucked my nipple, and swallowed my low moan. My hips jerked against his thigh, trapping my hand against the fly of his jeans, rubbing my center against his muscle.

His hips pushed forward, pressing into my hand as I came down from my orgasm. As lovely as it was, it wasn't nearly satisfying enough. I wanted Hayes Walker in my bed, moving inside me. Now.

"Mmm. Thank you, Tommy," I said as my eyes came open to see the amused look on his face.

"You just had to, didn't you?" He chuckled low and dangerous.

"Well, duh." I stuck my tongue out at him. "Seriously, we need to go. Before I start taking your clothes off because I need to feel your face fur on my thighs."

His eyes shot wide. "Is that so? *My* face fur, right? Because *Tommy* doesn't have any face fur."

I pressed my lips to his. "Of course, your face fur. Only your face fur."

He smoothed down his shirt looking proud of himself. "Well, you're in luck. I just happen to be giving away beard rides tonight. I've also got this piercing I'd like to show you…"

My eyes went wide, my mouth falling open. "SAY WHAT, NOW?"

When Hayes slipped his knee out from between my thighs, I'm not at all ashamed to say I grabbed him by the edges of his leather jacket and yanked him toward the parking lot. "Let's go, Walker. You're making good on that offer. And I need to investigate this piercing you speak of."

Letting me jerk him along, he laughed. "Yes, ma'am."

Chapter Nineteen

Déjà vu, part one

Hayes

We were on our way back to Olive's place when the call came from my agent. Luckily, I checked the number on the caller ID and sent it to voicemail, but it had me antsy as fuck. I hadn't told anyone that I'd been looking to get on with another team—not even Brody—and I was glad for it, because Olive had me questioning everything.

I'd been almost certain at this point that the call would never come. I thought it was highly likely the decision to stay retired had already been made for me. It's the only reason I let myself ask Olive out, to prove to her who I was. That's why I'd bared my soul tonight, too. I hoped context would help her understand me. God, why was it easier when I felt like it had been taken out of my hands?

Because you think it would absolve you of the guilt you feel for not putting your family first.

My conscience was an asshole for spitting that up right now. I shouldn't be letting this screw with me. I loved Olive, she's what I wanted. And yet, going after what *I* wanted felt selfish. Choosing her felt like I was failing my family. Choosing my family meant I failed Olive, but I'd also lose my chance to be happy. No matter what I did, I'd let someone down.

You're knee-jerking here, dude. It was my default after all. I fucking resented my mother. That I felt trapped in this circle with her. That I couldn't make myself happy until I knew for sure everyone else was taken care of. My sister was an adult now, my mother always had been, relatively. I had no one to protect at home anymore. Why did choosing Olive feel like shirking my responsibility? What Sharlene did to me was emotional fucking blackmail. Didn't I deserve to live my life how I wanted to live it? Do what made me happy? Here, with Olive. I could give Sadie the home she deserved, and just maybe, Olive, too. Olive's presence made me see things differently. I was less impulsive, and I thought about what *I* wanted out of life. About my own future, because I always pictured it with her.

Still, my gut churned when my voicemail dinged.

"Do you need to listen to that?" Olive's gaze sparked with each passing streetlight, setting my world back to rights.

"Nah. It'll keep. Tell me more about Cassie. She was a rescue dog, right?"

When I glanced her way, true fondness had colored her face. "She was…a bitch, for real, but she was my bitch. Casshole was five when I adopted her from the Dachshund rescue. She was an owner-surrender. They said she was untrainable, but no." She shook her head. "She was smart and could think for herself."

"What made you decide to get a dog?"

"You did, actually. Well, in a roundabout way. When

you'd talked about taking care of the strays that came around, how you turned in your neighbor for keeping her dog on a chain and not feeding her. I promised myself after I got the doors open on the consulting business, I would rescue a dog of my own. Besides, I spent so much time working for the first five years that Cassie was my only real companion."

"What about friends, dating and stuff?"

"I didn't have time, but I made time for Cassie. When I first got her home, she was a holy terror, and I didn't know what I was doing." She chuckled. "I had to learn right quick, though, so I started reading books, learning about Dachshunds. Little heifer kept digging holes in my carpet, through the bottoms of kennels, everything. I didn't know it was because Dachshunds were bred to go after burrowing prey. I got her some puzzle games that she'd have to bat around to get treats out of. I even made a ball pit for her so she could dig. I did everything I could to give her outlets for her instincts, and it helped. But, oh my God, that dog hated puppies." Olive let loose a genuine laugh that had my chest warming. "Like, HATED, hated, and I still have no idea why. But if a puppy so much as looked at her, she'd throw paws. She's the reason the Unruly Dog has their No Greeting Between Dogs policy." She cackled, wiped at her eyes. "Ah, God, that dog. I can't even count how many poor baby puppies she probably scarred for life. It wasn't funny then, but now… The more time she and I spent together the closer we got. She loved ice cream and belly rubs. Lying on my lap to watch *The Bachelor* and attacking my fuzzy house slippers like they were rabbits. Her very existence made me smile, ya know?"

I lifted her hand, kissed her knuckles. "How did you get into agility?"

"I found the Unruly Dog Training Center when I was looking for basic training classes so I could take her to work with me and not have to worry about her eating my office furniture. You know Carrie, right?" She raised a brow.

I nodded. "Last year when dogs kept showing up at the practice facility, one attacked my truck's front tire. It was hurt, but I was half-afraid if I got out, it would either run off or bite me, and it needed a vet. So I called Brody, who called Lily, who brought Carrie to come pick it up and get it to Gina's office. They named him Max. He lives with Carrie, Everett, and their host of dogs now."

She nodded. "Sounds like her. Her grandson was a client of mine for a time, and—"

"Wait. Who's Carrie's grandson?"

"I can't tell you that!" She slapped my arm. "It's none of your business. Anyhow, long story short, Carrie told me about the Unruly Dog and the different classes they offered. I thought it would be a great way to channel some of Cassie's instincts. We enrolled in their beginning training classes and swept through those, then started rally and it took us no time to get our first rally title. Next, we tried agility and she learned unbelievably quick. She had zero fear of everything but the teeter. Once we got past that, she had her Novice title inside of three months. So, we kept going. We tried nose work, Barnhunt, Earthdog, fly ball, obedience. She soaked up everything I threw at her, and I made friends in the community. People like Lily and Gina, Carrie and Everett. Melissa and Kate. The sports became my escape from putting in sixty-hour weeks, and Cassie was my little four-legged whirl of chaos."

I shut the engine off. "Sounds like she was a good dog."

The fondness on her face was genuine. "She was amazing. The goodest girl. I still miss her so much. Truthfully, I've missed that little bit of unpredictable she brought to my life." Olive's face saddened, and I stroked her cheek. "It's getting better, though. I laugh more than cry when I think about her. Life goes on, but we have the memories forever. So." She wiggled her eyebrows. "Would you like to come in? And by come in, I don't mean for a nightcap. I mean for the sex. Lots of sex. Hot, nasty, sweaty, dirty-talking, multi-orgasm-inducing monkey sex that leaves hickeys in hidden spots and handprints on ass cheeks."

I choked on a laugh. "Umm, yes? Thank you for asking."

She didn't wait for me to come around and open her door but jumped out of the truck and met me at the sidewalk. "Good. Glad we're on the same page." Olive ran her hand over my ass, grabbed a handful. "Consent, you know. It goes both ways."

"I appreciate that. Tell me, can I squeeze your ass like you just squeezed mine?"

"Yes, yes, you may." She giggled as she slid her key into the lock, and I cupped the bottom of her butt.

We stepped inside and I looked around. Lots of white with gray and black tones, black and white photographic prints with one huge painting in the foyer that was a riot of abstract color. It was perfectly Olive. "Will there be hair pulling with this monkey sex?"

"That's riiight." She tapped her lip. "You do like it when I pull your hair. I can accommodate this request."

"Ohh, sweetheart. I'm fairly sure you were the one that liked having your hair pulled, and your ass swatted." Looking cute as fuck as she played coy, Olive pulled her jacket off, laying it on the table next to her keys. Then she turned, pushing mine off my shoulders. "You also like to bite, scratch, and ride the edge."

"True." Sliding her hands down my chest, she caught her fingernail on the barbell in my nipple and her eyes flared. "But so do you. You also like a little more teeth than is polite downstairs, and doing the finger thing."

"Hey, the finger thing goes both ways. We both like that." I wrapped my hands around her waist, digging my fingers into her soft hips as my mouth ghosted up the side of her neck.

"Mmm, do that again."

"What? This?" I gave her hips another squeeze. "Or this?" Sliding my tongue out to wet my bottom lip, I put an openmouthed kiss over the pulse in her neck.

"Yeah." Her breath fanned across my collarbone and sent a pulse of chills down my torso to land directly in my cock.

Olive took a step backward, clenched my T-shirt, and took another. "C'mon."

"Wait, can I get a glass of wine first?" I didn't want a fucking glass of wine. I wanted inside this woman. "Maybe at least you could tell me I look pretty tonight?"

"I'll get you a glass of wine later. But you do look very pretty tonight, Walker. Now, is that enough fluffing for you, or shall I continue?" She never stopped walking, leading me through a living room, past the kitchen, and down the hall.

"Will you respect me in the morning?"

"Geez. When did you get so high-maintenance, dude? Hell no, I won't respect you. Will you respect me?" Olive opened a door, flipped on a light, but honestly, she could have walked me through a goddamned brothel, and I wouldn't have noticed because she was all I could focus on.

"Always, sweetheart. I'll always respect you. Just as long as you tell me how much respect you want. Slow and teasing, long, languorous, or do you want it the way I know you like it."

"And how do you think that is?"

"Biting, hair-pulling, and not nearly enough spanking for your taste."

"Mmm." Spinning to face me, she grabbed my shirt by the hem and lifted it over my head. "Christ, Walker. I wouldn't have thought you could have gotten hotter over the years, but all this ink is really hitting me right in the panties. I want to trace it all. With my tongue. So, how about a little of each and we play it by ear?"

"I'm sorry, my brain got stuck on the 'with your tongue' part. A little of each what?"

She circled behind me, dragging her fingertips along the ridges of my back. "A little of both? Jesus, Hayes, I could just stand and look at you all night. You're a goddamned piece of art."

Leaving my feet planted while turning at the waist, I took her wrist in my palm and pulled her around to face me. "A little of both it is."

Olive peered up from under her lashes as her fingers rimmed my jeans. My pulse went insane.

I skated my palm up her back, into the mess of hair at her nape to tug her head back. Warm brown eyes turned almost black as they met mine with heat and need and a little bit of challenge. Her mouth opened on an inhale, and it was all the invitation I needed. The kiss was a jumble of tastes and tongues, slips, and slides, nips and bites and sucks. Teasing, exploring, relearning every dark corner of each other while savoring every new discovery. Flicks. Nibbles. Moans were given and taken freely; gasps swallowed down whole.

Kissing Olive was religious—it always had been. From our very first kiss as I watched her lie on her back to look up at the stars. Her laugh was a humid summer breeze as the moon turned her eyes from dark chocolate to melted caramel.

Lying on my side, I propped my head up on my hand. When her laughter stopped, our eyes met, and I found myself transfixed. I brushed a knuckle along her cheek. "Would it be okay if I kissed you?"

"You'll stop if I say stop."

"Of course I will."

"No, no. That wasn't a question, my friend. It was a warning. You will stop if I say stop, or I will slap your nuts with all the power I put into a jump serve. Got it?"

Ouch. The grin claimed my face in a slow sweep from one side to the other. "That's...vivid, and cringeworthy. But, yes, I've got it. For the record, I would never try to force anything on you that you didn't want."

Her eyes got a little dreamy. Niiice. "Okay."

"Okay." I brushed my thumb at the corner of her mouth before dropping my lips to hers. That first touch was overwhelming. I felt like I'd taken a jolt from a downed power line because Olive was a fucking revelation. Sweet and just a little shy with something hidden underneath. Something spicy and wild. I ran my

*tongue along the seam of her mouth and her lips parted
for me. When I pulled her bottom lip into my mouth for
a gentle suck, the sound she let out shot straight down
my spine to the base of my balls. Slithering my tongue
between her lips, I dragged it across the length of hers,
slow and soft, as she curled her tongue around mine.
The sweet, wet dance went on and on. Advance and retreat, realigning of lips, reangling of heads.*

*Then I did something that let all that wild out of her
without even knowing it would.*

I sucked her bottom lip between my teeth. And I bit.

*Olive gasped, and I pulled back. "Good gasp or
bad gasp?"*

*She threaded her fingers into my hair, brought my
mouth to hers and bit my bottom lip, letting is slowly
glide from between her teeth.*

"Shit, Olive. Do that again."

"Yeah. You first." She laughed against my mouth.

It was my favorite make-out session ever. Until now,
when I decided to do the same thing I'd done years
before. With a last stroke of my tongue along hers, I
sucked her bottom lip in and bit, letting my teeth scrape
over the delicate flesh before it popped free.

Olive's eyes flared, her hands going to my belt to
fumble with the buckle. I couldn't help the grin. Knowing exactly what would turn her on, but rediscovering
it again was a heady rush. But I didn't want it going by
too fast. I wanted to savor, to explore. To play.

"Olive, slow down," I said, stilling her hands. When
her gaze met mine, I cupped her cheek. "For more than
a decade I've thought about this, about you. Missing
you. Knowing exactly how stupid I was to let you go.
We are not rushing this."

She nodded, and I could see it in her eyes. She'd thought about me too over the years.

"Turn around, sweetheart."

She did, slowly, with seduction in her movements as she cast a glance over her shoulder.

Slipping my arms around her waist, I pushed up her shirt and stroked her soft belly before I unhooked her bra. I let my hands drift beneath it to cup her generous breasts, rolling her nipples between my fingers, listening to her sigh as I palmed them and squeezed.

So round and heavy, perfect in my big paws.

Olive dropped her head back against my shoulder, exposing the column of her neck as she arched into my palms. Taking my time, I worked my mouth up the length tasting her, sweet and salty, letting her scent fill my nose. A nip here. A lick there. I kissed my way back down her golden skin, biting that spot where her shoulder met her neck that I knew would make her shiver.

"You remember." Her voice was throaty, her ass pushed against me as she wiggled in my hold.

"I told you I remember everything." I let my hand drift down to the button on her skirt, slipping it through the hole, and pushing the zipper down. I used my other hand to palm her neck, applying a little bit of pressure. "Is that too much?"

"No. It's not enough."

"Patience." I nipped her ear. Slipping my hand into the waist of her skirt, I toyed with the edge of her panties keeping steady pressure on her neck—just enough to let her know I had her.

Olive's breathing deepened, her chest rising and falling. "Hayes, touch me. I need you to touch me."

"Here?" I asked, skimming my thumb over the pulse

in her neck. "Or here?" Pushing my fingers under the waistband of her panties, I stroked her short, damp curls as I brushed the tip of my finger over the swollen bud trying to peek through her lower lips.

"Yesss," she hissed, rolling her hips against my hand. Olive reached behind, gripped my thighs to pull me against her ass as she widened her legs. "Right there, baby."

"Mmhmm." I stroked, and stroked again, strummed, trailing my finger up the length of her slit only to wiggle the tip just past her lips to brush her clit. "Like that?"

"Jesus, Hayes. Just like that." Her eyes were glazed, hips seeking more pressure that I wouldn't give her as I rubbed my aching cock over her backside.

"So fucking wet, Olive. I'm not gonna let you come like this. Not until you know what my beard feels like against your thighs, tickling over that wet pussy, stroking against this. Sweet. Hard. Clit." I punctuated each word with a tap of my finger on the sensitive nerve endings.

She bucked against me, let out a frustrated growl when I extracted my fingers from her skirt and lifted her shirt over her head. "Turn and face me."

She did, and it stole my fucking breath straight out of my lungs. God she was beautiful. Standing there like a Roman goddess, giving me fuck-me eyes as her tongue snaked out to wet her lips. Wild dark hair around her shoulders windblown from the concert and lipstick long ago kissed away. Big, tan nipples tipped her plump breasts, puckered and swollen from my fingertips. The dip of her waist and flare of her hips, the gentle swell of her belly. She was fucking everything.

Olive shimmied her skirt off while I watched her gorgeous tits jiggle. I wanted to see them move like that when she rode me. "Woman, I wouldn't have thought it were possible for you to get any more beautiful than you were in college, but now…" I used her line on her, but it was true. She was…all grown up.

Unbuckling my belt, she pulled it through the loops in one smooth move. "Mmm. This body is chubbier than the one you knew. Meanwhile, you've gotten leaner. Harder. Bigger than you were in college, where I have curves in places I didn't before."

"I *love* those curves. Lavish, sinful. You're so fucking sexy it makes me want to blow in my pants." I gripped a whole handful of her ass as she unbuttoned my jeans. "Your body is gorgeous and I want to relish it. I want to worship you, sweetheart. The way a goddess deserves to be worshiped."

Grinning, she chose that moment to push her hand inside my boxer briefs. "Mmm, shit. Olive." I squeezed my eyes shut, head rolled back on my shoulders. My jaw locked as she stroked her thumb over my piercing. When I looked back down, refocusing on her face, my cock throbbed under her fingertips and her eyes were blown wide.

Chapter Twenty

When order meets chaos...

Olive

My eyes went huge when I felt the balls. No, not those balls. The little hard ones made of metal that were about the size of a pencil eraser. One piercing ran through the center of the flared part of his cock head with the metal balls on either side. The other did the same, but was positioned on the underside of the head. "Ohmygod, I want to see it!"

His Adam's apple bobbed, and a smile stretched his lips as he tipped his head down to look at me. "Later."

Hayes wrapped his arms around my waist and lifted, walking me to the bed. He sat me on the edge and pulled off my boots before toeing off his shoes. God, he looked gorgeous. I wanted to examine each tattoo and hear the stories behind them. He'd had a couple in college, but now he had them everywhere. Over his shoulders and arms. His neck and those big hands. His chest, and back. Down one side of his ribs and over his abdomen.

"Now..." He gripped my thighs as he went to his

knees between my legs. "I felt how wet you are for me, and I really, really want to see it. Taste it."

"Oh, God," I muttered, pushing myself up the bed. So much had come rushing back to me when Hayes and I kissed. Not the accident, not anymore, but the way he knew my body and played it with precision. How he always seemed to know exactly where to put pressure and how much. When to speed up and slow down. Exactly where I wanted his lips, his mouth, his fingers and hands.

Of course, I'd slept with other men since college, and I was quite sure Hayes hadn't been a monk—for fuck's sake, he'd pierced his penis!—but nobody had ever satisfied me like this man had. Nobody had engaged my body and my senses, my emotions and brain and heart the way Hayes Walker had. I'd compared every man I'd been with to him.

I'd admit, it was totally unfair to them. Perhaps I'd just built Hayes up into something unreal in my mind. Unattainable. But I was dying to find out.

Grabbing both corners of my panties, Hayes slipped them off my hips. Pushing up with my arms, I lifted my butt for him to slip them underneath and down my legs. I knew how wet I was—just the slide of my own skin was goddamned maddening—but Hayes didn't go straight in. He pushed my knees wider and inhaled through his nose.

Christ, I'd forgot that about him. "Damn, I love that scent, Olive. It's sex and spice and fucking Christmas cookies. Pull your feet up, sweetheart. Let me look at you. I need to get reacquainted with this pussy."

When I looked down, there was amusement in his eyes. "That wasn't cheesy at all, Walker." Grabbing the pillows from the head of the bed, I stuffed them under my shoulders, then pulled my feet up to rest on the edge.

"Call it cheesy if you want, but I'm about to spend some quality time down here." He looked up from under hooded eyes as he dragged the edge of his beard along the inside of my thigh. Then he did it to the other side, his hands grasping the backs of my legs as his thumbs played along the edges of my swollen lips.

The man was a tease.

"Hayes."

"Nope. Still not going to rush this." When I met his eyes, I knew he meant business. "Lie back and enjoy. You know I'll get you there. I always do."

"Well, except for that one time." I quirked my lips.

His eyes widened. "What one time?"

"The first time."

"Oh…the *first* time. You mean *your* first time. I believe I made you come like three times before I pushed inside you, and then again later that night from penetration. Woman, do you even know how many girls come their first time?"

He was telling the truth. I couldn't help the giggle, and it got me a light swat across the inside of my thigh with the flat of his palm. The bit of sting vibrated into my core, making me hiss and arch, hoping for more.

The tickle of beard over the heated spot was a riot of sensation only outmatched by Hayes's skilled tongue snaking out to flick at my clit. Once, twice, then long, sweeping strokes up and down my crease before his rough thumbs opened my sensitive lips. "Fuck, Olive." A little shiver worked through me when I felt his breath against my skin. "I'm sure you've been with guys since me, but I have to tell you, I've always thought of this, and of you, as mine."

Reaching down between my legs, I ran a fingertip along his cheek. "Same."

With that, he dipped his head and put an open-mouthed kiss directly over my folds that was so intense, it had me clamping my legs over his ears and pushing against his mouth. "Sweet Jesus." The words came out husky and dark as his mustache tickled over my little bundle of nerves. Strong hands pulled my legs further apart, but I was already rocking my hips against his mouth chasing my release. "Hayes, yes."

"Fuck, I love how you taste. How pretty you are. Here." He ran a finger down my center, pulling a squirm from me. "Everywhere."

I expected him to put his mouth on me again. Instead, he pulled back, let my legs go, before he rolled to his feet. *The fuck?* I sat up, started to protest. But he crawled on the bed, lay at the headboard all casual-like, one knee bent, his forearm rested on his head. "Come on." Hayes patted his chest. "I want your ass right here with your knees by my ears."

"Umm, wait, what? When you said beard ride, like, I didn't actually think *beard ride*."

"Oh, that's exactly what I meant. Now get that sweet ass up here, Ollie."

I thought about it. This wasn't something I'd ever done before. Hayes must have seen my hesitation.

"I want to see your face, Olive. I want to watch you come against my mouth like the spectacular fucking queen you are with your hips bucking and your tits jiggling. I want this new memory with you, sweetheart."

I raised an eyebrow. "Aww, that was really beautiful and all, Hayes, but will you do the finger thing?"

His eyes crinkled at the corners and the bed shook as he laughed. "Christ, woman. I will do the finger thing. Promise."

I loved him like he was now. Relaxed. Not carrying the burdens he'd hidden from the world. That weight on him had been so much harder to see back in college, but time always had a way of making the load heavier to carry. Rolling on to my stomach, I pulled myself up on my knees and crawled to sit on my heels next to his ribs.

His eyes were dark and heated. "Stand up, sweetheart. Use the headboard to lower yourself over my face while you slide your feet under my shoulders."

I did as he said, getting to my feet and stepping across his chest as his gaze dragged up my body. His mouth opened on an exhale. When those electric blue eyes landed on mine, I couldn't look away. Not when I lowered myself over him, not when I adjusted my legs under his shoulders, and definitely not when he gripped my thighs and his breath fanned over my sensitive skin.

My brain coughed up only one thought.

This is where we belong.

"Sit back. Right on my chest."

I did, slowly, and when Hayes opened his mouth to put it over the center of me, those beautiful blues were fixed on my face. It was intense, meaningful, weighted. I felt the connection deep down. A connection that—I was beginning to understand—time and space had no bearing on. It was a vacuum, where he and I existed only for each other.

"Hayes," I whispered, feeling both pulled apart and put back together. I ran my fingers through his hair, over his brows and cheekbones. When he finally licked into me, my inhale was so sharp it made me a little dizzy and a lot drunk. "God, baby, that feels so good."

When his eyelids slipped closed, I reveled in being able to watch him. The way he hummed when he put his tongue to clit. The line that appeared between his brows, and the growl that rumbled against me, making my hips jerk. It was too much, watching this beautiful man between my thighs.

He squeezed down on my hips and tipped his chin back to speak. "Don't you dare look away. I want you to watch me, because I fucking love tasting you. Seeing you like this. Trying not to roll your hips against me when that's all I want you to do. Roll your hips for me, Olive. Chase what you want."

When he dipped his chin again, he pushed on my ass with strong arms, sliding me forward until I could feel his mouth but not see it. God help me, I rolled my hips. Once, twice, then over and over into a rhythm as I moaned and shook. My body tensed until the ache in my channel was so damn strong, but I needed something. I moved faster, spread my thighs further apart, put his tongue right where I needed it and pumped my hips. Hayes's cheeks flushed, his hair all kinds of fuck-me mussed as I gripped it between my fingers and pulled probably a little too hard. But those eyes were burning hot as he stroked up and down through my slick pussy, making the ache coil tighter and tighter.

"Hayes, fuck. Feels so good. So close."

He let go of one of my hips, lifted me enough to shift his shoulder, then I felt his hand between my legs with his mouth.

"Oh, that's it." Knowing what he was doing, I leaned forward, steadying myself with one hand on the headboard, the other gripping a handful of blond hair. "Yes, please."

Hayes growled, vibrating against my pussy as he pushed his thumb inside me, his finger rubbing small, soft circles against the pucker between my cheeks. "Oh…holy…fuck." He wiggled his thumb and his tongue at the same time as he sucked on my clit.

I came with the kind of force I didn't think was possible. The kind that made things fuzzy and dark around the edges. Where you lose control of your body and your thoughts are blissfully blank. All I was, all I felt, were contractions so sharp, they were pain before the pleasure, and those waves of pleasure set my sheath to clenching in time with every flick of Hayes's tongue.

When I finally came down, I crashed to the side unable to catch my breath.

"So," I said between gasps for air. "That's a beard ride. Huh. I'd do it again." I was twisted, my upper half on my back, my hip to the bed, eyes closed.

I didn't even notice Hayes shifting to his side to look at me until he spoke. "I did the finger thing," he said, sounding pleased as punch.

"You combined it with a new thumb thing. A finger-thumb combo if you will."

"Finger, thumb, mouth. I think I'll call it the Triple Lindy."

"Apt. That's some world record shit right there, baby."

Hayes snorted. I rolled my eyes open with great effort, turned to take him in…and now I was embarrassed. Half the man's face was wet. All in his face fuzz and over his lips, the tip of his nose. I'd come harder than I could remember and the evidence was all over him. Self-conscious, I slapped a hand over my eyes. "Ohmygod, your face is covered in me. Like, a ridiculous amount of wet." I peeked through my fingers as he stroked his beard.

"Excellent beard conditioner."

I rolled my lips in, trying not to laugh. "We should get you cleaned up."

"That's a thought. But I'd rather fuck you first, then clean up."

Oh Jesus, I haven't touched him. Poor guy. "Tell you what? I'll get a washcloth to wipe your face fuzz, and we'll go from there." After I wet a washcloth with warm water, I proceeded to clean him up. "I don't think I've ever made that big of a mess out of a man."

Hayes stilled my wrist as I made a last pass over his beard. "Messy can be a good thing. Messy is unpredictable, exciting even."

Sitting up on an elbow, he pulled my nipple into his mouth and pinched the tip between his teeth.

I sucked in a breath. Lord. "I don't mind getting a little messy. With you."

"I'm so glad to hear you say that because I love making a mess with you, Olive Russo."

The man moved slow, measuring and calculating and stalking as he lifted off the bed and stood before me. I reached for his fly, already half-undone, the waist on his jeans sitting loose on his hips as his cock stretched the fabric.

Fishing his wallet out of his back pocket by the chain, he produced a foil packet, throwing it on the bed next to me. "Go on and have a look then. I know you're dying to see it." The grin he gave me was all kinds of sexy.

Biting my lip, I slid his zipper the rest of the way down before I pushed his jeans down his legs. After he stepped out of them, I rubbed my palm over the bulge in his underwear, slipped my fingers in the waistband to pull them over his hips.

His cock popped free, the head slapping against his stomach. God, he was stunning. His thick, veined shaft, the ruddy crown wet at the tip. But I was mesmerized by the piercing. The silver balls were the size of a pencil eraser, one on the front side of his flared head, the other behind it, against his shaft.

"I forgot how big you are."

"Always nice to hear, but you staring at me like that is a problem."

I looked up his torso. Hayes's face was a dark mask of heat and need. Taking him in hand, I wrapped my fingers over the piercing and stroked.

"Fuck, Ollie." His stomach pulled tight, his head dropping back on his shoulders.

"Is this where it is for the reason I think it is?"

Hayes rolled his head forward, glazed eyes meeting mine over his abs. "Yeah."

"Won't, um, the condom kind of dull it?"

He nodded. "A little."

"Let's have the talk, then. When were you last tested?"

"A year ago. All good. Keep doing that. Just like that. Unh, fuck."

"A year. That was quite a while ago, Hayes." I thumbed both silver balls at once.

He let out a half moan, half grunt. "I haven't had sex with anyone in almost a year and a half." The way my mouth popped open had some kind of effect on him because his cock jerked in my palm, and he brought his fingers up to stroke the corner of my lips.

Yeah, I was picking up what he was putting down. "I'm all clean, too. But you're going to have to be careful with me, baby. It's been a long time for me, too."

"So, no condom? You sure? What about pregnancy?"

"The pill," I answered. "Unless you'd like to double up, which I totally understand."

His grin was sex personified. "Hell no." Hayes bent to kiss me, and my brain went offline. Unfortunately, I didn't get to put my mouth on him because he crawled over me, on top of me, nudging my thighs open with his hips.

My hand went to his sides without thought, my fingers exploring his lean ribs, the sculpted lats, the delineations of his stomach as he seated himself between my legs and that thick cock rested against my folds.

I rolled my hips along his length without thought and his mouth parted. I felt like my body had finally taken over and was controlling my brain, but the look on Hayes's face…

Intense and heavy-lidded. Blond locks in complete disarray. Wet lipped and eyes sparking like lighting in a night sky. Holding his weight on one hand, he slid the other up my shin, stroking my scars with his thumb before gathering my knee to push it next to his rib cage.

Hayes curled his hips, running his length back and forth through my wetness, nudging at my clit with the head. "I wish I could tell you how many times I've thought about this." Dipping his head, he pulled my nipple into his mouth and gave it a quick suck before letting it pop free.

"I know. Me, too."

With a curl of his hips, Hayes pushed the crown inside of me.

My head rolled back against the mattress, body bowing off the bed. So much stretch with a bit of sting, and it was fucking perfect. "Christ, more. I want to feel you stretch me."

Hayes's eyes twinkled with laughter. "She always wants more." When he started rocking his hips in shallow, even strokes I couldn't draw breath. I could feel it, the piercing, moving back and forth over the little rough patch inside me.

"Gooood, Haaaayes," I keened.

"Mmm, like that, do you?"

I couldn't answer. I arched my back, increasing the pressure in exactly the right spot and Hayes kept up those maddening shallow strokes.

"Sweetheart, I'm not going to last. What do you need?"

"The angle, more pressure."

Sitting back on his knees, Hayes wrapped his arms underneath my legs. With a quick jerk, he pulled my ass atop his thighs.

"That's it. God, that's it. Right there."

He pumped into me in short intense strokes as my orgasm built. The tightening in my abdomen was unreal. But it wasn't until Hayes circled my swollen bundle of nerves with a finger that the orgasm blasted through me. "Fuck. Coming." My eyes watered, those first contractions were so hard, my whole body jerked with each pulse as my legs shook and my hips bucked.

That's when Hayes buried himself in me. To the hilt. I was so damn wet and ready, the pressure was euphoric.

"So fucking hot. Jesus, Ollie. I don't... I can't..." Hayes met my gaze and pushed up on his arms, letting my ass slide back to the bed. Forehead to forehead he stroked deep into me over and over, his eyes full of an emotion I wasn't ready to name yet. "There's nothing like being inside you. Nothing like feeling you squeeze me. It's so..."

"Powerful."

"Yeah. So fucking powerful."

"I'm close again."

"Jesus. Thank fuck. Give it to me. Let me feel you come on me." Dropping a bit of his body weight on my abdomen, Hayes stroked in and out rubbing the base of his shaft against my swollen clit.

"God!" My channel fluttered around him, rippling as I tried to draw breath and a haze of pure bliss raptured my body.

"Mmmm, goddamn." Hayes's voice came out shaky. He dropped his mouth to mine. With our lips brushing, he pushed into the root. "So fucking good. Perfect, Olive. You're perfect." With every pulse of his orgasm, his hips curled deeper inside of me, giving me everything, until there was nothing left for him to give.

When he finally stilled, Hayes rolled to the side to let me breathe, but we were both spun out.

Arm still extended, legs tangled with mine, he looked like a god lying there in my bed. Neither one of us spoke as I nuzzled into that spot on his neck that was made for me.

He wrapped a heavy arm over my shoulders, putting his lips to my damp forehead.

There were no doubts left. Neither of us had come out and said it tonight, but Hayes Walker was my beginning and my end. I knew in my bones that I'd never stopped loving him, and I never would.

We were two halves of a whole, right where we were supposed to be.

The perfect balance of order and chaos.

Chapter Twenty-One

Surprise, it's a girl!

Hayes

I slept in fits all night long. I'd never stopped loving Olive, of that I was sure. It might have been the only thing I was sure of. Being with her had been like coming home again, but seeing Aaron's number on my caller ID had shook me. As much as I loved Olive, that pattern of running to take care of my family was harder to break than just saying the magic words and poof it was gone.

Truth was, I'd been enabling my mom. It was a lot easier to say you were going to end it than to actually follow through. Because my impulse—that circle I'd been stuck in to buy Sharlene's approval—was ingrained. I didn't flake on family. It was my responsibility to take care of them, to be there to rescue them.

I knew it needed to stop, I just didn't know if I had the wherewithal to do it.

"Psst."

I didn't open my eyes, but she knew I wasn't asleep.

"PSST!"

"Hmm. Go back to sleep," I mumbled, not able to feel my arm from where she'd slept on it all night.

"I can't. I'm volunteering at the shelter today and I have to get my ass in gear."

I slipped my half-dead arm out from under her, cracking my eyes open to see her face. Her cheeks were pink and sleepy, her lips red and swollen, her hair a mess of wildness.

This is where you belong, Walker. "I was going to drop by this afternoon to spend time with Sadie. Will I see you there?"

"I'll be there all day. Lily and I are going over numbers from the State Fair fundraiser, and then I have Charlie, the photographer, coming in to take pictures of the dogs from the shelter that closed to get them up on adoption sites. I've got a social media strategy for them that will get them adopted out in no time, and given the concert you arranged, I think the rescue will be more than flush for the next operating year. I ran numbers in my head. The concert could raise a huge amount of capital. Plus, we'll still have the Gala, too, as the feather in our crown."

I nodded. "Besides, with the check Matthew McKinley wrote, I bet we broke seven figures at the fair."

"Easily." Rolling onto her elbow, she dragged the sheet over her breasts. "I still can't believe Shane Jackson is adopting Dogzilla and Kevin. He seems like a good dude."

"He is. His daughter fell in love with Kevin at the fair. They're talking about changing his name to Fang like the Neo in *Harry Potter*. Honestly, I hope they don't. I love the name Kevin for that dog. And Shane and Zilla…that was love at first sight. As long as they get along with his other dog, they're good to go. I think Shane is going to look into more agility classes with his Lab mix, too."

That made her smile. "Really? That's awesome."

I nodded. "It's great news about exceeding our goal, too."

"Yeah. Thanks to you. Without all those players signing and taking pictures? We wouldn't have pulled in a twentieth of that and Matt might not have come."

"If you want, I'm sure I can talk to several of the guys about the date auction. I've got a ton of memorabilia from the team for the silent auction, too. I was even planning on dipping into my personal stash. I've got some things in storage collecting dust that I know would do well with serious sports collectors."

"Umm, yeah." She sent me a *duh* look. "What about you? You're going to participate in the date auction, right?"

I turned, smiled. "You trying to get rid of me already?"

She pushed my shoulder. "Don't give me that. You know how hot you are."

"I'll do it, but only if you bid on me."

Olive sat up, crossing her legs. "Hayes?"

"What, sweetheart?"

"You said you hadn't been with anyone in a year and a half. I always kind of figured all you guys manwhored around like Brody used to."

"And you want to know why I didn't."

"Yeah, I mean, did you ever?"

Nodding, I stroked her arm. "Not like most of the

guys. I was pretty tame in comparison. I don't know. Sleeping around felt empty to me. Like, no matter how hard I tried, how many women I went out with or relationships I had, they didn't fit. Not like this does. Not like you did. Maybe it's because I knew how a real connection felt, but it all just felt so...hollow. There were a few women I dated seriously, but nothing stuck. I couldn't get invested. Part of that is because I think I didn't care enough to put up with my mom, but the biggest piece was because none of them were you. I don't think I realized that until you came back into my life. That I was chasing something I've only ever had with you."

She rolled her lips between her teeth and I could see the tears she was fighting. She wasn't expecting the answer to revolve around her. Then again, neither was I until it came out of my mouth.

I shifted onto my side, putting my head on my hand. "Three years is longer than a year and a half."

"Man, did I need to get laid." She huffed out a laugh. "I tell other people my job is demanding, and it is. I like things my way, too, but given the right person, I could have made room in my life. I could have bent, but I never found anybody I wanted to bend for, you know? I've had a couple relationships. One even lasted a year, but we were too much alike. Sixteen-hour days and more convenience than romance. It was never really a relationship. I tried, once, to date a guy who was a 'free spirit.' A guy that didn't fit the control-freak mold. But it wasn't the same. He never made me feel the things you made me feel."

I huffed on my fingernails, rubbed them on my chest. "That good, am I?"

"Such a guy thing to say." She rolled her eyes and leaned to the side, mirroring my pose. "I mean, I was a little afraid of who I was capable of becoming, but more so, I think he didn't stick because of who I *couldn't* become with him? You have a way of challenging me to be present in my life, Walker. Nobody else has done that, forced me to stop and smell the roses, so to speak, save Cassie. It's not anything as trite as 'you complete me.'" She tugged at her lip with her finger. "It's more like you complement who I am in a way nobody else does. Those other relationships felt like carrying a fake Fendi—sure, it looked good, but I knew it wasn't real."

This woman... My heart skipped in my chest, cracked wide open for her. I'd had it right all those years ago. Olive Russo was the one. There would never be another like her. Hers was the only laugh I wanted to hear. The only smile that mattered. The only lips I ever wanted to kiss again. Every woman I'd been with over the past decade, every single one I'd slept with, I'd only ever seen Olive.

I needed to be in her orbit, to breathe the same air as her, and that pull was strong all the fucking time. Magnets, the two of us. I was her negative and she was my positive and we would always gravitate to each other.

Something about that calmed me, settling the cacophony of conflicting voices in my head that had kept me up all night. For her, I could figure it out. I could break the cycle.

I wondered where we'd be now if I hadn't let her go that night. "Come here." Slipping my hand into her hair, I brushed my mouth to hers. "I'm falling for you again." I couldn't tell her, yet, that I'd never fallen out of love with her. Not until she'd had some time to process where we were now.

She nodded. "Me, too. It's scary."

"It is, but it's exciting, too. You make me see things, think about things I haven't maybe ever."

"What things?" She cocked her head.

I kissed her pert nose. "The future."

It wasn't until I was on my way home to change that I pulled up the voicemail to listen. "Hayes, my man. I didn't want to leave this on your voicemail, but I'm heading out of the country. Looks like New York is going to wait and try to ride out the storm. David Standhope will likely go free agent this spring unless New Orleans can meet his contract demands, and New York doesn't think they can. I'm sorry, my friend. I've heard some things about Denver, though. Looks like LaMarcus Taylor might be leaning toward early retirement. I can't tell you how I know that, but stay fit."

I knew exactly how he knew that—Taylor was a client with another agent at his firm. I wasn't at all upset that New York had passed. I was relieved. I'd reconnected with Olive, and I liked my life in Dallas.

Maybe I'd even keep coaching. I'd made up my mind about my mom, too. I was finished trying to buy her approval, but there was still the issue of forcing her to live within her means. I wouldn't put my mother out on the street. She'd need at least some time to adjust.

I had Jessica to think about, too. Columbia's medical school was one of the most expensive in the country and living in New York City didn't help matters. I loved my sister. She was a good person, and I didn't want her starting her career 300K in debt. I wouldn't have much savings after all was said and done, but I should have enough to cover her last year of tuition before she started her residency.

For the first time in a long time, I had hope. It felt good setting foot on that path to my future.

After I finished team meetings and game films, I pointed my truck in the direction of the rescue center to see my girls.

"Hayes, hi!" I found Lily in with the photographer and Tucker, the black Pit Bull from the TV shoot. Beautiful dog. Sweet fella, too. He'd been an owner surrender at the other shelter before it closed for good. Tucker sat in front of a lavender backdrop like a good boy waiting for instructions. When he'd come to the rescue, he'd had zero training. His owner had been an older lady who passed and the dog was a little bit heartsick, but working with Lily to learn agility had brought him 'round.

"Hey, Lil, can you put the flower crown on his head? Will he sit still for that?" Charlie asked as she snapped away. "Hi, Hayes. Good to see you again."

"You, too. Charlie. Cute setup."

"Thanks."

"Are you going to see Sadie?" Lily asked me as she sat a crown made of peach and yellow flowers on Tucker's head while he stayed put like the good boy he was. "Tucker, stay."

"Yeah. I thought she could use some one-on-one time. I was going to spend time with a couple other dogs, too." Lily had told me long ago that one of the hardest parts of working with shelter dogs is that they can start to mentally decline because of limited stimulation, and when that happens some become unfit to adopt. Because of that, and their socialization needs, all of us volunteers spent one-on-one time with several dogs. But no doubt Sadie was my favorite.

Lil nodded, told Tucker to stay again as the photographer snapped several close-ups. It was a really cute way of presenting the dogs. It made the bullies look softer, like the family pets they had become. "I need to talk to you before you leave," Lil said.

"Okay. Where's Olive?"

Tucker took that moment to break his stay to visit with Charlie, who turned on a megawatt smile.

"She's in my office, finishing up some numbers. Hayes, she told me about the Urban Legend concert." Lily's face lit from within. "Thank you. Thank you for everything." She took three steps, and I was wrapped in a spider monkey of a hug. "You are a good man. And an amazing friend."

"Shh, don't tell anyone," I whispered, and squeezed her back.

"Get your hands off my woman, Walker." Brody came through the door.

"Well, in that case…" I hoisted Lily up and pretended to walk away.

She giggled and Brody shook his head. "You rang, my lovely bride-to-be?"

I set her down. "Yes, I had an idea. You know the fireman and puppies calendar hanging in my office?"

"Yes." He rolled his eyes.

"Since Tucker will have a hard time getting adopted, I thought you might take your shirt off and help him out?"

"Really, Lily," I said. "You want dad bod over here when you could have asked *me*?"

"Dad bod, my ass." Brody whipped his shirt off. "Where do you want me, Charlie?"

I had to give it to Brody. Even though I gave him shit on occasion, he'd stayed fit. Poor Charlie. She stood there with her mouth hanging open and a possible sliver of drool on her chin as she stared at the half-naked former linebacker. I was about to go double or nothing on her.

I grabbed my T-shirt over the back of my head and down my shoulders before I kicked off my running shoes and socks. "Shaw, ditch the Nikes."

"Why the hell would I do that?"

"Because there are a lot of people out there with a thing for jeans and bare feet."

Brody shrugged and did a quick heel-to-toe, getting rid of his shoes as I walked over to the backdrop and called Tucker to me. "Where do you want *us*, Charlie?"

Her eyes bulged, traveling back and forth between me and Brody.

Lily tried to hide her grin with her hand but was doing a piss-poor job.

Seconds ticked by... Lily even shot off a quick text, but Charlie didn't respond.

"Umm, Charlie?"

"Present!" Her eyes snapped up from my stomach. "Umm, okay both of you squat down on either side of Tucker." We did, and she snapped a couple photos.

"Hang on, let's just..." Regan moved forward, positioned Brody's chin, turning him a bit. "Now, um,

Hayes, sit on your heels, one hand on Tucker, one on your thigh."

Olive chose that moment to come in and immediately burst out laughing. "Oh my God, you two are waaay too easy." Reaching into her pants pocket she pulled money out, handing it to Lily.

"Told ya," Lil said.

"There's an extra ten in there for sucking Hayes in, too. Hang on, Charlie. I know what this picture needs." Olive walked over and bent down in front of me, giving me a perfect view of her tits in her pink V-neck sweater. She trailed her fingers below my belly button, reaching for the snap on my jeans with a sly grin.

"Enjoying yourself, sweetheart?"

Sporting a shit-eating grin, she unhooked the button on my jeans and pulled my zipper down about an inch.

"Well, you two banged," Brody announced to the whole room.

"Brody!" Lily shushed him.

But my girl only tossed him a saucy wink as she walked back out of the shot.

Fifteen minutes later Tucker was playing ball with Charlie when Lily stopped me and Olive before we went to see Sadie.

"What's up."

She took a cleansing breath. "I had an application come in for Sadie."

I felt all the blood drain out of my face, my stomach bottoming out somewhere around my knees.

"It's a couple in their late forties. No kids. He's an engineer who works remotely whenever he wants. She's a writer who works from home all the time."

Olive slid her hand around my bicep.

Brody nodded as he met my eyes. "They saw her at the fair and asked to meet her, quietly. The couple paid zero attention to the circus going on and focused solely on Sadie. They're nice folks, Hayes. Lily and I did the home visit yesterday. Nice house, big yard. They lost a Clumber Spaniel not too long ago and said they're ready for another dog. They also have a rescued Cane Corso who's having a hard time not having a sibling so, they have experience with bully breeds. They've never surrendered a dog and know they'll give her a good home for the rest of her life."

No.

I no more than thought it than it popped out of my mouth. "No. Sadie has a home."

Lily put her small hand on my forearm. "This is not a home, Hayes. The rescue is not a home. She belongs with a family who can love her. Where she can curl up on the couch or on her human's bed at night. Where she deserves be showered with love every hour of every day."

Even I could hear the desperation creeping into my voice as my stomach churned with the thought of losing her. "I can give her all that and more, Lil. Promise. No, you can't adopt her out. Sadie is my girl." Even as I was saying the words, I knew it was true. Sadie was mine. My life was changing, and I could give her the home she deserved. "Olive and I talked about this. She agreed to be Sadie's co-parent when I have to travel with the team. Let me give her a home." I wasn't above begging.

Lily turned her attention to Olive, and the two women were sharing a whole secondary conversation with looks alone.

"Are you sure you're ready for this?" Brody asked, eyeing Olive.

She nodded, slipped her hand into mine. "Yes, I'm sure. I love Sadie, too. I spend nearly as much time with her as Hayes does, now, and I can't imagine her going to a home where I couldn't see her. It may not be ideal, but when Hayes travels, she can go to the office with me during the day. Besides, with Hayes and I... together, it's a good fit."

A smile crossed Lily's face. "*Together*, together?"

I nodded, glanced at the woman holding my hand. "We hadn't really talked about it, but given last night, I'm not sure we need to? Yeah, we're going to try and do this. For the record, I'm not even sure if I want to keep coaching at this level, and if that's the case, I won't be traveling nearly as much." I lifted Olive's knuckles to my lips. I wanted to add that I hoped we'd be moving in together and consolidating homes, too, but I thought it best to have that conversation with Olive first.

"Okay. I'll tell the couple Sadie's no longer available. She's been adopted." Lily absolutely beamed.

As Lily embraced a delighted Olive, they both had tears in their eyes. Brody pulled me in to a bro hug. "Good man, Walker. Congratulations, your girls are amazing." He thumped me on the back.

"Thanks, man."

Lily was next, wrapping me in a warm hug I had to bend over for. "I'm so happy for you, Hayes. I always thought she belonged with you," she whispered. "And I'm talking about both of the *shes*."

I kissed her cheek. "Can I take Sadie home tonight?"

"No. Go spend some time with her today, then go

get the supplies you'll need before you bring her home. You can take her home tomorrow evening."

"Thank you, Lily. I owe you."

"You don't owe me anything. Just give her the best possible life and spoil her rotten with love."

It sounded like Lily's words were meant to be about Sadie—and I was sure they were—but I didn't miss the way her eyes slid to Olive, too.

"Always. I promise."

Chapter Twenty-Two

A freedom ride and a free ride

Hayes

Fall turned into winter in Dallas practically overnight. There was a nip in the air, but not a cloud in the sky as I drove into downtown to meet Olive at the gala venue and watched the suburbs turn into the city. The event was creeping up quickly. Single plates were selling for fifteen grand, and to buy a whole table, you had to have pretty deep pockets. Olive said it was all people were buzzing about.

It had been nearly six weeks since Sadie's freedom ride, too, and it was fucking glorious. Olive couldn't get out of a meeting, but my baby girl had a grand time. I only wished I'd done it sooner.

For far too long, I'd been holding on to the present too tightly, so I didn't have to think about my past or future. Adopting Sadie required me to take on more responsibility. Not easy when the word *responsibility* had become synonymous with obligation and burden in my mind, and generally made me feel like a fucking failure. Being with Olive again, the past had been easier to face, and the future gave me hope. She was the motivation I needed to start dealing with my shit and learning to move on.

Wiggly-butted and lolling-tongued Sadie jumped into the passenger seat of my truck, sticking her head out the window like she knew she belonged there. Lily and Olive would kill me if they knew I'd let her ride up front when I picked her up from the rescue but watching her lips flap in the wind and slobber fly down the side of my truck as we took the back roads home—it was the best feeling. She was loved, and wanted, and everything about her demeanor said she understood that. I was starting to understand that feeling, too.

Which got me to thinking as I pulled up to The Statler to meet Olive and the event planner. Maybe it was time to talk to Olive about moving in together. I liked having both of my girls safe under my arms. We'd been nearly inseparable anyway. I knew Olive would need time to consider it and weigh the pros and cons. I'd like to do it before the gala, but I was prepared to give her as much time and space as she needed.

I wasn't going anywhere.

I still hadn't called my agent to let him know I wasn't going back to playing yet either. It was a big step. Moving on from that part of my life didn't come without anxiety. Leaving things with my agent a little longer was my safety net until I was sure the changes I needed to make were in place, and everyone I cared about would land on their feet. Baby steps.

The Statler was nifty as hell. It was a historic hotel that got a makeover, and some upgrades a few years back. They had restaurants, nightly rooms, residences, and a large-capacity ballroom. It also had lots of history and that mid-century modern cool that sprouted the gala's theme—we were going full on Rat Pack with a kitschy Vegas vibe. As I walked past the vintage cars outside the lobby, I knew we'd picked the perfect spot. We were meeting with an event planner. Another favor she'd called in for the Unlovabulls Rescue.

Truthfully, she really didn't need me for this stuff. She had it handled, but I wanted to be there every step, and she insisted I might be useful in helping charm the planner if necessary.

The lobby interior was all old-school wood, cursive script, and marble and gold accented with geometric shapes. My boots thumped on the floor as I headed for the walnut and marble reception desk next to the Lubin abstract mural they'd found hiding when they started renovating the place. The whole vibe was Rat Pack cool. I saw Johnathan waving me down from the stairs just as my phone rang and I put up a finger to tell him I needed a minute.

"Hey, Mom, what's up?"

"Neiman's canceled my credit card, and when I went to make my car payment this month, you only deposited half of what you normally do. When are you going to transfer the rest? I have rent to pay. I was able to cover the car out of my savings, but I can't cover rent, too."

I'd hoped to do this in person as opposed to over the phone. Weaning my mother off sponging off me wasn't going to be easy. I'd known that from the outset. It's why I'd never bothered to try before now. "We talked about this, Mom, I can't afford for either of us to live that lifestyle anymore. I'm still paying Jess's tuition and expenses and trying to keep myself from living in a cardboard box. You have to cut back."

"WHAT? YOU DID THIS ON PURPOSE!" Her shriek into the phone was loud enough that I had to pull it away from my ear. "I never. How could you do this to me? I gave birth to you and put a roof over your head. Kept you in clothes and food at a time in your life where feeding a growing teenage athlete was no easy feat. And you cut my money in half?"

Her money. Jesus.

She'd always refused to call it an allowance, but that's what it was. Really, it was more like hush money, or protection money, take your pick, because that was the truth—my mom was shakin' me down every month. But that was over. I could continue to give her a partial allowance for the next six months until she could get on her feet. She was my mother, after all—I wasn't going to put her out on the street.

If Sharlene was smart, she'd dump the apartment and car now and save that cash. Though, apparently, she already had savings. Which prickled. Half the time she'd come to me for extra cash because she'd said she'd overspent... I'd always caved. Frankly, it was a hell of a lot easier to pay her off than it was to let her lay into me. But if she had savings, she wasn't overspending nearly as much as she'd led me to believe.

Sonofabitch—quite literally, actually.

I was done being played. It was fucking extortion and I'd let it go on way too long.

"You have savings." It wasn't a question. "How'd you manage to save money when you constantly come to me because you couldn't afford one thing or another that you couldn't live without?"

"I... Just... None of your damn business, that's how. You think I'm stupid, son? That I didn't know one day you'd do me exactly like your daddy did? I will *not* feel guilty about putting some of my money away to take care of myself when that happened." I could practically see the filterless Marlboro she'd smoked when I was young hanging from her lips.

I could walk this path with her, argue until I was blue in the face, but it wouldn't do me a damn bit of good.

"You know what, Sharlene? Keep it. You have six months to get your act together and start paying your own way. After that, you're on your own. I'll be letting the tenant board and the car dealership know that if the leases aren't rolled into your name by then, they can do what they gotta do. I'm also canceling your Neiman's card all together. I'll pay the final bill because the account is in my name, but this is the last time."

"Hayes Edmond Walker, you'll do no—"

"Yes. I will. I don't play football anymore, and I'm not going back just so you can keep spending money like water. I like Dallas. I like coaching, and I'm not gonna tear up my body year after year so you can keep buying Hermès and Chanel." I could feel my temper rising, my voice getting louder. The kind of rage I'd once had on the football field clawed at the surface to get free. I tried to moderate my tone and failed. "The free ride is over. Six months. If you're smart, you'll save every dime you get between now and then."

She huffed. "Who are you kidding? Football was, and is, the only thing you'll ever be any good for. I always knew you'd turn out like your old man in the end. Worthless."

"You know what? I actually understand perfectly why he dumped you and left us."

I jammed my thumb onto the end-call button, wanting

to hurl the damn thing through the plate glass. Then, I'd punch the window next to it until my fist went through and my blood coated the jagged edges. As my eyes darted around, I saw people looking at me with fear in their eyes. It wasn't a feeling I liked. Drawing in one deep breath after another, I tried to steady myself but wasn't sure how long I stood there before I got a handle on my temper.

A warm, familiar hand pressed against the back of my shoulder, and I reached over to cover it with my palm.

"You okay, baby? You look like you could do murder."

I grinned at Olive's use of my own words; the rest of the anger faded into the background, the knot of anger in my sternum easing at her touch. Turning, I put my arms around her waist, pulling her to my chest. "Yeah. Yeah, I think I'm okay. For the first time in maybe ever, I think everything is going to be okay." I brushed her lips with mine. "I'm excited even. About the future, me coaching, and Sadie is doing so well with us! I was thinking on the way over. Maybe it's time to talk about our living arrangements. What do you think?"

Olive's eyes turned into Popeye's after he's had his spinach. "I... Wow, you really know how to spring something on a girl. I..."

"Take your time, sweetheart. And if now isn't the right time, we can reevaluate later. I'm not going anywhere. You are *it* for me. I love you, Olive Russo. I always have."

I smiled at her, then tucked her into my neck so she wouldn't see the frustration and worry. As hard as I was trying to escape, to tell myself that Sharlene's approval wasn't important to me, the guilt and shame still bubbled up, and I wondered if that reaction might never go away.

Chapter Twenty-Three

"It's hard to talk with a mouthful of dong."
—Olive Russo

Olive

Holy shit. He loved me. And he'd suggested we move in together, all in the same breath. It was… A lot to digest. As I stood there in Hayes's arms—the place I knew in my heart was home—I knew I loved him, too.

"I love you, too, Hayes Walker. You've always been the only one for me. And yeah, let's talk about living arrangements."

His face softened, a smile blooming that made his eyes crinkle at the corners, and the strong arms around my waist gave the slightest squeeze. I heard the news alert on my phone, but I ignored it. There'd be time later to worry about whatever trouble one of my clients was in. Planting a kiss on his lips, I patted his solid chest. "Let's go meet with the party planner. We can talk about living arrangements later."

"We have to get a king-sized bed if we live at your place," he teased. "You and Sadie both sprawl."

I chuckled as I led him by the hand up the stairs to meet with the planner.

Later, while meeting with the event planner, discussing arrangements and place settings and centerpieces, two more alerts had come through on my phone. I ignored them until the flowers had been selected and Hayes and I were on our way back out of The Statler. In addition, I now had three voicemails. "Shit," I said as we pushed through the lobby doors to a cool Texas evening.

"Everything okay?" Hayes's face held genuine concern.

"Mmm, I have several news alerts and a few voice-mails from the office. I need to go back to work for a bit to handle whatever this is." I grinned, a tired but happy grin. Because Hayes Walker loved me. "It might be a late night for me. You and Sadie should stay at your place."

His eyebrows shot up. "You sure? I could whip up some dinner for us at the town house. Pasta? I could even pick up that chocolate bag cake thingy from Tru-luck's?"

I gave him a little side-eye. "You don't eat sugar."

"Me? I love sugar, I've just always had to watch my intake to stay fit. I can splurge a little more often since I'm not playing anymore."

This man... I palmed his fuzzy cheek. "Yes, I'm sure. I don't know how late I'll be. But I can try to swing by when I'm done if it's not too late. Besides, that way you'll get a decent night's sleep in your king-sized bed."

He lifted my palm from his cheek, kissed it before he held it against his chest. "Okay. Take care of whatever you need to and then come by. I love you, Olive."

A warmth radiated from the center of my being. "I love you, too."

Hayes walked me to my car before he left. I got into my Audi, started the engine, and began checking the alerts to see what was happening. The first one I tapped was from *Dallas Life & Style*'s website. When the site popped open, I didn't realize what I was seeing at first then it slowly dawned on me. My heart plummeted into the immediately sour pit of my stomach. "No, this...isn't happening." I scanned it again to make sure I hadn't made a mistake. "Motherfucking shit fuck." Shocked stupid, the phone slipped from my hand, and I made no move to pick it up from my lap.

There we were—the photo was a little grainy, like it had been taken on a cell, but it was definitely me and Hayes.

Spotted: Urban Legend concert at Dos Equis Pavilion—Public relations maven Olive Russo of Russo Image Consulting getting cozy backstage with former Dallas Bulldogs tight end Hayes Walker after the band announced a limited-seating concert to benefit one of Russo's pet projects. Should be interesting to see how she spins PR that's taken a decidedly personal turn.

I could see Hayes's knee between my legs plain as day, one hand disappeared from sight, the other framing my goddamned "O" face!

The phone vibrated in my lap, and I thought about leaving it there while I had myself a good fucking cry and hid away in my house with my pajamas on for about a year. Then I remembered who the hell I was.

Clearing my throat, I answered Johnathan's familiar number. "Yes, I've seen it."

I could hear every bit of the panic in his voice. "What

the hell do I do, Olive? How could they do this to you! Like, HOLY SHIT! What am I supposed to tell clients? Will they walk over this?"

It was time to do what I did best and compartmentalize the shit out of things even though all I wanted to do was crawl under a rock and hide. The shame… my wholly conservative, uptight parents who already thought I was a semi-disappointment—they would see my fricking "O" face, for Christ's sake. And with Hayes. Who they'd always blamed for my so-called fall from grace. I was… I felt… I felt all the things I had no time to feel at the moment.

Shaking off the panic, I had a sense of stepping outside myself as the plan began to formulate in my head and I laid down my marching orders. "Johnathan, calm down."

Pfft, me telling my staff to calm down when this was my goddamned life! "We treat it as if we're doing damage control for any client in crisis. Call *DL&S* and find out who took the picture. I want to know if it was one of their staff photographers or not. If not, I want to know who they bought it from. Hayes is a celebrity." I should have known better. "The magazine named him one of their Hottest Bachelors in Dallas this year. Chances are most of my clients won't care. The man is hot, unattached, and we were both fully clothed. We made out in public." At least that's all a reader would be able to deduce. "Couples do that every day." Thank God this was only the Spotted column. If they'd done any digging…

"But, but…" I could imagine his scrunched-up face and the trembling in his hands. There was something he wanted to say and was desperately trying not to.

"Spit it out."

He blew a heavy exhale into the phone. "IS THAT YOUR 'O' FACE, OLIVE?"

My jaw cracked as I ground my teeth together and let my head drop into my palm. *Yes, yes, it is, Johnathan.* I let my tone harden on purpose. "That's not your business. Call Stephany." She was one of my senior associates. "She has a solid connection over at *DL&S* that did the Hottest Bachelors rundown. Ask her to find out where the photo came from."

The thing was, I was usually off-limits with *DL&S* or with most media outlets for that matter—because of my connections, and the number of celebrity photo ops they received ahead of time as a result. Besides, personally, I was boring AF. Until now. Until Hayes. The thought simultaneously made me want to grin and recoil. This wasn't who I was supposed to be. I was the one controlling the crisis, not at the middle of it. I was supposed to be in control at all times, and the minute Hayes arrives, out comes the recklessness, blowing my carefully created control all to hell.

Damn it. Why do I let him do this to me?

"Johnathan, make the call to Stephany. Have her leave the info on my voicemail, then go home to your hot husband and forget about this until tomorrow. I am allowed to have a life and our clients know that. Most will understand. I can only think of a couple pearl-clutchers who might yank their business, and honestly, the shit their kids and grandkids have done is way worse than making out at a concert."

He didn't answer. I loved the guy, but I was beginning to wonder if he was cut out to be an associate at Russo Image Consulting.

"Johnathan?"

"Yeah, yes." I could tell he was trying to get it under control.

"Draft a response to any questions you might get from concerned clients and email it to me. Make it light-hearted. We're laughing this off. The boss is allowed to have a life and a little fun." The man was a hell of a writer. That was his wheelhouse. "Email it over and I'll look at it tonight. Roll any client calls concerning this issue into my voicemail and we'll get to them tomorrow morning."

"Okay, I'm...I'm upset for you, Olive. Not at you. Never at you. I want to send my husband to teach whoever did this a lesson." He let out a shaky sigh. "I'm an empath, and I know you're controlling your emotions right now, so I'm upset in your place, okay? Just tell me whose ass I need to kick, my love. I will send my husband to kick it."

That made me grin. "You are a true friend, Johnathan. Thank you for the offer."

Loyalty. That was also in his wheelhouse.

Forty-five minutes later, I pulled into my parking spot at home and saw Hayes's truck parked on the street.

I told him to go to his place. It irked me. This was *my* space.

Opening the door, I set my work bag on the entryway table. Sadie crawled off the couch to greet me.

"Hey, I wasn't expecting you so soon." His voice grated on my nerves. "I made enough for two. Angel hair with diced tomato and asparagus in garlic sauce."

Dammit. I needed time and space to pull myself together, but with Hayes around those were the last things I'd get. Evidenced by the constant ping of notifications on my phone.

"Hey," I finally said, but I could feel the line between my brows.

"You want a glass of wine?"

"No. I thought we agreed you'd go to your place tonight." I knew my tone was cold. Walking around the counter, I opened the fridge and grabbed a bottle of water.

Hayes must have heard the annoyance. When he turned the look on his face turned calculating. "You said you'd be at the office late. I was going to leave this in your fridge, so you'd remember to eat when you got home."

"Look, I'm tired, okay? I was expecting the place to be empty."

His eyes turned shrewd. "I've seen you deal with some client shit before, but I've never seen you look like this."

Nice, dude. "How do I look?"

"Beautiful. Always beautiful, my Ollie." He turned the stove off and came around the counter. "But you look dejected, and annoyed. Tell me what's going on."

With a big sigh, I tried to let go of my ire, but it didn't quite take.

"It's not a client. It's about me. *Dallas Life & Style* got a hold of a photo of us backstage at the Urban Legend concert. They posted it in their Spotted column. It's my fucking 'O' face, Hayes."

His jaw audibly cracked under the stress of his teeth. Nostrils flared, a vein jumped out of his head. "This is because of me, isn't it." He wasn't asking a question. "Olive, I'm sorry. I should have been more careful. Will this upset your clients?"

"No, I don't think so. There's nothing wrong with

me having a personal life. I just didn't account for my being involved with a celebrity and I should have. I won't make that mistake again."

Standing there, Hayes locked his hands behind his head as he tried to cool down. "What did they say about this?"

"Most of them?" I pushed up on my kitchen bar stool. His hands immediately came down to cover my shoulders. "'Way to go, Olive. You bagged one of Dallas's hottest bachelors.'" I grinned. "I don't know, I may lose a few of the Bible-thumping old ladies' grandkids, but I highly doubt anyone else would walk."

"You're pissed at me, though."

"Yes. No. I… It's on both of us. What bothers me is if the photographer had dug deeper, dredged up my past and turned it into a feature…" I shook my head.

Hayes's arms wound around mine as he pulled me into a hug, but I was just in a pissy mood.

"Plus, you dropped the *let's move in together* bomb on me. It's a lot."

"I see," he said, letting me go to sit on the stool next to me. "Let's talk about it."

I met his eyes. "I'd like to hold off on the living arrangements thing until we can do it quietly and not in the spotlight." Plus, I needed time to think. I knew that I loved Hayes, but today was taxing. I may have put everything from my past out in the open with him, but that didn't mean I'd forgotten it, apparently.

A wrinkle appeared in his brow but was just as quickly gone. "When are you thinking?"

"After the gala in February. This will be old news by then, my clients will have forgotten about it or fully embraced it, but given my past I don't want to whip things up even more than they already are. Besides. It's not that far off."

He ran a palm over his beard as he studied my face. He was seeing through me, but goddamn it. Wouldn't anybody hesitate? I had a past I wanted to stay buried, and there I was in a gossip column making out with one of the city's most eligible bachelors, while my "O" face was on display for the whole world to see!

"Okay. We introduce the idea slowly instead of giving them another reason to snoop. By then we'll be a couple in the media's eyes. Boring."

"Exactly. Boring is good."

"Olive, I love you, which is why I'm about to say this, but secrets never stay buried for good. We should have a plan for if your past ever bites you in the ass."

My eyebrows shot up. "Look at you, all about the plans."

He brushed a kiss against my lips. "I learned from the best."

God, he was sexy. I was still annoyed with him, but now I wanted to fuck him, too. For real, fuck. Hard. Like, not quite hate-fucking, but definitely taking my frustration on him. He must have seen the heat on my face because something sparked in his eyes. Letting my hand drift down his T-shirt, I grabbed the buckle of his belt, but he stopped me.

"No. You're pissed at me that this happened, Olive, and I understand that, but I think you're really pissed at yourself, too. You're scared of what this means about you as a person. You have to get out of that pretty little head of yours so I'm going to give you exactly what you need, sweetheart."

A sinful smirk covered his face as he dragged his finger over the tip of my breast. "Stand up and strip."

God. Why did that make me so wet?

I did as he asked, standing and sliding the zipper down on my dress. With deliberate moves, I pulled it off my shoulders and let it puddle on the floor to reveal lots of black French lace.

Hayes's voice dropped low and dark. "Good girl." I'd never thought I had a praise kink until he said those words and my lower belly tugged tight. "Now. Take my belt off and tie your wrists."

Slowly, I undid the buckle and pulled the leather from his jeans. The way he watched me, missing nothing, eyes hooded and mouth parted, it made my nipples pearl into hard points.

With a few quick loops, I had the belt around my wrists. Looking him dead in the eye, I tightened it with my teeth.

"Goddamn." Hayes looked at me from under hooded lids, his eyes glowing with heat. "You have to tell me yes. Tell me this is what you want tonight."

"I want to be fucked. Hard. Don't you dare be gentle. I want pink cheeks and swollen lips and that delicious soreness between my legs that reminds me who my man is. That enough permission for you?" I cocked my head at him.

One move was all it took, and his hand was firm but forgiving around my throat, his rough thumb stroking the corner of my mouth. "Then that's what you're going to get."

Hayes's lips crashed down on mine and my nipples chafed against the lace of my bra. It was exactly what I wanted, all tangled tongues and clashing teeth, nips and bites, and deep and demanding. We both warred for control of the kiss and in the end, Hayes would come out with it, but I wouldn't go down easy. That was the whole point. He'd relieve me of that burden for a little while. Because he knew that's what I needed to get out of my head.

I slid my bound hands under his shirt and scrapped my nails over his stomach a little harder than was necessary as I nipped his bottom lip.

Hayes hissed. "Fuck, Olive."

"Too hard?"

"No." Letting go of my neck, he pulled his shirt up to reveal the faint red marks. "Just right."

With rough hands, he grabbed the belt between my wrists, guided me back to the hooks next to the front door where he kept Sadie's leash. Hayes yanked my arms above my head, wiggled the leash hook through one of the snug loops on my wrist.

"Clever, but you know I can pull that hook down."

Reaching behind me, Hayes unhooked my strapless bra and my breasts bounced free. "No, you can't. It's screwed into a stud."

"I'd like to be screwed into by a stud. But he's taking his sweet time about it."

Putting his chest against mine, he grabbed my jaw with a rough palm as he slid his hand into my panties wearing a smirk on his face. "Spread 'em wider. Brat. Now."

I did, and his fingers danced along my wet skin making me cry out while he dragged the thumb on his other hand across my mouth.

When he tried to do it again, I caught it between my teeth and bit down on the fleshy pad.

"Ahh! Damn it, woman. Are you trying to make me insane?"

"I want your mouth on me." Oh, no. I shouldn't have said it out loud. He'd never do it now.

Hayes stepped back, eyed my panties while stroking his beard. "Mmm. Tempting, but no. Say, are those expensive?"

I glanced down. "What? My underwear? They aren't from Target if that's what you're asking."

"Shame. They look kinda flimsy to be expensive."

"Hayes…" I warned. But it was too late. He dug his hands in at the waist at both hips, gripped firm and yanked the lace apart, letting it fall to the ground. "Goddamn it!"

"Jesus. Will you fucking look at that. You're soaked, sweetheart. I don't even have to get close and I can see it on your dark curls." He breathed in deep. "My dick's hard as a fucking rock over here and you can't even touch it." Unbuttoning his fly, Hayes pushed a hand into his jeans with a hiss.

My lips went slack, eyes heavy and glued to where the head of his cock played peek-a-boo with his underwear, and my already wet pussy ran slick all over again. "Show me, baby. Please."

Reaching over his head, he tugged his T-shirt off, giving me way too much to look at all at once. I pulled against the hook, needing to touch, to explore, to have my mouth on all that beautiful hard muscle, but it didn't budge an inch. "Sonofabitch," I spat.

"As much as I'd like to drag this out…" He freed his length from his pants and resumed stroking from root to tip. "I can't look at you all splayed out for me much longer without coming in my hand, and I'll be damned before I let that happen. Not when I have so many snug, wet places to choose from."

"Oh, thank God."

Palm never leaving his shaft, Hayes used his other hand to slide two fingers through my wet curls only to smear it over his thick, purple crown before guiding himself to my entrance.

He nudged at my opening and my head hit the wall behind me. "Fuck, Hayes."

"Shit, Olive. So slick."

I let out a long low moan as he pushed the head past my lips and inside my channel. "That is—"

"Mmm, yeah it is."

I rotated my hips, trying to push more of him inside, but he refused with a wicked smile until he was damn well ready. When his hips finally jerked forward and his cock filled me up, my eyes rolled back and my head smacked the door. "Jesus, Hayes... Fuck me. Hard."

"Lift your leg, put it on my hip."

I did and it stretched my opening wide. Hayes slid his forearm under my knee and wasted no time curling his hips into me with fast, deep strokes. "Oh holy... That feels amazing, Walker. Just like that."

My hands were beginning to tingle, my breasts damp with perspiration rubbing against his chest as he met my hips with those endless strokes that set my nerve endings on fire. I'd never been so angry for putting myself in a position where I couldn't touch him, because Hayes Walker was goddamn glorious. His electric eyes met mine before drifting down our bodies to watch himself disappear inside me, daring me to do the same. "Look at it, Ollie. God, that's hot, seeing my cock disappear inside you."

I sank my teeth into my inner cheek, tried to keep from crying out or watching what he was asking me to. I knew when I did, the pressure would stop building and bubble over. And that ache… That sweet fucking ache, and the heaviness as my nerve endings coiled tighter and tighter. It was completely divine.

"Come for me, Olive. Let me feel you come. You know it's mine. They're all mine."

I looked down between us as Hayes thrust his hips up, watching his cock disappear inside me until his pelvis rasped against my aching bundle of nerves. Once. Twice.

The third time, I broke. "Oh fuck… Coming."

"I feel it. Uhn, goddamn."

Lights flickered in the apartment. Or maybe that was the hardwiring in my brain shorting out. I was nothing but a pile of feral, uncontrolled movements and deep aching spasms that were sheer bliss. I knew I was talking. Saying things like come for me, to come in my pussy. That all of my orgasms were his, like he said. Words fell from my lips like rainwater from a roof, but I couldn't really hear them. I was a mass of sensation, writhing, trying to draw every last bit of pleasure out of my body.

When I finally started to come down, it took me a few seconds to realize that Hayes hadn't finished. It was all the opening I needed. "Let go of my leg, baby."

He did, eyes like blue pools, his breathing deep and audible. The man looked like he could devour me whole, but I had just the opposite in mind. With a quick twist of my wrist, I freed myself from the belt and prowled toward him.

"You got out."

"Yes. I could always get out."

"Sneaky, sneaky."

Putting a hand on his stomach, I worked the heels I still had on as I guided him backward until his ass hit the back of the couch. "Among other things. Like talented. With my mouth."

"Get on your fuckin' knees."

"No, I don't think I will." With that, I pulled down the jeans and underwear that were barely hanging on to his hips and dragged my lips and tongue over his neck. A nibble on the collarbone. A bite to one pec. A swirl around his nipple that made him pull in a sharp breath. Teeth over the abs and nails over the muscles at his hips as I dropped into the kind of squat on my heels that any stripper would have been damn proud of. Then, I took his still-wet, still-hard length into my hand.

"Holy… Olive."

Sliding my lips over the crown, I rolled my tongue against the piercing on the underside, catching the one on top very carefully with my teeth.

"Oh, goddamn." They were guttural, those words. Shaky. From deep in his abdomen where the muscles tensed under my fingers. When I pulled him back to nudge at my throat, the sound was half grunt, half *unnh* that was deeper than his normal tone. I loved that sound, wanted to hear it again and again as I worked my mouth and my hand in sync, and he stroked his thumb along at the edge of my lips.

When his hips started to swing in time with my mouth, I knew he was close. Meeting his eyes over his abdomen, I let my hand fall from his cock and took him back as far as I could, sliding my fingers to the skin behind his tightened balls. When he spread his legs wider, I pressed up, rubbing firm, small circles.

Hayes's legs sagged. "Fuck. Me."

I knew that was my two-second warning, but I didn't pull off. Instead, I opened my throat.

"Jesus. Christ. Woman." He grunted, his abdomen contracted, and his cock jerked. His piercings on both sides hit my teeth, causing him to hiss and his hips to swing forward as throb after throb filled my mouth and throat and we locked eyes. "I love you."

I couldn't say it with a mouthful of dong, but I sure as hell thought it.

Same, big guy. I love you, too.

Chapter Twenty-Four

Fuck around and find out

Hayes

Stretching out my hamstring at the head of the crushed granite path, I waited for Brody to show for this morning's run.

I understood Olive's hesitation. The whole photo thing had really thrown cold water on the two of us moving in together, but a part of me—a big part—had wanted Olive to say fuck it, let's start combining households. I was disappointed, sure, but I also understood my girl's need to take things one step at a time. Especially with the photo in *DL&S*. I could tell the picture had her shook. The way she'd fidgeted, and smoothed her hair, the mood, being so irritated with me. The ordeal was making her panic about being with me, and what that meant about who she might become. I knew she'd pull away from me if I didn't do something to stop it.

When I'd taken control, she'd willingly handed it over. Sometimes she just needed to set down the weight to quiet her brain. She'd always be cerebral, always get in her head about things and play it close to the vest. It was who she was. But if I took control like I had, for a little while at least, she didn't have to be the one with all the answers. That's what I'd done—helped her calm her thoughts enough to see that the picture of us was not a head-on collision, but a bump in the road. I wasn't a violent guy off the field, but seeing how that picture had shaken her up? Yeah, I wanted to throw somebody a beatin' for hurting her like that.

Whipping my foot up, I grabbed my ankle and stretched my quad to loosen my bad knee. I wished things were moving quicker between us, but the end of December had crept up, quickly. The team was only two weeks out from the first playoff game, and the gala was only six weeks away.

I was up to my eyeballs in football, and I'd waited over a decade for this woman. A couple more months wouldn't hurt.

As I let my ankle go my phone vibrated in my long-sleeve jacket. It was cold this morning and I knew Shaw would have some damn excuse to stay in bed with Lily while I was out here freezing my nuts off. I hit the talk button. "You goddamned pussy. Go get your balls out of Lily's purse and get your ass over here. Now."

"Uh, I'm sorry?"

"Whoops. Aaron. I thought you were Shaw calling to tell me he's skipping our run." Out of the corner of my eye, I saw Jensen Bishop pull into a parking spot at the path head in what would be a Honda Civic if not for the rust eating away at the body. Brody told me he'd invited Jensen along this morning. He was a good guy, talented player. Hard worker. I respected that. Waving a hand at him, I turned back to my call. "What's up, Aaron?"

"Are you fit, my man? Because Denver wants you. Badly. LaMarcus Taylor is announcing his retirement in February. Rodriguez will move into the vacant starting position, but he's still a little wet behind the ears. They want someone to back him up that can bring him along and they think you're the guy. Are you ready to put the pads back on, my friend? I've got a solid offer— 1.6 million for one year. Six hundred and fifty thousand dollars guaranteed with an option to extend."

Whoa! That was good money for a guy my age. Even more than what I'd been hoping for a few months earlier and it was tempting as hell. I'd be able to do so much with that kind of money. Erase my mother's debt, pay my sister's tuition, and set myself up with a nice little nest egg. But all that was from before I'd reconnected with Olive. Before I'd adopted Sadie.

I had different priorities now. Still, it wasn't easy to walk away from that kind of quick fix for my family. Old habits, and all that. And yeah, it made me jittery to know I had the option. It was a lot easier to walk the new path when I thought I hadn't had a choice.

Now, that choice was staring me in the face. The thought of not taking it, not being able to fix the problems with a hastily spoken *yes* was making me jittery.

Except I'd lose Olive, my mom would never let up, around and around we'd go. As much as I felt the pull to take the job and solve my money problems, it would only be superficial. The problem was deeper than that, and I was getting off the merry-go-round.

Something else occurred to me, too. Me not calling Aaron to tell him I was officially retired, leaving that door back into playing football cracked, however small, was a cop-out. A way for me to not fully commit.

If I'd learned anything from football, it was that you chose a path up field and took it. Courses could be corrected, adjustments made on the fly. But you couldn't just stand there with the ball in your hands—you'd get clocked every time.

I'd chosen my path, and yes it made the insides of my brain a little itchy to shut the door on playing, but it led to Olive.

"That sounds like a great offer, Aaron. I appreciate it, and the work you put into making it happen, but I've decided to stay where I am and keep coaching. I think my playing days are over. Dallas is home."

Jensen lifted his chin in a silent hello as he pulled on a thin pair of gloves. Brody had backed in next to Jensen's car and stepped out of the cab.

"Well, I'll be damned," Aaron said. "Hayes Walker is hanging up the cleats." He paused, seemed to be considering whether or not to say something. "Are you sure about this? It's exactly the type of deal you wanted. One more year, two at most. Short and sweet. Then you can retire to Dallas and spend all your time at that dog rescue."

I liked Aaron, but I knew if I didn't get paid, he didn't get paid. "Yeah, I'm good where I'm at. Content. I miss playing, but I don't miss the way my body felt the day after. As it turns out, I'm not too shabby as a coach."

He sighed. "I could see that. McManus is shaping up into quite the tight end. That kid had a reputation for being uncoachable, but you've kicked his ass into line. If you're sure that's what you want, I'll let Denver know."

By the time I hung up, Bishop and Shaw were both looking at me with slick grins.

"Your agent, huh?" Brody asked.

"Yeah. Got an offer from Denver to play."

"Not taking it?"

"Nah. The life I've got here—Olive, Sadie, the rescue, even you fucksticks. Some things are more important than money."

"Indeed, they are," Jensen added.

Brody nodded, eyed the empty trail where our feet would pound the crushed granite. "You love her?"

"Yeah, I do."

"Good. Glad to have you here for good, brother." He chucked me on the shoulder. "Now shut up and run, Karen."

And I was at peace with my decision. My playing days were over and I was looking forward to what the future held. Maybe for the first time.

Olive

"I'm sorry you feel that way, Mrs. Stillwater, but I understand and I'm happy to recommend someone else for your granddaughter to work with."

Two clients. That's how many were walking. They were long-standing, exacting clients with a lengthy history in this town that, had my business and reputation still been in the early stages, would have hurt me significantly to lose. Now it simply made room for me to choose two new clients to work with. So far, I'd gotten three calls from well-known Dallas socialites about setting a meeting to discuss their PR concerns and goals.

I'd also heard from my father, who'd called me an embarrassment to the family, reminded me that my Roman Catholic grandmother would spin in her grave, and asked me not to come home for his birthday because it would be too untoward for his asshole friends.

Whatever. It was what it was. I was forever tarnished in their eyes long before those photos went public.

After I hung up with Mrs. Stillwater, I gave Stephany a quick call only to find out that the photo had been sold to the magazine. It hadn't been one of their staff photographers or even someone they contracted with. But they'd refused to tell her who sold it to them.

It was time to muscle them. I hit the intercom button on the landline. "Johnathan, get me Anthony Clark at *DL&S*."

Anthony was the *Dallas Life & Style's* editor-in-chief. I wanted answers, and to nip this in the bud before anything else cropped up. Given where Hayes and I had been when the photos were taken, there was no expectation of privacy. I couldn't get them to pull the photo down, but I could make sure they didn't post anything else about me, and that it stayed out of the next month's print issue.

"Olive, I have Anthony on two."

I hit the speaker button on my phone. "Anthony, how are you? Well, I hope."

"Ms. Russo. Can't say I wasn't expecting this call." His cigarette-worn voice was a little hesitant.

"Then let's cut through the bullshit. Who'd you buy the photo from?"

"Correction. Photos. And you know I can't tell you that."

"The hell you say. Now spill. Or I will take all my clients and beat feet over to *Big D Journal*. You'll get no more tips from me. No more photo ops. No more party invites or breaking stories. I will take that and more over to *Big D*, and we both know a long-standing publication like that will be able to bury a trendy competitor like you in no time flat." I was pissed, and every bit of my accent was pouring into my threats. "Not to mention that Russo Consulting doesn't chase the market. We lead it. When I walk, it's only a matter of time before the other PR firms start to follow. I didn't want to do this, but if you won't give me a name, I for damn sure will."

A heartbeat ticked by, then another. Finally, a throat-clearing cough came through the line. "One of the new editors I just hired from a tabloid slapped it up on the website before I had a chance to review it. I gave her a talking-to. Told her we weren't that kind of publication. It wasn't the first time she'd done something like this, but I give the Spotted writers a certain amount of autonomy with their column. Otherwise, they'd keep me up all hours of the night getting approval on posts."

"I wouldn't ask you to fire her, Tony. I just want to know who sold you the photos, and I want your assurance that you won't publish any more. I won't have damage done to my business, my clients, or my pro bono work because I'm seeing Hayes Walker. I realize he's a celebrity, and I will give you the first appropriate photo op of our relationship in return. Though, I do find it odd that the write up focused on who *I* was instead of who he was. So long as you give me that name, the rest of the photos, and you don't post anything else about Hayes and me between now and the gala I'm planning for the Unlovabulls Rescue. I'll even sweeten the deal. I'll give you access to the gala in six weeks. It's going to be one hell of a star-studded event. After that, you can write a fucking feature about Hayes being off the market if you want."

"So, he is? Off the market?" His voice sounded way too perky.

"The name, and your word. I guarantee what I'm going to give you will sell a hell of a lot more magazines than pictures of me kissing Hayes."

"Damn it, Olive. I've never given up a source."

"I don't care. You take what I'm offering, or I take my clients and walk."

"Fuck," I heard him say under his breath. A moment went by, and another. "Crystal Vincent. She took them to the same editor that published the photos of her and Michael Seaton."

My mouth dropped open. Fuck. Me. *That little twunt did this to get back at me.* And it wasn't about Hayes at all, which was why the write up focused on who I was. She was trying to screw with me. The parallel of the photos hadn't escaped me either.

Anger was bubbling in my veins, my voice deadly cold. "How much did you pay her?"

"Five hundred."

Then it was solely about revenge. I was fit to be tied. "Get your editor under control, Tony. Or you're going to end up with a reputation as just another gossip rag. I have a relationship with you because your publication is otherwise a classy outfit. But if you keep posting this kind of shit, it won't be for long. I'll be expecting the rest of the photos."

I hung up and spun around in my chair, kicking off my heels to look out at the city. That little heifer had caused me one headache after another. Vindictive little witch. Still, it hadn't caused me to lose credibility like I'm sure she hoped it would. It had just been embarrassing.

Man, had it been a long day. The sun was starting to slip lower in the sky and parts of the city fell into shadow as my phone buzzed yet again.

"Olive?"

"Johnathan, can you roll it to voicemail? I'm exhausted."

"Erm. There's someone here to see you. She doesn't have an appointment."

"Who is it?"

"Sharlene Walker?"

The fuck? Hayes's mother, who I'd never met, and was the reason Hayes dumped me? I did not have the patience for this shit after the day I'd had. But I did what Olive Russo does and slid back into my four-inch heels and smoothed my ponytail using my reflection in my laptop.

"Send her in." I looked at the sky outside. *Lord, grant me the strength to not knock this abusive bitch right the fuck out here in my office. Amen.* With that I spun my chair around to face the door.

Sharlene was pretty, but slight. She looked young for her age—or very well-refreshed—dark hair just past her shoulders, and a Birkin slung over her forearm. Hayes said he took after his father, but his eyes were all Sharlene. The look on her face said she did not come here to apologize for convincing her son to dump me, nor would we ever be braiding each other's hair.

"Olive. Well, look at you. Aren't you just a big strapping farm girl." Her voice was all cigarette smoke and dingy roadhouses.

"Sharlene. Won't you come in?" I said, ignoring the

insult. There was no smile on my face or warmth in my voice, but I chose to stay seated behind my desk. Both to remain in a position of power, and to put distance between us so I couldn't wring her neck like I was itching to.

"Ms. Walker, if you please." *Oh, this bitch...* "Let's not waste time. I wasn't sure exactly what was going on with my son, why he was pretty much kicking his mama out on the street with nothin' but the clothes on my back. Then, I saw the picture, and it all made sense. Hayes has got himself mixed up with you. Again. And, well, I've come to tell you to stay away from my boy. He's easily swayed, you see, and I think you've done quite enough damage both then and now. You have a way of turnin' that boy inside out so that he doesn't think straight."

"He's easily swayed? Don't you mean manipulated?" I crossed my arms over my chest. "From what I've seen, only one person has ever been able to manipulate Hayes, and it wasn't me."

Her lips pursed, revealing the age lines around her mouth. "You do know Hayes has a sister."

"Yes, of course."

"Jessica is attending medical school at Columbia University. It's very exclusive, hard to get into."

"I'm aware of Columbia's prestige."

"Yes, well. Prestige comes with a hefty price tag. One that Hayes has been paying. Did he tell you that?"

I tapped my fingernails against the desk. "That's his business. I don't know the ins and outs of Hayes's finances."

"Did you know that in college, Hayes took a job two towns over from the school, where he was paid under the table, in order to send money home to his family? And he did it at the risk of his scholarship. Or at least he did until he met you. Then the money stopped coming. He stopped coming home. Didn't call often, and when he did, he spent most of that time talking to Jess. He left his mother and his sister—his blood—high and dry."

Truthfully, I didn't know any of that. It didn't surprise me that Hayes would do something like that at the risk of his scholarship, or that he let the job go when he met me. He'd started thinking about himself and what he wanted. What did surprise me was that there seemed to be a lot Hayes did, then and now, that I wasn't aware of. "No, I didn't know about the job, but he's always been generous to a fault."

I could see the anger in Sharlene's eyes and did my best to keep my cool as she threw an arm up and a vein bulged in her head. Hayes had that vein. "You walk back into his life, and he's all about that piece of ass again. He's threatened to kick me out of my loft, let my car get repossessed, and if he doesn't give me the money for his sister's tuition soon, they could bounce her out of the program!

"I don't know what kind of magic you got between your legs, girl, but you gotta stop gettin' in my boy's ear and turning him against me. You're trying to cut me out of the picture! His mother! Don't you think that's a little selfish?"

Lordy, that was a lot of screeching. And I was being selfish? No. "First of all, I did no such thing. Your son is a kind and intelligent man despite his upbringing who, when beyond your reach, is beginning to understand what he wants from his life. I'm sorry that doesn't include continuing to fund your lifestyle, but unlike you,

I'd never manipulate Hayes into cutting anyone out of his life. However, if that's what he wants to do, then I will stand with him. You, and Jessica for that matter, are both grown women. You should damn well be able to fend for yourselves instead of *you* financially and emotionally blackmailing your son into doing it for you."

She pointed a finger at me. "Don't you dare talk to me like that. You don't know my life or what I've been through. What that boy owes me." Putting both palms on my desk, Sharlene leaned down to get close to my face. "You do not want to go toe-to-toe with me, girl. You will lose."

I'd had about all I could take. Uncrossing my legs, I rose to my full height—which towered over Sharlene—then mirrored her pose, dropping my head to make sure she saw my eyes. "This is not a fucking contest. Hayes deserves better than that from his own mother. Make it about money if you want. Tell everyone who will listen that I'm the reason your son cut you out if that's what helps you sleep at night. Make no mistake. You've used him, manipulated him, made him believe he was worthless if he couldn't play a damn game, and emotionally blackmailed him by withholding your love. Hayes has decided to put up boundaries with you for his own reasons. That is on you, and you alone. And stop calling him boy. He's a grown man. A good man with a good heart you've taken full advantage of."

I straightened to my full height again, closed the notebook on my desk, slipping it into my work bag. "You can show yourself out, or I can do it for you, *Sharlene*. Big ol' farm girl like me has definitely got a few pounds on you."

"Are you threatening me?"

I sniffed, glanced up into her shocked face. "Yes."

Rolling her eyes, she waved me off as she marched to the door. Before she could slam it, I made damn sure she heard my last words. "Oh, and Sharlene? I won't tell him this time."

She paused, keeping her back to me.

"Don't come here again and pull this woe-is-me bullshit. If you think for one minute Hayes doesn't know you've been manipulating him all these years, then you greatly underestimate the man's intelligence. As for you trying to manipulate me? Next time I won't be so polite. I'm in his life to stay, *Mom*. Get used to it. Because you won't rip us apart again."

She threw a look over her shoulder. "We'll see about that." The glass door shut behind her.

No wonder Hayes would've rather paid her than deal with her.

Narcissistic bitch.

I knew Sharlene was all about the Benjamins she skimmed off her son I'd discerned she lived off him from what he'd told me the night of the concert, and I was glad Hayes was putting his foot down with her. But why hadn't he told me he'd cut her off, or about the job in college, or his sister's tuition? What else wasn't he telling me?

Chapter Twenty-Five

What kind of fucking name is Wrangler?

Hayes

My mom had only called to bitch at me once in the last couple weeks and Olive had handled the photo situation like a pro. Things were going smoothly, though I could tell Olive was a bit hesitant with me in public. We'd been photographed once in a restaurant for Spotted, which Olive had set up, but it was all on the up and up. Nothing embarrassing.

After leaving Sadie with Olive, I packed up for The Bulldogs playoff game. Throwing my stuff in my truck, I headed for DFW airport to make the team plane. We'd gotten lucky, turning a wildcard berth into a second game. It was a long shot. We were sixteen-point underdogs going into Denver, but the Bulldogs were scrappy like that.

I was extremely proud of our guys—particularly McManus. He'd really pulled his head out of his ass and started playing for the team instead of himself.

I was getting ready to board when Jess called.

"Hey, Nugget. How are you? How's Moose?" The

basset hound I'd given to her was now fully grown, but mentally still a big puppy who got in lots of trouble, and he was funny as hell.

"He's good. Chubby. My roommate won't stop feeding him French fries. He's a bad influence on my sweet boy. I keep telling them those things are awful for both him and my dog, but Kyle still gets one order for himself and a second for Moose. I swear, we're nearly third year, Hayes. You'd think the guy should've learned by now that putting that stuff into your body is a bad idea."

"Oh, yeah. You mean all the stuff that tastes the best? Worth it."

She sighed. "You two are impossible. I'm going to start making KYLE WALK MOOSE!" she yelled, I'm sure to get under her roommate's skin.

"What's up, kid? I'm about to get on a plane."

I heard a door close on the other end. "I know. Denver, huh? I saw the New York game. You guys kicked ass. Proud of you, bro."

"Yeah, thanks. Speed it up, kid. They're holding the team plane."

"Umm, I've run into a problem here at school. I keep getting bills at my campus address for last semester's tuition and housing. I ignored the first one because I figured, *Mom*, you know? She does stuff like that. But the second one came with a decent-sized late fee, so I called her, and she said it slipped her mind. Now I've gotten a third bill, tuition will be due again soon and if she doesn't pay them both, they'll boot me out of the program."

"Goddamn her." Hand on my hip, I stared out the terminal window trying not to lose my temper at the airport and get hauled off by TSA.

"Yeah," Jess said. "I called her to ask where the payment was, and she said she'd forgotten and would send it right away. Now she's not answering when I call. She sends me to voicemail."

"You've got to be fucking kidding me. I gave her the money for your fall tuition back in August. I wonder where the hell *that* eighty grand went." I hadn't heard from Sharlene since I'd told her she had six months to get her shit together. It was time to have our come-to-Jesus. "You owe the school 160K." I didn't have that much. It would drain every last bit of the money I had stashed and still not be enough. I had my coaching salary, but I couldn't write a check to cover Jess's tuition both semesters.

I'd have nothing. What the hell was I supposed to do?

"Give or take. Plus, late fees for last semester. I'm so sorry, Hayes. I double-checked with the financial office to make sure they didn't screw something up. They never got a payment. Now interest has accrued on the late fees. I wasn't sure what else to do but call you. I should have just had the bills sent directly to you given how squirrelly she's been since she started seeing that new guy. I don't know what she's thinking."

I pinched the bridge of my nose. "This new guy…is this Dylan or whatever?"

There was nothing new about my mom having yet another boyfriend. She'd liked them young and ever rotating for as long as I could remember.

"No, there's another one. Wrangler? I think that's his name. They've been together for seven or eight months now. Hayes, this is my fault." Jess blew out a heavy breath. "I never thought Mom would do this. She's always paid my tuition, even if it's a couple days late, but this?"

"Yeah, my guess is she doesn't have the money I gave her." I wanted to put my fist through the window. "It's not your fault, kid. Sharlene doesn't think about anybody but herself—she never has. Have the college bill me directly from now on. I'll...figure something out. Don't worry. Just focus on your third year."

After I let Jess go, I got on the plane, slipping on a pair of headphones so I didn't have to talk to anyone. What the hell did Sharlene do with the money? She'd always been a problem for me, but never in a million years did I think she'd take Jess's tuition money.

What was I gonna do? I could cover the back tuition and part of the current, but not all of it. I could max out the credit cards I had and make payments.

That seems like a bad idea, paying fifteen percent interest. It would only make matters worse in the long run.

Maybe I could make payment arrangements with the college, but that would take a sizable chunk out of my regular salary. Would I have enough to live on?

You could let Jessica take out student loans. She's a big girl, after all.

No. None of this was Jessica's fault. I didn't want my baby sister starting her career off under a mountain of debt. Next year she'd be starting her residency and could afford to take on some of her own costs, but if anyone was going to take on debt, it would be me.

You know how you can make this work.

Leaving Olive? Beating on my too-old-for-this-shit body again? Besides, I doubted the offer was still on the table. *That's not the answer, Walker.*

Isn't it?

Chapter Twenty-Six

Complete chaos

Olive

It was a warm, early-January day in Dallas while Hayes was freezing his balls off in Denver preparing for the Bulldogs' playoff game. Things were moving right along on the gala; ticket sales and donations were rolling in and our guest list had a number of names on it that I thought might give Lily an aneurism.

So of course that's when the bottom fell out of everything I'd built over the past decade.

I had flipped open the glossy pages of the February issue of *Big D Journal* that had dropped this morning when I saw the article.

Walker Is Finally off the Market: All about the PR Mogul with a Checkered Past.

"Oh no. No, no, no." As much as I wanted to throw up and hide, not necessarily in that order, I couldn't look away from my own personal train wreck.

It seems Hayes Walker likes his women tall, dark, and powerful with a questionable past. Big D has discovered that he and former college flame Olive Russo—

sole owner of the well-known public relations firm Russo Image Consulting—have rekindled their decade-old romance that began when they attended Oklahoma University together. Walker, former tight end and current assistant coach for the Dallas Bulldogs, has often been referred to as one of the most eligible bachelors in the city since his trade to Dallas three years ago. Coach Walker, however, has rarely been linked to women and has remained both intensely private and careful about who he steps out with.

Russo, who generally stays behind the scenes for her clients, has built a stellar reputation in the public relations field in the DFW area with a list of well-known, highly visible members of the community including sports stars like basketball player Alonzo Whitley and Stanley Cup MVP Edouard Morin. Her list of socialite clients is even more impressive and exclusive. But has Russo's squeaky-clean image always been a sham?

After recent photographs surfaced of Mr. Walker and Ms. Russo in a more-than-compromising position, buzz started to swirl about the new-old lovebirds. Fortunately for us, an exclusive source provided Big D with court documents that confirm Ms. Russo used to be very naughty, indeed.

Her criminal record involves convictions for the misdemeanor charges of driving under the influence as well as reckless endangerment stemming from a late-night crash outside Pilot Point, where she ran another car off the road before crashing her own into a tree. Both convictions carry heavy penalties in Texas, remain a part of your criminal record indefinitely and often come with jail time. Police reports indicate Ms. Russo sustained serious injuries and totaled her vehicle. The *occupants of the other car had only minor injuries. Her blood-alcohol content at scene was a staggering .16.*

How did she keep the conviction quiet for so long? You'd have to speak with her father—now federal judge Mario Russo of the 362nd District Court.

It went on about women Hayes had been linked to in the past, his playing stats, et cetera, and was accompanied by a picture of Hayes and I looking cozy in the lobby of The Statler.

Bile rose in my throat and toyed with my gag reflex. I barely grabbed the trash can in time for it to catch the contents of my stomach. There it all was for everyone to see—the past I'd tried to keep buried. The DUI conviction. The reckless endangerment. Was Crystal the source again? When the concert photos had backfired, maybe she'd dug until she found my secret. No, something told me the girl was neither smart enough nor determined enough to pull this off. Did it even fucking matter who the source was?

This was all my fault, anyway. I'd made bad choices. *Because you're involved with Hayes Walker and did something impulsive at a concert.*

I, of all people, should have known that dating Hayes could thrust me under the microscope. I'd been rash at the Urban Legend show, thought only of what I'd wanted in the moment, and now I'd pay for it with my career. My business that I'd built from the ground up.

Hayes Walker equaled poor decisions.

This wasn't the concert photo all over again. I'd lose clients right and left and I could only hope it didn't blow back on the gala for the Unlovabulls. Shit, people might pull out of that. I had clients who'd paid for plates and tables. I hadn't asked, or even pushed them to attend, but it was an event Dallas's elite wanted to be seen at. Or at least they *had* wanted to be seen there. Now...

Plus, the humiliation that came with this level of exposure. Everyone would know what I'd done. How foolish I'd been. Everyone would bear witness to my biggest regret in every word on the glossy page.

DUI. Reckless endangerment. Conviction. Record. They were the words my brain coughed up over and over as I retched into the trash can a second time and my ears rang with shame. A quick glance at the phone on my desk, and I could see all the lines lit up. Someone put a cool towel on my neck as I rested my head on my forearm against the edge of my desk.

Johnathan's voice. My staff knew. They looked at me with pity in their eyes. My humiliation was complete. I don't know how much time went by, but I heard Johnathan say my name into a cell phone and talk about getting Hayes back from Denver.

"NO! I don't want Hayes here for this. I need time to think. And this is a playoff game. He can't miss that."

Johnathan nodded, curled his mouth in a sad smile before he spoke into the phone. "No, don't come. She said she needs time to think and plan."

After that, things started to come back into perspective, my brain sorting itself out and rebooting. It was just about that time I heard two familiar voices.

"Out! Everyone out. Johnathan, can you get everyone moved out?" Lily said in the tone she used to correct a dog's unwanted behavior.

He nodded, clapped his hands and started shooing people toward the door. "Everyone out now. We've got damage control to do, people. Into the conference room. I want to know who their source is and why they felt the need to do this. Mark, call *Big D*. I want to talk to Danielle Roderick, their chief editor. Ashley, I want Crystal Vincent on the phone yesterday. Marnie, clients only into my voicemail. I'll draft a response to give to them and deal with them personally..." Johnathan's voice trailed off as he closed the door behind him.

My bottom jaw was on my desk. "Holy..."

"He's like your Mini-Me," Gina said.

"Yeah, don't sell that one short yet, Olive. He's got potential," Lily added.

I let my head fall in my hands. "Lily...the gala. I don't want this to blow back on the rescue."

"Shhh. Don't worry about the rescue. Let's get you sorted. What can we do?"

"I...nothing?" I met her violet eyes before glancing over to Gina's golden brown. "I need to handle all this. There's so much to do."

I felt Gina's hand on my shoulder. "Honey, I hate to burst your bubble, but Mini-Me is on top of things."

"Was that Hayes on the phone with Johnathan?"

"Yes. They just got into Denver and he wanted to get a flight back. That's a good man, right there," Gina tacked on.

Lily nodded.

"He is a good man. This isn't on him. He'll think it is. But it's not about him at all. I just make these terrible decisions when I'm with him. Stuff I would otherwise never do. I don't make mistakes when he's not in the picture."

Lil rolled her lips together and tapped her finger against her chin. "What you're saying is that when Hayes isn't around, you're a perfectionist. This single facet of your personality. But when Hayes is around you give yourself permission to be human and whole?"

I opened my mouth to disagree. Closed it. Opened it again. Lily grinned as I shut it one more time.

Gina flopped into a chair she'd pulled around my desk and took my hand. "You are allowed to make mistakes, Olive. Everyone does; it's the reality of life. Nobody is perfect. Does it blow that your mistakes are playing out in a magazine? Yes, but if you continue to beat yourself up over what happened years ago, how will you ever move on?"

"You won't," Lily added. "It's okay to be human, Olive, and to forgive yourself for not being perfect."

I nodded, and the tears started to fall. It was such a heavy weight, that fear of letting down everyone around me. Of letting myself down. Didn't I deserve to be forgiven for the sins of the past? The only forgiveness I needed was my own.

This wasn't about Hayes at all. It was about me being unable to forgive myself for being human. People made mistakes. They learned and they moved on and it was my job to help them when those mistakes played out in public. That was what I preached to my clients when they were in some kind of PR crisis, yet I'd never extended that courtesy to myself.

I would lose clients because of this—lots of them—but I couldn't deny there was a measure of relief in finally having it off my shoulders for the moment. "I'd... Anyone up for ice cream and vodka at my place? I think I could use another girls' night."

"Absolutely."

"I'll call Brody."

Scooping up my work bag, I got to my feet and carried my heels under my arm. I made one stop before leaving the office. With a tap on the glass, Johnathan looked up and walked to the conference room door. "Everything okay, boss?"

"Yeah, I've got a lot of thinking to do." I pointed a thumb behind me at the girls. "I'm going home for the day. Gonna have some ice cream and figure out how to save my business after all our clients leave."

"Eh. Tonight, focus on the ice cream. Think about the other part tomorrow. And don't you worry. I got this until you're ready to come back."

I slid an arm around him and squeezed. "I know you do. Thank you."

Chapter Twenty-Seven

In the blink of an eye...

Hayes

"Shit. They're gonna blitz." And McManus didn't see it. Nobody did.

I'd been concerned about Olive since the article came out. I wanted to be there for her, not in Denver, but I also knew my girl. If she said to stay in Denver, I should stay in Denver, give her time to process and keep my mind on the game. After all, this was Olive. She was the strongest person I knew.

"They're not showing blitz." This from the Bulldogs head coach.

"Look at the strong-side linebacker. His feet are shifty. It's a tell. They need to check off. Somebody's going to miss their assignment."

He nodded. "Send it in."

The assistant coach tried to get the attention of the quarterback to call an audible or a time-out, but he'd already started his count and the referees were focused on the line of scrimmage. It was too late.

The blitz came and the offense wasn't prepared. As

our quarterback took his drop steps, they were overwhelmed on the right side where McManus had lined up. Between the right tackle and the guard, a hole opened up, and the linebacker with shifty feet shot the gap.

I saw what was coming next about the same time McManus did. Our left-handed quarterback never saw the linebacker coming with the open receiver he was targeting along the right sideline. He started to cock his arm back to fire the ball.

And got leveled. The ball popped up into the air and McManus managed to get under it, pulling it in to avoid the fumble. He did everything right.

When he didn't have a path up field, he made for the sideline on the diagonal, but one of Denver's safeties was target-locked on him. Daniel couldn't turn the corner around the other player.

Instead, he got clocked. The guy dove at him, catching him around the hips right in front of where I was standing. The hit was clean. But I saw McManus twist on his planted foot, and I heard the almost simultaneous pop as he landed out of bounds at my feet and grabbed for his right knee.

"Sonofabitch," I spat. That sound hollowed my gut.

Daniel did what we all did when we were hurt. Gut check—he got up slow and limped off to the bench. But he was hurting. He had to be.

"Cortez!" I yelled at his backup. "Get your ass in there! Don't do anything stupid. Play it safe."

With only a minute fifteen left in the first half, Cortez took the field, and I went back to the bench where McManus had landed on his ass. "How is it?"

"S'okay. Need a minute."

His face was turning green. "Okay, my ass." I cranked my head around to yell for Darius, the head trainer, but he was already there next to me.

"What happened, my man?" he asked Daniel.

"I, uh, just, pfft…you know."

Darius gave me a knowing look. McManus was babbling because he couldn't focus through the pain.

"I heard a pop," I told the trainer.

Darius didn't wait. He pulled out a walkie. "Get the ortho to the locker room and get me a cart."

At the half, I went straight into the training room to see what was going on. And I was pissed at what I found. McManus was sitting on the table, the lower half of his right leg under the arm of the head doctor while he checked for stability in the knee.

And Dick—that short, sweaty, greasy, JR-Ewing-motherfucking-look-alike—was standing at the head of the table next to Daniel.

The doctor set Daniel's leg down, pulled his glasses off with a sigh, and wiped them clean before setting them back on his nose. "I'm going to leave it up to him," he said to Dick.

"Leave what up to him? And where's Darius?" I demanded as I walked in and over to the table.

Doc looked up at me. "Could be just a sprain. Or, it could be cartilage, or an ACL."

I crossed my arms, set my feet apart. "I heard the pop, doc. It was loud enough to make my stomach turn."

Dick's lipped thinned.

The doctor looked to Daniel. "You hear it pop?"

"No, but with the helmet and the hit and everything, I guess it could have." I was glad he sounded a little clearer than he did on the sideline.

Dick stepped around the end of the table in front of me. "We don't need you in here, Walker. Go do your job."

"I'm not going anywhere. This is part of my job. Protecting my players. Besides, what are you gonna do, Dick? Toss me out? Good luck with that." I towered over the GM.

The doctor's gentle voice turned my head. "Daniel, I won't stop you if you want to play—"

That's when I started to lose it. "You want to shoot him full of drugs and send him back out on the field? I'm telling you I heard the fucking thing pop." I pointed at Dick. "You're going to end his goddamned career before it even starts!"

"But," the doctor continued. "If your coach heard something, I think playing is bad idea. You need an MRI, son."

Dick's face turned the color of a tomato. "Damn it, Walker! Mind your own fucking business. If he wants to play, that's his decision. Daniel." He turned to the kid. "There's a good chance that if you don't go back out on that field, we won't advance. Your teammates need you, son. Are you gonna let them down when we're so close to a conference championship game?"

Oh, this slimy bastard. I pointed at the tight end. "I'm telling you, something's fucked up in that knee. I'm certain. It's your career, McManus. Your decision. Ask yourself, do you want to risk the next ten years for one game? You're a talented player, brother. There will be other playoff games for you whether they're with Dallas or elsewhere. But not if you let him shoot your right knee full of drugs and tear it apart because you can't feel anything. You'll get plenty of runs at getting your ring, but you've only got one right knee."

The doctor sent Daniel a questioning look.

Several seconds passed before he finally spoke up. "If Coach Walker says he heard it pop, I believe him. I'm not playing without an MRI."

"Goddamn it!" Dick stormed out of the room, pushing past me.

"Good decision, my man. Well done."

"I agree," the doctor added, clapping him on the shoulder. "We'll get it set up for as soon as we get back to Dallas. In the meantime, I'm going to put you in a brace and I want you to stay off of it."

"Doc," I said, drawing his attention. "Darius knew about the pop. I'm guessing that's why Dick didn't let him in here. Keep that in mind, okay? I trust Darius with player health. After all, I was one of them."

He nodded. "I hear you, coach."

We lost the game thirty-one to twenty-one.

While we were shaking hands with the other team, Denver's head coach found me on the field.

"Sorry about McManus. Kid has lots of promise. You've done a great job with him."

"Thanks, Ian. And congratulations. Give Chicago hell for us." I clapped him on the shoulder intending to move on, but he didn't let my palm go.

Pulling me in, Ian lowered his voice a notch. "That offer's still good, Walker. I need experience on my side right now. Not youth." He slapped me on the back. "Have your agent call me."

After he walked off, I stood there a bit stunned as I realized something.

After losing the game with the backup tight end—

because I'd had to play hero and keep the needle out of Daniel's knee—something profound occurred to me.

Playing football in Denver was going to be my only way out of the hole my mother had dug.

I'd done the right thing in that locker room, and it was going to cost me my job. The chances of me paying my sister's tuition with no paycheck coming in were zero. I might have saved McManus from causing further damage to his knee, but there was a good chance it could cost me the woman I was in love with.

Chapter Twenty-Eight

This little piggy went to the market

Olive

Having the girls over had helped. For a little while. But eventually they had to go home, and I was left to my own devices. Sadie crawled in bed with me, and that's where we stayed. I got up to feed her and take her out and that was it.

She was faithful. By my side the entire time, head or paw or back always touching me. She listened, didn't judge, gave me kisses and her special brand of doggie hugs. She even had her own bowl of strawberry ice cream. I loved my friends, I was in love with Hayes, but as much as I wanted to share with them the intense shame of the whole ordeal, I knew all they would do was tell me to let it go. And I couldn't. That wouldn't come until I was ready to set it down.

And I just wasn't ready yet. I had to let myself feel all the things before that. The shame and anger, the fear that I would lose my business. The disappointment in myself that I was wallowing while someone else tried to keep things afloat for me. The sadness for what I'd done all those years ago and the ghosts of the pain I'd felt when they dislodged my mangled leg from the steering column to pull me from the car.

In the back of my overactive brain, I knew I wouldn't be able to heal until I'd let it run its course, so that's what I did. For several days I loved on my dog, I slept, and I ignored the outside world. I watched the Bulldogs lose their playoff game and I slept some more.

Until Johnathan came by the house.

"How many clients did we lose?"

Lips pursed, he let his eyes fall to his crossed legs. That's what I thought. "Is there anyone left?"

Uncrossing his legs, he scooted forward in the leather chair to take my hand. "Yes. So far about half have canceled their service contracts, and most of those were older, long-standing clients. About half our clients are waiting to hear what you have to say before they make any decisions. But…" He didn't finish the sentence.

"But what, Johnathan? I need to know."

"Stephany, Brian, and Aleta have turned in their notice. They don't think Russo Consulting can rebound from this and they no longer want to be associated with the company. They're afraid it will damage their reputation. Stephany said it was the fact that they felt lied to most of all. Between the three of them, they're taking a fair number of clients. I reminded them that according to their contracts, they can't poach clients if they leave, but they have a list and enough clients to start their own PR firm."

I waved it away. "They can have them. I won't fight it. If those clients don't want to be associated with Russo Consulting, then I don't want them. Any other staff?"

"Mostly, the staff wants the one thing I can't give

them. Direction from you. We all want to hear from our fearless leader. The damage is done, the buzz is no longer at its peak. But there are several high-profile clients and a number of our staff that are waiting and watching, wanting to hear what your plan is and what you have to say. A lot of clients have been in similar situations, Olive. Which is why they hired a PR firm to begin with."

I nodded. As good a job as Johnathan had done trying to keep the ship afloat, I was the captain, and it was my job to correct course. I'd been hiding here, wallowing, when I should have been doing what I did best. Planning. Working through the angles and deciding how to approach this disaster like the PR badass I was. I needed to compartmentalize and get the fuck back to work if I wanted to save my business.

Pulling the hair tie off my wrist, I gathered my messy locks in a low ponytail at my nape and perched on the edge of my couch. "The gala. How is all this affecting the gala sales?"

Johnathan shrugged. "Honestly, it hasn't slowed. I dropped the announcement about Tommy Jane and Urban Legend participating in the date auction and sales actually picked up. It's almost sold out. As far as the silent auction, we've already collected on ninety-five percent of that stuff. Nobody has backed out."

Oh, thank God. "That was a great idea. In fact, I owe you, Johnathan. You've handled this like a true public relations pro. I don't think I've been giving you enough credit. With three associates leaving, I'll definitely be looking to promote from within and you are at the top of my list."

His eyes lit. "We're sticking around, then? Not going to close up shop?"

"When have you ever known me to go down without a fight?"

He squeezed my hand. "Glad to hear you say it." A pause ensued, and I could tell he was weighing his words. "Hayes has called me several times, Olive. He's worried you're not taking his calls. I think he feels responsible for all this."

Well, of course, it wasn't Hayes's fault. "When does he get back?"

"The team plane arrives tonight at DFW."

I nodded. "Don't worry. I'll talk to him. As for the office..." I pulled my work bag off the table, produced my laptop. "...send me a list of everything you've done so far, any releases you've drafted and a list of clients we've lost along with those who you think are on the fence about leaving. I'll deal with Stephany, Brian, and Aleta first thing tomorrow morning after I'm up to speed. In the meantime, I want us to focus in on promoting the gala. Get ahold of our contacts at every news outlet and send them a list of the most eligible men and women who will be participating in the date auction. It's okay to let slip one or two of our big donations for the silent auction as well to both *DL&S* and *Big D*. Perhaps the all-expenses trip to Fiji and the numbers matching GTO from Jay's collection."

Johnathan whipped a pad of paper out of his own bag with a small smile on his lips and made notes.

"What? What's that smile about?"

"Nothing. Just glad to have the badass back."

After a shower—because I smelled like ass—I left Hayes a voicemail telling him to come by. I'd been so busy wallowing that I hadn't even acknowledged they'd lost their playoff game and their star tight end, Daniel McManus, had torn his ACL in the second quarter.

When Hayes showed up, he had dark smudges under his eyes and his hair was disheveled. It looked like he hadn't slept in days, and he didn't bring his bag in when he came to the door.

He brushed a soft kiss against my lips. "How are you?"

"Better. I've drowned my sorrows in ice cream for long enough. It's time to get my ass in gear and figure out how to save my business. I'm sorry I didn't take your calls while you were gone. I shut my phone off. Honestly, I just wanted to be alone and have my pity party for one."

He pulled me into his arms, held me tight. "I was worried about you, sweetheart. If you hadn't started seeing me, none of this would have happened. Not all those years ago, and not now."

I fisted his T-shirt against the small of his back. "No, this is not on you. You even warned me that secrets have a way of coming out. You were right. I'm starting to feel lighter about it. Like, now I realize not everything has to be perfect, you know? That it's okay to be human and make mistakes. You learn from them and move on. The standards I hold myself to sometimes are unrealistic. It's kind of freeing having everyone know I'm not perfect. That I screw up, too. Now, I just have to figure out how to save my business and hold on to my remaining clients."

He kissed my head. "I'm glad to hear that. Can we go sit down? I'm beat."

"Of course. Do you want a glass of wine?"

The sound of doggie paws padded down the hallway. Sadie must have finally heard his voice and made her way out of bed. She was a sound sleeper and she'd been sleeping more recently. I attributed it to my own lazy ass and her age.

"No, I'm good. I need to go home tonight. I've got too much to do tomorrow to stay here. Hey, girl!" Hayes got a welcome home with a wiggling rear end and kisses on his face. "Were you a good girl for Olive? Did you keep her company while I was gone?" He patted her side. "It's beginning to look like you're getting too many biscuits, baby girl."

I sat down beside them. "The ice cream this weekend didn't help, but yeah. I was thinking the same. We need to cut the treats back a bit." I patted the couch and she jumped up between us, laying her head on Hayes's leg. "I'm sorry about the game and McManus. Is he going to be okay?"

"Yeah. He's having surgery first thing in the morning, but recovery shouldn't be too bad. Used to be a torn ACL was a career killer when I was his age. But with the way treatment has advanced, he should be back next season."

"That's good at least."

"Yeah, I'm going to go check on him in the morning then I'll be tied up at headquarters all day with team shit. I'm sorry I wasn't here for you when all this went down."

I waved him away. "It's okay. I just wanted to be left alone anyway. You look like you haven't been sleeping well. Was it the game? Worrying about me?"

He leaned into my palm as I ran my fingers through his mussed hair. "And then some."

"Talk to me."

He huffed out a laugh. "My sister called. Our mother didn't pay her tuition, which is now a semester behind. Almost two. I gave that money to Sharlene to make the payment back in August and I've got no idea what she did with it. None." Leaning forward, he put his elbows on his knees. "It was nearly eighty grand."

That bitch. "Holy shit, Hayes. That's nothing to shake a stick at."

His head bobbed up and down and he looked like he had more to tell me but thought better of it. "I've got to go see her tonight, now. Find out where the money went. I'd given her six months to get her shit together, but she just forfeited that time. I'm done."

One, I can't believe she came to me and acted like Hayes hadn't given her the money. She'd likely wanted me to tell him about her visit to me so he would pay her to leave me alone. Two, I hated this for him. Hated her. Wished I could take it for him or that I'd given her a beating the moment she stepped foot in my office. Narcissists, man. I felt my jaw clench, my nostrils flare as I did my best to bring my temper down to a simmer. "What are you going to tell her?"

"That I'm finished. That if Jess needs something, she'll come straight to me from now on."

Leaning over the dog, I rubbed small circles on his back. "If there's one thing I've learned in my business, there's a lot of truth to the saying you can put lipstick on a pig, but it's still just a pig. People only change when they're ready, baby, and some never do. Some come to me genuinely wanting a better public image because they're not that person anymore—the one who ran a car off the road and was convicted of a DUI. Others come to me with no intention of ever changing—they just want someone who can hide it for them, sweep up the messes. Clean 'em up and put lipstick on the pig. Those clients always, always end up back in the mud. When that happens, sometimes it's best to slaughter the hog and fry up some bacon."

A laugh burst through Hayes's lips. "Ahh, God, Olive. I needed that laugh."

"Anytime, baby. Anytime."

Chapter Twenty-Nine

Who wants a BLT?

Hayes

I couldn't do it. I couldn't tell her about Denver's offer, not yet, when there was a slim chance I'd get to keep my job. But my mother had to be dealt with right away. Pulling open the door to Sharlene's building after I left Olive's place, I nodded at the concierge and took the elevator up to the thirty-second floor as a wave of exhaustion poured over me. I was weary, and worried, and at the end of my rope trying to juggle everything and not drop the balls.

When I tapped on her apartment door, nobody answered, but I could hear people inside. I whipped out my key and pushed it into the lock, popping the door open with a soft *snick*.

"Hey, what the hell, man? How'd you—"

Wrangler was tall, somewhat muscular, and all-around douchy with his *Urban Cowboy* vibe. I held up my key. "Where's my mother?"

"Oh." He stuck out a hand. "You're Hayes. I'm Wrangler. I'm your mom's—"

"Save it. Where is she?" I instantly didn't like him, and his face was asking to be punched.

Sharlene came into the living room, lips pinched, ire on her face. Six months I hadn't seen my own mother—who lived in the same city as me—and she was annoyed she had to look at me.

The feeling is mutual, Mom.

She wasn't a big woman. Five foot four. Thin. The hair that brushed her shoulders was the same chestnut brown as my sister's. But she had bright blue eyes the same color as mine. She looked like she'd lost weight since I'd seen her last, and there were dark smudges under her eyes she'd tried to hide with makeup.

"Hayes. We were just leaving. You should have called." Her cigarette-worn voice made the hair on my neck stand up.

"Tough shit. We need to talk." I met her determined gaze with my own resolve.

"Don't take that tone with me," she snapped, but I saw the moment she resigned herself to dealing with me.

"Wrangler, why don't you wait downstairs." As soon as the door shut behind him, she started. "You can't just drop in unannounced. I have a life."

"Oh, yes I can. I paid the rent."

She turned hard eyes on me. "I said don't you talk to me that way. Don't think you're too big for me to pop in the mouth, Hayes Walker."

The thought made me flinch, but I wasn't a boy anymore. There was nothing left for her to hurt me with.

"Now, what do you want?"

I couldn't look at her. Instead, I peered out of the floor-to-ceiling windows outlining the city lights.

"You never paid Jessica's tuition for last semester. Where's the money I gave you?"

She rolled her eyes, turned away.

"No, Sharlene." I used a tone that brooked no argument. "Don't walk away from me. Tell me where the money went."

She flipped around, pointing a finger at me like she was wielding a broadsword. "None of your business."

Damn, this woman. "That money was for my sister's tuition. Well, now you're screwed, Mom. Because I have no more money to give you. It's gone. No more allowance, no more car or apartment. No more secret savings you sponged off your son."

"Fine! Wrangler, he got in debt with some bad people. I cleaned out my savings, but it wasn't enough."

"Jesus." I ran a hand through my hair. "Never in my life... You've done some stupid stuff, but taking Jess's tuition money to help a boyfriend? Draining me is one thing, but you and I..." I gestured between us. "We had an unspoken agreement. You leave Jess alone and focus on me. You broke that."

"I'm not standing here while you insult me. Wrangler ran into some trouble, and I helped him out, that's that. I planned on paying Jess's tuition when he paid me back, but he's not been lucky at the tables." She picked a handbag up from her glass coffee table, stood there like I was eating into her manicure time.

"The tables," I whispered letting my head drop forward to stare at the floor. "I'm done. Paying for your lifestyle and my father's sins. As of now, you're cut off."

"Excuse me?" Fury lit in her eyes that I flat-out ignored.

"Jess's bills will come straight to me. And I suggest you start looking for another place to live or figure out a way to pay your rent on your own. I'm canceling this lease. I'm also canceling the lease on your car, and no more allowance for living expenses."

Her eyes went wide, glassy. "I always knew you'd turn out like your father. When I told him I was pregnant, he said he'd take care of me, then he ran out the first chance he got. Go on, then, walk out on me like he did."

"You know, all I ever wanted from you was your approval, or for you to acknowledge that I was more than your ticket out of that Oklahoma trailer park. Now, all I have to show for my career are bad fucking knees." I shook my head. "After I get Jessica's tuition caught up, there will be nothing left. I can't give you what I don't have."

Striding across the room, she got in my face. "How am I supposed to live, Hayes? On my feet waiting tables, or slinging drinks at a roadhouse at my age? If I hadn't pushed you the way I did, you wouldn't have a ring to your name. Hell, you'd probably be an outlaw like your father, doing a stint for one thing or another.

"All you had to do was play football, son. Something you were already good at, already enjoyed, and I made damn sure to clear your path of anything that might stop that. I deserved to share in your success." She pointed a finger at me. "I'm responsible for that success, after all."

I felt my jaw crack as I ground my teeth together. I don't know if it was because I had family and friends here that I knew loved me, but it all clicked. Sharlene had never cared about me. She probably never would. She resented me because she thought I'd ruined her life. I was nothing to her before football came along, and now that I couldn't write her checks, I'd be nothing to her again.

Olive was right. It was time to slaughter the hog.

"I have a ring to my name because of my own blood, sweat, and tears. I worked my ass off for it, not because of you, but despite you. I will not let you take that away from me and make it your own.

"But just to be clear, because you think I owe you for the years of abuse that made me the fucked-up man standing in front of you, consider my debt fully paid, Mom."

She switched tactics, turned on the crocodile tears. Or maybe they were real because she finally realized I wasn't going to cave. "And just what am I supposed to do now?"

I made for the open door. "I suggest you start selling your Birkens."

Pausing at the door frame, I turned. "I truly hope you get your shit together and don't end up back in the trailer park, Sharlene. I won't be your ATM anymore, but if you decide you'd like to have a son instead, I'm around."

I tapped the door frame and disappeared down the hall.

The following day, I checked on Daniel. He'd come through his surgery with flying colors. The doctor was giving him six to eight months before he was field-ready. After that, I went to the team meetings and waited for the axe to fall, but it didn't. Not right away.

In true Dick Head fashion, the general manager waited until Friday afternoon to fire me.

Luckily, Olive was too busy with her own shitshow to be overly concerned with the amount of time she and I weren't spending together since the Bulldogs season ended in January. I still hadn't told her I'd gotten fired. Only Brody knew. With the gala so close, and her business struggling, I didn't want to add to her stress.

So, yeah. I'd been avoiding her like the great big pussy I was.

Because I was going to have to tell her that I had no choice but to take the offer from Denver.

Olive knew something was off, though. When she did ask me over, I made excuses. When we were together, she'd asked if I was okay, or if something was bothering me. She'd even told me I was a bit distant. When I told her it was nothing, she took me at my word and let me have my space.

But now football season was over, the big game had been played, the world champions crowned, and it wasn't Denver—they'd gotten knocked out by Chicago.

The second Saturday of February was upon us, and tonight was about the Love for the Unlovabulls Charity Gala and watching my girl shine. I was showered, trimmed, styled, and had on my tux. Tonight was for dancing and drinking, fundraising and toasts. Tonight was for my girls. Both the four-legged and two. I would freeze-frame each one of Olive's laughs into my brain, each of her smiles and sultry looks, each time she took command of whatever hiccup arose throughout the night, just in case it was the last time.

She was still struggling with how to save her firm, but it was my mission to help her forget about the future and the past, and live in the moment with me, tonight, and maybe, just maybe, tomorrow…she'd agree to come with me.

It was my best play.

It was my only play.

Chapter Thirty

Kick ass and take names

Olive

I knew how to save Russo Consulting, I'd developed my plan, and it was time to execute. The gala would be packed with celebrities and socialites, athletes and musicians, actors and personalities. I had my whole business riding on tonight, the connections I could make, and I'd even spoken with Lily and Brody, who had zero issue with me chatting up potential clients.

Good friends, those two.

I'd been able to hold on to the rest of my clients after I went back to work. It wasn't nearly as hard as I thought it would be. It came to me naturally during the first conversation I'd had with my firm's first client: he'd been the enforcer for a professional hockey team with a penchant for bar brawls before he came to me. Now, he was a network commentator.

"It doesn't look good, Olive," he'd said.

"No, it doesn't, Liam, and I'm not going to try to make excuses. I'm also not going to try and sell you. You know damn well what I'm capable of."

"I get that, but I worked hard to clean up my image and my life only to find out that you're not the person I thought you were."

"None of us are, Liam. Not a single person," I'd said with a sigh. "I mold and shape, create opportunities for clients to reflect the person they want to be or have become. Do you think I'm good at that because I was squeaky clean, or do you think I'm good because I understood your situation on a visceral level?"

I'd leaned forward, elbows on my desk. "We all fuck up, buddy. Every one of us. Including me. That's why you should stay with me. Because I've been there. I know what it's like to have secrets, or be ashamed, or wish people saw me differently. But, if you think my expertise is no longer a good fit for your brand, I'll understand." I'd put a hand to God. "No hard feelings. God bless."

I'd been there. I'd made the mistakes many of my clients had made, and that was going to save my business. I'd had only one other client decide to leave after hearing me out, and it wasn't Liam Dansworth. Tonight, I'd pitch some of the biggest names in Dallas–Fort Worth and replace the ones who'd left.

After perfecting the wing on my eyeliner, I took my time applying my signature red lip. First to arrive and last to leave, I'd booked a room at The Statler for Hayes and I. Sadie would be staying with his neighbors for the night. I loved that man something fierce. It was visceral, like the realization of why I was good at my job. He made butterflies swim in my stomach at his every touch, but something was off lately.

Hayes had been withdrawn, the light in his eyes a

little dull. I intended on getting it out of him before the night was over, even if it required sexual favors.

Smoothing the midnight-black shantung of my solid-colored ball gown, I took a last check in the mirror. It was stunning. Spaghetti straps. Triangle-cut cups that connected to the A-line plunged to the waist in between. A full, floor-length skirt was slit to the crease where thigh met hip. Serious Old Hollywood glamour. Red peep-toe Loubous under my arm with my matching clutch, I stuck my feet in my bunny slippers and went down to the ballroom to make sure everything was coming together.

"Oh. My. God."

I turned at Lily's voice as my party planner put the finishing touches on oversized red centerpieces.

"This is stunning, Olive! Absolutely stunning!"

Large gold palm trees lined walls covered in a black and white harlequin material. Tables were set with gold bamboo-style chairs, black tablecloths with white toppers and gold place settings. Each table's centerpiece was an oversized frosted martini glass overflowing with scarlet red blooms that wound around the stem and trickled onto the table. The bartenders were 1950s gangsters in black shirts with white suspenders and black fedoras. The waitstaff wore white waistcoats and pristine gloves with 1950s hairstyles. Crystal chandeliers floated above a black and white checkerboard dance floor next to the stage where the big band was setting up.

It had even exceeded my expectations, and those were high. "Yeah. The planner really outdid himself. This fundraiser is going to be the talk of the town for the rest of the year. Attendees will be clamoring to get tickets to next year's gala before this one is even in the books."

She slipped a hand around my waist. "I don't know how to thank you for all this."

"You don't have to. That's what friends are for." I squeezed her tight. "Besides, I should be thanking you. This gala may very well save my business."

"You don't have to. That's what friends are for." She nudged me with a shoulder, and I couldn't help the laugh.

"Where's Gina? I thought she was coming with you guys. And Brody?"

"Brody's parking. Gina's bringing a date."

My eyes widened. "A date?"

She nodded. "That paid for their plates."

"Holy shit, Olive! You look smokin' hot!" Brody burst into the room with two garment bags slung over his back and a fedora on his head. "I mean, my fiancée will always be the prettiest girl in the room, but you're comin' in a close second in that dress, girl." He kissed my temple. "Hayes here yet?"

"Thanks, and no. He was changing before he came."

Brody hip checked his fiancée. "Did you tell her who Gina is bringing?"

Lily rolled her eyes. "You do it. You've been dying to anyway."

Brody's face turned bright with glee. "Jensen!"

I slapped his chest, playing it up. "Get out! Dead ass?"

"Yup!" He squeed like a teenage girl.

"Huh." I grinned. It was impossible not to love the man.

"Hey, where can I put this stuff?"

I fished in my clutch and pulled out my key card. "Here, y'all can use my room to change. But stay out of the bed. I have plans for that later that involve Hayes and a finger thing."

It took a second, but Brody's face changed, a line forming between his brows.

"What's with the face?"

"Nothing." He snapped out of it. "Just... TMI. Come along, dahling. We must get changed." He skipped off. Literally.

Lil sighed. "He's a doofus, but he's my doofus and I love him." She went after him.

"Didn't you say that about Mack once?"

"More than likely."

I was still smiling after them when the familiar hand wound around my waist. "Hey, beautiful."

I turned in his arms. "Hellooomygod, look at you!"

Christ, he was hot. All black-on-black tux laid open at the neck, ink peeking out from his cuffs and collar.

He whistled low and long. "No, look at you, sweetheart. That dress is a beatdown waiting to happen."

I arched a brow. "Why would you say that?"

"Because at some point tonight, some drunk rich fucker is going to hit on you and I'm gonna have to throw hands. So help me God, if Tommy Jane so much as casts a flirty glance at you—"

"Shhh, baby." I put a finger on his lips as I slid a hand inside his jacket and around to his ass to give it a squeeze. "I only have eyes for you."

"I'm particularly fond of the bunny slippers."

"I thought you would be. Speaking of, what time is it?"

Hayes fished his phone out. "Six thirty."

The band choose that moment to start warming up. In another twenty minutes the early birds would start trickling in, though things weren't supposed to get rolling until seven o'clock.

"Olive?"

I turned to see my party planner. "Yes?"

"Sorry to interrupt, but the step and repeat is ready to go, and the photographers are getting antsy for people to show. They were wondering if they could get you out for photos now?"

"Sure. Give me just a minute. I'll be right there."

Holding on to Hayes's bicep, I slipped my bunny slippers off and my peep-toes on.

"How far does that slit go up, anyway?"

My lips curved as I buckled the strap on my shoe. When I stood back up, I dragged my hands over my leg all the way to my hip bone. "About there."

"Niiice. Dance with me, before you have to go out there and pose for the cameras. One dance before anyone else gets here while the room is all ours."

"Okaaay," I drawled as he tugged me to the floor.

Hayes turned to the stage. "Say, you guys know 'Wonderful Tonight'?"

The band started to play, and Hayes wrapped his arms around me.

I rested my head on his shoulder. "This was our song."

"Mmhmm. Remember when we heard it?"

I nodded. "After the frat party. We were in your car after making out under the stars. You took me home and this was playing on the car radio when you kissed me good-night."

"I was gone for you right then, Olive Russo. Totally in love with you from that night on."

"I was slower to come around to it. But, yeah, I think I knew it, too."

He chuckled. "Of course, you were. You wouldn't be the girl I fell for if you didn't take some time to process things first."

I kissed him. "You wouldn't be the guy I fell for if you didn't think it was love at first sight."

"What a pair we are. Opposites attract, I guess. Yin and yang. Impulsive and meticulous. The rich girl and poor boy."

"The last one doesn't apply anymore."

Hayes stiffened. "I, ah… I need to talk to you about something—"

"Olive, the photographers?" came the voice across the room.

"Okay," I called over my shoulder before turning to Hayes. "Come with me for photos? We can talk tomorrow, and you can tell me whatever it is, why you've been a little distant?" I wasn't quite sure what had been going on with Hayes, lately. It wasn't like him to pull back instead of charging forward. But I wasn't worried. Together, we could get through anything.

Chapter Thirty-One

The Principle of Centrifugal Force

Hayes

Letting Olive go, I ran a hand over my beard, sucked my bottom lip between my teeth and bit. Nothing got by her. She'd just been giving me time to work through whatever it was she thought was bothering me because that's what she would've needed. Truthfully, I'd been lucky the Bulldogs wanted it kept quiet until they could slide someone new into the coach's position. They wouldn't have wanted to explain I'd been fired because I refused to let them shoot an injured player full of enough drugs to medicate a horse.

I'd been about to tell Olive everything standing right here.

Instead, I pitched her bunny slippers around the corner of the stage, looped her arm through mine, and put on the easy smile I'd gotten so good at faking for all these years. "Okay, sweetheart. Let's go."

Olive worked her magic all night. Floating around the room from person to person with ease and grace.

The woman was far too good for me. But I'd take it and take her with me if she'd let me.

The night hadn't all gone off perfectly. We ran out of whiskey. A couple got into a loud argument in the lobby, and the staff complained that a drunk woman had scratched up the hood of one of the classic cars they kept parked outside, but the only real drama went down in private. When one Michael Seaton had arrived at the party with the chick who had sold the pictures of me and Olive to *DL&S*, a very drunk Amanda Baker-Seaton had knocked the shit out of her in the bathroom.

Lily waved me over frantically, ushered me in to help get the soon-to-be former Mrs. Seaton under control and out the back way so she wouldn't be photographed. When she'd seen Olive, she'd used both hands and feet, à la a cartoon character, braced against the doorway.

Looking Olive dead in the eyes, in a drunken slur, she said, "This is your fault. If you hadn't put that harlot in my husband's sights, I wouldn't be humiliated and filing for divorce. That's why I sent your record to the reporter at *Big D*. My daddy is a higher-ranking judge than your daddy. Nanny nanny. And that's the only reason I bought a ticket to this thing. So I could punch her and tell you off!"

Olive's face turned a shade of plum I'd never seen before and I'm fairly sure I saw steam come out of her ears. Mrs. Seaton was damn lucky Olive didn't haul off and lay her out. That's when Lily piped up. "Get her the fuck out of here before I hit her myself. And thank you for the donation. Twunt."

Jesus. I was beginning to learn that professional football wasn't nearly as brutal a sport as Dallas society. They were fucking merciless.

But Olive was a vision working that room. Speaking with one guest after the next effortlessly, pretending that the weight of the world wasn't on her shoulders. When her eyes landed on someone new, that person immediately stood a bit taller, gravitated in Olive's direction as if pulled by a magnet. That's how she was, she drew people in and didn't let them go.

When the rest of the thousand-dollar high heels had been discarded under tables and the fedoras abandoned to the tabletops, Olive still carried herself like her feet never tired and her dress never creased.

We danced, everybody danced. We raised money for a hell of a cause. No lot left unauctioned, no date gone without bid. I would guess that we'd raised enough money for the Unlovabulls that this gala would be the only fundraiser the rescue would need the following year.

I watched Brody swing Lily around the floor one last time while the band played "One for My Baby" and the singer crooned. Guests filtered out long after Gina and Jensen snuck out the back door, happy and tired with much lighter pockets than when they came.

Jacket discarded and shirtsleeves rolled up, finally I felt that familiar palm slide around my waist to rest on my abs, her chin on my back.

"They look happy. Content."

"Yeah, they do. I'm glad for them."

"I'm glad for us," she said with a kiss on my neck. "Take me upstairs, handsome, and peel me out of this dress. I think you'll like what's underneath."

Turning my head, I arched an eyebrow over my shoulder. She was a little shorter than she had been earlier in the night. "I will, will I? Need a lift?"

"Mmm, my feet would like that."

I bent my knees as she gathered her dress behind her legs then hopped up on my back. "At your service, sweetheart."

"Oh, bunny slippers."

We waved at Brody and Lily, I grabbed the bunny slippers, and we went upstairs. As much as I wanted to peel her out of that dress just like she'd asked, I wouldn't.

I still had cards left to play. "Sweetheart, there are things I need to tell you that won't be easy."

She sat on the edge of the bed and rubbed her feet. "What's going on?"

Sitting next to her, I pulled them into my lap and set to work on them, but I couldn't look at her. "The Bull-dogs let me go."

"What? Why?" Her voice was a little higher than normal.

"Officially, I'm not a good fit for the team. Reality is during the playoff game with Denver when McManus took that hit next to the sideline, I heard his knee pop. They wanted to give him the needle, but I convinced him to refuse it. Then we lost, and some of that was be-cause his backup played sloppy football."

I felt her hand on my cheek. "Hayes, I'm so sorry. You did the right thing. You probably just extended his football career several years because you kept the needle out of his leg. You shouldn't beat yourself up over that."

I shook my head. "I'm… I did, but it's set off an ava-lanche in my life." God, I didn't want to tell her this. The shame churned in my gut. "I told you about Jess call-ing me, about my mom not paying her tuition. What I didn't say was I'm very nearly broke. I was foolish with my money, didn't plan, didn't save, gave way too much of it to a woman who seemed to always need more. God, I hate saying this to you. Now, I'm in a position where I can't pay Jess's tuition without my coach's salary." When I finally met her eyes, I saw what I'd been avoiding all week.

Shock. Sympathy. Pity. It killed a little part of my soul. A lump formed in my throat that I nearly choked on. As bad as I felt in that moment, it was about to get worse.

Olive

I felt horrible for him. He was broke, and he knew he wasn't blameless, but I knew his mother was the one to suck him dry. So I said exactly the wrong thing to a beautiful man with very wounded pride. "Do you need money?"

"No." He said it softly.

I kept right on rattling. "I can help you, Hayes. We can get you moved into my place, and I can give you enough to cover Jess's tuition."

"No." This time his voice was a little more forceful. But all I wanted to do was fix it for him, solve his problem, because that's who I was.

"I'm sure you won't have an issue getting on with a college team around here if that's what you want. You could even pay me back if it would make you feel better about it. Call it a loan. Tell me how I can help, Hayes. I just want to help."

The wrinkle between his eyes appeared and he stood

to pace. "Damn it. I said no. I don't need your pity, Olive. Or your charity."

The way he snapped at me set my eyes wide. "That's not what I meant at all."

Falling into the chair in front of me, he put his elbows on his knees and dropped his head. "I know. You just want to help, but you can't fix this for me. I have to do that myself."

"Talk to Jess, Hayes. She's not like your mother. Maybe it's time she takes out student loans or looks into financial aid, maybe a scholarship or two. She's reasonable."

"No. I have a solution, and Jess doesn't need to know about any of this. She needs to focus on school, not how to pay for it."

That made me hesitate. "She doesn't know, does she. That the money is gone. Why don't you tell her? I'm sure she wouldn't want you to continue to pay for her schooling if she knew you were struggling. Why can't she pay her own way?"

"Because." His voice was getting louder. "I don't want her to."

So was mine. "Why, Hayes?"

Still, he didn't lift his head to look at me. "Because it's my fucking job to take care of my family. To protect my sister, and I will goddamned do my job!"

Now I was full-on upset I wasn't getting through to him. "Even though your sister is a grown woman who is fully capable of taking care of herself, tell me, how do you propose doing that?"

When he finally brought his head up, his eyes were beyond sad, defeat plain on his face, and I knew what he was planning to do.

"Oh." My heart immediately jumped into my throat as my stomach rolled. He needed to fucking say it. "Say it, Hayes. Have the balls to say it to my face this time."

The silence in the suite grew deafening as a minute ticked by, then two. And that was that. He'd made his choice, and it wasn't me. His family—the family that drained him—would always come first. "Where?"

"Denver. It's just for one year. I love you, Olive. But you have to understand, this is who I am." He met my eyes and I saw the waterline against the blue that matched my own.

"No. This is what you do. Not who you are. But apparently the man you are now is stronger than the desire to become the man you want to be. I don't need that in my life. I love you, too, Hayes. But you see only what's right in front of you and knee-jerk to it. Have you already told Denver?"

He nodded. His voice came out raw, choked. "I fly out day after tomorrow for clearance and to sign the contract. Aaron negotiated a small signing bonus. That's how I'm covering Jess's tuition."

Tears fell down my cheeks. Maybe it was selfish, but I wanted him to see my pain. My words sounded tortured to my own ears. "You didn't even talk to me. You just made another snap decision that affects all these lives around you, and you didn't even think to talk to me." I crossed my arms over my chest, tried to fight the tears filling my eyes. *How can he do this to me? Again.*

My knees gave and I dropped to sit on the bed.

Rising from the chair, he came to stand in front of me. "Come with me, Olive."

I looked up. "What?"

"Come with me to Denver. You and Sadie. When the year is over, we can move back."

I knew he could see the horror on my face by the look of disappointment on his. "How can you ask me that? I have a business here, people I love, a home and friends. You think I'm just going to walk away from all that because I've hit a rough patch? So you can continue to pay a grown woman's tuition by playing a sport you don't really want to do anymore?"

Hands in his pockets, he stared at the floor, refusing to look at me, refusing to answer.

"Do you even hear how ridiculous that sounds, Hayes? *Olive, pick up your life, give up on the business you've built, and move with me so that I can take care of my able-bodied baby sister because I have a hero complex and an abusive witch of a mother.*"

"Yes, but I'm asking anyway because I can't not ask. I love you too much not to try. Please. Come with me." He offered me a hand.

I shook my head, sniffed back the tears. "No, Hayes. And that's not why you're asking at all. You're asking because you're still stuck in a loop where you have to rescue your family to feel worthy of love, and you're looking for the easy way out so you don't have to make the really hard choices. You believe that cutting your mother off was the last big step. The piece that means you've broken free. When the truth is, this test is much harder because it's your sister."

"What would you have me do, Olive?" His voice was so soft, so tortured as a fat tear ran down his cheek. "I can't choose between you and her. It's fucking impossible and unfair to ask." Turning away, he walked to the window to stare out into the city at night. Seconds, minutes, maybe hours ticked by before he broke the silence. "How am I supposed to do that, huh? Tell me what I'm supposed to do here. No matter what I do, I'm going to let somebody down."

"Hayes, look at me." Finally, he turned. I could see he was wrecked, but so was I. "Stop it. You don't get to pretend you don't have a choice. You always have a choice. Given that we're here, arguing, and Jess has no idea any of this is going on because you've sheltered her from everything her whole life, I'm inclined to think you've made that choice."

Hayes's lips thinned, his jaw clenched as shook his head and tugged on his beard as if he was damned if he did, and damned if he didn't. But that was bullshit.

"I will not play second fiddle to your mother or your sister over and over again, and you've had ample opportunity to show me that I'm just as important to you as they are. But that's not even the real decision you should be making here. This was never about choosing between me and your family, Hayes. The only way you get off the hamster wheel is by choosing between your family and *you*. You have to choose your own happiness. You've got to put yourself first for a change. I thought we could do this together, break that cycle you're stuck in, together, but I was wrong. It has to be all you. And as much as I wish you could do it, you're not ready for that." I glanced down at my lap.

Coming to stand in front of me, Hayes tipped my chin up. "Olive, don't do this. Please. I won't put them ahead of you. This is the last time, I—"

I met his eyes and let him see all the pain, naked and intense. "Just stop, Hayes. Don't make promises you won't keep. And I know you can't keep it. Because if you can't choose to make your happiness a priority, how could I ever believe that you would choose us?"

"Olive…"

Balling my fists in my dress, I tried to steady my voice. "You should go."

He nodded. "You keep Sadie. She'll have a better life with you. More stable. I'll say goodbye tonight. You can pick her up tomorrow from my neighbor." He slid his hands against my cheeks, turned my face to his. "I love you, Olive. More than anything. I always will."

With that, he placed a kiss against my lips. I tasted salt and sadness. Regret and heartbreak. Frustration and so much despair. All without knowing which emotions belonged to whom. I was absolutely heartsick as he let his hands fall away and I watched his back disappear through the door.

I thought I'd been in a dark place when my business faltered. Tonight, I'd saved it. I'd set up meetings with some of the most prominent figures in the city. But I felt no joy.

I only felt tired. Hopeless.

Hope, happiness, contentment, love—some of the cruelest fucking emotions the human psyche could experience. Why? Because they led to sharing your heart. The result? You lost control of it. I'd bottled those emotions once. Buried them deep down only to have Hayes dredge them back up.

It was time to do it again.

It was time for me to take back control.

Chapter Thirty-Two

Ruminate on that shit, Karen

Hayes

Brody and I thumped the ground as we padded along in comfortable silence. It was a new path. One he'd chosen. I'd told him everything. He'd called me a stupid motherfucker then pulled me in for a bro hug.

The air was crisp, but the sun was shining, and I had a plane to catch in four hours.

To sign my contract.

To give up everything I loved. For money. The thought turned my stomach. Olive had every right to say the things she'd said to me. It was college all over again. Perpetuating a cycle that I started because of my mother, and that I was passing on to my sister. I did have a fucking hero complex, but I didn't understand: why was the compulsion so strong to take care of someone who was essentially an adult?

"Am I doing the right thing?"

Brody sucked in a breath. "Only you can decide that."

"This is the last time. Next year, Jess will be a resident. She'll have a salary. My mom is out of the picture now, too. I'll be able to stash a little and live comfortably. Even move back here to Dallas."

Brody huffed, pulled up to a stop, sticking a finger in my chest. "All right, I'm sick of this shit. I'm about to drop some hard truth on you so feel free to punch me when I'm done, but you're going to listen now."

He rested a hand on his hip, looked me dead in the eyes. "Yes, you have a hero complex. Yes, your mom fucked you up, but you're not the first and you won't be the last to have a shitty childhood. Losing your position screwed with you, and I know losing the coaching job is doing a number on your head, too. But you are more than football. I think you need to hear that. You're going to lose Olive because you're scared of changing, not because of money or football. You're scared of letting your sister stand on her own, too, and that makes you as chickenshit a motherfucker as I've ever seen, Karen.

"Olive is the best thing to ever happen to you, bro. You see who you want to be when you're with her, and you're going to shelve that shit so you can play Superman to someone who doesn't really need it. Olive sure as shit can't fix you or be the Magic 8 Ball to all your problems. You have to do the work on your own. Trust me, I know. But the changes you made when you started seeing her? They were for the better. You're about to ruin the best thing you've got going for you by getting on that plane, because I guarantee Olive Russo will not be giving you a third chance in a year or two. This is it. It's the only one you're gonna get. And you're fucking it all up." He poked me in the chest. Again.

"Hey! Are you guys who we think you are?"

We both turned to see who yelled. There were three high school–age boys in pads on the practice field next to the trail that looked like they were about to get in deep shit with their coach.

Brody slapped my chest with the back of his hand. "Now, ruminate on that shit. Hey, let's go crash their practice."

"Shit. Okay." We jogged over to join them.

Coach wandered up to us, shook our hands. "This will get them fired up," he said.

"Mind if we watch for a bit?" I asked.

"Not at all."

The boys lined up, running blocking drills, but I could see exactly why everyone was breaking 58's tackles. "Hey, 58!" I waved him over and caught Brody's grin out of the corner of my eye. I knew he was right. I knew what I needed to do. And I knew I couldn't get on that plane. "Just...stop smiling. Smug asshole."

As soon as we were done goofing around with the high school team, I needed to make a few phone calls: the athletic director at UNT, Denver's general manager. My agent. But first I needed to call Jess.

It was time to break the cycle for good. Brody was right. I was tired of carrying the weight. Olive couldn't fix what was wrong with me. I had to fix that myself, but I could do it with her by my side. If she'd have me. If she could forgive me. I was hardwired to gravitate to whoever I thought needed me most in the moment. Olive was such a strong woman, so smart and capable, such a fighter who had her shit together, that I never prioritized her as one of the people who needed me.

Or maybe she didn't need me at all. She wanted me. She chose me. When she didn't need anybody or anything, the woman chose me. And I'd thrown it in her face because she didn't make me feel like a hero?

Yeah, okay. I needed to find a good therapist. No shame in that. I needed help to unpack my baggage like lots of people did. I'd maybe try Brody's guy, or the one Lily saw.

Because it was time to stop looking for the easiest way to handle the situation and start putting in the work.

Olive said she wasn't a quitter. I wasn't either.

Chapter Thirty-Three

Hurricanes and shit

Olive

I was tired, cried out, and basically a walking zombie. Sleep escaped me. When I closed my eyes, I saw Hayes. Heartsick was definitely a thing. All I wanted to do was stay in bed with Sadie and cuddle as I drifted in and out of sleep and isolated myself from the world.

But I had a business to run and potential new clients to meet with. Covering my raccoon eyes with makeup, I pulled my hair back and picked something out of the closet that wouldn't make me look too…puffy-eyed and bloated from ice cream? Loose green pantsuit it was, and after the previous night's dancing marathon, I opted for flats. Packing up my bag, I called for Sadie, who still wasn't out of bed. She wasn't a morning doggie at all.

Honestly, I was thankful Hayes's neighbor had agreed to drop my sweet girl off. I didn't want to run into Hayes if I didn't have to. "Sadie, let's go, lazybones! Time to go to work!"

Still, she didn't come, and I walked back to the bedroom to get her. Eyes open, chin on the bed, she had an odd set to her ears. "Honey? Are you okay?"

I sat down, petted her noggin and she lifted it to nuzzle into my hand, but when I called her off the bed again, she tried to stand and wobbled before lying back down.

My first call was to Staci, Hayes's neighbor. "She seemed fine last night. Calm. Though now that you mention it, she lay on her bed a lot, didn't eat much of her dinner, but I thought it was because she missed you guys."

My second call was to Gina. "What color are her gums?"

I lifted Sadie's lip. "They're definitely a little pale."

"Any weight gain?"

"Yes. Hayes and I were talking about that a while back. Her tummy is rounding out a bit. We thought she was getting too many treats."

"Dammit. Yes. Bring her over right away. I'll fit her in."

Thank God I was "a big ol' farm girl" because Sadie had a hard time standing up on the bed. As gently as possible, I picked her up, carried her out to my SUV, and slid her into the back seat with her favorite blanket and ball. She whined a bit. "Shh. It's going to be okay, sweet pea. Gina's going to fix you up in no time." I smiled at her with tears in my eyes. Sadie was nine or ten at least. This couldn't be a good sign.

I got to Gina's office in record time. Me, the woman who didn't speed, because car crashes would do that to a person. A vet tech helped me get my girl out of the car and into the clinic, straight back to an exam room where Gina was waiting for us.

"Hey, beautiful girl! I hear you're not feeling well." Sadie lay on the table, nub tail twitching and head raised at Gina's voice, but she made no move to get up.

The fear welled in my gut like a fucking balloon getting too close to a needle. "What do you think's going on?"

Gina ran her hands over her belly, listened to her heart, lungs, the sounds in her abdomen. She checked Sadie's gums. "Her blood pressure is low."

"But why?"

"She's developed a large mass on her spleen I can feel when I palpitate her abdomen. I believe the mass may be bleeding. It's also what the symptoms point to. I need to get her into ultrasound right away to determine if we can remove it. That okay with you? I'll give her some light sedation, and I'll need to start an IV. If it's operable, we'll need to get it out quickly."

What the hell was a mass doing on her spleen? "I... What? How did this happen?"

Gina stopped, looked away from Sadie and into my eyes. It wasn't the face of Dr. Avalos. It was my friend, Gina. "The symptoms are often subtle until it gets to this stage. It isn't something you did or missed. It just is. Dogs are more susceptible to these masses than humans are."

"Is this cancer? Does she have cancer?"

"I don't know that yet. I'm going to draw blood and look for indicators. But I have to get her into ultrasound to confirm the mass size and whether or not it's ruptured." She looked over her shoulder, giving directions to the vet tech before turning back to me. "We're going to take this one step at a time, Olive. Give your girl some pets before we take her back, then call Hayes and loop him in. Okay?"

I nodded, kissed Sadie's snout. "You be a good girl for Auntie Gina. Okay? Such a strong girl you are. I love you, my sweet pea." Standing, I wiped away the tears. "Okay. Go. Save my girl."

"I'll do everything in my power." Gina gave me a quick hug, then slipped out with the tech and my baby girl on a gurney.

I was beside myself. How could this happen? When it rained it fucking turned into a goddamn hurricane, didn't it. I had no idea what to do with myself. I felt powerless, completely without control, and there was only one person I wanted to be with. One set of arms I wanted to feel wrapped around me. Yet, if I called him, I'd get exactly that. And then he'd leave again. If he wasn't already gone. I understood why he'd chosen to give me Sadie. It was a truly unselfish choice. He'd have had to board her for away games, he'd be constantly gone for practices, and I wouldn't be there to back him up.

But I knew how much he loved her. He did what was best for her like he did for his sister, by sacrificing his own happiness. Unfortunately, he never seemed to save any of that for himself or for us. Or better yet, not sacrifice at all. He wasn't selfish. He was impulsive and he had a deep-seated need to rescue those he didn't believe could care for themselves. In a way, it was a backhanded compliment. Hayes knew I was strong and didn't need to be rescued.

I'd never asked anyone to be my knight in shining armor. I'd asked for a fucking broadsword instead. Hayes needed to feel both needed and acknowledged for more than football. I needed to feel both in control and like what we had mattered to him.

Jesus, we were both so broken. Some of the breaking we'd done alone, some together, and some was the fault of our families. But Hayes deserved the opportunity to be here if things didn't go well for Sadie. I had to give him that. He loved her as much as I did. She was his dog, too.

Stepping outside the building, I dialed his number.

It went to voicemail. "Hayes, I'm at Gina's clinic with Sadie. She was acting a little off this morning, so I called Gina and brought her in. Gina said our girl has a mass on her spleen, and she believes it's started bleeding into her abdomen. She's taken Sadie back for an ultrasound and then straight into surgery—if it's operable, that is. Or at least that's how I've told Gina to proceed. If you haven't left yet and you want to come to the clinic… Well, I know you love Sadie, and I could sure use someone to hold my hand right about now. Okay. Bye."

With a deep breath, I went back inside and waited to hear something.

Chapter Thirty-Four

When Basset Hounds Attack

Hayes

"Why are you waiting until just now to tell me this, Hayes Walker! You've protected me my whole life, sheltered me from our raging bitch of a mother, and sent me off to college with a silver spoon in my mouth, and I never asked for any of it! How could you let her do this! I never, never, never would have taken one damn penny if I knew you were in this kind of financial trouble."

I pulled the phone away from my ear. My sister had the same voice as my mother, just less smoke damaged. "Yeah. Jess, I'ma need you to bring that down a bit. The neighbor's dogs are starting to howl."

"I'm pissed off!"

"I can tell. I'm sorry I can't afford to cover tuition for the new semester. I can help you cover the back tuition, though."

"No, asshole! I'm pissed at Mom, and at myself for every time I came to you when I needed money. I can take out a goddamned loan—that's what everyone else does, for Christ's sake." I could practically see her waving her arms around in a huff. "Besides, I have stellar fucking credit thanks to your overly generous big-ass self."

"Yeah, I've found something here in Dallas that I just… I know I'll never find it again. I have a family here, Jess. Not just Olive, but the rescue and Sadie. Brody and Lily and the rest of the crew. It's a—"

"It's a home."

"Yeah."

"The one we never had beyond each other."

I nodded even though she couldn't see me.

"I get it. I've found one here, too. With Kyle and Moose. The rest of these people that I have to spend more time with than any people should ever be forced to spend together." She paused. "Hayes, I know what you did for me growing up, how you handled Mom, what you've done for me all my life. But it's time for you to live your life for you and not for me and Mom. In fact, I think you should have kicked Mom to the curb a long, long time ago."

"I worry about you is all," I said it in a soft voice.

"I know you do. I worry about you, too. I worry about the damage you've done to your body playing football, and how you took the brunt of our mother's… well, everything, so I didn't have to. Most of all I worry that you're missing your life because you've been living it for other people. You need to do what makes you happy. Besides, I'm much stronger than you give me credit for. I'm a bit of an ass-kicker, you see."

I smiled at the words, the way they were nearly identical to what I used to tell Olive. Man was I a hypocrite. "You are, are you?"

"Yes. In fact, I've trained Moose to attack on command."

I laughed out loud. "Oh, really? What does he do? Flop in front of would-be assailants?"

"No. He gets nervous and farts."

I busted out laughing.

Jess giggled. "It's noxious. Like, it could easily knock out a grown man. You can ask Kyle. Big brother, stop worrying about me. It's time to go get your girl. I can't wait to meet her. Maybe Kyle and Moose and I can drive down during break. I'd like to meet Sadie, too."

"Hmm. So… Kyle, huh?"

"Yes. Kyle."

"Do I need to give him the talk?"

"No. Besides. He's nearly as mountainous as you are. I don't think you could intimidate him."

Something about that bit of knowledge made a knot unwind in my shoulders and a smile cross my face. "We'll see about that."

It felt good, setting down that mantle. It felt right.

I was about to call the athletic director's office at UNT when I noticed a new voicemail.

Olive.

I listened to the message and was out the door before she'd gotten the very short first sentence out.

I burst into Gina's office twenty minutes later not thinking for a second about my size or the way I must have appeared. Other folks in the waiting room looked like they thought I might rob the place. I didn't care as I stormed up to reception. "I'm with Olive Russo."

"Sadie's dad?"

I nodded. "Where is she?"

"The vet tech took her back a few minutes ago. Follow me."

The receptionist opened the door and there was Olive,

my amazing strong woman, sitting there, looking so small and half-panicked. I was sure whatever therapist I chose was going to tell me this was absolutely the wrong impulse or whatever, but maybe for the first time I could see it. In that moment, Olive needed me. To hold her, to let her cry and tell her everything would be okay.

Shooting out of her chair, her shoulders started to tremble. "Hayes?"

It was my name, but it was a plea as well. I took one step and wrapped her up tight in my arms. "I got you, sweetheart. Let it go."

She did and so did I. Her tears soaked the fabric of my shirt as mine fell slowly into her hair.

"I can't… I can't do anything. I can't help, and I can't be there. I can't make a plan because we don't know what Gina will find. I can't help. I need to be able to help, and I can't."

"Slow down. Take a deep breath. Tell me what you know." It would give her a chance to focus. To realign whatever part of her brain compartmentalized and helped her analyze.

Backing up, she wiped her eyes and took a deep, shaky breath. "Gina just left. Sadie does have a mass on her spleen that burst, and she was bleeding internally. They're taking her into surgery to remove her spleen. They won't know for sure if it's malignant until they get in there and get it out. If it's cancerous and it's metastasized, the prognosis isn't good, but she could still take the spleen and give Sadie more time with us, pain free. If it's malignant and *hasn't* metastasized, then they remove the spleen anyway and she could live for several more years without her spleen, but even if it's not cancerous, the spleen still has to come out or she'll bleed to death. Gina said I caught it early. The weight we thought Sadie put on?" She shook her head. "Her belly was swollen from all this. It's also the reason she's been tired so much lately."

Olive had a task to focus on—bringing me up to speed—and it had steadied her. "I didn't know if you'd already be on the plane or what. I was afraid you wouldn't come."

I waved it away. "I promise I'll always come. My new therapist may get pissed about that, but for you, I'll always come. No matter what. I wished I could have seen her before the surgery, though. Damn it. I broke about every traffic law in existence on the way over here."

"Wait, what?" Her face was a comical mix of tears and *what the fuck* that made me grin.

I slid into a chair, patted the one adjacent to me. "I got a wakeup call. But before I tell you about it, I need you to know that I am here to stay. In Dallas. Even if you don't like what you hear, I'm not going to Denver, and I'm not going back to playing football. Ever."

"What the hell are you talking about, Walker? God-damn, you are a fickle fucker, you know that. Change your mind again, have you? Let me cry my eyes out about you leaving me. Again. And then decided not to go?"

She ripped the hair thingy out of her hair. Let it tumble over her shoulders. God, she was magnificent. "Yes, I changed my mind again. But this time it's made up for good."

She threw a hand in the air, got up, and paced the two steps across the room. "Whatnthehell brought on this change of events?" Oh, the Texas twang was coming through loud and clear.

"You did."

Chapter Thirty-Five

Déjà vu, part two

Olive

This fuckin' guy...

"I left the hotel room last night already knowing I'd fucked up. That I'd chosen wrong. I always choose wrong when it comes to you. You are my opposite in every way, Olive Russo, and that included the fact that you didn't need me. Not one bit. You are this magnificent creature who is tough as nails, strong as steel, and self-assured beyond compare. Remember when we met?"

"Yeah, the party."

"Where I took a drink away from you, so you didn't get roofied. That was the first and last time you needed me, sweetheart. You were right. I have that superhero complex or whatever you said. I gravitate to people who I think need me, and I never drew lines with them. With you, I never had to worry because you're Olive fucking Russo."

I cut him off. "No, I didn't need you. I'm self-sufficient like that, and I'm a fuckin' queen over here. But what you don't realize is that because I didn't need you, I could choose you."

"Yes, but that's a relatively foreign concept for a guy who's spent his life trying to buy the affection of someone who didn't really want me around but needed me around anyway. When Jess called about her tuition, I'd been working that out on my own, but it snapped me right back into superhero mode. 'Jess needs me, I must fix this for her. I must swoop in and save her.'"

"It doesn't explain why in the hell you throw me over anytime someone else needs you," I snapped. "I know my worth, Hayes. And I do prioritize my happiness."

He put a hand up. "You have every right to be angry. I would be, too. Remember I told you I do think about the consequences of my actions, it's the priorities I get wrong? I don't have to worry about you. I think about you. I love you. I'm in awe of you. But I know no matter what, I know you will be okay. Because you're the strongest person I know."

I dropped back into the chair. "So, what... I'm too strong a woman for you? Too independent? I get deprioritized because I can handle my business? That's some bullshit, Hayes. I'm being punished for being strong."

"No. I mean, yes, but... Shit. With you, I *was* beginning to break that cycle. I was starting to become the guy who thinks about who he is and who he wants to be. That knows he's more than just football. I was able to think about those things for maybe the first time because I don't have to worry about you, because you come equipped with your own fucking broadsword. Not having that worry with you is what helped give me the space to start thinking about who I wanted to be and how I wanted to live. Because you're so strong, I was able to prioritize my own happiness for once. You can't fix me, sweetheart. I have to do that myself, like you said, and I think I need a professional to help me sort through all my reasoning on a deeper level. Still, I may always have the urge to run and save my little sister, just like you will always need a certain amount of control. But I'm willing to do the work. When I made the decision to take the job in Denver, I was still afraid to put in that work to make the changes I needed. But the moment I stepped out of that hotel room, I started questioning *why*. *Why* did I need to rescue Jess; *why* couldn't she pay her own tuition? And when I went running this morning with Brody, I got that wake-up call. Brody will think it was because of him, but it wasn't." Hayes grinned.

"We ran by a high school football field. Some kids having an 'unofficial' practice. The minute I stepped on that field and started helping them improve technique or adjust stance, I knew this is where I needed to be, that was what I wanted to do, and I belonged here. With you. Nowhere else with nobody else. You and me and Sadie. I called Denver and backed out. I called my agent and told him I was finished. I called my new PR manager and he's gonna hunt up some endorsements for me. And I called Jess to tell her I wasn't going to be able to pay her tuition, and that I'd cut my mom off completely."

The problem was how could I be sure he wouldn't scoot me to the back of the priority line again? "What did Jessica say?"

"She reamed me for letting it get to this point, bitched about me trying to tear my body up for her sake, and wanted to know why in the hell it took me so long to

come to my senses and start living the life I wanted."
Sliding his hand into mine, he met my eyes. "This is
the life I want. Here. With you."

"Hayes, I love you, I can see that you're committed,
and I understand what you're saying about me being
strong enough that you could think about yourself for
a change. I like what you're saying about therapists
and belonging here. I just... How can I be sure that you
won't break my heart again because I can take care of
myself? That you won't run off to rescue someone else
and push me, push *us*, back down that priority list?"

"I wish I could tell you there's an easy way to make
that happen. I'd love to give you the assurance that you
need when all I can give you is my word—but you have
it. I promise that you will never come in second to my
family again. You, and I mean *we*, are my number one
and that includes Sadie. I hope to one day expand that
group of *we*. If, at any point, you think I'm slipping up
on that, you can kick me square in the nuts or come
with me to see my currently hypothetical therapist."

I held his hand. Chewed my bottom lip. It was a leap
of faith. But wasn't love always a leap of faith? To walk
off the so-called cliff with your heart exposed and pray
the bridge appeared underfoot, or someone was waiting at the bottom to catch you? Without risk, there's no
reward. And without throwing in a little chaos, there
was no risk.

My life could be safe, boring, unremarkable, and my
heart would be intact, or I could jump, allow the chaos
in, and hope Hayes was at the bottom to catch me.

*He's here, isn't he? He's saying things that make
sense. Shouldn't you at least give him the chance to
prove he can do it?*

No. No, I wouldn't do anything ever again because I should or shouldn't.

But I would do it because I damn well wanted to.

"Okay," I said in a low voice. "But I reserve the right to both kick you in the nuts and tell your therapist about it. Nonnegotiable."

"Done." Hayes slid off his chair to bend over me and rested his forehead against mine. "I will not fail you again. I love you, my Ollie."

I wrapped my arms around his neck and he lifted me from my seat. "I love you too, Walker. Always have. Always will." Our lips had barely touched when the door opened. I held my breath as Gina untied the mask around her face.

"Your sweet little girl no longer has a spleen. She had a sizable mass that was, indeed, ruptured. I don't see any obvious signs of cancer, but I'll be sending a biopsy to pathology to determine whether or not it's malignant. If it is, I think we caught it early. I didn't see any signs that it may have metastasized, though it doesn't mean they aren't there. If pathology comes back malignant, I'll want you to take her to the specialty clinic in Addison to have a full MRI."

Hayes cleared his obviously choked throat. "So, she's okay? For today, I mean?"

"Yes. She'll need to spend a day or two here. I want her to have a blood transfusion and we'll need to watch her to make sure she's stable. It doesn't mean we're out of the woods, because of the possibility of malignancy."

"And if it is malignant?" I asked.

"If it hasn't spread, she has an excellent prognosis, and there's a good chance we got it all. If it has spread, then you will still have time to spend with your sweet girl before you would have to make the hard choice. At least six months."

A sharp inhale caught me off guard and Hayes squeezed my hand.

Gina cut in. "Don't go there yet, guys. Wait for the pathology. Even then, it's not assured you'll lose her that quickly. Like I said, no obvious signs it's spread."

"How long will pathology take?" Hayes asked.

"I'll put a rush on it. Hopefully not more than a few days, okay? We're okay. She'll be able to come home in a day or two, but you can go see her before you leave if you like, though she probably won't be awake yet."

After we visited Sadie, Hayes followed me back to my place.

"She scared the hell out of me." Olive huffed out a weary breath.

"Me too, sweetheart. How 'bout I whip up some pasta and you can put on those satin jammies you like so much."

I grinned, kicked off my flats, and dropped my jacket. "How about I get into my satin jammies and you can rock the gray sweats you left here. *I'll* make the gravy and you can make the noodles."

"Why do you always get to make the sauce?"

"Uh, my grandmother would spin in her grave if she saw you use those canned tomatoes. You have to use fresh tomatoes. That's why your gravy sucks. You've got no taste for spices either. Waaay too much oregano."

He faked a wounded look. "You're killing me over here, woman."

I sent him a look. "I'm sorry, it's the truth. You're not paesano therefore your sauce sucks. I make the sauce."

With that, he burst out laughing.

"What? What's that about? That laugh."

Winding his arm around me, he hauled me in until our bodies were aligned. "Déjà vu. I love you, Olive. You own my heart for all time."

I kissed his lips. "And mine, yours. I love you."

Epilogue

Olive
One Year Later

Hayes, right there. Yes, that's it. Right. There. Wait, how are you even doing that up next to my armpit? How do you even have that many hands? What, are you like that chick in The Incredibles?

Hayes opened his mouth, and a soft puppy whine slipped through his lips.

Wait. That couldn't be right. Something was very wrong with this scenario.

Slowly, I came around to the sunlight streaming through our bedroom window and heard the back door slam. I turned to find Hayes out of bed already. But he would be. It was Saturday. Not just any Saturday, though. It was Safeway Bowl day—Southern Methodist University Mustangs versus the University of North Texas Mean Green. A long-standing rivalry in North Texas, and my man would have too much nervous energy to lie in bed with me this morning.

The soft whine I'd heard in my dream came again and I turned my head to find Sadie's nose burrowed into my armpit as she sprawled across the king-sized bed. I couldn't begin to explain how scary it had been for us while we waited the few days for the pathology to come back. When it came back malignant, I may have eaten my weight in ice cream. Well, Sadie's weight anyway. But we'd gotten very lucky. Nearly two-thirds of dogs with hemangiosarcomas didn't make it. But we caught it early, and the scans showed it hadn't metastasized. We were a year out since Sadie's spleen had been removed and she was back to chasing balls and going to the office with me. "Morning, sweet pea." I patted her tummy. "Are you having dreams?"

Slowly, she cracked one lid open and gave me the stink eye. "Still not a morning dog, are you?"

It had been a good year for us. Hayes actually enjoyed therapy. The therapist he saw was a football fan. And a jock. It was a match made in heaven. I'd even gone with him a few times. Not because he was slipping and I owed him a kick in the nuts. Because I was curious. I was seeing a therapist now, too. She was helping me deal with the whole control thing. Nobody forced me or even asked me. I just liked the changes Hayes was making and how much lighter he'd become. He really was the easygoing guy now that he used to pretend to be. He didn't bottle things up or hide them anymore.

I rolled around Sadie, slid my arm under her head and cradled her. "Mmm, baby girl. I smell corn chips." I buried my nose in the folds of her skin and inhaled. Yes. I was a weird dog person. I didn't care who knew it. I was going to be turning into a weird baby person, too, in about eight months, but Sadie and I were keeping that under wraps until after the game tonight.

Last thing I wanted was to distract the coach. Coach had done well for himself in the absence of his job with the Bulldogs. He was pulling a good salary and had signed on to be Johnathan's first client, after I'd promoted him to associate. Hayes was endorsing a deodorant and an athletic brand that was aiming to pull in the older weekend warrior or athlete. And they were beyond happy with the results.

I heard the footsteps in the hall and closed my eyes. Ever since I sold my condo and bought Lily's house, we had this morning routine where he woke me with a kiss before his morning run. He said he had to stay fit because of the endorsements, but I think he just loved working out. I worked out, too. But I did it because I had to. He actually looked forward to it.

I also think he just liked his bro time with Brody and Jensen.

Instead of a kiss, I was hearing an awful lot of shuffling and muffled directions. Finally, I got my kiss and opened my eyes to find Iris staring at me with something perched on her nose.

"Stay, Iris. Good girl. Be still," Hayes whispered. The man was buck ass naked to boot. That was something I'd learned since we moved in together. Hayes preferred to be naked. All. The. Time.

Not that I minded. Except I walked around all the damn time wet and ready to bang.

Tomorrow I was going to ask him to cook bacon for breakfast just so he'd put some clothes on.

The more my eyes focused, the more I realized what I was seeing. We'd adopted Iris after Lily had finished with her training. She was my agility dog, and she was fast for a Lab. We'd whizzed through Novice and were very close to getting our Open class agility title. Strong, smart, quick, and eager to please, that was Iris. I'd had to step up my game to keep up. We thought she was about five years old. The same age Cassie had been when I rescued her.

"Is that…" My eyes popped wide as I stared at my dog's nose. "Is that a ring on her nose?"

Hayes grinned his sexy grin. "So, do you wanna?"

"Do I wanna what?"

"Marry me, Olive. Be my wife."

I eyed him like I was thinking about it. "Yeah, okay. I guess." I knew I wasn't supposed to screw with the coach's head before a game, but it seemed like the appropriate time. "Given I've got a bun in the oven, it's probably a good idea I make an honest man outta ya."

"YOU WHAT?" Hayes's eyes might as well have popped out of his head like a cartoon.

I laughed long and low. "I'm pregnant. About eight weeks."

At this point, Sadie snored, and Iris whined with the beautiful emerald-cut solitaire she was balancing on her nose completely forgotten about by her people.

Sliding my arm out from under the Boxer, I sat up on my elbows as Hayes put his eyes back in his head and reached for the ring, but it was too late. I saw the quick twitch of her eyes. The way her nostrils flared.

With a quick flip of her snout, she shot the ring up and snatched it out of the air, swallowing it in one gulp.

"Ahhh! Iris!" Hayes went mouth diving to see if he could get to it before she swallowed, but it was long gone.

I cracked up laughing. "Ahh, God. That's a pretty ring. The answer is yes, but you better clean the hell out of that thing before you put it on my finger."

"Yes?" Hayes gave me his sexy grin as he crawled into bed with me.

"Yes, Hayes Walker. Kindest man I know. Let's get married. And then pop out this kid."

He notched his hips between mine and laid his half-hard cock against my sex with a wiggle of his ass.

"Mmm, that's nice, but between you and me? I'm worried. We are not small people, Hayes. This baby is liable to come out twelve pounds and thirty-six inches. I know I can carry a big kid—I got them childbearing hips you're so fond of, and all this boobage should feed a big baby just fine, but I'm not looking forward to pushing *your* kid through my vagina. Not one bit."

He wasn't half-hard anymore. Hayes was fully erect as his slid a hand up my sternum, pushing my sleep shirt up to my neck to palm said boobage and suck my nipple into his mouth. "Ahh, do that again."

He did, and I rocked my hips, feeling his piercing slide over my clit.

"I don't know. I think you'll be okay. You're pretty used to having big things…" Curling his hips back, he pushed them forward when he grazed over my entrance and pushed into me to the root. "…up there. Jesus, you feel good." Hayes pushed in and out in that slow, lazy Saturday-morning sex way with the sun shining on the side of his face.

This man. He was everything.

I wiggled my fingers through his beard, let the tip of one play with his bottom lip.

Catching it between his teeth, he swirled his tongue over the sensitive skin before he let it go.

"A baby," he said, a look of wonder on his face as one of his palms covered my stomach. "I am in awe of you, Olive. I don't think that will ever go away."

"I love you, too." He pushed in deep, held there while

he slid his hand down my stomach to circle my clit. "Mmm, yeah. That's it. Just like that."

"What do you want, girl or boy."

"I want an orgasm."

"I think I'd like a girl. She'd be a badass like you. Wouldn't have to worry about her playing football."

"Why can't girls play football? She can play football if she wants."

He grinned. Nodded. "She's your daughter, she'll do whatever she damn well pleases, including playing football."

"Bet your ass she will."

Hayes arched his hips, hit that spot that only he seemed to be able to find. "God. Coming."

My channel started to flutter around him, and my body shook with the force of my orgasm as Hayes thrust in deep and slow and moaned as he came pulsing inside me.

As we came down together, he rolled to the side, putting a hand on Iris, who'd curled up on his pillow. "Shit. Literally. I guess I better walk Iris soon and get your ring back. Labs, man. They will eat anything."

"In a minute," I said. "C'mon over here and warm me up."

Hayes wrapped his big body around mine, his hand drifting protectively to my stomach. Sadie snored into my side while Iris shared her pillow with Hayes.

This was how families were meant to be. This was, and would always be, our happy place. A couple of dogs, a kid or two, and Hayes and me.

Unequivocally and irrevocably in love.

* * * * *

Acknowledgments

Opposites are definitely my favorite characters to read and write. In truth, my life is really one big opposites attract trope. My husband and I have been together for twenty-six years and come equipped with our very own meet-cute.

I'm a writer (obvi). I tried various professions, but everything stifled me until I started writing. It took me half my life to figure out it's what I was meant to do. My husband is a mechanical engineer. He knew early in life that it was exactly what he wanted to be. He's the logical left brain in our relationship and I'm the creative right brain. He is the grounded one and I am the whimsical other. He is consistent and I am unpredictable. He is the analytical to my emotional. He is the calm, and I am the storm.

Many people have wondered how it works when we're so different. All I can say is that…it just does. There are two things I strongly advise against in an opposites attract household, however… One, never try to do home remodeling together. And two, never go canoeing down a shallow river two days before a knee surgery.

Yet, I know, as a hotheaded, knee-jerking, sweary,

all-the-feels writer, I wouldn't have been able to chase my dreams if it weren't for the calm and collected, analytical, much less sweary, doesn't-take-it-personally engineer I married over two decades ago.

Thank you, Mike. For being my balance and having faith in me even when we don't always understand each other. I love you an immeasurable amount, my polar opposite.

I'd also like to thank my editor, Stephanie Doig, and Carina Press for helping me stick this one out during a time when the poo rolled downhill, and I was at the bottom of a mountain. Also, thanks for not cutting my fart jokes... Yeah, my sense of humor belongs to a thirteen-year-old boy.

Thank you to my All The Kissing and Pitch Wars sisters: Alexa Martin, G.L. Jackson, Lindsay Hess, Maxym M. Martineau, and Stella Becks. I would have put down the laptop long ago if it weren't for you all. To Rebecca Yarros, thank you for helping guide me through the industry. To my Pitch Wars mentee, Sarah Burnard, I have no doubt I will see *Batteries Not Included* on a shelf one day soon.

To my townies and bike-racing family. I'm in awe of how y'all continue to support me. It leaves me speechless. Same goes for the Roadies. Cassie S., Dawn C., Mary, Missy, Angie, Deena, and so many more, thank you for your vehement support. Huge thanks to my OG agility crew—Kim, Antoine, Michelle, and Connie— and their doggos. You all keep me sane.

To my parents, thank you for having unending faith in me, and for helping me become the person I am. I love you.

Last but never least thank you to my Brennie. My

big, intimidating-looking sweet pea of a Cane Corso who was the inspiration for the Unlovabulls series. And to her brother, Smitty—my cute and floofy little hellion of a Clumber Spaniel that rarely lets his mama write in peace.

See? Even my dogs are a study in opposites. I couldn't get away from this trope if I tried. Heh.

About the Author

Tricia Lynne is fluent in both sarcasm and cuss words—a combination that tends to embarrass her husband at corporate functions. A tomboy at heart, she loves hard rock, Irish whiskey, dogs, and Vans (shoes). She's drawn to strong, flawed heroines, and believes writing isn't a decision one makes, but a calling one can't resist. She currently lives in the Dallas area with her husband, the world's sweetest rescued Cane Corso (Brennan), and a completely terrifying Clumber Spaniel (Smitty) affectionately referred to as Smithole.

For the latest on releases, bonus material, giveaways, and appearances, sign up for her newsletter at tricialynnewrites.com. You can also find her making an ass of herself on TikTok, Instagram, and sometimes Twitter. But where the really good stuff happens is in her Facebook reader group, The Jam Session.

If NFL player Brody Shaw wants to retire from his hometown team, the Dallas Bulldogs, he needs to keep his head down and his nose clean. But when the stray dog he rescued bites the pet sitter, it sets off an avalanche of bad publicity, and it's time to bring in a professional...who just happens to be the most beautiful woman he's ever seen...

Keep reading for an excerpt from Protective Instinct, *book one in the* Unlovabulls *series by Tricia Lynne.*

Chapter One

Murphy's Law: Shit can ALWAYS get worse.

Lily

"Oh, goddamn. I ain't got time for this now." I clenched my teeth as traffic slowed to a crawl. Heading south on the Dallas North Tollway—yes, I knew how ridiculous that sounded but it was accurate—I was late to a meeting with a new client. At four p.m. on a Friday, you could always expect traffic going north on the tollway, but going south? Frisco was far enough from the city that it shouldn't have been a problem. Instead, there I was, doing five goddamned miles an hour.

"Well, shit." I pulled the rubber band from my hair and regathered it at my nape.

I hated Dallas traffic on a good day. Today it was the cherry on top of my shit sundae.

It had started first thing this morning. I'd been in Starbucks when an asshole in a dually parked so close to my driver's side door that I didn't have a prayer of squeezing my butt through the opening. Already running late to teach my morning puppy kindergarten class, I crawled across the passenger seat. As I was shimmying over the console, I kicked over my coffee. Then, the dually driver emerged, glanced through my window, shrugged, and left.

Next, I got peed on.

After puppy class ended, I was speaking with Pickles the Pupper's mom when Cassie (or Casshole, as her mother referred to her, because of her need to destroy all puppies in her general vicinity) came through the door. Cassie was nearly thirteen. She had agility and nose work titles, and she'd earned the right to be a bitch if she damn well pleased.

She was also the reason the Unruly Dog Training Center had a no-greeting-between-dogs policy.

The next part happened in a matter of seconds. Pickles the Pupper's tail started wiggling at helicopter speed as she pulled her leash tight toward a barking Cassie. Knowing the dachshund's barking wasn't a friendly hello, but an *Ima tek yo face off, puppeh!* I quickly scooped up Pickles as Casshole snapped out, nicking the puppy's lip.

That was when Pickles peed on me. Down the front of my last clean work shirt, over my khaki pants, and right on the inside of my sneaker.

Now, I'd hit traffic when I was late to a client meeting. *Can this day get any worse?*

The cosmos threw her head back with a witch cackle. *Oh child, ask and you shall receive. Muahahahaha!*

Contemplating the merits of anger-management classes, I didn't bother to check the caller ID when my phone rang. I hit the Bluetooth button on the steering wheel and immediately wanted to punch myself in the face.

"Yeah?"

"'Yeah'? We don't say 'yeah' when we answer the phone, Liliana." My mother's voice was like nails on a chalkboard sending hair on my nape up.

"What do you need, Mom? I'm late for a training appointment."

She huffed. "That's why I called. Your father—"

"Stepfather. Dick is not my father." My father was Billy Costello—one of the foremost linebackers in Dallas Bulldog history. Unfortunately, he'd died when I was younger. Not long after he passed, my mom turned to Dick as her meal ticket.

A weary sigh filled my car speaker. "Please stop calling him Dick. Richard detests when you do that. Speaking of training appointments, don't you think it's time to let the dog thing go?"

"Umm, no? Is that why you called? To harass me into working for *Richard*? Because you might as well stop there. I won't work for the team."

"Liliana, the Dallas Bulldogs have been good to us. Your stepfather needs someone he can trust in the head trainer's position, and…well, playing with dogs all day instead of using your expertise…it's an affront to the family."

"Hmphf. To Richard, right? Don't you mean it's an insult to Dick?"

Her voice got higher. I could hear the annoyance. "We've discussed this. You are the daughter—"

"Stepdaughter."

"*Step. Daughter.*" I was sure that ugly vein in her overly Botoxed forehead was starting to bulge. "As the stepdaughter of the general manager of the Dallas Bulldogs football team, you knew Richard expected you to use the degree *he* paid for by working for the team."

Dick needs someone he can trust in the head trainer's position. Uh-huh. Sure, he did. Dick could give a good goddamn that working with dogs was what made me happy. He saw me as a tool he could use to better the team—*that* was the reason he'd paid my tuition. Now, he was pissed he wasn't getting any return on his investment.

"I'm not having this argument again." I seriously thought about beating my head on the steering wheel. Instead, I looked over my shoulder and turned on my signal, trying to nose my way into the exit lane. No one was budging.

Yes, I had a master's in kinesiology, but my undergrad had been in political science. I'd planned to go to law school, but a guy happened, and law school didn't. Long story. Anyhow, when I was little, my real dad took me to the *Bodies* exhibit when it came through Dallas—you know, donated human bodies dissected, preserved, posed, and displayed? I'd been fascinated with human mechanics ever since. Instead of applying to law schools, I applied to the Master of Science in Kinesiology program at UNT.

Dick had almost been as gleeful to have me slotted in the head trainer position for the Bulldogs as he was to have a lawyer he thought he could bring on staff. I never had any intention of working for my stepfather. As it turned out, I didn't have the highest peopling threshold. Hence, me not using said degree. Besides, Dick had shady written on his forehead. He had to have an ulterior motive for wanting me working for the Bulldogs— Dick didn't do anything that didn't benefit him—I just didn't know what the reason was. Best guess was because of who my father was, but I didn't think that was entirely it, either.

Why were most humans such asshats?

Like the person driving the F-150 sitting in my blind spot. *Ignoring. My. Turn. Signal!* Dogs, however, were as close to the divine as people would ever get. If they only lived longer…

"I'm not going to work for the team, Mom. I don't want anything to do with the Bulldogs. Ever. I don't give two shits *who's* disappointed in my job choice." Dammit, if this jerk would only speed up or slow down…

"Language. I raised you better." *Screeeeech*, went the nails on the chalkboard. "Besides, isn't it about time you let all that ugliness go?"

Raised me? Ha. I raised myself. And ugliness? She made it sound like a pimple on prom night. Not only did Dick have the word *shady* written on his forehead, the Dallas Bulldogs employed my cheating, creepy ex-fiancé. I'd rather dig out my eyeballs with a spork than work for the team that employed *that* prick. The little voice in the back of my brain told me this conversation would go a lot faster if I kept my mouth shut.

"Liliana, Richard is serious. He made it clear that if you refuse to work for the team, we'll be forced to cut you off financially."

Oh, whatever. "Okay, thanks for the info gottago-byeeeee." I pushed the hang-up button, shooting metaphorical lasers with my eyes at the pickup truck driver through its tinted windows. Cut me off, financially? I didn't know why they thought that would work.

Why the hell was he so desperate to have me work for him, anyway? I wasn't buying the whole you *owe me for paying for college* thing. As far as money went, besides tuition, I'd only asked my mother to help financially when my dog, Joker, had needed surgery, and when a couple of my foster dogs needed medical help I couldn't afford. Even with the expensive surgery, I still lost my boy, Joker. But both of the rescues went on to forever homes. The couple of times my mother *had* helped me out, Dick admonished her for "setting a bad precedent and using his money to do it."

My mom was a lot of things. Vain. An unfit mother. A social climber. A former Dallas Bulldogs cheerleader who moonlighted as a jersey chaser.

Audrey Costello-Head may have been a flake who needed a man to take care of her so she could go shopping at Neiman's and get on the committee for the Cattleman's Ball. Still…

She wasn't a Dick Head.

Finally! Someone left me enough room to squeeze in behind the jerk in the pickup. "Yassss, biiitchesss!" DFW drivers believed our daily commute was a contact sport. As such, we took that shit as seriously as we took our Friday night football or the Red River Rivalry. Pushing my way into the exit lane felt like my very own touchdown dance. Slowing down, I moved over to the right, rounding the truck on its left side. The pickup driver turned on their signal to move into the lane in front of me. Refusing to let the truck over, I pulled even with the passenger side, rolled down my window, extended my left arm, flipping the driver off with enough force that surely the sonic boom reverberated through his cab.

Asshole.

Yet, somehow, he managed to slip in behind a Tesla two cars back. I didn't think anything of it until I took the right toward the apartments where my appointment was, and the truck turned behind me.

Oh, shit.

There was a scene in *Miss Congeniality* where Sandra Bullock tackled a guy in the crowd during the talent competition. She told the pageant director that the dude had a gun. The pageant director replied that in Texas everyone has a gun.

Yeah. *That.*

I tried to hold it together, except when I turned in to the garage for the building, the truck followed. Convincing myself I was being paranoid, I found a guest spot and put the car in park. It was a nice building. The first floor had a gym, spa, coffee shop, restaurant, dry cleaner. Good. That meant people were close by. A thought that gave me little comfort when much to my horror, the truck whipped into a numbered spot catty-corner from me.

Fuck. I double-checked to make sure my doors were locked then put the car in reverse. The truck bounced as the sound of the driver's door shutting echoed off the concrete walls, and a large man in basketball shorts walked to the bed and grabbed an athletic bag.

I knew that neck-length messy black hair. That scruff. Those wide shoulders. The breath rushed from my chest. I rested my forehead against the wheel hoping he wouldn't notice me. Only, when I chanced a peek, his maple-syrup-colored eyes met mine, his pink lips turned up at the corners. Shit. I would have rather faced a gun.

Shutting the car off, I grabbed my bag while he leaned against the bed of his truck. I made my way over knowing I wasn't getting out of this without saying hello.

"Well, well. Liliana Costello. Fancy meeting you here." Brody Shaw's voice was all dark, sweet hot fudge, and I was the ice cream melting under the sound.

His lips curled in something like flirty amusement. "Especially after you flipped me off."

My heart sped up. "Hi, Brody. It's been a while." The term "sex on a stick" was invented for this man. At six foot three and 252 pounds, Brody used to run the forty in five seconds flat. The man was built like a brick shithouse. Though he'd had shoulder issues the past couple of seasons, Brody Shaw was the archetypal middle linebacker for the Dallas Bulldogs. Big and fast, he had a Mastiff-sized set of shoulders and his ass resembled two bowling balls trapped in a pair of football pants. The man's arms were surely a gift from some long extinct Roman god, and those legs…oh my God, they were my crack. I had a thing for strong legs—the kind of thick, ripped thighs a guy only got from squatting four hundred pounds or digging into the turf to push other men around.

I know. Very cavewoman of me.

We'd chatted a few times before, when my mother forced me to attend team functions. I knew the dude was witty, quick with his devastating smile, and flirty as all get-out.

The first time we talked, he'd approached me during a rooftop gala. I knew him, of course, but he didn't realize who I was at the time. He'd spent a solid thirty minutes making me feel like the center of the universe. We'd discussed politics, books, a shared love of the TV show *Supernatural*, and the foundation we were there to support—an organization working to minimize the instances of concussions in high school sports. He'd even asked me for my number before one of his teammates interrupted and mentioned I was the GM's stepdaughter.

An hour after that convo, he left with a tall blonde he hadn't arrived with. Not that I would have given him my number, anyway. I didn't date my stepdad's players—if being Billy Costello's daughter had taught me anything, it was that football players were fickle, hedonistic, and volatile.

It didn't stop Brody and me from gravitating to each other at any and all subsequent events before he inevitably left with a different woman. Between that, and the very recent fantasy suite scandal, it was clear Brody Shaw was bad news with a capital Bad Boy.

Fun to look at, even to flirt with on occasion, but that's where it ended.

I swept a stray hair behind my ear as I tried not to stare. It wasn't easy. "Yeah, I'm sorry about that. I'm running late for an appointment. In fact, I should get going. It was good to see you." I started to sidestep him to head for the elevator. Brody slung his bag over his shoulder and matched my strides. The lines in his forehead deepened as he squinted an eye shut, catching his bottom lip between his front teeth.

Jesus. Ten years into his career and he looked even better than he had in college. The laugh lines, the bronzed skin, and hard muscles underneath. I'd watched Brody play football at UNT when I was a student. *That* Brody was a boy. A boy who did things to my lady parts, granted, but still a boy. This version of Brody was a man. The sharp jaw, the crooked nose with the scar across the bridge, the dimples hidden by his dark scruff and eyes that warmed every part of me.

My breath came out in a pant. Annnd *that* wasn't embarrassing at all.

"Lily, aren't you a dog trainer?"

I peeked sideways as I pushed the elevator call button. "Yes. And a certified canine behavior specialist."

A grin crept over Brody's face.

No! My mouth fell open. Not long ago, Brody had made the news when his dog bit a pet sitter. "Are you... Erica?"

"Yep." His smile was enormous. "Well, she's one of my neighbors, but yeah. My publicist made the appointment for me. I had no idea it would be you. She always gives my neighbor's name and address to make sure I don't get psycho fans knocking on the door."

No. This cannot be happening. The elevator opened, and we stepped in. *Not no, but hell no.* I needed to get through his dog's evaluation and recommend another trainer for Brody to work with. Given my body's reaction, Brody's reputation with women, and his affiliation with the Dallas Bulldogs, this was a really bad idea.

Really. Bad. Idea.

Don't miss Protective Instinct, *book one
in the* Unlovabulls *series from Tricia Lynne,
available now wherever Carina Press books are sold.*

www.CarinaPress.com